The Socialite Spy

In Pursuit of a King

THE
SOCIALITE
SPY

IN PURSUIT OF A KING

SARAH SIGAL

LUME BOOKS
A JOFFE BOOKS COMPANY

LUME BOOKS
A JOFFE BOOKS COMPANY

Published in 2023 by Lume Books

ISBN 978-1-83901-531-1

Typeset using Atomik ePublisher from Easypress Technologies

www.lumebooks.co.uk

For my mother and my grandmother

'In wartime, truth is so precious that she should always be attended by a bodyguard of lies.'
—Winston Churchill

'I adore artifice. I always have.'
—Diana Vreeland

January 1936

Gertrude Leigh stood on the train platform at West Hampstead. She pulled back a brown leather glove and looked at her watch. She had been waiting four minutes already. There must have been a delay. It was a Sunday evening and there were always fewer trains on Sundays. Besides, there had been strikes that week so the service was unpredictable. London's population had ballooned but the transport system hadn't been able to keep up. And while the Mayor of London had vowed to expand the Underground, any progress in that direction was yet to be seen.

Gertrude was thinking about trains. Her next novel took place on a train. There was a murder, of course – the daughter of a diplomat from a Central European country. Perhaps Czechoslovakia. And a missing diamond necklace. The mystery would be whether the murder revolved around international diplomacy, theft or both. And Miss Virginia Dalkeith – her perennial heroine-detective – would solve it. Though whether she would just happen to be on the train when the murder took place, or the train just happened to stop in the village where Miss Dalkeith lived, was also still up in the air. Either was a slightly absurd coincidence, but her readers never seemed to mind those. Knowing a foreign language would play a part in solving the murder. Could Virginia speak Czech? A product of having a Czech grandmother? No, no… too much of a stretch. But perhaps she spoke German. After all, German is widely spoken in Czechoslovakia, and a more commonly spoken language generally. She could have learned it in school.

Gertrude shivered and pulled her tweed coat tightly around her, wishing she had worn her Melton instead. She felt a droplet on her cheek. She looked up at the inky black sky. Rain. Or perhaps sleet. Why hadn't she brought an umbrella? Gertrude felt silly. A coat not warm enough for a cold January evening and no brolly.

The freezing rain started to fall harder. She walked down the platform and headed towards the bridge so she could shelter under it. But suddenly she felt woozy. She blinked her eyes a few times as the West Hampstead sign on the platform opposite swirled. And then came the stomach pains. Unexpected, urgent cramping. Gertrude looked around for a bench. Or for someone to help her stay upright. But there was no support to be seen. She could make out a figure at the far end, just descending the stairs, but it was too far away.

Then she heard the sound of a train coming down the tracks. Relieved, Gertrude thought that if she could at least get herself onto the tube carriage there'd be someone who could help her.

The lights of the Metropolitan line train pierced through the night but strangely, Gertrude couldn't make out the sign for the destination on the front. She felt another woosh of wooziness and wobbled, but pulled herself back from the platform edge. Gripping her handbag in her left hand, she put the right one on her stomach, willing it to be calm.

And then, from behind, she felt a shove.

February 1936

I

King George had hardly been dead a few weeks and already people were saying that it was the end of an era.

It's the end of an era. We'll never see another one like him. Time marches on. Pamela didn't like knee-jerk sentimentality and found those kinds of maxims tiresome. She had sighed when she discovered Cook crying in the kitchen just after the death was announced on the wireless, but made sympathetic murmurs and fixed her a cup of tea nonetheless.

In the upstairs study, Lady Pamela More sat at the George III desk – another, earlier King George – with the fire blazing on a bitter February afternoon. She tried to write, but instead watched the people passing by in the rainy Belgrave street below. Many wore black armbands.

'How strange to mourn for someone one doesn't know,' she said.

'Everyone has someone they don't know personally but feels a strong attachment to, for one reason or another. For instance, I'm sure you would be quite inconsolable had the BBC announced the death of Clark Gable,' her husband Francis replied from across the room, as he puffed on his pipe and read the paper.

'Oh, pish posh. Who wouldn't be?' she retorted.

As she re-read what little she'd managed to write for this week's column for *The Times*, she considered how strange it was that the perpetually boyish Prince of Wales was now King Edward VIII. The previous title had suited him better. With his youthful looks, he was like a prince in a fairy tale.

'One wonders if the poor chap will be able to stick it,' Francis mused. 'They say he went into an absolute panic when his father died, realising he would finally have to take the throne.'

'That's rather odd – the man is nearly your age.'

'Two years my senior, actually.'

Pamela looked at Francis's bald spot. Perhaps face powder would take the sheen off.

'Well then, even odder. The man has had forty-two years to become accustomed to the idea.'

'They say it's why he used to try to break his neck riding in point-to-points,' Francis sighed, flicking through the paper.

'What, so he wouldn't have to become king?'

'So he wouldn't have to face the responsibility. His father predicted disaster within a year of Edward taking the throne. Said he was sure to ruin himself.'

'Well, I'm not unsympathetic. It does sound like a terrible amount of pressure.'

Francis grunted in reply.

Despite the fact that the newly minted King of England had a good thirteen years on Pamela, she felt as if they belonged to the same generation; whereas Francis was nearer in outlook to the deceased George V – tweed, shooting, walking sticks. She was fascinated by the glamorous bachelor's film star-type persona: nightclubs, polo, love affairs.

'He's a modern monarch for a modern age,' she continued. 'Less

Zeus and more Apollo.' She paused. 'I should write that down. The Apollinaire Prince. The Apollinaire King. Nightclubs and Nightstands: The Racy Life of the Palace Apollo.'

Francis looked at her with a raised eyebrow.

'Too much?' she said.

She looked at the balls of paper crumpled up on the study floor and sighed.

Pamela had met the new king a few years back at the Coconut Club when he was still the Fairy Prince. Francis had just gone to the bar and Flossie Brackenberry was banging on about trying to get rid of her pregnancy weight. ('I simply must reduce, Pam!') Pamela realised she had a cigarette but no light. With the holder clenched between her teeth, she was about to turn to Jack Harris when a slight but debonair gentleman lit her cigarette.

'Allow me,' he drawled.

'Thank you,' she drawled in reply.

It was the dinner jacket she noticed first: a classic Frederick Scholte London drape. Roomy, soft shoulders (no padding), tapering into a V-shape, giving him a deceptively athletic build. Distinctive tailoring lately made popular by a certain member of the Royal Family.

Pamela took a better look at the gentleman's face and, as she suspected, found it was the Prince of Wales. She jabbed Flossie in the side. Flossie turned to look at her, confused, then realised who was standing in front of them. The two women curtseyed. Flossie was so nervous that she nearly lost her balance.

'Pamela, Lady More, your Highness.'

The prince smiled and said, 'Charming... charming...'

And then walked off, leaving Pamela wide-eyed and Flossie open-jawed.

He had been a trifle shorter than she'd expected, Pamela remembered as she poked at the dying fire in her study. Certainly, a change from his father, with his bushy beard and deep-set eyes. He looked like a boy who had become hardened by life. She couldn't decide if he was old for his looks or young for his age.

Pamela looked out the window again. A man in a flat cap, an overcoat and a tartan scarf was leaning against the fencing around the garden in the square. He had been there when she first sat down to write over two hours ago and was still there, hardly having moved. It was bitterly cold out, much too cold for a man to stand outside without reason. It almost seemed as if he was watching her house. Pamela tried to get a better look at him. He looked suspiciously like a man she'd seen a number of times – or at least, thought she'd seen. Outside the paper. When she was shopping. Once in the park. But maybe she was imagining things. Francis always told her she read too many novels. After all, who would want to follow her?

II

Pamela hurried up the grand staircase at the House of Hartnell, pausing to check her appearance in the mirrored wall. She was already late for the spring/summer collection show but didn't want to make an entrance looking frazzled in front of the good and great of the London fashion scene. She shrugged off her sable – she was now overheated and clammy from all the rushing about – and tugged at her sea-green belted dress with a lavaliere neckline. Pamela despaired at the state of her permanent wave, her brown hair already frizzing and resisting the confines of hairgrips. Maybe she could pass it off as a look à la Fay Wray after the ravages of King Kong.

She slipped in through the back of Norman Hartnell's showroom. The salon was full to bursting and the show had not even begun. The couturier had recently created the bridal gown and bridesmaids' dresses for the wedding of the Duke of Gloucester – now third in line to the throne – and Lady Alice Montagu-Douglas-Scott – daughter of the Duke of Buccleuch. Becoming dressmaker to the Palace was the best publicity Hartnell could have hoped for.

A sea of expensively dressed, immaculately coiffed women chattered softly in hushed anticipation while looking around the room to see who else was there. Pamela groaned inwardly at the thought of having to stand for the next half hour, head throbbing from too little sleep and too many cocktails at the Café de Paris the night before. Francis had left early – as he often did – scuttling off somewhere, leaving his wife to carry on with her friends and drink too much.

As she lit a cigarette and scanned the room for an empty chair, she spotted Johnny Ashton-Smythe, who was waving so frantically he looked as if he was drowning. As she climbed over socialites, fashion editors and department store buyers – all glaring furiously at her – Johnny moved his coat off the chair he had gallantly saved.

Only twenty-one and fresh from the quadrangles of Cambridge, Johnny had been foisted upon Pamela by her bossy mother's even bossier friend, Camilla Ashton-Smythe. At first, she resented the imposition, yet after a while she found she had quite got used to having him around. Johnny was shy and often behaved as if he'd never encountered a woman before but was surprisingly competent with cameras and rather clever.

'You are a darling,' Pamela said as she petted Johnny's cheek. She opened her silver cigarette case and proffered it to him. 'Cigarette?'

Johnny shook his head and fiddled with his Leica. 'No, thank you, Lady Pamela. Are you well this morning?'

'The less said about my health this morning, the better,' she replied as she fished in her handbag and found a dusty, lint-coated aspirin.

Johnny sneezed and then loudly blew his nose into his handkerchief. The platinum blonde in a mink stole sitting in front of them turned around, affronted. Johnny inched down in his seat in embarrassment, but Pamela glared right back at her until the woman retreated.

The setting was perfect material for Pamela's column: 'Agent of Influence'. A combination of fashion editorial, social observation and gossip. 'Who's where and who's wearing what', as she put it. Pamela joked that she was like a sartorial spy, reporting back on what women were buying, sporting and coveting, as well as being a subtle but artful influence on her readers, passing judgement on trends and rumours alike. She signed off each column: 'Lady Pamela, Your Agent of Influence'. Pamela stubbed her cigarette out in Johnny's empty tea cup sitting at her feet, and retrieved a notebook from her pocket ready to get to work. As the show began, she scanned the room.

Daisy Fellowes. The Anglo-French heiress to the Singer sewing machine fortune, Elsa Schiaparelli's greatest patron and, until recently, the *Harper's Bazaar* Paris correspondent. As the models paraded down the catwalk she angled her lithe body towards them, revealing a close-fitting jersey dress that showed off a large, glittering Cartier necklace, said to have been made especially for her. Pamela noted that the rumours were true – Daisy *had* had her nose 'fixed'. It seemed as if the new trend for plastic surgery was a by-product of the recent psychotherapy craze (and thus an overabundance of introspection). And then of course there was the *other* gossip that swirled around Daisy. That she wore only a cellophane cape when she received guests, fresh from the bath and au naturel underneath. That she had several volumes of leather-bound pornography. That she spiked the drinks of people she didn't like with Benzedrine and cocaine. Truth, tales fabricated by jealous society rivals or self-made propaganda – who could say?

Across the runway from Daisy sat the statuesque, six-foot tall Nancy Cunard. Estranged daughter of London socialite Emerald (of the Cunard shipping line), poet and self-identified anarchist. Wearing a headscarf, leather jacket and arms full of carved African bangles, Nancy looked bored, her kohl-rimmed eyes nearly closing. No wonder. Nancy's bohemian life in France consisted of taking up political causes, publishing incendiary works and courting controversy with her continually changing procession of lovers. Looking at London's latest frocks must have seemed dull in comparison. People might look askance at her lifestyle but she'd been photographed by Cecil Beaton, and Boucheron had made a series of bracelets inspired by her bangles. Her mother Emerald had cut her off without a penny after discovering her affair with an American jazz musician. Pamela had heard Nancy used her heavy bracelets as weapons in fights with her lovers.

And front and centre, in the place of honour, was Madge Garland, *Vogue*'s formidable editor-in-chief in London. She wore a striking, asymmetrical knit top, an Eton crop and a slash of blood-red lipstick. Her enormous eyes never wavered from the models and the clothes they wore as they stalked down the catwalk. Who would have guessed an Australian lesbian would be running *Vogue*? Despite a tumultuous and controversial history, Garland was *the* word in London fashion – even Virginia Woolf took style advice from her. She had started off assisting then-editor Dorothy Todd, who soon became her lover. Condé Nast then sacked Todd for trying to make *Vogue* too 'literary'. And then hired Garland in her place. And then sacked Garland. And then rehired her years later. This was all in spite of the fact that Nast had threatened to expose both women's 'morals' – the scandalous nature of their relationship and that Todd had a secret, illegitimate child – when Todd wanted to sue. (A bit rich coming from a notorious philanderer whose second wife had been thirty-five years his junior.)

Perhaps buoyed by its recent good fortune, the House of Hartnell was embracing a romantic mood: an array of long, elegant skirts and gowns in lace and silk – longer hemlines than last season to suit higher heels. Although there were a number of sensible day dresses and light spring jackets for Hartnell's matronly clientele, there was also a bevy of evening gowns for their debutante daughters who were getting ready to be presented when the Season began in May, as had been the case for their mothers, grandmothers and countless generations before them.

Pamela noted the small capes that matched the dresses, the jaunty hats and tiny belts. She was amused by what people were calling 'house pyjamas', designed to be worn indoors and out – the latest word in hostess attire, lately popularised by Joan Crawford. Though if you didn't actually resemble Joan Crawford already, you'd risk looking as if you've just rolled out of bed.

As the show drew to a close, the final spectacular ensemble was presented to the audience: a wedding gown complete with an enormously long veil and even longer train. Pamela couldn't help but roll her eyes at the staid predictability of the practice of every fashion house ending with a bride. As if nothing significant in a woman's life preceded or succeeded marriage. Looking at all the long, flowing skirts and gowns, she felt nostalgic for the bygone days of shorter, flapper-length skirts that one didn't have to keep from dragging in the rain or being trodden on by a dance partner. Did she miss the more carefree era or simply her own younger years? After all, she was turning thirty this spring and had recently spent nights lying awake, worrying if thirty was the start of Middle Age.

March 1936

I

Pamela was late. Again. This time for a meeting at *The Times* building on Printing House Square; the office was a large, ornate edifice with the paper's name emblazoned across its façade. She trotted down the corridor, the sound of her heels click-clacking on the linoleum echoing the click-clacking of dozens of typewriters as dozens of journalists churned out stories in the adjacent newsrooms. She entered through a side door to the meeting room as cigarette and cigar smoke and the funk of sweaty, overworked men poured out.

She took a seat next to her editor Percy Blakely, who gave her the fish eye. He was dressed more sombrely than usual in a muted grey suit for the occasion, but still wore a rebellious bright pink pocket square and enough cologne that Pamela was immediately enveloped in a cloud of it.

Lately, Pamela had been bunking off meetings. She resented having to listen to the editor-in-chief Geoffrey Dawson's smug droning and the similarly smug droning from all the other editors giving long-winded reports. She rarely spoke because she knew no one would listen to her anyway – even on the occasions when the men humoured her, either no one took her seriously or they would patronisingly try to explain things to her, correcting what she had just said.

When she was younger and had just been hired by Percy's predecessor – a friend of a friend from her deb days – Pamela had been keen
to stay on top of current affairs, to prove her mettle as a journalist. She
read *The Times* every day, in addition to the *Manchester Guardian* and
several others. She had wanted to show that she wasn't simply the wife
of a peer with an eye for frocks, that she was a shrewd woman with
insight and intelligence and judgement. Someone who could casually
but deftly discuss things like diplomatic relations, and trade agreements.

But when she tried to do so, Pamela didn't find encouragement
anywhere. Her friends weren't interested. ('Don't be a bore, Pam.') Her
mother actively discouraged it. ('No one likes a woman who thinks
she's cleverer than she is.') And the men at the paper would nod and
smile politely before turning to each other to have serious discussions.
('Yes, very intriguing. Anyway, what was I saying?') Now, Pamela only
read the paper occasionally, listened to the news on the wireless distractedly and generally fell out of the habit of trying to keep up with the
world's increasingly complex and seemingly ever-changing political
developments. Francis always seemed content to discuss politics but
he always knew so much more about every political development
than she did that it sometimes seemed impossible to catch up; she
preferred staying silent to risking looking a fool. So, she retreated into
the realm of fashion and cocktail party gossip, where it was safe, if not
intellectually stimulating. While her column proved to be an exciting
outlet for her ideas and desire to write in the first couple of years, her
enthusiasm began to wane once she banged her head on the ceiling
of the format, readership and editorial direction one too many times.

And so, the Peer's wife with an eye for frocks decided that her
time spent in meetings would be better used elsewhere. But Percy
whinged and wheedled.

'Come on, ducks, you can't make me go to those dreary, hideous things on my own. I need someone to keep me amused. Besides, it's good to make an appearance from time to time in front of editorial. Remind them you exist.'

Pamela didn't think the editorial staff very much cared if she existed or not but agreed to humour Percy, even if only to keep him on side. (Being a somewhat unpredictable person, he could be trying if Pamela didn't make an effort to stay in his good books.)

She settled herself into the uncomfortable wooden chair at the end of the long table and turned to Dawson. Pamela didn't especially like him and found it concerning that the editor-in-chief of such a large and important paper could have so little eye for detail that he always wore badly tailored suits.

'It is important that we encourage our readership to understand the possibility of an alliance between Britain and Germany, a nego-tiation of equals through pacific means,' Dawson said. 'Germany is not to be feared as an enemy but rather should be seen as a modern, industrial powerhouse forging a path into the future. For example, today marks the maiden voyage of the Hindenburg zeppelin, which may well revolutionise air travel.'

Pamela didn't really understand why anyone needed zeppelins if they had aeroplanes. She also didn't understand what seemed like, in certain circles, the increasing allure of Adolf Hitler. She had always found him boorish and nasty, especially since his rise to power – the means by which everyone seemed to have conveniently forgotten. But German politics were always so complicated. People she knew who had been to Germany recently said the cities were cleaner, the streets were safer, and you didn't see a tramp around every corner anymore – a great contrast to how things were during the last government. Though she still couldn't help but feel the whole thing had a bad smell about it. The rallies, the saluting and the marching. All that leather. The lurid uniforms with the skull insignias. And that curious little moustache – like the bristles on a toothbrush.

Francis always said Hitler was a thug and not to be trusted – probably no better than Stalin. To Pamela, a choice between the fascists and the communists didn't seem like much of a choice at all. Rabid, swivel-eyed Nazis in macabre uniforms versus po-faced, bloodthirsty Soviets in shapeless tunics. Just the idea of Britain being overrun by Bolsheviks was enough to make any aristocrat's blood run cold. Everyone remembered the shooting of the Russian royal family in that basement – especially the children – like it was yesterday.

Dawson elaborated on Hitler's great economic vision for Germany, his spectacles sitting on the end of his nose.

David Stern, a diminutive foreign correspondent who always looked dishevelled in his rumpled suit, said, 'We are turning a blind eye to the terrible laws Hitler's imposing on his own people. And to the speed at which Germany are re-arming.'

Dawson retorted, 'David, no one is turning a blind eye to the religious persecutions but it's a complicated situation. And someone needs to take the reins in Europe before we have another crash, which would be disastrous.'

The two middle-aged men stared each other down for a moment until Dawson turned away and moved the discussion to the situation in Spain, the strikes and ongoing political unrest. A man in a pinstripe waistcoat sitting on the other side of Pamela rolled his eyes, muttering about unions and agitators. The discussion then carried on to other political topics that Pamela, much to her chagrin, realised she only had the vaguest of ideas about. She prayed that someone would bring in tea, but no one did.

Pamela's eyes drifted around the room. She wondered if everyone knew how much they gave away about themselves with every creased suit, scuffed shoe and loosened tie. Henry Rake, an editor who had been given a formal warning for coming in to work drunk, claimed he was back on the wagon but Pamela could tell from his too-tight trousers and mis-buttoned waistcoat that this was entirely untrue. A staff journalist, Fred something-or-other, was rumoured to have a wife who was leaving him for someone else at the paper. Pamela guessed she had already left by evidence of the fact that he wore mismatched socks. It was whispered that Beryl Collins – a bossy spinster in the secretarial pool, sitting in the corner taking the minutes – had a mysterious, secondary source of income. Pamela knew it must be something lucrative, given the new and obviously expensive Lalique necklace she was wearing that she would never have been able to afford on her salary.

Pamela found the combination of male chattering, the warm room and lack of fresh air lulled her to sleep. She awoke with a start, her head jerking upwards in surprise when Percy kicked her under the table. He glared at her and pointed to Dawson, who was looking at her.

'Pamela, your feature will be called "A Week with Wallis".'

'Wallis who?' she asked, wondering how long she'd been asleep.

'Wallis *Simpson*, Pamela.'

Percy kicked her again and glared at her. Pamela rubbed her wounded shin and glared back.

Oh yes. The American favourite of the King.

Dawson explained that there was a gentleman's agreement on a blackout regarding press coverage of the relationship between the King and Mrs Simpson who, as a twice-married American adventuress, was not considered an appropriate royal companion.

Doris – Dawson's secretary with a penchant for ostentatious brooches – snorted loudly, muttering, 'Companion my foot. If she's only the King's companion then I'm the Queen of Sheba.'

A few people tittered. Dawson glowered and they fell silent.

'I was hesitant to suggest it, but Mr Blakley felt it would be good for increasing numbers in female readership.'

Percy smiled. He had been brought over from the *Tatler* two years previously to persuade more women to read *The Times*. He managed to toe the line between not so much gossip as to compromise their reputation but just enough that they didn't lose readers to the *Daily Mail*.

'It was originally going to be Mrs Leigh's piece, but...' Dawson sighed, removed his spectacles and rubbed his eyes wearily. His facial expression suddenly turned to one of worry. A few people began to whisper and he held up his hand. 'And before you ask, I'm sorry to say that Mrs Leigh is still in a coma. Her sister says the doctors are uncertain as to the progression of her condition. She was transferred from Hampstead General to UCL Hospital last week.'

'Blimey, that doesn't sound too hopeful, does it?' Percy muttered to Pamela.

Pamela bit her lip and fiddled uneasily with her bracelet. She felt very odd indeed, inheriting a piece from the comatose columnist in question. Gertrude Leigh had never been one of her favourite people. A strait-laced, tight-lipped, somewhat humourless woman in her late-forties, she had written an advice column called 'A Word in Your Ear', where she seemed to play agony aunt to half the country. It was incredibly popular and *The Times* postroom was flooded with people seeking her advice on anything from marital strife to workplace grievances every day. Considering how haughty and condescending Gertrude could be in person, Pamela was always surprised at the warm, considerate tone she used in her responses to those who wrote to her.

Being two of the very few women at *The Times* who weren't secretaries, cleaners or switchboard operators, one would have thought they would have made an alliance. But Pamela always got the feeling that Gertrude looked down on the world of fashion generally and her in particular. She was always secretly worried that if the paper were to face a downturn and had to trim its sails, she would be one of the first to get the chop. Whereas Gertrude, due to her popularity, was safe and secure in her position.

But Pamela had never wanted her to end up like *that*, lying in a hospital bed. Did she even have anyone to visit her? Pamela knew she had been married to an older man who had died several years before. No children that she was aware of. Though perhaps she had other family, and friends. She had a sister, at least.

There had only been one witness when Gertrude had fallen from the train platform, but it was dark and he was too far away. It had been an icy, wet night, so he assumed she must have slipped. So, no one really knew what had happened. Pamela felt terrible for her.

'Anyway, the general consensus is that the Simpson woman is meant to be something of a...' Dawson searched for a phrase, '*fashion plate*. So as long as you are tactful, do not mention the King and simply write about what the woman wears, we won't be breaking any confidences.'

Pamela wanted to be more enthusiastic about being given a feature – something to sink her teeth into – but instead felt a sense of disappointment. She didn't see what all the fuss was about with

Wallis Simpson. When he was the Prince of Wales, HRH ploughed through a number of mistresses. Freda Dudley Ward. Thelma Furness. The Princess Fahmy who murdered her husband in the Savoy. He preferred the married ones who fussed less when he dropped them unceremoniously. Thelma had said she learned about the end of her romance from the Palace telephone operator. ('Madam, I have orders not to put you through.')

Leaning back in her chair and gazing absently at a damp spot in the ceiling, Pamela thought, it will all blow over and someone else will be flavour of the month soon enough.

Once the meeting had ended, Pamela strode down the corridor, eager to get out of the stuffy building and, if she was honest, to forget about the tragedy of Mrs Leigh. People pushed past her in the lunchtime crush, ducking in and out of offices and newsrooms. The lift appeared to be out of order so she took the stairs down to the ground floor. The stairwell was empty but suddenly, a floor above her, she could hear footsteps – at first descending the stairs slowly but then getting faster and faster. Pamela felt uneasy for some reason and found herself speeding up too. Though she didn't know why, she felt a strange sensation that she needed to get out of the building as quickly as possible. When she got to the reception, she could still hear the footsteps behind her. She sped up her pace a bit more as she walked quickly out of the building. The footsteps continued to follow her, growing closer and louder.

'Excuse me?'

Pamela kept going. Her heart was pounding.

'Excuse me! You dropped your glove!'

As she exited the monolith of *The Times*, she turned around. A young man in a striped V-neck jumper and shirtsleeves was, indeed, holding one of her long, brown, calfskin gloves. She gratefully accepted the glove and thanked the man, feeling somewhat foolish.

II

Pamela returned home that afternoon to find yet another postcard from her sister Charlotte on the side-table in the entrance hall. Charlotte was a relentless sender of postcards. There was nothing she liked more than making other people envious.

Hello from Mongolia! We had the most wonderful yak soup, which was just delicious after a long hike in the mountains!

California is so sunny and warm. Peter's friend who makes darling little films introduced us to Fred Astaire!

Tuscany is gorgeous this time of year. The wine is fantastic, the tomatoes are in season and we've been listening to Il Duce on the wireless!

Charlotte's husband Peter did 'something in business' (what exactly had always been a mystery to everyone) so the couple were constantly abroad, a lifestyle which had turned Charlotte into a self-proclaimed expert on everything. How to pack for a Kenyan safari, or what to order at Raffles when one is in Singapore, or the best way to avoid rush-hour traffic in Manhattan. Charlotte had told her she really needed to see more of the world – 'travel broadens the mind!'

The two sisters had been prone to quarrelling ever since they were children. Her sister always managed not only to get under her skin but also make her look irrational if she reacted to her provocations at all. Francis was insistent that Pamela try harder to rub along with Charlotte, if only for the sake of Christopher and Alexandra. Her nephew and niece had been bundled off to school at the earliest opportunity; Francis thought they always looked a bit forlorn and underfed.

Lately, Francis had struck Pamela as being moony around children. He took any opportunity to play with other peoples' offspring, dandling babies, cooing at new-borns. Which would then encourage their friends to ask her questions like, 'when will it be your turn?' On the cusp of thirty, Pamela sometimes became overwhelmed by the friends and family who continually felt the need to tell her what a blessing children were, to whisper in her ear 'don't leave it too late'.

Chance would be a fine thing.

But Pamela had never been truly interested in having her own, and had heard such ghastly things from other women about their pregnancies.

Being ill in the morning, and the afternoon, *and* sometimes the evening. Pamela's own mother was bedridden the entire time she was pregnant with both Pamela and Charlotte.

Monstrous foot growth. Flossie Brackenberry was horrified to find she couldn't wear anything but her wellies after she had Elizabeth. The doctor had told her it was just water retention but she found her feet had actually permanently expanded after the birth.

Speaking of which, of course, uncontrollable weight gain. Some women never managed to lose the weight they had gained during pregnancy. When Charlotte had Christopher, she managed to retain her trim figure – she was one of those women who hardly showed until she was practically due. But when she had Alexandra, she was an absolute whale. She had been so smug the first time; it was downright exciting to see her get so fat the second time round.

And once you had them, you had to look after them. Engage nannies and governesses and choose boarding schools. Make sure they had something to do in the school holidays. Not coddle them too much but not allow them to grow up to be sociopaths. Pamela hadn't a clue what to do with children. It was always awkward when faced with someone's child. Did one try to play with them? Or make conversation? If so, what was one meant to talk about?

Francis was quite keen and frequently made comments about how lucky they would be if Pamela were to fall pregnant, what a perfect addition to their family a baby would make. And while it had been several years since they had been married, he said nature would one day take its course. Eventually.

The telephone rang, interrupting Pamela's train of thought. It was her mother. She sighed. Her mother was always the last person she wanted to hear from. Fortunately, the connection was poor and she could hardly hear a word she was saying over a good deal of interference and a strange, occasional clicking.

'Sorry, Mother, can't hear you! Terrible connection. I'll ring you back later,' Pamela said with relief as she hung up.

She made a mental note that if it happened again, that she would get one of the servants to make an inquiry with the telephone company.

III

Percy had woken up late from a party the night before and had rung Pamela to meet him in a café in Covent Garden instead of his office. He always went to the same café for a fry-up when he was hungover; Pamela thought the place rather cheerless, uninspiring and very much like any other café in the city, but Percy swore up and down they made the best sausages in the city.

He fluffed his polka dot cravat, peered at Pamela through bloodshot eyes and said, 'I have someone I'd like you to meet. A bit rude, drinks quite a lot but marvellously dishy. And terribly good at what he does.'

'And what exactly is it that he does?'

'He's a photographer.'

'Yes, I suppose we could use one of those.'

'Well, yes but he's also a devastatingly attractive, available man…'

Percy sipped his tea and raised his eyebrows at Pamela behind his tea cup theatrically. He had been hell-bent on her having a love affair and thought her rather a stick for remaining faithful to what he thought was a dull husband.

'What a nice cravat you're wearing this morning. Very Noël Coward. Or is it Ivor Novello who wears cravats?' Pamela replied as she took one of Percy's cigarettes from the pack sitting on the table.

'Don't change the subject!' Percy retorted as he playfully smacked Pamela's hand.

'Percy, you have enough love affairs of your own to occupy yourself. Besides, some people might object to me having an affair with a drunken photographer.'

'Some people object to absolutely everything.'

'Speaking of which, are you still seeing that theatre critic at the *Daily Express*?'

'You know, I do believe the man is a Soviet spy.'

It was best not to ask how Percy knew this. Percy knew everything. That was partly because he was a highly social creature and partly because he was a blackmailer. Pamela was the only person in his life who knew this, and she was strangely unperturbed by it. He told her it was necessary as insurance against ending up in prison for his nocturnal activities. Percy was from Wolverhampton, which meant his accent was as fake as his background. Pamela wasn't sure if Percy Blakely was his real name. He even dyed his prematurely grey hair. But she liked him all the same. He was a sharp editor; he knew everyone and he gave charming cocktail parties in his Bloomsbury flat where one could meet the most unusual people.

In between eggs and toast, they dissected the photos Johnny had taken at Lady Harborough's wedding at the Brompton Oratory.

First, fashion.

The bridesmaids wore Vionnet – pale pink Brussels lace. The mother of the bride wore Fortuny – subdued but elegant navy. And the bride had been dressed by Charles James – eggshell white, full skirt, embroidered bodice.

'I don't know if I find Charles James particularly exciting, do you?'

'No, but he's been quite the thing ever since he designed Cecil Beaton's sister's wedding gown, hasn't he?'

Then, gossip.

They each eyeballed the faces in the wedding party. That one's inherited an enormous fortune ('typical'), those two are getting a divorce ('Isn't everyone?'), this one's rumoured to have killed her husband ('delicious').

'Is the bride barefoot?' Percy wrinkled his nose in distaste.

'She felt she had to – the groom was awfully short.'

'Is this a trend now? Barefoot brides? Rather Pre-Raphaelite.'

'Even if it is, let's not write about it. I don't want to encourage women forgoing shoes to satisfy the neuroses of their husbands-to-be.'

Percy sighed, leaned back and then ate a forkful of sausage. He looked around the café, spotted someone and turned to Pamela.

'Do your little thing, Pam.'

'My what?'

'Your little party trick. Where you do a character assassination of a stranger.'

Pamela tapped her red manicured fingernails on the table in exasperation. 'I don't do *character assassinations*.'

'You know what I mean. Your decoding. I'm just in the mood.'

Pamela rolled her eyes. Percy scanned the room for victims. He pointed to a table in the corner. A woman in a thin dress wearing a tremendous amount of makeup was sitting with an older man in a brown suit.

'Them. Is she a tart? Is that her client? Or her pimp?'

Pamela waved her hand at Percy. 'Keep your voice down, please, Mr Blakely.' She peered at the table in the corner. 'Why would a tart take a client to breakfast?'

'Maybe he's taking her to breakfast?'

'Why would a tart *want* to have breakfast with her client?'

'Then he's her pimp.'

'I don't think she's a tart.'

'So much slap though. Trowelled on. Makes her look so much older than she probably is.'

'I'd put her at twenty-three.'

'Thirty if she's a day.'

'No older than twenty-three or twenty-four. It's stage makeup. I'd bet money that she's an actress. We are in Covent Garden, after all. And stage makeup always makes women look older than they are. And it's…' Pamela glanced at her watch, 'nearly eleven o'clock. So, a bit late for someone to be having breakfast, unless they're hungover…' she gave Percy a look, 'or exhausted from a performance the night before. And she might be wearing her stage makeup because she has a matinee in a few hours. She did it at home because didn't want the fuss of having to come in early to the theatre for makeup, because she had a breakfast meeting. Which means whoever she's meeting with now is somewhat important, otherwise why would she bother with a meeting when she has two performances in less than twenty-four hours? So perhaps he's a producer... although not in that suit. Nor a director either. My guess is that he's her agent.'

And without a word, Pamela rose from the table and walked over to the table in the corner of the café, lingered a moment and then continued on to the ladies' room. When she returned, she looked at Percy with a cat-like smile.

'Exactly as I had suspected. He was talking to her about a casting.'

Percy leaned back, folded his arms, smiled and said, 'Very good, pet.' He looked back at the photos on the table from the wedding and said suddenly, 'Oh, look! There she is.'

Pamela scanned the pictures. 'There *who* is?'

'The notorious Mrs Simpson,' he purred.

She squinted at a petite woman with a severe centre parting and an elegant bias-cut gown.

'Can't fault her for taste, I suppose.'

'I haven't met her myself,' Percy said as he primly took a sip of tea, 'but it sounds like she has an air of the demi-monde about her: a penniless childhood of shabby gentility, a violent first husband, tours of the brothels of the Far East. An operatic femme fatale. And she must have such excellent Palace gossip. Not that we can publish any of it.'

Pamela put the picture back on the table. 'What would happen if we did?'

Percy raised an eyebrow. 'Why do you ask?'

'I must say, I don't understand this fuss over the Simpson woman.'

'Do you want to lose your job, darling?'

'It isn't as if he hasn't had married lovers in the past. Even married, American lovers.'

'Ours not to reason why, ours but to do and die. And bring readership numbers up.'

'It seems rather odd, all the mystery over this woman.'

'Well, he is king now. You can't go gallivanting around with anyone you like when you're the king. Wouldn't be decent.'

'I'm just not sure what I'm going to write that's of interest if all the interesting things are off-limits. Mrs Leigh was awfully good at making the utterly banal enticing.'

Percy paused and looked at the picture of Wallis on the table. 'I do have a friend I can ask. About *her*. See if he has something we can use. He's another journalist. Foreign. Always seems to know everything and everyone.'

IV

'Maeve found a gentleman's calling card in the pocket of an evening jacket belonging to Stephen Tennant, the son of Baron Glenconner.'

Jenny, Pamela's maid, looked through her notes, written in crabbed handwriting so tiny no one could decipher it but herself. She perched on the chaise longue in Pamela's bedroom.

Pamela was continually impressed by Maeve the laundress's fountain of knowledge, and Jenny's seemingly endless ingenuity. Their arrangement had been working out well for both of them. Unbeknownst to Francis, for the past two years, Pamela had been secretly paying their maid a small commission for the most interesting society gossip she could track down. It seemed that 'pas devant les domestiques' had gone the way of the horse and carriage because Jenny seemed to be able to report back on every cocktail and dinner party in town.

Pamela lit a cigarette and then gave one to Jenny, who fished a lighter out of her apron pocket and lit it.

'Lady Diana Cooper's maid Annie reports that Errol Flynn was a dinner party guest the other night. Drank too much, got into a scuffle and broke a vase.'

'This is what comes from inviting Hollywood film stars to dinner.'

When Jenny turned out to have an extensive network of contacts, not only with servants and tradesmen, but also cutters, fitters and seamstresses who staffed the London fashion houses, she started bringing Pamela trade secrets too.

'Rosie, the pattern cutter at Victor Stiebel, says everyone is going to be wearing floral by summer.'

'Floral for summer. How predictable. I think Stiebel is losing his edge.'

'Deb, my friend at Lachasse, says Hardy Amies—'

'He's so terribly young to be a managing director.'

'He's going to make sage *the* colour next year. Especially with tweed.'

'Sage? Hm.'

Pamela handed Jenny a few coins, who discreetly slipped them into her apron.

'Jenny, do you ever hear anything about Wallis Simpson? American. Lives behind Marble Arch.'

'Is she the one the King's been hanging around with?'

'I've been asked to write a feature on her so can use all the help I can get. Keep an ear out, will you?'

Jenny nodded and stubbed out her cigarette in the grate. She was about to leave but turned around. 'Oh, and Madam...?'

'Yes, Jenny?'

'You know how you said there was interference on the telephone line? A clicking sound?'

'Yes?'

'If you hear clicking on the line, it could be that someone is listening in. To your telephone calls.'

'Someone is what?'

'Listening on the line. It's called wiretapping.'

Pamela took a long drag on her cigarette.

'And how do you know that?'

'My best mate Polly, she's a telephone operator. That's what she told me when I asked. Just thought you might want to know.'

Jenny gave Pamela a little nod of her head and exited into the hall.

V

Pamela had just dropped off her column for the week with Percy and was walking down the corridor when she passed David Stern. Another rumpled suit, she noticed – grey this time. And a stain on his tie. (Wife ineffective, absent or non-existent.)

'Ah! Mrs More,' he said, turning around.

Pamela was so surprised that anyone on the editorial staff wanted to speak to her, let alone remember her name, that she stopped walking.

'Oh. Hello, Mr Stern,' she replied.

'Mrs More, I have a question for you.'

Pamela tilted her head to the side in curiosity.

'What do you make of Baldwin's policy of appeasement?' Stern asked.

Pamela suddenly felt nervous and was already starting to regret entering into the conversation.

'Policy of appeasement?'

'With respect to the Hitler government, I mean. Well, specifically, what do you think of Dawson's editorial approach to it? To me, he seems wholly uncritical.'

This was all very odd. An editor stopping her in a corridor to ask for her opinion.

'Dawson has known the Prime Minister socially for a number of years…' She drifted off, realising she didn't know quite where to go with this.

Pamela kicked herself for not having read a paper for the past week and worried the more she opened her mouth, the more she would look a fool. To make things worse, she felt as if she was, for some reason, being appraised.

'So, because he is friends with the PM, our editor-in-chief, a man who runs a newspaper with the largest circulation in the country, need not be critical of the government?'

'No, of course not. But I would imagine it would make dinner parties with Baldwin and his wife rather awkward if Dawson was seen to be disagreeing with him in a public arena? And besides,' she added, 'isn't it this inside track, so to speak, that gives us an advantage over other papers?'

'That kind of relationship has its advantages,' Stern said thoughtfully. 'However, if his relationship with Baldwin is as cosy as you say, that presents a conflict of interest for our journalistic integrity.'

Pamela looked at her watch. She felt too out of the loop to comment intelligently – and also, late for lunch with her mother. It seemed best to extricate herself as politely but as quickly as possible.

She tried to edge her way closer to the lift as she said, 'I don't know that anyone cares what I have to say on the subject. According to the people who work at this paper, I only write a fashion column.'

'Mrs More, I believe it is our duty not only as citizens of a free, democratic country to voice our opinions but especially as journalists to do so, so that we may inform the general populace. There are many countries who do not allow their citizens those freedoms and we should cherish and honour them.'

Stern continued and asked if she had seen the headlines about Hitler violating the Treaty of Versailles by marching into the Rhineland. Pamela nodded, hoping he wouldn't ask her for a detailed evaluation of German foreign policy.

Instead, he asked, 'What, in fact, do you make of Adolf Hitler?'

'I don't think I really know enough about the situation to be truly well informed. The German Chancellor certainly has managed to pick the economy back up and keep the communists at bay, bring down crime, and so on.' She paused. 'But, as I say, I feel more information on his policies and so forth would be rather useful. But…' She paused again. 'Well, to be honest, *I* wouldn't especially like to have Hitler running my country.'

'The economy is certainly more stable than it was under the Weimar governments. Hitler *has* overthrown the communists, but that's because everyone's been imprisoned or killed.'

'But that's… terrible.'

'I find it troubling that Dawson seems more concerned with rapprochement and appeasement than exposing the truth of these crimes. What do you think?'

'To be perfectly frank, Mr Stern, as I said, I can't imagine many people here, especially Geoffrey Dawson, cares what I think. As

I said, and as you know, my job is to write about fashion and socialites.'

'But, you see, many of those socialites admire Hitler very much.' Stern looked at Pamela directly. 'And the fate of our country could rest in their hands.'

Pamela looked around. Usually bustling, the corridor was eerily silent and empty. 'What do you mean?' she asked.

'There are a number of people in high places who are in favour of Hitler's government and the Nazi Party. If it came to shielding Britain from a Russian infiltration or invasion, they would happily make the alliance.'

'I don't know if I blame them. As unsavoury as they are, I can't imagine the Nazis are a worse alternative to the Bolsheviks. They killed rather a lot of people in their revolution.'

'Mrs More,' Stern said gently, 'Hitler is pursuing policies designed to exclude anyone not supporting the Nazi Party. Repression of dissent, violence, internment. And worse, far worse, the Nazis are eliminating anyone not of the Aryan race, people they consider unfit to breed. German Jews are being sacked from their jobs, their shops closed down, their children turned out of school. The Soviets aren't the only ones who have stripped their own people of their rights. An alliance with Germany would not only be playing with fire, it would be downright immoral. Crime is down in Germany because the criminals are in the Reichstag.'

'How do you know all of this?'

'I have cousins who live in Berlin,' he replied.

Pamela was at a loss. But what can *I* do, she thought? I don't even know any Jews. Suddenly she realised that Stern himself was probably Jewish.

'Do you have children?' he asked.

Pamela shook her head, curious at the turn in the conversation.

'Well, let's say you did. And let's say that one of those children had been born with some developmental problems. And then the state offered to take the child away. For treatment, they said. But really, they were having the child sterilised. Or euthanised.'

Pamela dropped her handbag and all her things fell onto the floor. Stern stooped to help her collect them.

'Imagine this… you're shut out by society… you're dismissed from your job… there are certain areas from which you are barred. What would you do?'

'I… I'm sure I don't know. Go out to the family home, I suppose. In the West Country,' she said feebly.

They stood and faced each other.

'Mrs More, what if nowhere was safe? What if there was nowhere to hide?'

VI

Sitting across from her mother at Claridge's, Pamela wondered if she had worn her fox stole on purpose. The two fox heads always seem to stare accusingly across the table at her with their beady little eyes.

'Had a dreadful time getting here from the station,' her mother groaned as she sipped her wine. 'I couldn't get a taxi for love or money. Traffic was impossible. And the smog! I don't know how you can stand it. I would never come to London if it weren't for the shopping.'

Alma Plumbly was forever campaigning for her daughter and son-in-law to remove themselves permanently to the countryside. Trees. Fresh air. Hunting. Meetings with the local horticultural society. Calls to the vicar's wife. Pamela spent her entire childhood in the fresh air and had had quite enough of it.

'Did you hear Lady Althorp's daughter Minerva had a little boy?' Alma asked pointedly as she inspected a piece of wilted lettuce from her salad with her fork.

Minerva and Pamela had been schoolfriends and came out the same season. She married a man Flossie and Pamela used to refer to as 'the chinless horror' who trod on everyone's toes at debutante balls.

Pamela wasn't in the mood for one of her mother's usual lectures on becoming a 'woman of responsibilities' and how she and Francis lead separate lives. How she was a spendthrift and she ran in a 'fast' crowd with dubious morals. (Everyone knew people with dubious morals were the most interesting people.)

The thought of spending every evening by the fire next to one's husband in deepest Gloucester, making nonsensical chit-chat about the day you'd had arguing with the gardener, was enough to drive one to drink. Which was probably why so many people in the country did.

'What is it that you *do* all day?' Alma asked. 'You can't be serious about that little column you write for the paper. It isn't as if you *need* a job.' She ate a forkful of potatoes and made a face. 'These are cold. Excuse me! Waiter!' Alma waved to a passing server, pointedly ignoring the fact that he was carrying a tray full of drinks.

Pamela didn't actually know why her mother insisted on seeing her whenever she came to town. It wasn't as if they enjoyed each other's company tremendously, and Alma always complained regardless of where Pamela took her for lunch, afternoon tea or supper.

'I don't like the new décor – it's far too modern. And the food...' Alma rolled her eyes. 'Why couldn't we have gone to Rules?'

Pamela gripped her fork in irritation. 'Because the last time we went, you said it was too dark and you couldn't see what you were eating.'

'I don't remember that. And besides, the crowd here is rather...' Alma looked around in disdain as a stunningly attractive woman in a leopard print coat walking a small, white poodle passed their table. 'It seems like the sort of place where men take their mistresses.'

'Doesn't Rules have a secret room where Edward VII used to bring Lillie Langtry for dinner?'

'That was years ago.'

Alma looked up and impatiently called for the waiter again. A young man with heavily Brilliantined hair came over.

'My potatoes are cold?'

Alma's use of a question mark was almost menacing at times. The waiter apologised, bowed and tried to take her plate.

'No, thank you, I'll keep it for now. I would like a chance to eat my chicken. Just bring another plate with the new potatoes, if you please.'

The waiter glanced at Pamela and she made a sympathetic face.

Pamela's mother then turned to her favourite topic: her favourite child. Pamela sighed. Charlotte and Alma had always had a strong bond and her mother never failed to remind Pamela that her sister already had two children, despite being two years younger than Pamela.

'Did you know Peter is building a factory in Milan and another in Rome?' she said, taking a mouthful of cold potato. 'Perhaps you, Francis, your father and I could go to Italy this summer. He and Charlotte are desperate for us all to visit.'

Pamela knew this to be patently untrue, and what's more her father hated travelling as much as her mother hated foreigners, so fortunately, this plan was unlikely to come to fruition. She resisted the urge to remind her mother how gauche and nouveau riche she used to find Peter.

'Your Aunt Constance is coming back to London, or so her letters claim,' Alma said through gritted teeth.

Now we're coming to the point. Pamela watched her mother's face tighten at the very notion of her aunt. Probably her entire reason for wanting to meet for lunch.

Aunt Constance. The former suffragette who used to chain herself to railings of government buildings, go on marches and get arrested. She had been living in India for many years, running a girl's school and raising money for various causes.

Alma sawed angrily into her coq-au-vin. 'Can you believe that she had already boarded the ship to England when she wrote to me? Clearly all very badly planned and last-minute. Like everything she does.'

Pamela's mother had always been very firm that she and Charlotte not take their aunt as a role model. They were to marry and lead respectable lives. She hadn't wanted her spinster sister rubbing off on her daughters, which was probably why Pamela always got along better with her aunt than her mother.

'I believe she's going to be spending her time in London, though for how long, who can say? You know what she's like. Completely unpredictable. We will see each other at some point but in the mean-time, perhaps you can,' she sighed, '*entertain* her.'

Pamela found herself buoyed by the thought of her eccentric aunt, who she hadn't seen since she was a girl. What would she be like now?

Alma suddenly looked up from her plate and peered at Pamela. 'Have you done something new to your hair?'

'Well, I—'

'Because I'm not sure it suits you.'

Pamela realised her martini glass was empty and signalled the Brilliantined waiter. She ordered another drink and her mother continued, expounding on the gossip in her local village – who had moved away, who had moved in, whose extension to their house was in terribly poor taste, who was having an affair. Pamela sighed and let her mother carry on, knowing it was easier to feign interest than try to stop her. She looked around at the other diners, wondering if she might know anyone there, someone who might be able to intervene and make luncheon a little more bearable.

And then Pamela did a double-take. It seemed as if the man at the table behind her, who had appeared to be reading the paper alone, was watching her over its top. She just caught his eye for a moment before he returned to his reading. Was she imagining things? Of course, people watched each other all the time in hotel bars and restaurants, something she was aware of more than most – everyone knew hotels were extraordinarily good places to watch people. But Pamela could have sworn the man who had been watching her looked exactly like the man who had been standing in the square looking up at the house.

VII

Pamela didn't quite know what to expect from Wallis Simpson. She had looked dark and mysterious in her photographs, so perhaps she would turn out to be a tragic operatic heroine after all. She was, of course, an American, but from what she had heard Pamela didn't expect her to be one of those loud, uncouth Americans one so often encountered elbowing their way into the Royal Enclosure at Ascot or bidding on the contents of a stately home at Sotheby's.

At first, she had been somewhat resentful of the assignment – American nobodies from nowhere seemed rather a waste of time if one wasn't to write about their royal assignations. And it seemed a bit roundabout to write a piece on someone who was, as far as the unsuspecting public were concerned, a minor figure in society, whilst simultaneously winking at gossip and scandal. How thoroughly like Percy in many ways – a wink and a nudge to those in the know, a flirtation with the forbidden. Because, as Dawson had said, the Simpson/HRH affair was off-limits to the press.

But then something made her look at the story in a different light. There were two strange things about it.

Firstly, it was curious and surprising that the King had focused his desires on someone like that. Not an heiress to a great fortune. Not a foreign princess. Not even a glamorous film star. How *had* Mrs Simpson ended up where she was? What was the allure?

Secondly, the capricious love life of HRH had never been any great secret, nor was his father's disappointment in his son's lack of interest in marrying and continuing the royal line. (After all, King George had dutifully married his brother's fiancée Mary of Teck when he died suddenly of influenza and had expected his son to be similarly dutiful.) And where they'd hardly bothered with the Prince's previous lovers, the Palace seemed especially eager to keep this affair out of the papers. So why then was the Palace dead-set on covering up the Simpson affair? Because she was American? Because she had been divorced and remarried?

It bothered Pamela that she was hampered with this so-called gentleman's agreement between the Crown, Westminster and Fleet Street. Perhaps David Stern was right, that it was their duty as journalists to inform the public about what was happening in the country. The

British people had a right to know what their sovereign was about. For all they knew, Wallis Simpson could be a secret agent in the employ of the Americans.

Riding in the taxi up Marylebone High Street, Pamela cursed the weather. She had been caught unaware in a brief but sudden downpour and had become somewhat sodden in the moments between struggling to open her umbrella and attempting to hail a taxi – which, of course, everyone else was doing at exactly the same moment. Fortunately, she had put on a good, sturdy, waterproof Aquascutum raincoat that morning when she looked out the window and saw grey skies. If she learned anything from growing up in the countryside, it was that it was worth sacrificing glamour for practicality if it meant not having to be wet. Her hair and face, however, were somewhat the worse for wear, so she reapplied her lipstick, powdered her face and tried to make herself look more like a respectable woman and less like a drowned animal.

They pulled up in front of Princess Elena Andreyevna Tarasova's modest atelier, where Pamela was to meet Mrs Simpson for their interview. The Princess was a White Russian aristocrat Pamela had met through Percy at one of his Bloomsbury parties, and did a trade in tailoring and also copying the latest couture fashions for those who couldn't afford the originals. She was discreet, since she herself knew the humiliation of falling on hard times after years of growing up in gilded splendour.

Pamela entered the shop and was ushered to a fitting room at the back by a young Russian woman with a long blonde plait and a steely eye. A tall woman with copper hair streaked with grey, Princess Elena embraced Pamela and gave the customary three cheek kisses. She then introduced Pamela to Wallis Simpson, whose gown she returned to pinning.

Pamela was surprised to meet a somewhat severe-looking, slender American with a hard mouth and a square jaw. Bright blue eyes and dark brown hair. Older than she had expected, closer to the King's age than Pamela's. Perfectly correct posture. The Princess was hemming a dark green crepe de Chine gown with a high neckline. It looked like a Molyneux, but if Wallis was having it tailored by the Princess it was likely to be an excellent imitation.

Pamela noticed a diamond bracelet with little crosses made out of gemstones, which made her wonder what the financial arrangement was with regards to Wallis and HRH. The Princess's handiwork might be so good as to obscure the provenance of a dress, but Pamela could spot Cartier a mile off.

'Now that His Majesty and I are such close friends, he insists that I accompany him everywhere. Of course, one cannot possibly be seen in the same gown twice, and we ladies of Baltimore know how to dress,' Wallis explained.

Where indeed was Baltimore?

Pamela removed her raincoat and hung it on a coat stand by the door. She turned to face Wallis, who was suddenly alert, her large, dark eyes focused on Pamela's dress.

'Schiaparelli. Last season?'

Pamela was impressed. She was indeed wearing a navy-blue wool crepe dress with a pussy bow collar. It was subtle, not one of the more dramatic creations for which Elsa Schiaparelli was generally known. Not everyone would have spotted it. Pamela often wore such outfits on the job – well made, by a good designer, but not ostentatious. Tasteful ensembles were reassuring to those she interviewed.

'You have an excellent eye,' replied Pamela as she sat in a chair in the corner of the fitting room and took out her notepad.

'Schiaparelli is my favourite designer,' Wallis replied as she inspected her gown in the full-length mirror.

Pamela was tempted to ask if she could actually afford her, or just admired her collections from afar.

Wallis carried on, talking about her friendship with the King in a way that seemed to Pamela both casual and calculated, as if to impress the listener while obscuring the true nature of the relationship. She told a few stories from Fort Belvedere, the King's favoured retreat in Windsor.

'It has all the latest conveniences. Central heating. A bath for every bedroom. A swimming pool. Very different from Windsor Castle or Buckingham Palace.' Wallis's way of speaking was staccato, with the occasional, explosive burst of ragged laughter. 'His Majesty just loves the little American touches I've brought to the place.'

It was well known that Wallis's predecessor, Thelma Furness, was responsible for the modernisation of Fort Belvedere.

'Do you know,' she said, 'I've even taught the kitchen staff how to make sandwiches. They're perfect when we screen movies for his friends.'

The Princess wrinkled her nose at the mention of sandwiches. Pamela couldn't imagine that was how she would spend her tenure as the King's mistress.

After the fitting, the three women moved into the front room of the atelier and drank tea poured from a samovar by the steely eyed young Russian. Once again, Pamela had a sudden, uncomfortable feeling she was being watched. She noticed the Princess looking in the direction of the front window. As Wallis chattered on in her staccato fashion, Pamela spotted him. A man in a bowler hat and a trench coat, leaning against a lamppost, was clearly watching them through the window. It was the same man from the square and Claridge's. Pamela just knew it. It was probably some awful little gossip-monger from the *Daily Mail* trying to jump on her story.

Pamela thanked the Princess and Wallis for their time and made her exit. As she stepped on to the high street, she saw the bowler-hatted man was still there, reading – or pretending to read – a newspaper. She *had* seen him before. It was the man from the square and the hotel and probably several other places. The nerve, the cheek of him, leeching off the hard work of a rival paper. She wouldn't stand for it.

Pamela turned left towards Oxford Street and subtly glanced behind her. The man had begun to follow. She quickly slipped around the side of a building. As the man paused to see where she had gone, Pamela sprang out from the shadows. And whacked him over the head with her umbrella.

'Take that, you two-bit hack!'

Whack.

'How dare you spy on me? Think you can steal my story, do you?'

Whack whack.

'Think you can hang around, taking advantage of good, honest journalists? I've seen you before – don't think I haven't!'

He cowered and covered his face with his arms.

'Go back to the *Daily Mail* and tell your editors never dare to tread on the toes of *The Times* ever again!' she cried as she gave him a good sound thrashing.

'Lady Pamela, stop hitting me with your umbrella! I am not a journalist!' the man replied, under a hail of blows.

Pamela froze, holding her weapon aloft.

'How do you know my name? Who on earth are you and why are you following me?'

She considered calling for a constable but thought better of it when she got a better look at him. He was an unassuming, well-spoken man of medium height, with a mop of wavy brown hair and bright blue eyes, who looked to be a few years older than Pamela. His trench coat was a bit worse for wear after the surprise attack but rather smart and clearly made by Burberry. She knew he couldn't be a tabloid hack with a coat like that.

'Come with me and I'll explain everything,' said the man.

He took Pamela to a dingy little café near Marylebone Station. Apart from an elderly couple having a cup of tea together in the front window, it was empty. He walked to a table at the very back. They sat down and he leaned in closely. It was so surreal, she felt as if she was in a film. Suddenly she felt self-conscious in her sturdy, sensible raincoat and wished she had worn something more glamorous for this mysterious assignation. She quickly took off the coat and hung it on the back of her chair, then fluffed the bow on her dress and subtly (she hoped) checked her hair. She crossed her legs to the right and then remembered her left profile was the better one.

The man introduced himself as Charlie Buchanan. Even though he showed her an MI5 identity card, Pamela still wondered if it was his real name. He explained that he worked for the Security Service and had been assigned to watch Wallis Simpson. And now Pamela, who his handlers had decided was a potential asset.

'So, someone *was* following me, listening in on my conversations, watching my every move! Meanwhile I thought I might be going mad. And it was you, wasn't it?'

'Not just me. There have been others too, engaged in the surveillance operation.'

'Have you people been tapping my phone line as well?'

Charlie frowned. 'Not to my knowledge, no.'

Perhaps Jenny had been wrong about the phone-tapping. Maybe the clicking was simply a fault on the line.

'Well… I can see why one might want to keep an eye on Mrs Simpson. I suspected she was an American agent all along. But I don't see why—'

Charlie looked at Pamela in surprise and laughed quietly. 'It's actually precious little to do with the Americans. You see, certain parties believe our king is not fit to rule because he's too sympathetic to the Germans. And if the situation in the Rhineland comes to blows, Germany will be our enemy once again.'

'I thought this was the kind of thing the League of Nations was meant to settle. Why on earth would our king come into it? He doesn't have any real say in politics. I mean, for heaven's sake, it isn't as if he's Charles the First.'

Charlie lit a cigarette and then offered another to her. She leaned across the table to accept it and got a better look at his face. He was slightly older than she had first thought, the beginning of crow's feet forming around his eyes.

'The King has become rather attached to Mrs Simpson. And Mrs Simpson has become rather involved with a number of people who appear to be more loyal to the Nazis than our own government. High-ranking, influential British subjects as well as German diplomats and aristocrats.' Charlie inhaled deeply. 'I'm sure you can imagine why the King of England cannot be involved with a woman closely connected to such a cabal. Mrs Simpson is privy to state secrets because the King is careless with papers sent over from Downing Street. It's bad enough that he has his own flirtation with the Germans but it would be a disaster if she was able to pass information to Hitler's government.'

'You give her an awful lot of credit, considering the woman is nothing more than an overly ambitious American housewife.'

'You'd be surprised what people are willing to do in the name of ambition.'

Pamela watched the smoke she exhaled drift up to the café ceiling. She noticed the stain from an old leak and wondered who lived in the flat above. She looked over to Charlie, who was watching her.

'We've been observing them both for the past year. And her husband, of course. The Prime Minister himself has an interest in Wallis Simpson's relationship with His Majesty. It all began when the King – when he was still the prince – began giving Mrs Simpson certain expensive presents.'

'The jewellery, you mean? Yes, I thought she was wearing an awfully valuable Cartier bracelet earlier,' explained Pamela as she took another sip of tea. 'I wasn't aware that *Mr* Simpson was in a position to be making gifts of such expensive baubles. I heard the two of them had been rather strapped for cash since the stock market crash. They live behind Marble Arch – not London's most fashionable address. And she avails herself of Princess Tarasova's services, so it doesn't seem as if her wardrobe is full to bursting with Paris couture.

'If I had to guess, I would say that the King buys the jewels and if she's wearing a reproduction, or a lesser-known label, the husband buys the frocks. Though if she starts looking as if she's stepped off the Champs-Élysées, then we'll know His Royal Highness is investing in her sartorial happiness as well. Which would lead one to question the motivations of the affair. Is she in it for the glory? The social cachet? Knowing that the King could pop round at random to their flat for cocktails or dinner on a regular basis certainly has made the two of them rather popular. Or is it simply the money? And in that case, with a financial incentive, perhaps Mr Simpson is in on it too.'

Charlie smiled and tipped his head at Pamela in recognition.

'Very well observed. That was our thinking as well. You see, we became concerned when expensive little gifts to Mrs Simpson led to many thousands of pounds more. Though it's not only the expenditure that raised eyebrows. We have also discovered Mrs Simpson is rather partial to the company of men. We believe the King isn't her only lover.'

Suddenly, it all made sense as to why the Palace would want to cover up the affair.

'That does sound complicated,' replied Pamela. 'So, the objective, as it were, would be for your people to somehow dislodge Mrs Simpson from the King's life.'

'Rather the opposite, actually. Our mission is to ensure the success of their romance, encouraging it as much as possible, even to go so far as to hope for the prospect of marriage.'

Pamela was so surprised by this that she nearly knocked her teacup to the floor.

'But he can't marry her. For one thing, she's already married. And for another, I can't imagine the King of England would be allowed to have an American divorcee beside him on the throne. It isn't as if she could ever be queen.'

'Exactly so, Lady Pamela. Exactly so.'

It was like having a conversation with the caterpillar from *Alice in Wonderland*.

'But that doesn't make any *sense*.'

Charlie stubbed out his cigarette and folded his hands together in front of him on the table. He waited, watching the couple put on their coats and exit the café, the little bell attached to the top of the door ringing behind them.

'Look at it this way: His Majesty is a liability because of his fascist leanings. Mrs Simpson is too, not only because of some of her less salubrious connections and dubious background, but also because of the effect she has on the King. It is almost assured that he would not be allowed to marry her and make her queen. But perhaps, if he was enamoured enough, he might give up the throne for her.'

Pamela looked across the empty café with its tables sporting neat little red and white tablecloths and small vases with single carnations. A waitress with dirty blonde hair and a floral apron cleared the vases off the tables, getting ready to close up for the afternoon. She came over to the table and asked if they wanted anything else. Charlie politely declined and she returned to the kitchen.

'What you're telling me,' Pamela said quietly, 'is that you want the King to become even more entangled with the Simpson woman, so much so that he sacrifices the throne for her?'

Charlie smiled. 'You've hit the nail on the head, Lady Pamela.'

'I still don't understand how I come into it.'

Charlie leaned in. The faint smell of stale coffee and burnt toast mingled with the sweetness of his cologne.

'Being a person so at home in society, you could be very useful to us. We want to recruit someone with the right contacts, well placed to infiltrate that social circle. Not only in relation to Mrs Simpson, but people like Lady Cunard, Viscountess Astor, the Duke of Westminster. We need to find a way of increasing surveillance without arousing their suspicion. And someone like you… someone who is already known in society… someone they'd never suspect… whose job is already to gather information and insert herself in various social situations.'

Feeling self-conscious, Pamela straightened up and smoothed her hair. 'Yes, well, I like to think I've always had an eye for detail.'

'And most importantly,' Charlie continued, 'you are a woman.'

'I would imagine that we do well undercover, don't we? No one takes much notice of most women anyway.'

'Yes,' replied Charlie. 'The advantage of a female agent. But we also need a *canny* woman. Someone who can win Mrs Simpson's trust, become a friend to her. Encourage her romance with the King.'

Become close to the severe-looking woman with the ragged laughter, to encourage her to divorce her husband and marry the King. Pamela felt a bit ill at the prospect.

She shrugged her shoulders and replied, 'Surely this will soon be yesterday's news. His Majesty does have a reputation for being rather a bounder. I'm sure he's bought expensive presents for many of his lovers.'

'The King has made it known – in certain circles – that he is very serious about Mrs Simpson. He refuses to be separated from her,' replied Charlie.

'His Majesty is a confirmed bachelor. He's notorious for his love affairs. You don't imagine after all of that he would fall prey to *that* kind of woman?'

Charlie looked Pamela in the eye. 'Our sovereign is an easily influenced dimwit interested only in his tailor, golf and sunbathing on the Mediterranean. If he's idiotic enough to fall for the charms of such a person as Mrs Ernest Simpson of Baltimore, USA, then what else might he fall prey to?'

What would happen if it was discovered that the wife of a peer was found to be instrumental in a plot to de-throne the King of England?

Charlie stood. 'Take some time to consider our offer. But keep it under your hat.' He began to walk away but unexpectedly turned around. 'Isn't your column called "Agent of Influence", Lady Pamela?' he said with a slight smile.

'Oh, well… yes. But that was just a joke between—'

But Charlie had already disappeared.

VIII

Once again, the silence was broken by another banshee-like wail.

Flossie dandled her baby George while he cried mercilessly. Both mother and baby were red-faced with exhaustion. Pamela looked up sympathetically from the rug where she played dress-up with Flossie's daughters Margaret, two, and Elizabeth, five.

They were like hairless pets, just less well behaved.

'He simply won't stop crying, Pam,' Flossie said, a note of desperation in her voice.

'Isn't crying what babies do?'

'But neither of the girls were like this. It's utterly endless.'

Pamela spotted Nanny Flynn out of the corner of her eye, hovering anxiously around the side of the doorway.

'Perhaps now might be a good time to call for the nanny?'

'Mummy loves you… Mummy loves you… Mummy loves you!' Flossie repeated over and over, alternatively stroking, bouncing and patting baby George. 'I just want to be able to soothe him myself.'

For a moment, George stopped howling and looked at Flossie. She smiled.

'There's my good little chap.'

But it turned out that he was only pausing to draw breath and start all over again. Flossie sighed and continued to stroke George. She looked over at her daughters; Pamela was demonstrating to them how to wear pearls and a tiara.

'Margaret has been terribly slow in everything – walking, talking. Albert insisted we take her to a specialist. He said she may just be later than other children her age to develop. Or she may have some... problems. He says it's too early to say.'

'Well, she is only two years old,' Pamela said gently. 'You can't expect too much of her yet. Maybe she's simply taking her time.'

Flossie forced a smile.

'No, I suppose you're right. It's just very upsetting, the thought that one's child might be... that she might turn out not to be like other children.'

Pamela suddenly remembered what David Stern said about the children in Germany. She looked at Margaret as she pulled on a pair of tiny, opera-length gloves.

George continued to bellow in Flossie's face.

'Oh, Pam, I'm utterly hopeless at this mothering business.'

Elizabeth presented Pamela with one of her dolls, which she had stripped naked. Pamela rummaged around in the doll clothes and suggested some options to her.

'But you're so good with the girls,' Flossie continued. 'They are terribly fond of you. I know you don't think so but I think you'd be a wonderful mother.'

Pamela felt her shoulders tense.

'And surely, when the time comes, you'll give up the column and devote yourself to the children. Of course, with a nanny and then boarding school, you and Francis will still have plenty of time to yourselves. And just think, if you were to fall pregnant soon, how wonderful it would be if our children could grow up playing together!'

Pamela was rescued from having to respond with another ear-piercing wail from George. Flossie sighed and called for Nanny Flynn.

'How is Albert?' asked Pamela.

'In rude health as always. And pleased as punch to have manoeuvred himself on to a special committee. Something to do with improving relations with Germany that will be bound to be good for business.'

Pamela turned to look at Flossie.

'Oh yes?'

'It's called the Anglo-German Fellowship, which is meant to help improve trade links and that sort of thing. A bit of a feather in Albert's cap.'

Recalling her encounter the day before with Charlie, Pamela started to think of a question to ask Flossie. But then Nanny Flynn entered, looking as anxious as ever about baby George. Flossie sighed with relief as she handed him over.

'Do you think it's too early for a sherry?' Flossie asked.

'I'll fetch the decanter.'

IX

'You've beaten me again!' Pamela cried as she clapped her hands.

The dark-haired eight-year-old boy in the Argyll-patterned jumper sitting across from her smiled shyly. He struck Pamela as especially small for his age and seemed dwarfed by the enormous carved oak chair in which he sat.

'Shall we play another round? Best three out of five?'

The boy nodded. As Pamela reset the draughts board on the table between them, she wondered if she would be doomed to entertain other people's children for the rest of her life. She looked out the library window and watched the drizzle come down outside, grateful she had found an excuse not to go hunting.

Francis had wanted to catch the end of the fox hunting season, so they were spending the weekend at Irene Curzon's house in the heart of Melton Mowbray hunt country. Hectored by her parents and sister, Pamela had endured years of hunting during her childhood and adolescence and had long decided that she needn't risk breaking her neck as an adult. She had seen Francis off at the stirrup cup that morning and somehow been saddled with Jamie, the little boy, when his pony bucked him off before the hunt had even begun.

Unheated houses, wet dogs everywhere and all anyone could talk about was horses. Pamela was bored to tears, though draughts was preferable not only to hunting but also to the new Barbara Cartland she had been trying to read, which was left in her bedroom by a previous house guest. It was about romance in country houses, which was ironic considering all anyone seemed to do all weekend – when not riding or talking about horses – was drinking and bed-hopping. Shuffling down the cold, dark corridor to find the lavatory the previous night she had bumped into several people furtively ducking in and out of bedrooms. No wonder this was where HRH had switched his attentions from Freda Dudley Ward to Thelma Furness several years ago.

Pamela watched Jamie furrow his brow, concentrating on his next move, and wished she had remembered to bring the Graham Greene novel she had been reading. Her mind wandered and she found herself thinking about Charlie. Maybe MI5 was watching her at that very moment. She couldn't decide whether she found the idea disconcerting, exciting or both.

She had been weighing the pros and cons of his offer in her mind all weekend.

Pros. It could be exciting. Assignations in darkened bars, writing letters in invisible ink, leaping into getaway cars. An adventure, a chance to do something different with her life. An opportunity to serve her country too, of course. And for once she, not Geoffrey Dawson, would be the one with the inside track on current affairs, the possibility of which made her feel quite smug.

Cons. Pamela had to admit that she had no idea what she was getting herself into. What if she unseated the King just to find out it had all been a misunderstanding or, worse still, she had been some kind of pawn in a political plot? If she was exposed, it would be a terrible embarrassment to Francis. The whole thing would, of course, make life more complicated because she would have to lie a bit to her friends and family.

At dinner that evening, Irene discussed her most recent jaunt to London. She'd been to Nancy Astor's for a dinner party and most of the European ambassadors, the League of Nations Secretary-General and Alfred Rosenberg, the man in charge of Hitler's foreign office, were there. Irene commented that she found it interesting that Nancy was on quite good terms with him and was evidently determined to insinuate herself with the Germans.

Pamela was surprised to find things were more as Charlie described than she'd imagined. But this only increased her sense of worry. Did she really want to put herself, not to mention her family and possibly her friends, at risk for the sake of some sort of internecine war between the government and the Palace? In books and films, innocent people who got caught up in political intrigue generally met a bad end. Spying could be awfully dangerous. (Look what happened to Mata Hari.)

Pamela shivered. No, no... it wasn't worth it. The liability, the entanglements... perhaps even the threat to her life. Maybe she was overreacting but surely it was better to be cautious in such a situation.

The next time Charlie (or whoever MI5 sent) approached her for her answer, she would say no.

X

Francis's friends were different from Pamela's; they tended to be older and a good deal more subdued. Friends from school, the army, the Lords, the Commons, his club. Well bred, well read, intelligent. Not dull per se, but Pamela usually didn't have much to say to them and vice-versa. At the mention of the cocktail party, she thought, oh no, not another tedious evening with cantankerous MPs and their bored wives. She was about to invent an illness so she could get out of it when Francis mentioned that the host was Sir Alan 'Tommy' Lascelles. Francis had known him in the war and Tommy happened to be the King's Private Secretary. Pamela had made up her mind about the offer from MI5. But she was curious to know if there was any truth to the things Charlie had said about the King.

Pamela was surprised to see how run-down Tommy looked. He had dark circles under his eyes and projected an air of despondency. Though being a courtier of the highest order, he was, of course, immaculately dressed in a well-cut dinner jacket with a high thread count (probably Dege and Skinner).

'I hear you're working for His Majesty again,' said Pamela.

Tommy had been HRH's secretary before, in the previous decade when he was the Prince of Wales. The job had been so arduous that King George had awarded him a medal for his services to the Royal Family. Tommy had said it was the hardest earned medal he'd ever received; quite a statement, coming from someone who had won the Military Cross. He was an erudite man with a strict moral code, a lover of books, classical music and history. As different from Edward as one could imagine. The Palace had assigned Tommy to the prince in the hope that his sense of duty would rub off on him, but he ended up resigning in frustration. After some time in Canada, he became Assistant Private Secretary to King George. And then, a year later, when the King died, he was obliged to take up his previous post as Edward's secretary.

'It is utterly exhausting,' said Tommy as he rubbed his brow.

'Is His Majesty... demanding?'

'There was a reason why I resigned as Private Secretary, all those years ago. He's an absolute...' Tommy stopped himself and instead took a swig from his glass.

'I understand His Majesty is rather different from his father,' offered Pamela hesitantly.

'Different from his father! My god. He leaves official papers everywhere. He has no understanding of what confidential means. He takes nothing seriously. It is as if he's been *inconvenienced* by having to take on the responsibility of being king, in which he has no interest whatsoever. He just wants to know what he can get away with.'

'I'm sorry to hear things are so difficult for you,' Pamela said as she put a sympathetic hand on his arm. 'I have heard His Majesty has fallen in with some... unsavoury people.'

Tommy finished his drink and lit a cigarette, puffing away angrily, moustache bristling.

'God knows who that woman is passing information on to,' he said, running a shaky hand through his hair. 'The League of Nations is meeting to discuss the Rhineland today and he doesn't give a damn about anything but her. I've heard things from footmen. One of them walked in on him, on his hands and knees, painting her toenails. Her toenails!' he hissed. 'He keeps insisting they are merely friends but I find *that* as easy to believe as if someone told me they'd seen a herd of unicorns grazing in Hyde Park.'

'At the end of the day, surely he has the best interests of the country at heart. Perhaps he's simply a new kind of king, less bound by convention?'

'The only best interests that concern him are his own. You don't understand. No one does.' He paused. 'He is like the fairy king who has been given every gift except a soul.'

'Oh dear.'

'I should have bred racehorses. Or cart horses. Any sort of horses. I wish I'd never met the man.'

Later that evening, after the party, Pamela undressed for bed. She called to Francis to ask him to help her with the zip on her gown, and he entered the room in his shirtsleeves, puffing away on his pipe.

'The last time I tried this, the dress got stuck in the zip and you weren't very pleased with me.'

Francis undid the zip and then allowed his hand to linger on her back for a moment. Pamela took a step towards her dressing table and removed her earrings.

'You looked very lovely tonight, as always,' he said. 'Is that a new frock?'

'*The Times* fashion columnist can hardly be seen in any old thing, can she?'

The evening news on the wireless floated in from the next room. The BBC broadcaster reported on the negotiations going on between Britain and Germany regarding the Rhineland.

'Francis,' Pamela started. 'I was wondering, now that the prince is king… you know he's had all these love affairs and so on, over the years. And he's been going about with this divorced American. Well, she was divorced from her first husband but now she's remarried to her second.'

'Yes?'

'I was just wondering if there's any chance of this woman becoming queen. If he asks her to marry him and she divorces her current husband.'

'That would be impossible. A twice-divorced American. It would need the approval of the Archbishop of Canterbury as the King is head of the Church of England. And I can't imagine that would go over well. Commoner, divorced, foreign. Unless they agree to a morganatic marriage, which I can hardly imagine.'

'What's that?'

'In theory, if the sovereign were to marry a commoner, that person wouldn't be able to take a title, nor would their children. I suppose there was Mrs Fitzherbert – the commoner George IV married in secret – but she was a Catholic, so it had to be annulled. Otherwise, he would have lost his place in the line of succession.' He paused. 'Why do you ask?'

'Oh, no reason… curiosity.'

Francis smiled and kissed the top of her head. 'Pamela…'

'Yes, darling?'

'Do you think we could… consider the possibility of trying for a child again?' he asked hesitantly.

It was such an inappropriate moment, but all Pamela could think of was the King on his hands and knees, painting Wallis Simpson's toenails.

XI

'Darling!'

Aunt Constance clutched Pamela to her bosom.

Pamela had forgotten how much her aunt liked to embrace people. Apart from an array of Indian jewellery and a deep suntan, she hadn't seemed altogether changed. Aunt Constance had always exuded an air of wildness about her, like a bird that had flown into a house through an open window.

'Everything is so clean and modern here! There are so many people going around in an orderly fashion, queuing up in little straight lines, very polite, very quiet. Nothing out of place. And the air. The *air*! I'd forgotten how dirty it was. Clean streets, filthy air. I can hardly breathe. Oh, and the meat! One can hardly move for meat pies and meat-filled sandwiches and so on. I've practically become a vegetarian living in India.'

She waltzed around Pamela's morning room, picking up objects and putting them down, looking out the window, barely pausing for breath. She kept pushing her curly, unruly brown hair back from her face.

'It's funny what an Englishwoman I feel over there and what a foreigner I feel here. Can you imagine? I can't believe how much I've missed you! You have been terribly, terribly missed – I want you to know that,' she said, taking Pamela's hand. 'But I really did have to go when I did. There was nothing for me here anymore and everyone was so very disappointed in me. And I didn't fancy going to America.'

'America?' said Pamela.

'I had offers from friends who'd emigrated. I fantasised about going out West, to see the mountains and the plains and the canyons!

How romantic, to become a cowboy, or cowgirl, as it were. Can you imagine? Me, roping cattle? Galloping over the open horizon?'

Aunt Constance laughed and flopped down on the chaise longue.

The idea of her aunt on a horse, with a lasso and a holster, didn't seem that far-fetched. She remembered being a little girl and Aunt Constance coming for dinner and arguing with her parents and grandmother about the Vote. She shouted and banged on the table, upsetting everyone. It was always rather exciting.

Aunt Constance peeled off her cardigan unceremoniously and fanned herself. 'I'm awfully hot! Are you hot? It's rather stuffy in here. Obviously, England is *much* cooler than India but everything is so stuffy and I can't remember how to dress for the weather!'

'Perhaps if you sat away from the fire, you might be more—'

'Oh!' Aunt Constance exclaimed suddenly. 'I nearly forgot! I have presents for you!'

She leaned over to root around in a bag she had brought with her and presented her niece with an elegant blue and gold sari and a little wooden statue. Pamela held it up to the light and inspected it.

'This is Ganesh,' Aunt Constance said, 'an Indian deity, the Hindu patron of wisdom and remover of obstacles. Very powerful.' She took it from Pamela and set it on the mantelpiece. 'It should be kept in a prominent place in the house for good luck, otherwise you won't be able to absorb its energies.'

Pamela made a mental note to remember to take Ganesh down before Francis came home.

'It's a wonderful country, you know. Very exciting and wild, all the animals and the colours, the kinds of flora and fauna we'd never have here. Incredible beauty. And the people! Such wonderful, generous people. Rather different kind of mentality from here. And they are

58

much kinder to us – the British, I mean – than we deserve.' Aunt Constance went to the window, watching the people walk by on the pavement. 'Look at them. All those people.' She turned back to Pamela. 'They have no idea.'

'No idea about what?'

'About the way the British government has been treating Indians. And about how poor people are over there, how much less they live with.'

'Is it really so terrible?'

'No, it's far worse. Take this tea, for instance,' she said as she lifted the cup. 'It's Indian, I'd imagine. Produced under ghastly conditions. And of course, they say they've built the railways, created jobs, outlawed suttee and so on. But really, all they've done is strip them of everything they have. Highway robbery!' She paused. 'I want to start another school for girls, just like the first Lydia and I have been running. For Indian girls. But I need to raise the funds, which is partly why I've returned to Britain. I'm hoping to throw a benefit, some kind of charity event. And I thought perhaps you could help me. I don't want to put any pressure on you, but you know quite a few people and if you had the time… Well, if you could see these girls back in India, Pamela… If you could see how much a good education has meant to their lives. Sometimes I wonder what a rather better education could have meant to my own life.'

Pamela sighed and said, 'I'll see what I can do.'

Aunt Constance came over and embraced Pamela tightly, stroking her hair for a moment.

'You are a darling.'

Then she stood, put her hands on her lower back and stretched like a cat.

'I can always feel it in my bones when I haven't done my yoga. Make sure you stretch your muscles every day, Pamela, otherwise one day you'll wake a stiff, bent-over, miserable old woman! Speaking of which, how is my sister?'

'The same as ever. Though she is looking forward to seeing you.'

'I can't imagine there's anyone she wants to see less. She says she doesn't come down to London often so I'm going to take myself out to Gloucestershire. Whether she likes it or not.'

As a young woman, Aunt Constance was forever running away. From parties. From people she didn't like. From home. Escaping out back windows and running through fields. She had been a great beauty but always said the wrong thing to prospective beaux. She had wanted to go to Paris to be a painter but her parents wouldn't hear of it. They finally allowed her to take some classes at the Royal College of Art, where she discovered an entirely new and bohemian way of life. Artists, writers, socialists, and then the suffragettes, which had been the last straw for her family.

Aunt Constance went over to the gramophone and looked through Pamela's record collection. (Francis didn't own any records.) She took out a Louis Armstrong record and put it on.

'American jazz music! What a treat!'

'I've quite taken to jazz over the years, going out to nightclubs. Though Francis isn't wild about jazz. Or dancing. And I know Mother wouldn't approve,' Pamela said with a smile.

Jenny brought in some biscuits and tea. She gave Pamela a brief look of surprise as Aunt Constance danced around the room to the music.

'Your mother doesn't approve of anything. And as for your husband... Golly, I realise I've never even met him! Isn't that strange?'

Aunt Constance sat down and poured the tea. 'What is he like? Is he a nice chap?'

Pamela took a sip of tea. 'Oh yes, quite nice.'

'You must be very much in love to have settled down as you have,' said Aunt Constance.

Pamela frowned. 'I don't think I've *settled down*...'

Aunt Constance took Pamela's hand and looked into her eyes. 'I know my sister would have seen to it that you were married sooner or later. But I remember when you were going to be a writer. Short stories and that sort of thing. I remember when you were a girl and talking about going to the London University to study literature.'

When she was younger, Pamela had harboured secret dreams of becoming the next Rebecca West (minus the illegitimate child), Virginia Woolf (minus the crippling depression) or Katherine Mansfield (minus the tubercular death).

'Mother was very determined to keep me on the straight and narrow, especially after you left.'

Alma had been terrified that Pamela would end up like her sister, a subject of gossip or worse, a spinster.

'I'm sorry I didn't stick around and help you fight against the old battle-axe,' Aunt Constance said sadly as she took Pamela's hand. 'Your generation had a chance after the war that no generation before you had. There was a whole civilisation to be saved and remade.' She paused. 'It's never too late, of course.'

'Too late for what?'

'To do what you want to do. To make a difference,' she replied.

April 1936

I

As she cut through Hyde Park one afternoon, a man bumped into Pamela, nearly knocking her over.

'Oy! Watch where you're going!' he snapped.

'Perhaps you should watch where you're going, considering it was *you* who ran into *me*,' Pamela retorted loudly.

The man turned around, looking surprised at first, and then glaring at her. He wasn't very tall, but stocky and muscular. 'What?'

'I said, it was *you* who ran into *me*,' she said as she drew her shoulders back.

The man took a step towards her. 'If you were my wife, I'd give you a slap for a mouth like that.'

The man had taken off his cap and was twisting it tightly in his hands.

Pamela's instinctive response was to back away. But then she started to feel indignant at being bullied by a complete stranger. She took a deep breath and put her fists on her hips.

'Whoever your wife may be, I feel well and truly sorry for her.'

The man was about to take another step closer to Pamela when, to her relief, a constable walked by. The man took a step back, gave her a dirty look and walked away.

Pamela noticed that in his rush, he had dropped a pamphlet on the ground.

KEEP OUT ALIEN JEWS!
Support these protest meetings.
Hear British Union of Fascists speakers put the case against alien
Jewish immigration into Britain.

The pamphlet went on to list a series of rallies being given by the BUF, and then an encouragement to join the Union. Pamela looked up and saw a crowd gathering in the distance. Curious, she walked in the direction of Speakers' Corner.

A young man with blond hair in a Blackshirt uniform was giving a speech in front of a small crowd while another passed out pamphlets, like the one Pamela had in her hand.

'Our government is run by old men who allow the economy to lie fallow and our army to grow weak. We have no one to protect us from the threat of economic collapse, from unemployment, from immigrants – parasites that stream over our borders. Plain, honest Englishmen are suffering, unable to feed their families. There is a conspiracy against these hard-working men.'

He looked no older than eighteen or nineteen and it was startling to see so much venom coming from such a young person. She wondered if he truly understood and believed what he was saying. Two Blackshirts flanked the speaker, like Roman sentries. Pamela had passed Speakers' Corner and its would-be prophets on many occasions, but this was the first time that she'd felt so uneasy.

She looked around at the crowd; it was mostly men, with a handful of women, all different ages. To Pamela's surprise, they all looked rather ordinary, even respectable. She had assumed that BUF supporters were people who lived on the fringes of society, but many in the crowd looked like they could be accountants, typists, doctors – anything. Were these people simply curious passers-by, idly listening to the angry young man on their daily travels? Or had they come specifically to hear the speech? Was this what they wanted, this anger? Did these people believe what they were being told? And if so, did it mean that they would go back to their lives after this, to their friends and families, repeating this BUF propaganda? She looked over at the thuggish man she'd encountered earlier, his eyes fixed on the speaker, attention rapt.

Pamela felt a shiver go down her spine. A sharp wind picked up and the clouds above darkened. Pamela turned and walked briskly towards Park Lane.

A tramp, wearing a greatcoat from the last war, called out to her. 'Spare a penny for an old soldier, ma'am?' He held out his cap. Pamela rooted through her handbag and found a few shillings to give him. 'Kind of you, ma'am, god bless you,' he said.

It began to rain. Pamela opened her umbrella and hailed a passing taxi. As it pulled up to the kerb, she climbed in. She was startled to find Charlie sitting in the back. He was wearing the Burberry trench coat and held his bowler hat on his lap.

'Well, this is a surprise, isn't it? For me, anyway,' Pamela said with a raised eyebrow. 'I'm sure you're rather practised at this sort of thing.'

Charlie nodded enigmatically, but said nothing.

'Where are we going anyway?'

'That depends on your response to our offer, Lady Pamela.'

Pamela briefly weighed up all the factors. The morality of undermining one's monarch and spying on one's friends and associates. Having to lie about what she was doing, where she had gone and who she had seen. The situation in Europe, and indeed, what was happening at home, in her own country. She looked out the window at the park, trying to catch one more glimpse of Speakers' Corner.

Would MI5 protect her if something went wrong?

Then she thought of what Aunt Constance had said about Pamela's unfulfilled potential. And of what Tommy Lascelles had told her, about the careless king with no sense of duty. The British Union of Fascists and their supporters, including the man who had threatened her.

As if reading her mind, Charlie looked out the window of the taxi and said, 'Mosley likes to send his young foot soldiers out into the public. That one looks like a Boy Scout. Innocent. Very clever of them.'

Oswald Mosley was the leader of the British Union of Fascists. Pamela had never met him personally, but had seen him from afar. He had been a Conservative, then independent, then a Labour MP, before forming the BUF.

'Yes, I've heard he's rather Machiavellian. After all, when he was married to Lord Curzon's daughter Cimmie, he'd had a number of affairs, even when she was on her death bed. With her own sister and stepmother, no less. Everyone knew it had been a marriage of convenience – at least for him. Very useful for advancing one's political career, marrying the daughter of the former Viceroy of India when one is merely a baronet.'

Charlie smiled at Pamela. 'It seems as if you have more intelligence on members of the ruling class than we do.'

'If by "intelligence" you mean gossip, then yes,' she replied.

Pamela and Charlie sat in the stationary taxi, looking at one another.

'What about my position at the paper? Would I be obliged to step down?'

'On the contrary,' said Charlie, 'journalism is the perfect cover. It gives you the opportunity – an excuse, really – to go places, speak to people and do things you might not otherwise be able to do.'

Pamela enjoyed the idea of having a secret life no one at *The Times* would know about.

'Well, this is clearly a very important mission. And if you really feel I'm essential to the cause of protecting crown and country from nefarious elements, how can I say no?'

'Excellent, Lady Pamela. Those above me will be very glad to hear it.' Charlie looked at the driver. 'Thames House, please.'

As the driver started the engine, Pamela asked, 'Where are we off to now?'

'Headquarters. So we can brief you on your mission. And to sign the Official Secrets Act, of course.'

Looking in the rear-view mirror, Pamela patted her hair and adjusted her hat. 'Yes. Of course.'

That evening, she stealthily made her way down to the kitchen. Cook had gone home and Jenny was sharing a cigarette with a young man in a flat cap in the doorway of the servants' entrance. Flat Cap spied her first and froze. Jenny turned and looked at her, surprised at her mistress's presence below stairs.

'Don't mind me,' she chirped. (She already knew about Jenny's sweetheart.) 'Just a quick word in your ear, Jenny.'

Jenny quickly stamped out her cigarette while Flat Cap (herringbone tweed) guiltily skulked in the corner of the stairwell. She approached uncertainly, clearly having put on a bit of rouge for the occasion. Pamela took out her notebook and ripped out a page where she had written a list of names.

She handed Jenny the list and said, 'I need as much information on these people as possible. For an article for the paper,' Pamela added quickly.

Jenny and Flat Cap watched her with curiosity. She suddenly realised how she must have sounded. You must remember to try to be your usual self as much as possible. Mustn't give the game away.

II

The theory making the rounds at Security Services was that the closer Mrs Simpson became to the King, the more vulnerable she was. She didn't have the social or financial security of the King's previous mistresses – no title, no great fortune. And she wasn't so established in London that the friends she had acquired through the King wouldn't drop her if – or perhaps when – the romance lost its allure.

Though Wallis wasn't known to be the kind of woman who liked other women, she was notoriously snobbish in the way that those born on the fringes of good society often were. With her title, wealth and social profile, someone like Pamela was well placed to gain the trust of Wallis Simpson. And then there were the clothes. Wallis, like Pamela, had a well-known love for fashion and jewellery, and so they could be easily drawn together through flattery and a shared admiration for couture.

Pamela was surprised at how little preparation or training Charlie gave her since it seemed too important a mission and too delicate a situation to leave to the luck of a rank amateur. He had told her to act naturally, to be entirely herself, and to go about her daily life whilst trying to see if she could get closer to Wallis in order to encourage the American to confide in her. Nonetheless, Pamela had taken it upon herself to do some research. She had spent a week of afternoons by the fire in her study, flipping through an assortment of spy novels, combing them for tactics, details, protocol and lingo:

Eyes only – intelligence intended to be seen only by a specific person or people but not discussed

Paroles – passwords used to identify one agent to another

Swallow – a female agent employed to seduce a target to gain intelligence

Agent of influence – a person who uses their position to influence public opinion or national policy

And then there were the bits about camouflage and costume, which she found particularly intriguing.

The wrong clothing for a certain situation, environment or country could give a secret agent away. An out of place label or a too-new article of clothing could cost a life.

Agents should always be prepared for a quick transformation and carry things like scarves and newspapers. Newspaper could be folded up and tucked into shoes to make the wearer look taller or into the shoulders of a coat to make their shoulders appear broader.

Soot, coal dust or burned matches could be used to darken hair and eyebrows.

The heel of a shoe could be hollowed out and used for hiding things.

What looked like a lipstick could really be a small pistol with a single shot.

Even everyday accessories were deceptively useful. A handbag or a briefcase could be used as an incendiary device; one could hide the battery and wiring in the lining and use the clasp as a switch.

And one book seemed to suggest that if a female agent wanted to go unnoticed, she should aspire to look mousy, dumpy or old. Pamela felt this was overkill, considering that most women went unnoticed much of the time anyway, however well or badly dressed, however unattractive or beautiful they were.

Charlie taught her to write invisible letters. The process involved a copy of the original letter, which appeared blank until one shook graphite powder onto it, revealing the writing. The graphite would stick to the wax on the copy, left over from the wax paper the writer had laid in between the original and the blank copy. A clever trick but awfully fiddly.

Pamela passed messages to Charlie through what was called a 'dead letter box', which was essentially just a kind of post box. Their dead drop was a space behind a loose brick in the side of St James's, the Christopher Wren church on Piccadilly. The brick was in the side of the church that faced the courtyard, shielding Pamela from busy streets. It was in a convenient location and sat next door to Fortnum and Mason, so if Pamela thought she was being followed, she could always duck into the department store to lose her tail.

Charlie indicated when he wanted to meet by sending a signal to Pamela through a stout, balding Lancastrian called Fred, who sometimes posed as a gardener in the square outside Pamela's house. (Exchanging messages in person was called a 'live drop'.) If it was a regular meeting, Fred would ask about Pamela's geraniums. If it was urgent, he would say he was worried about the state of the chestnut tree in the square.

Now that she had made first contact with Wallis, Charlie wanted Pamela to arrange to meet her again, ostensibly to follow up on her piece for the paper. He suggested asking to meet at Wallis' flat, so Pamela could cover her taste in interior design. (Pamela couldn't help but think Charlie would make a decent lifestyle editor if he ever needed another line of work.) While she was there, she could ingratiate herself with Wallis and see what she could get her to reveal, off the record. Which she could cross-reference with what Jenny had discovered about her. (Not that she had told Charlie about Jenny's involvement. She assumed it was best to keep that detail to herself.)

III

'Lindbergh Baby Murderer Executed by Electric Chair.'

Francis had a habit of reading the most shocking, gruesome titbits from the paper aloud to Pamela, taking particular pleasure in emphasising the gory details. It sometimes seemed that the only news coming out of America was to do with murderers, mobsters or movie stars. Though she did fancy the idea of visiting New York, with its glittering skyscrapers and department stores.

After all, now that she was a secret agent, she needed to become a woman of the world by seeing more of it. And perhaps buy some new luggage. (She quite fancied the new Louis Vuitton range.)

'Francis, wouldn't it be fun to go to New York one day?'

Francis harrumphed over his paper. At least he hadn't said no. Pamela found a harrumph could be turned into a yes over time.

Jenny brought in the evening post and Pamela discovered she'd received another postcard from Charlotte.

Hello from Istanbul! Rather sunny here, wonderful weather for trotting around the Grand Bazaar. Impossible for Peter and me to

*come back to Britain to pick up Alexandra and Christopher. Would
you and Francis be darlings and take them for the Easter hols?*

'She's put in the bit about the Grand Bazaar to make me jealous. She
knows my weakness for markets,' Pamela said to Francis. 'She always
does this. Makes her children our responsibility. I'm tempted to write
back and tell her to send them to our parents for Easter.'

Francis looked up from his paper and smiled. 'Nonsense! Of course
we can take them. They're very sweet children.'

'Yes, I know but you know what Charlotte is like. Before we know
it, they'll practically be living here.'

IV

Christopher, who was eight, was blond and pale, like his mother.
Alexandra, seven, was dark like her father. At first, Pamela was resentful
of having to take on her sister's children, find activities for them to
do and generally rearrange her schedule to accommodate the needs
of children. But when they arrived, they looked peaky and underfed.

Francis was clearly thrilled to have them, as he always was with other
people's children. Pamela hoped it wouldn't lead to another conversation about the possibility of offspring, and for a brief, mad moment,
wondered if they should simply adopt her sister's children. Peter and
Charlotte didn't seem especially interested in them and perhaps Francis
would find it a satisfying project. Pamela did think sometimes that he
needed more to do. He spent a good deal of time at his club, and was
at Westminster a fair amount. And, depending on the season, went
hunting and golfing and shooting, like so many other men in their
circle. But she often felt a hobby of some sort would make him happy.

Or happier, in any case. It was often rather difficult to make Francis happy. Although relatively easy-going, Francis often suffered from a melancholy disposition. Pamela hadn't known him before the war so couldn't say what he was like back then, but it had been impossible to miss comments here and there from his friends and family about the man he used to be, before he was sent to France. He was a kind man with a nurturing instinct – far more so than most men she knew of his background – who enjoyed gardening when he was in the country and doted on Patricia, their retired foxhound. She knew he would likely be happier with something – or someone – to look after.

'They seem abnormally quiet, Pam,' said Francis after the first day.

'With Charlotte and Peter for parents, I can't imagine they get a word in edgewise.'

'And they're surprisingly uncomplaining about spending their holidays with their aunt and uncle and not their mother and father.'

'Well, would *you* want to spend Easter with Charlotte and Peter?'

Cook did her best to fatten them up. Francis took them to the pictures and the zoo and the park. Pamela played dolls with Alexandra. Christopher wanted to play too but Francis insisted on showing him his boyhood train set. (Poor Christopher.)

One morning, the four of them were having breakfast together, with Francis reading the paper. He was agitated; Pamela could always tell the political situation by the number of breadcrumbs and coffee stains on the table cloth.

'Christ…' he muttered.

'Yes, darling?'

'The German Ambassador to the Court of St James has died of a heart attack. They found him in his bathroom. The door was locked so they had to break it down. They suspect foul play.'

'Really? Why? People have heart attacks all the time.'

'The same fate befell the German Ambassador in Paris, just at the end of last year. Sudden, unexpected heart attack.'

'Did they have anything in common?'

'Neither had been a member of the Nazi Party.'

V

In anticipation of Pamela's visit to Wallis Simpson's flat to discuss her wardrobe and taste in interior design, Jenny had compiled a list of titbits about her:

Her maiden name was Bessie Wallis Warfield. (How unfortunate.)

She was raised in a boarding house in Baltimore, Maryland by her aunt, also called Bessie.

Her first husband was a pilot in the navy and a violent alcoholic. Grim rumours of abuse.

Her second husband Ernest was a bit dull.

She was introduced to the Prince by Thelma Furness, who Pamela imagined must be kicking herself now. She didn't make an impression on him when they first met but somehow managed to develop a hold over him.

Many said the King was attracted to strong personalities and a firm hand, perhaps making up for some kind of weakness in his own personality – which would explain his attraction to Adolf Hitler.

She had managed to elevate her anonymous social status by becoming friends with people like Sibyl Colefax, Emerald Cunard, Margot Asquith and Nancy Astor. Her little suppers had become rather popular because everyone knew the King was apt to drop in at any time.

Pamela found her flat at Bryanston Court relatively modern with some traditional touches. Sleek, satin-upholstered club chairs mixed with Chippendale. Pale colours on the walls. A few nice Turkish rugs. Pamela noted that designer Syrie Maugham's influence was very much in evidence in the dining room, with its large mirrored table and metallic drapes; although she really didn't understand what appealed to people about creating the illusion of living in a nightclub. It wasn't a grand setting, but Wallis Simpson had clearly made the most of a modest budget.

A number of staff rushed about the flat, carrying bouquets of flowers, cleaning, cooking, arranging. Pamela couldn't tell whether they were in Mrs Simpson's employ or hired for the occasion.

'Lady More!' she cried as she appeared.

Wallis smiled and offered Pamela a bejewelled hand. Were the rings all gifts from HRH? In a quick appraisal, Pamela decided that two were real and two were paste. (They did make such good costume jewellery these days.) They were all sapphires, which, Pamela realised, were intended to match Wallis' demure, long-sleeved navy dress. (She had never been convinced of the merits of matching everything one was wearing to everything else.)

'Mrs Simpson,' she replied.

'Now remember what I said. I'm very American; I insist everyone calls me Wallis.'

Pamela found the practice of being on a first-name basis with people one hardly knew affected, but smiled and nodded.

Wallis turned suddenly and said sharply to a man setting a large arrangement of gardenias on a round table at the window, 'No, not there. I *said* those are for the dining table. In the *dining* room.'

The delivery man nodded but narrowed his eyes at her when she turned her back.

Wallis struck Pamela as somewhat different from the average London socialite. Of course, she was American, but there was more to it than that. Most women in the upper echelons of British society had a veneer, a coating of charm and politesse under which was a base layer of the rigid and complex etiquette drilled into them from a young age. It allowed them to move effortlessly from one social context to the next; but it also meant that their true opinions and emotions were largely kept hidden, far beneath the surface of these other layers. (Pamela knew she herself was no exception to this.) She recalled how Percy had described Wallis – the femme fatale with the penniless childhood and the abusive first husband. A determined woman, then. Without those layers of British social training, abrasive, somewhat hardened, a little lacking in polish, but also, perhaps, resilient.

'We're having a few people over for supper tonight. Even when His Majesty just thinks he might drop in, he sends a battalion of people with flowers and food and wine. He's such a peach.'

They moved to a sitting room and Wallis explained that she had tried to bring 'a touch of home' with her to London.

'For instance, tonight I'm serving fried chicken, potato salad and coleslaw for supper.'

'My, that sounds terribly... novel,' replied Pamela, thinking it sounded anything but. 'I must say, you've done such a fantastic job with your flat. Do tell me about your decorator.'

A doorbell rang and a maid announced that a Princess Stephanie von Hohenlohe had arrived.

'What a treat!' said Wallis.

An elegant woman about Pamela's age, wearing a mauve-coloured, square-necked blouse with matching skirt and a rather fine emerald brooch, entered the room. Wallis introduced Pamela to the woman, who turned out to be her neighbour.

'You told me you would be occupied this afternoon with the preparations so I wanted to see if I could help,' Princess Stephanie said.

Pamela couldn't quite place the accent, but she suspected that the blouse and skirt were by Lucien Lelong.

'Remember I said that Lady Pamela was coming over for the piece she's writing about me for the paper?' replied Wallis.

'Which paper, please?' she asked, looking at Pamela intently.

'*The Times*,' she replied.

'Ah! A very good paper. I am somewhat involved in newspapers myself. Do you know Lord Rothermere?'

'I've met him once or twice, yes.'

There was something odd about the woman but Pamela couldn't put her finger on what it was. She wondered if her title was real or invented. One never knew with displaced foreign aristocrats.

'He is a very dear friend of mine, very dear,' she said. 'As Wallis knows, it is very difficult to make connections, to make friends in such a large city when one is a foreigner. And Lord Rothermere has been terribly kind to me.'

They all sat down and Wallis rang for tea. Pamela positioned herself with her notepad at the ready. 'You were saying, about the decor, Mrs Simpson?'

'You must call her Wallis,' interrupted Princess Stephanie. 'She insists and everyone does. A charming American custom, though perhaps unfamiliar to Europeans like you and I.'

Pamela bristled at being lumped into the same category as this woman, who she already found somewhat disagreeable, but smiled and forced herself to comply.

'I've had some help here and there from knowledgeable friends – Syrie Maugham, Sibyl Colefax,' Wallis said. 'But mostly I've thrown everything together myself. Picking out pieces here and there that appeal to me, really.'

Thrown everything together. Was this affected casual posture an American habit or had Wallis in particular cultivated it to set herself apart from the formality of the people with whom she surrounded herself? Pamela was beginning to understand how Wallis had wended her way into the King's life.

'She has a… how do you say…? Knack! A knack for making things beautiful,' interjected the Princess. 'As you can see.'

The bell rang again. The maid interrupted apologetically to tell Wallis that her special delivery from the Palace had arrived. Wallis clapped her hands together like a delighted child.

'You'll have to excuse me for a moment,' she said. 'His Majesty does so enjoy making little contributions to my dinners. I'll only be a moment.'

Wallis exited and the Princess turned to Pamela. 'It is very unusual that English ladies work in newspapers, no?'

'I suppose it is.'

'Then you must be a very good writer,' she said, smiling at Pamela in a way that made her wonder what she wanted.

'I'd like to think I've managed the hang of it and have a natural sense of… people, fashion.'

'Ah, but of course!' she exclaimed suddenly. "Agent of Influence"! Yes, I have read it many times. Quite amusing.'

Pamela was more suspicious now, and with the distinct sense of being patronised. She looked down at her simple blouse and skirt and wished she had worn something a little more impressive. Though she had gone out of her way not to overshadow Wallis, she could have gone to greater lengths than a simple strand of pearls. Sometimes she wondered if her childhood in the countryside in twinsets and tweed had embedded a tendency to sartorial understatement in her.

'You could say I too work with newspapers. I am an advisor to Lord Rothermere. On European affairs. I am originally from Vienna and spent many years in France. I introduced his lordship to the German Chancellor myself.'

'You introduced Lord Rothermere to Adolf Hitler?'

The Princess smiled, almost coquettishly. 'Yes. I do not think it too forward to say that I count myself as a particular friend of Herr Hitler. I helped his lordship host a dinner party for Herr Hitler and a number of other people in his government in Berlin, at the Hotel Adlon. Do you know it?'

'I've never been to Berlin.'

Wallis re-entered the room.

'Ah, you must come!' the Princess said. 'You can be my guest! I am forever trying to get Wallis to come and visit.'

Princess Stephanie took Wallis' hand as she sat beside her on the sofa.

'I promise, I will soon. But with Ernest in New York so much on business, I have to hold down the fort,' Wallis demurred.

With Ernest frequently away on business in New York, Pamela assumed 'the fort' she really meant was Fort Belvedere.

'It is a marvellous city,' continued Princess Stephanie. 'And of course, much safer now under this government than in the Weimar days when you could not walk down the street without having your pocket picked. I would like to think I can do something here in London for relations between Britain and Germany. For peace.'

'For peace?'

'It is my wish that we may live in a united Europe, liberated from the fear of conflict. I was a nurse in the last war, on the Eastern Front for the Austro-Hungarian Army. It was a terrible, bloody business.'

'So I recall.'

'Germans and Austrians say the British do not understand because you did not suffer as we did; you did not lose your territories.'

'Certainly, His Majesty feels very strongly about the war,' added Wallis. 'It affected him badly, having to fight a country he'd always considered an ally.'

It was clear Wallis brought up the King at any opportunity because she knew how precarious her social position would be without the connection.

'I do not believe this country wishes for another dispute any more than we do,' said Princess Stephanie. She got up to pour more tea. 'Wouldn't you agree, Lady Pamela?'

VI

Pamela left a message for Charlie in their dead letter box, reporting on the Princess Stephanie and her connections to Hitler and Lord Rothermere. Charlie wrote back to say that she was known not only to British agencies but also to French intelligence, who threw her out of France when they realised she was spying for the Germans. Born and raised in Vienna, she had made a very good marriage to an Austro-Hungarian prince. Now divorced, she travelled back and forth between Britain and Germany having affairs with numerous people.

Charlie was interested to hear that she was so close to Wallis and asked Pamela to keep an eye on the situation. Ideas regarding ways of doing this, however, were not forthcoming, Pamela noted. He also suggested she cultivate an acquaintance with Princess Stephanie, which she found even less appealing than cultivating an acquaintance with Wallis Simpson.

Pamela rang for Jenny.

'Jenny, do you ever hear anything about… about people who hang around with… political types?'

Jenny raised her habitual eyebrow.

'Could you be more specific, Madam?'

'Foreign political types.'

'Any foreign in particular?'

'Germans, for instance.'

'Keep a lookout for people connected to Germans?'

'Yes.'

'Nazis?'

'Germans *and* Nazis. Not all Germans are Nazis, I don't think.'

'No, Madam.'

VII

Since their reunion, Aunt Constance had started insisting on taking Pamela with her on various excursions. That day they ventured into Essex to visit her friend Sylvia Pankhurst. Aunt Constance had first met her when they were art students – the only two women in their class – and then became involved in the campaign for the Vote, designing posters and banners together.

Sylvia had been excommunicated from the rest of her family by her mother Emmeline and sister Christabel for a number of sins, including her pacifism during the war, living with an Italian man to whom she wasn't married and having a child out of wedlock. She wore a tweed skirt, brogues and an old jumper.

The two women were very pleased to see each other after so many years apart. Sylvia insisted on having tea in the garden because it was sunny (albeit very cold).

'I simply can't abide being inside on such a beautiful day,' said Sylvia as Pamela pulled her coat tighter around her.

'Sod the tea, this calls for a real drink. Whisky?' said Sylvia.

'I really shouldn't but... oh go on then,' replied Aunt Constance. 'Isn't it a bit early in the day for—'

'Nonsense!' Sylvia said to Pamela. 'You're far too young to be such a wet blanket.'

Sylvia poured three glasses of whisky and she and Aunt Constance quickly became engrossed in old memories.

Pamela's mother and grandmother blamed the Pankhursts not only for her aunt's ruin but the downfall of all women. Raised hemlines, smoking in public, speeding around in motor cars. When it came to Pamela, Alma was spoiled for choice in terms of who to denounce. Her sister, who had passed down her wild, rebellious streak to her niece. Or was it the girls she had met when Pamela was being 'finished' in Paris? (Convinced the French had encouraged wantonness in Pamela, Alma sent Charlotte to Switzerland instead.) And she was certain the modish flapper culture of the time was also at fault for the proclivities of her daughter, who had obtained a reputation for being 'fast'. Easily bored at deb balls, Pamela would sneak out halfway through, dragging a nervous Flossie behind her, and talk her way into the Florida Club or the Café de Paris. She danced with the boys the other girls had labelled MTF ('Must Touch Flesh') or NST ('Not Safe in Taxis'). She flaunted her aspirations of becoming a writer in the face of her parents, threatening to become a bluestocking, and thus making herself unattractive to potential husbands. When she finally married Francis – well into her twenties, a far older age than all her debutante peers – Alma had been relieved beyond description.

Aunt Constance brought out her sketchbook of drawings from India, telling stories from her travels and her girls' school.

'But this is marvellous, Constance! You have continued our good work. Even if your family don't approve.' Sylvia glanced at Pamela.

Aunt Constance said, 'Pamela is nothing like Alma and my parents. She's more like us. Very clever. Independent. Makes up her own mind.'

Pamela suddenly felt a sense of pride. 'Oh no, I'm nothing like my mother and sister. Actually, I think Mother finds me to be a terrible disappointment.'

'That sounds familiar,' Sylvia replied.

'Do you ever speak to either of your sisters? Or was the rift a permanent one?' Aunt Constance asked Sylvia with a hint of sadness in her voice.

Pamela realised how lonely Sylvia and her aunt must have been, during all their years in the wilderness, cut off from their families for their political convictions and choices in life. She had a strong urge to tell both of them about her recent assignations. She wanted Sylvia to know she was different than other women. That she was doing something. That she had a purpose. And then she felt a wave of sadness that she would never be able to tell anyone.

Sylvia stood up and walked a few paces away to inspect her roses. 'There's too much distance between us now. They're like strangers to me. It's incredible to think we all wanted the same thing, once upon a time.'

'Is Christabel still going around with those mad evangelists in America?'

'She's returned to Britain. Think the evangelical bloom is off the rose. Did you know, she's being made a Dame of the British Empire? Mother would have been very proud. She did become so conservative in her old age – absolutely obsessed with the Bolshevist threat. I never forgave Mother for shipping Adela off to Australia. They've done something to her out there. In her last letter she seemed quite enthusiastic about Hitler.'

Sylvia finished her whisky and poured another, topping up her guests' glasses in the process. Pamela tried to stop her but was too late. She felt the whisky rising in her, warming her and dulling her senses slightly. A ginger cat slipped by her legs, rubbing on her. Pamela reached down to pet it and it rubbed against her hand.

'*Hitler*? Adela? I can't believe it,' replied Aunt Constance. 'How has it come to that?'

'The Nazis seem to attract people who are easily impressed and flattered. People who like strong personalities,' interjected Pamela. 'Even our own king seems to be drawn to them.'

Sylvia looked at Pamela, appraising her. 'I suppose my mother was a kind of dictator herself. She wanted us to be her obedient foot soldiers.'

Pamela finished her whisky and picked up the cat, holding it in her lap while it purred contentedly. She was awfully fond of cats but Francis was allergic so they could never have one.

'And most people *are* easily taken in,' Sylvia continued. 'That's the problem. Take the last war, for instance. Did the British people have any idea what they were fighting for? Did they go to the slaughter-houses regardless? And there my mother and sister were, handing out white feathers to every man between the ages of eighteen and forty. The war made senseless brutes of everyone, on the battlefield and off. And in the end, it was for nothing.'

Pamela rose and absent-mindedly walked around the garden with the cat in her arms. She remembered how furious her mother had been with Aunt Constance for taking the pacifist's stance with Sylvia, especially as their brother Edward and Pamela's brother William had both served in the army. Pamela's uncle had been killed early in the war at Loos and her brother towards the end at Amiens, though no one in the family spoke of them. It was as if it was simply easier to pretend that they had never existed at all, rather than raise painful memories. The whole family had felt Aunt Constance had disgraced their honour by being a conscientious objector.

'What are you campaigning for now?' Pamela asked Sylvia.

'Ethiopia,' replied Sylvia gravely. 'It's an abomination, what the Italians are doing. Everything has escalated so quickly. I had hopes that the League would do something but they've been useless while the Ethiopian people are left to fight for their lives. And of course, Britain is turning her back on them too. We're allowing everything to crumble to pieces around us, alone on our little island.'

Pamela thought sadly of William. It felt like an indulgence somehow, allowing herself to wade through the memories of their childhood together. The older brother who liked books and cricket and cats and dogs, who alternatively teased and doted on his little sisters. Despite their age difference of seven years, Pamela had been closer to him than she ever had to Charlotte. He died at the Battle of Amiens, in 1918, heartbreakingly close to the Armistice. He was nineteen years old. Pamela was twelve. She wondered if Sylvia was right, if it had all been for nothing.

May 1936

I

'It's not a *scandal*, Pamela. You're making awfully heavy weather of my engagement.'

'Do remind me, Evelyn,' said Pamela, 'how old is your child-bride?'

'She's not a *child*.'

'She is all of twenty years old!' laughed Diana Cooper. 'Which means she was... how old when you met her? Seven?'

'She was seventeen,' Evelyn Waugh replied primly, 'which is when most young ladies are introduced to society for the purpose of being married.'

Pamela was at the Savoy for luncheon with Evelyn Waugh, and Diana and Duff Cooper. They were celebrating the forthcoming publication of Evelyn's new book on his stint in Abyssinia. (The publication of which had coincided with the Italian Army's capture of Addis Ababa, Emperor Haile Selassie's flight into exile and Mussolini's proclamation of King Victor Emmanuel as the new Emperor.)

'You are glowing with smugness,' said Pamela. 'You have a new book, a pretty child-bride—'

'She's not a—'

'And now the second husband of your first wife, who jilted you, has now jilted her. Also for a pretty young woman. All these pretty young women!'

'Is it true she's a Lloyd's Bank Lloyd?' asked Diana.

Evelyn's first wife had also been called Evelyn. When they were married, their friends referred to them as He-Evelyn and She-Evelyn. Their marriage had only lasted a year before She-Evelyn left He-Evelyn for another man, who was now leaving her for someone else. Pamela couldn't help but feel a bit sorry for She-Evelyn, who had lost all the friends she had accumulated with He-Evelyn, in no small part down to the character assassination she received in his novel *A Handful of Dust* two years previously. (Everyone knew that the character of the heartless adulteress Brenda Last had been based on her.) It was a salutary reminder that one must be careful what one said around Evelyn Waugh, otherwise it might end up in one of his novels.

'I still have to get an annulment from the Catholic Church before Laura and I can be married,' Evelyn sniffed.

He had recently converted to Catholicism and had become rather pious. Pamela didn't think he would have leapt into the arms of the Catholic Church if his first marriage hadn't imploded, but she kept this to herself.

Evelyn sipped his claret and regaled the table with stories from his time as a reporter the year before. He leaned back in his chair and adjusted his natty polka dot bow-tie, which made him look somewhat youthful. It always amazed Pamela that despite not having a fixed abode for years, instead taking advantage of one friend or another's country house, he always managed to look smartly dressed.

'It seems to me that the Romans are following their destiny as empire-builders. Besides, Abyssinia is a run-down, dirty, savage place which

Signore Mussolini is doing well to take. When I was in Addis Ababa last year, I stayed in a flea-ridden hotel run by a misanthropic Greek.'

'What were the Greeks doing there?' asked Diana.

'It was just the one Greek. And a Russian. A Russian *prince*. He was running a tannery which sat next to the hotel. Like a tragic short story.'

'A *tannery*? What was on the other side? An abattoir?' Diana said, nibbling at her mushrooms en croute.

Evelyn paused for dramatic effect, to make sure everyone was paying attention. 'A house of ill fame!'

'Oh!' exclaimed Diana, both scandalised and delighted.

'Once the wireless station was shut, there was nothing to do with the other foreign press but drink and gamble. And I must say the girls weren't very pretty,' Evelyn added with pursed lips. 'But you know what Latin men are like: the greatest hardship for them is to go without a woman. They weren't very discerning.'

'I imagine it wasn't an especially nice hotel,' Pamela said.

'Pamela darling, guests introduced menageries of pets into their rooms and shot at the night watchman.'

'Sounds rather like a cowboy picture,' said Diana.

'Oh Evelyn, how can you condone such a brutal invasion?' asked Duff, frowning.

Evelyn primly ate a green bean from his plate while complaining that reports of Italian criminality were exaggerated.

'I read somewhere that the Italians have been using mustard gas,' Pamela interjected.

Evelyn's face fell and he spluttered, 'Well... the Abyssinians have committed atrocities too.'

'I don't think young boys wielding spears are a match for poison gas,' Pamela retorted.

Duff nodded. 'I remember the men who were gassed in the war. Absolute hell for them. The tragedy of this whole thing is how ineffective it has shown the League to be.'

Evelyn looked sulky, folding his arms against his chest. 'The League has always been ineffective. If anyone is to blame, it's Britain and France who could have blocked Italy in the Suez Canal but rather liked profiting from the commercial traffic.'

Pamela spotted Cecil Beaton out of the corner of her eye across the room and waved. Cecil waved politely but turned back to his table.

Evelyn spotted the snub and rolled his eyes. 'Cecil has never forgiven me for supposedly bullying him at school.'

'Well, *did* you bully him at school?' prodded Diana.

'Yes, mercilessly, but it was such a long time ago. Besides, I'm a Catholic now.'

'What's that got to do with it?'

'You have no idea how much nastier I would be if I was not a Catholic. Without supernatural aid I would hardly be a human being,' replied Evelyn as he reached for his claret.

As off-the-cuff and casually as she could, Pamela turned to Diana and asked her what she made of Wallis Simpson. (She and Duff had been to Bryanston Court several times.)

Diana dabbed her mouth with her napkin. She then pursed her lips and forced a small smile. 'She is certainly... different.'

As Evelyn and Duff argued about Mussolini, Pamela attempted to draw her out.

Diana looked around and whispered, 'No one will admit it, but it's plain to see she's bored stiff by him. I know it's a feather in one's cap to have His Royal Highness dropping by to say hello during cocktail hour, but I think the novelty's worn off. And her boredom brings out her Becky Sharpishness. Rather uncharming.'

'Do you think the bloom is off the rose for him too?'

'Oh no. For some reason, he's besotted. But I do wonder why she's been hanging around if she's so miserable,' Diana continued. 'I suppose the Royal Purse is an incentive. From the looks of things, it seems as if he's been buying Cartier's entire front window to keep Wallis interested.'

It was curious to Pamela that Wallis continued to see the King if she was indeed so bored and unhappy. Was Diana right? Were the social connections and jewels enough? Or was there something else afoot? Was it mad to think that Wallis had been planted by someone to infiltrate the British monarchy and gain influence over the King?

Either way, Pamela was going to find out.

II

It was typical that Charlotte and Peter were in London on a 'flying visit' when Pamela had a cold. Her sister had an unbroken record of making an appearance when she felt and looked her worst.

They bustled in to the house, looking as smart and healthy as ever. Charlotte was wearing what Pamela was certain was a new fur coat and a more platinum shade of blonde than the last time she had seen her. Both seemed to have the kind of glow that radiated outwards from the self-obsessed. And of course, they sported matching suntans. They had recently been on the Italian Riviera with someone in Mussolini's cabinet and his film star mistress. Pamela glanced at her reflection in the mirror in the entryway, lamenting her London pallor made worse by runny nose and red eyes.

Peter had brought a bottle of wine from the vineyard he had invested in and then proceeded to expound upon it for much of the evening, confirming Pamela's long-standing opinion of him as narcissistic, vulgar and a crashing bore.

While Pamela and Charlotte's parents hadn't been thrilled at the prospect of being linked to a nouveau riche family like Peter's, Charlotte had been dazzled by the wealth he had dangled in front of her. He had been a more alluring prospect than the baronets' sons saddled with their fathers' gambling debts she was wont to meet at garden parties and debutante balls.

As Peter droned on about tannins, bouquets and soil, Pamela looked at Francis, who was staring blankly into space. And then he began waxing lyrical about Italian food.

'You simply cannot get tomatoes here like the ones they grow in Italy.'

'Even the bread is the most divine thing you've ever tasted.'

'Christ, and the cheese. The cheese!'

'I don't know how anyone eats anything at all in this country. Diabolical.'

Pamela felt quite insulted on behalf of Cook and her efforts with the salmon that evening. Francis gave her a look from across the table.

Charlotte took up the mantle from her husband, talking about their recent travels to Capri and how delightful the weather was there this time of year – knowing full well that Pamela had always wanted to go to Capri. She had taken up swimming and enthused about how the stones had simply melted off her body.

Pamela sneezed.

'You should really leave England more often,' Charlotte said pity-ingly. 'It will improve your health. But then again, I suppose you always were a homebody, as the Americans say.'

Stabbing at her salmon violently, Pamela replied, 'We've been discussing a trip to New York, as a matter of fact.' She looked at Francis pointedly. 'Weren't we, darling?'

Francis raised an eyebrow.

Charlotte clapped her hands together and said, 'How marvellous! Your first trip to New York! I'll be sure to give you shopping tips.'

Before Pamela could lunge across the table for her sister's throat, Charlotte suddenly changed the subject. 'I've heard you've seen Aunt Constance. Is she as odd as ever?'

Pamela was guarded in her replies, not wanting to expose her aunt to criticism, but Charlotte picked up on her equivocation like a bloodhound.

'You always were like her, Pamela.'

'What do you mean?'

'Oh, you know, a bit rebellious, never did what you were told. And everyone assumed you'd eventually end up a spinster.'

Before Pamela could go on the attack, Francis stepped in diplomatically to ask how Alexandra and Christopher were.

'We'll most likely see them at the weekend but you know how busy we are when we're stopping through London,' said Charlotte. 'Very kind of you to take them over Easter. Peter had business in Istanbul and I don't like to stay in Rome by myself, even with the children. The problem is this palazzo we've taken—'

Peter looked up from his wine glass.

'Charlotte,' he interrupted.

'It's old as the hills, like everything in Italy. But it has a terrible aura.'

'Charlotte, not tonight,' Peter insisted.

'Peter doesn't like me to talk about it, but the house is haunted.'

Peter threw his napkin down on the table in a huff.

Charlotte had always had a weakness for the occult. It was the one influence Aunt Constance had had on her. When they were children, she used to read them stories by MR James and hold séances.

'Apparently, someone *died* in the house, sometime around the end of the last century. According to the housekeeper anyway.'

'Charlotte, your Italian is terrible,' Peter interjected. 'You've probably misunderstood her.'

'She says the daughter of the count who used to own the palazzo hanged herself because her parents forced her to marry a man she didn't love.'

'And you've *seen* this dead Italian girl…?' asked Pamela.

'I've *sensed* her. And I've heard things, late at night.'

'*I* haven't heard anything,' protested Peter.

'That's because she only makes herself known to those who are *receptive*.'

'Then maybe you could stop receiving her.'

Charlotte turned to Pamela. 'Elena – our housekeeper – wants to bring in a priest. For an exorcism.'

'I am *not* having a priest coming to my house muttering some mumbo-jumbo,' snapped Peter.

'And until you agree to let me bring in a priest, I don't feel comfortable staying there and I certainly don't feel comfortable having our children stay there.'

'I take one of the most beautiful places in one of the best neighbourhoods in Rome, where half of Mussolini's cabinet lives—'

'Which we could only afford because it's haunted by the ghost of a girl who killed herself,' Charlotte replied.

Peter was pacing back and forth along the length of the dining room.

'I'm sure I've heard stories of possession,' Pamela said. 'Of children.'

'Oh…' Charlotte murmured anxiously.

Francis gave Pamela a warning look.

'For god's sake,' Peter muttered angrily to himself as he lit a cigarette.

'Will you be returning to Britain again soon?' Pamela asked politely. 'Or do you have more business dealings ahead in Italy, Peter?'

Peter walked to the window and looked out into the street, as if he thought he might be watched.

'I've been arranging some investments in East Africa. Factories and so forth. For the Italians. So, it's likely I'll be spending some time there.'

'*We* will be spending some time there,' corrected Charlotte.

'My friend Evelyn was in Abyssinia recently. He says it's rather exotic. With some lovely little hotels.'

'How wonderful!' cried Charlotte.

'I'll have to get the names for you,' replied Pamela.

'We've discussed this, Charlotte. It's not safe for you there,' replied Peter.

'Peter, you're not leaving me alone in that house of horrors.'

Francis took a sip of wine and said, 'Peter, speaking from a political perspective, it's not wise to become financially involved in Ethiopia. There is, of course, the ethical dilemma, the way the Italians have treated the Africans. And there is also the issue that Britain and France have sanctioned Italy and put an arms embargo in place.'

Peter walked back around to his chair, threw his cigarette into the fire and sat down.

'That's why the factories we're building there are going to be making the arms. No need to worry about shipping routes and trade embargoes. And when everything gets settled over there, the British government will change their tune. They always do when they know which way the wind is blowing. After all, Mussolini's managed to do in six months what should have taken years. And even the King won't receive Selassie at Buckingham Palace.'

Francis sighed. Pamela could tell he wasn't in a mood to argue.

'You're not leaving me alone in Rome, Peter,' insisted Charlotte.

'If you don't like it, you can stay in London,' he replied.

'Of course, you can always have the priest round to exorcise the Canterville Ghost while Peter is away,' Pamela said to Charlotte innocently.

'What a good idea!' said Charlotte.

Peter glared at Pamela.

'I'll ring for pudding,' said Francis.

III

Hyde Park. The south side of the Serpentine. 5pm.

Pamela received the note one afternoon from Charlie via Fred the gardener. It was a bit inconvenient as Flossie and her husband Albert were coming over for supper at seven o'clock.

It would have looked strange if Pamela cancelled at the last minute. (Besides, Flossie's feelings were so easily hurt.) She tried to think of excuses to leave the house that wouldn't arouse Francis's suspicions. She spied Patricia lounging by the grate in her usual spot and announced to Francis that she was going to take the dog for a walk. Francis looked surprised. Pamela was not known to be a dog person. She snapped on Patricia's lead and the dog looked at her balefully. When they got to the front door, she resisted, planting her front feet on the threshold in defiance. Pamela felt guilty as she gave the lead a sharp tug and practically dragged her out the front door and down the street.

As Pamela walked into the park, Charlie was smoking on the bench next to the third lamppost on the left as agreed. He raised an eyebrow when he saw Patricia. Pamela attempted to behave as if she was hardly ever seen without a dog by her side.

'We need more information on Mrs Simpson – the situation is starting to move faster than we'd expected. It seems that abdication may become inevitable if the King doesn't give her up, and it is looking less and less likely that he will do so.'

'And what will happen if he does step down?'

Patricia pulled on her lead, trying to sniff out the squirrels and birds.

Charlie reached down to pet her and said, 'The Duke of York will take his brother's place and everything will continue as normal.'

Soothed, Patricia sat and looked at Charlie with her large brown eyes.

'Normal? For a king to abdicate for his American girlfriend?'

'As normal as possible.'

Pamela watched people walking past. A couple arm in arm. A governess holding two small children by the hand. A guardsman in regimental uniform.

'Do you think people might… find it odd? Or get upset? After all, the King is rather popular.'

Charlie turned towards her and leaned in. 'There are rumours of a coalition of Nazi sympathisers and British Union of Fascists members who feel aligned with the King and his politics, who may possibly even split from the Conservatives. We need to avoid dividing the country at all costs. Such a division would be a disaster and could weaken Britain irreparably.'

'And where do I come in?'

'We must gather as much information as necessary, of the King's devotion to Wallis, of her dubious motives, of his connections to the far right, so that if the time comes and he relinquishes the throne for her, we are prepared.'

'Dig up some dirt, you mean.'

Charlie smiled. 'Exactly. How like a journalist.' As Pamela looked at her watch, he caught her eye and said, 'Don't worry, I won't keep you much longer. The information you have been giving us thus far through the dead drop has proved very useful.'

Pamela thought about all the notes she painstakingly wrote in invisible ink and left behind the loose brick in the church wall. What Diana had said about Wallis being unhappy. Wallis's friendship with Princess Stephanie – Hitler's 'particular friend' – and the Princess's connection to Lord Rothermere (owner of both the *Daily Mail* and the *Daily Mirror*). Tommy Lascelles's stories about Wallis and the King.

Pamela felt the slip of paper between her fingers as she put her hand in her pocket. It was the list of names she and Jenny had put together. Anyone associated with Mosley, the BUF, Germany, German business interests. Anyone who had spoken highly of Hitler and even Mussolini. Persons of interest, they called it. She hesitated, wondering what she was getting herself into. What she was getting the people whose names were on the list into. Flossie's husband Albert, for instance. Peter and Charlotte – her very own sister. She suddenly felt terribly, terribly guilty. She took a deep breath and handed it to him.

'This may prove useful to your people.'

Charlie looked surprised. He opened the folded paper and read the list.

'Well done, Lady Pamela. An excellent start indeed.'

As Charlie began to stand up, she put a hand on his arm.

'I don't know everyone on this list personally. I suppose I know some in passing, socially. Some are acquaintances... people I've known for years through one thing or another. And I can't say I especially *like* them all. In fact, some of those people on that list are really not very nice people at all. But some of them are my friends. And my family. The thing is...' she trailed off, hesitating. 'I don't think it's unreasonable for me to be concerned. About the consequences. Of what I'm doing, in giving you their names. After all, I don't really know if anyone has done anything wrong. I'm not Scotland Yard. I don't want to get anyone... into trouble.'

Pamela wondered if she should have phrased that differently. She suddenly felt a bit silly. Maybe she was overreacting.

'You're concerned about betraying people you care about.' Charlie lit another cigarette. The smoke drifted off towards the horizon. 'Lady Pamela, we wouldn't be asking you to do this work for us if we weren't certain there was a tremendous amount at stake for our country. What no one understands is that the threat from within is the most dangerous one. There are quite a number of people with personal connections to Germany, business connections, with illusions of grandeur, who are abusing their wealth and power in ways far beyond our imaginations. You needn't worry about who's guilty or not guilty – we aren't asking you to be judge and jury. We're simply asking for your help. If you're able to be our eyes and ears and report back on the things you observe, that will be enough.' Charlie stood. He was about to walk off when he turned around. 'And you will have done a great service for us.'

Pamela watched him as he tipped his hat and walked into the darkening park. She stroked Patricia's head as she laid it in Pamela's lap.

June 1936

I

'But it *is* a summer party, Pam!'

'You know floral doesn't suit you,' Pamela said as she handed Diana Cooper a light green chiffon gown to try on.

She and Diana were in Diana's dressing room, picking out dresses to wear for Sibyl Colefax's party – the designer's last gathering before she moved out of her beloved and much-celebrated Argyll House.

'Do we know who's going to be there?' Diana asked.

'Evelyn, Cecil, the Churchills, Stephen Tennant, Harold and Vita. They say Artur Rubenstein is going to play.' In an attempt to make it sound like an afterthought, Pamela added, 'And possibly the King and his American.'

'She's everywhere these days,' sniffed Diana. 'Duff agrees with me that she's hard as nails and doesn't love him but doesn't want anyone else to have him. It isn't as if she's given up her own husband, yet she refuses to let him speak to Freda or Thelma.'

'Whatever will they do about Ernest Simpson? If the King is genuinely serious about her, that is?'

'He's never been serious about a thing in his life. But I did hear from Duff that he's tried to get the husband a diplomatic service posting in China, which would, conveniently, take him far, far away from Wallis for a very long time.' Diana examined herself in the mint-coloured gown Pamela had suggested. She wrinkled her nose. 'Not quite the thing, is it?'

'Try the purple,' Pamela said, handing Diana another gown. 'Do you think he would give up the throne for her?'

'Why ever would he do that? Would you be a darling and undo the buttons on this one?' As Pamela unbuttoned the dress, Diana turned her head and lowered her voice. 'We have heard some things, though they are rather... sensitive.'

'What things?'

Diana looked around and then turned back to face Pamela. 'Well... whenever Duff and I have seen them together, Wallis treats him like a child – tells him what to do, makes him work for her approval. Sometimes she even taunts him and makes him very unhappy.'

'Why ever does he put up with it?'

'I think it's one of those... sex things. Wanting to be treated like a little boy, controlled, spanked. He's terribly frightened of Wallis but from what I hear, he quite enjoys being frightened by her. You know what men can be like, looking for Nanny in every woman they bed.'

What would the Security Service make of this?

'Isn't it fun? Talking about sex! It's rather modern, isn't it? I don't understand what the fuss is about myself but bully for His Royal Highness if he's found what he's been looking for. Perhaps they both like it. Of course, you know all about that sort of thing.'

'*I* know all about that sort of thing?' Pamela replied, indignant.

'I remember what a wild girl you used to be when you were young!'

Pamela busied herself by looking through Diana's wardrobe.

'I was hardly *wild*, Diana.'

'I remember when you were running around with that Bunny Russell-Jones,' Diana said as she put on the purple gown.

'I wasn't *running around* with him. We were engaged. He was the one who was doing the running around...'

'Yes,' Diana sighed. 'Shame he turned out to be such a cad. Didn't he go off to Rhodesia or somewhere like that?'

'Kenya. Where, as far as I know, he's still living with his wife.'

'I've heard he and the coffee heiress are now divorced. And he's living in England.'

'Oh? Well, bully for him,' she replied, as indifferently as she could.

'And he's going to be at Sibyl's party tomorrow night.'

Her stomach tightened. Pamela felt sick at the prospect of having to see him. How was she supposed to defend the nation from saboteurs if she was busy dodging former lovers?

II

Pamela couldn't help but find Sibyl Colefax's party a bit tragic. Despite the fact that her business ventures in interior design had been going rather well, her fortunes had never fully recovered from the stock market crash. And then her husband, Sir Arthur, had died earlier in the year. Even though she was putting on a brave face and had clearly pulled out all the stops for the party with endless flower arrangements, champagne and canapés, Pamela knew her heart wasn't in it. Sibyl looked as if she was attempting an atmosphere of youthful abandon, but as Harold Nicolson once said, Sibyl didn't do youthful abandon. She had opened the doors to the garden, which was in full bloom, and laid scatter cushions on the floor for people to sit on. No one did, apart from Sibyl, who looked about as innocuous on the floor as if someone had laid an inkstand there.

Pamela decided that she would use *The Times* as her cover for the evening, asking other guests about their dressmakers and tailors, who they had come with, where they were holidaying this summer – her usual questions. She had even brought Johnny, who was dutifully making the rounds with his camera. Sibyl was thrilled he was there and monopolised his time, showing him around Argyll House and explaining what she had done to the decor over the years. At one point, Pamela spotted her sitting in the corner, holding his hand and regaling him with stories of parties gone by. She rescued him, with Sibyl in the throes of a highly exaggerated report of what a dear friend Henry James had been to her.

As Pamela and Johnny crossed the drawing room, she stopped dead in her tracks.

Bunny Russell-Jones.

She turned around, furtively, hoping he hadn't seen her yet, but ran smack into Johnny, who was walking right behind her. 'Sorry, Johnny.'

Johnny saw the look on her face. 'Something wrong, Lady Pamela?'

'No, no, everything is absolutely fine.'

And then she felt a hand on her bare shoulder. She turned around and found herself eye to eye with her old lover.

'It's such a pleasure to see you, Pamela. It's been so many years. Seven? Eight?'

His curly black hair, normally unruly, had been tamed and combed back, making him look older, more sophisticated, only leaving traces of his younger, boyish self that Pamela had known. His hazel eyes looked into hers in a way that made her feel as if she was completely naked.

'Bunny,' she replied, as neutrally as humanly possible. 'I trust you're well?'

He looked at Johnny and said with a wry smile, 'Bit young for you, isn't he?'

Pamela cleared her throat and said, 'This is Johnny Ashton-Smythe, my photographer. I work for *The Times* now – I have a column. Johnny, this is Mr Russell-Jones... an old acquaintance of mine.'

'Your own column!' Bunny said, appraising Pamela, hands in his pockets. 'Congratulations, old thing. I remember you always wanted to be a writer. And *The Times*, no less. Rather impressive.'

Although irritated to have been forced into the position of making polite chit-chat with a man she had hoped never to see again, Pamela also felt a surge of pride in her accomplishments. After all, Bunny's marriage had failed and he had been forced to come back to England with his tail between his legs. Whereas she was not only a columnist for the most widely read paper in the country, but also a secret agent defending her nation from encroaching threats, foreign and domestic. But it was also this pride that was the most dangerous sentiment. It stirred an old instinct in Pamela to impress Bunny, to be the object of his admiration, the recipient of his praise. For he was one of those people who was as quick to offer his approval as he was to rescind it, and it was this turbulence which had always kept Pamela in thrall to Bunny's whims.

'You look stunning, Pamela. You always did light up a room.'

Pamela flushed in embarrassment as Bunny openly appraised her. More attention, more praise, another rush of pride, of vanity. Where was this coming from? She hated that Bunny was giving her the attention she hadn't even realised she had been craving. She felt the frisson of the old flirtation, the old chemistry; as destructive as it – and he – had been to her life, it was still seductive, even after nearly ten years. Pamela felt like she was twenty years old again, caught between a burgeoning urbanity from two seasons out in London society and a lingering awkwardness about her sheltered, country upbringing. Bunny, a London-bred sophisticate who, even when they were hardly out of their teenage years, knew all the city's bolt holes and secrets, had conferred on her the kind of metropolitan glamour she had longed for.

Pamela looked around, desperately trying to find a way out of the situation before things got out of hand.

'I didn't know you were friends with Sibyl Colefax,' she said.

'Old Coalbox is a friend of Mother's,' he replied, rolling his eyes and smiling in a performance of forbearance. 'Ever the doting son, aren't I?'

'And how is your wife?' asked Pamela, feigning ignorance.

Bunny took a swig from his drink and said, 'Eleanor and I are divorced now. I'm surprised you hadn't already heard through the gossip mill. She's in Kenya, with her moustachioed army colonel.'

Johnny was trying not to look at them, but was clearly listening.

'That's a shame. I'm sorry to hear it,' Pamela replied primly. She then grabbed Johnny's arm and started to walk away with him.

But Bunny took a step closer, cutting Johnny out of the equation. 'Still married to Francis More?'

It felt strange, hearing her husband's name out of the mouth of her old beau. It had never occurred to Pamela that Bunny would have kept tabs on who she had married while thousands of miles away in Kenya. Again, she felt a wave of flattery, but this time with a sense of unease.

'I can't imagine how a firecracker like you ended up with a chap like that.'

'A chap like *what*?'

'Oh, come off it, old thing. Don't be cross with me. You know what I mean.'

'I think you'll find that my husband is a rather decent fellow.' (She was tempted to add 'and he's twice the man you are' but felt that was veering into the territory of cheap Hollywood dialogue.)

Bunny leaned dangerously near to Pamela and said, 'That decent fellow doesn't know how lucky he is.'

Pamela felt Bunny cup her elbow the way he used to do when they had been courting. All the little details of their love affair came rushing back in Technicolor. The sudden, intense attraction, the persistent attention, his frantic pursuit of her. And then, when she had let her guard down, the coldness, the distance, the humiliating indifference. Wanting what he couldn't have and rejecting it when it was offered to him. The arguments and the cajoling in his sports car after dark. The making up and the loving, or perhaps only the pretence of love. Her youthful insecurities. His admonishments, making fun of what he referred to as her 'country church-mouse priggishness'. And finally, his disinterest not long after she finally succumbed to his advances.

Bunny took another step closer. Pamela got a better look at him and realised his hairline had started receding already. His dinner jacket looked a little worse for wear, straining slightly against what looked to be the beginnings of a paunch. Peter Pan was already on the road to middle age.

'Men never know how lucky they are,' Pamela replied as she took her elbow away and stepped back from Bunny.

'Yoo-hoo! Pamela!'

She turned around to see Flossie stop dead as she spied Bunny. She blanched and looked at Pamela. 'Bunny. What a surprise.'

'Hello, Flossie,' he replied coldly. (Bunny had never liked Flossie and she had loathed him.)

Flossie took Pamela by the arm, who in turn grabbed hold of Johnny. 'Pamela, darling, I've someone I'd like you to meet.'

As the three of them walked away, Johnny whispered, 'Who was that?'

Flossie curtly replied, 'The Ghost of Christmas Past – never you mind.'

Talking to Flossie and Lydia Harkness a little while later in the garden, Pamela overheard a conversation between Francis, Harold Nicolson and Winston Churchill. She left Johnny with the ladies and floated over in their direction, hoping not to be noticed.

'I'm often accused of having a Foreign Office Mind, taking this sort of view,' said Harold, 'but how can we have any power if we do not maintain moral standards in Europe? The smaller powers need a measuring stick by which to test what is good in international conduct and what is not and we cannot be seen to be condoning behaviour like that.'

Winston listened, puffing away on his cigar thoughtfully.

Who were they were talking about? Pamela took a step closer. Johnny looked over at her quizzically and started to approach her. She gestured to him to stay back and he gave a baleful look.

Winston said, 'We hope that by appeasing the Italians we will make them more well disposed towards us, when really it will hardly deter them from making an alliance with the Germans, who have their eye on their own empire.'

'Anyone who was in Germany after the war knows how utterly humiliated they were,' said Francis.

'And besides,' said Winston, 'no treaty with Britain or France could hold, not with that defeatist, cringing attitude of Baldwin's.

How we cannot possibly do anything until British armaments are restored; how foreign policy is useless without backing from more powerful countries. Very backwards attitude, I say. Germany will continue to confront us with increasingly outrageous acts and an ever-growing military.'

Francis spotted Pamela and said, 'Darling, there you are.'

Harold and Winston bowed slightly. Winston kissed her hand. 'Looking ravishing as always, Lady Pamela.'

'Thank you very much. What was everyone discussing before I interrupted?'

Harold replied, 'Just foreign policy matters, nothing very cheerful.'

'I was in France the other week and saw Madame Chanel. How is the French fashion industry these days?' said Winston playfully.

They all looked at Pamela expectantly. She felt like a child who was being asked about her new school.

Francis smiled forbearingly and said, 'If my wife's investments in the industry are anything to go by, rather well, I'd imagine!'

They all chuckled.

Pamela's temper flared and she was sorely tempted to tell them that this simple fashion journalist was a person MI5 was employing to bring down the monarchy. She excused herself and took a walk around the garden to get her bearings. Doing or saying anything out of the ordinary would defeat the whole purpose of her mission. She went back inside to find Johnny, who was leaning against a wall, looking bored.

'Come, Johnny,' she said, 'we're going to look at gowns.'

Pamela was feeling shaken by her encounter with Bunny and irritated by Francis's remark. She did her reporting rounds with Johnny half-heartedly and felt as if she had achieved nothing whatsoever.

And then, after supper, the King arrived with Mrs Simpson, attracting much excitement. He seemed bored and continuously glanced around, probably looking for the exit, as Rubenstein played Chopin.

Cecil Beaton leaned over to Pamela and muttered, 'Never was one for high culture, was he?'

Pamela noticed that Wallis was at the King's side at every turn, almost like a puppeteer, and recalled what Diana Cooper had told her about their proclivities.

'What a coup to have managed to entice His Majesty,' Pamela said to Sibyl.

'Oh yes,' she said, pleased with herself. 'I'm on terribly good terms with Mrs Simpson. She's becoming quite a fixture on the social scene. And His Majesty has become awfully fond of her. I think she's been rather good for him – taking care of him, making his life more domestic. She's so funny and spontaneous.'

Pamela wondered at Sibyl's adoration of Mrs Simpson. Diana had said Wallis brought out the King's shallowness and spoiled, childlike demeanour.

'Sibyl, in your opinion, do you think she has a genuine affection for him?' (Pamela knew Sibyl loved being asked for her opinion.)

Sibyl beamed. 'Of course, she does! Mrs Simpson is a very genuine person.'

Noel Coward had taken Rubenstein's seat at the piano and piped up with 'Mad Dogs and Englishmen'. The King noticeably relaxed and looked to the piano.

Pamela made her excuses to Sibyl and waved to Johnny, who had now taken to gazing out the window dreamily, to join her. They made their way over to Wallis and the King.

Suddenly, the King erupted at the sight of her. 'What exactly do you think you're doing?'

Surprised, Pamela said, 'Your Majesty, Lady Pamela More. I write a fashion column for *The Times*.'

'A journalist,' he fumed. 'We thought as much. We are tired of being hounded by the press, having them poke their noses into everything we do. Even a king has a right to some privacy. There should be restrictions about where journalists can go. You cannot simply expect to write about whatever you like.'

Pamela was completely taken aback. Johnny cowered behind her.

Wallis put out an arm and said, 'Your Majesty, this is Pamela, Lady More. We're already acquainted. She's a fashion columnist. She wrote about me quite recently. It's all very innocent.'

'Ah,' he said. 'My apologies. You see, we are so often hunted down, like rabbits. There's hardly anywhere we can go without being bothered, when we are visiting our friends. We do not want our names splashed about in the papers.'

'Oh, no, sir. Of course not. And I hope you don't mind my saying, sir, but that is an exquisite dinner jacket. Frederick Scholte, I believe?'

He attempted half a smile. 'Yes, it is. I'm rather loyal to my tailors.'

'A beautiful cut, sir. And if I may say, Mrs Simpson,' Pamela added, 'your dress is absolutely divine.'

She smiled like a Cheshire cat. 'Wallis, please! Like I said, I'm on first-name terms with everyone. It's how we do things in America.' (The King beamed at this little eccentricity.) 'It's a Mainbocher. I got it in Paris just last week.'

They walked off and Pamela resisted the urge to sink into the floor. She bowed as they retreated, looking around to see if anyone around her had seen the encounter. Johnny glanced at Pamela nervously. She shrugged and gave him a reassuring pat on the shoulder.

Pamela watched Wallis glide across the room in what was undoubtedly a brand-new Mainbocher – a sleeveless, bias-cut silk gown in peach with a bateau neckline. The fact that the King was now investing serious money in Wallis's dress collection did not escape her.

III

Pamela received a note from Charlie the next day:

> *Nancy Astor is hosting a ball at Cliveden House this weekend. Sources say people connected to W, E and German Embassy will be there. Find a way to get an invitation.*

Although the Astor family owned *The Times*, Pamela only knew Nancy slightly. And she didn't like her. Nancy had been the first woman to sit in the House of Commons but she was always banging on about imposing curfews on women and banning makeup and short skirts. A teetotal Christian Scientist, the Viscountess didn't believe in alcohol or doctors, and was known to have a tendency towards spitefulness. She picked on guests at dinner parties for sport – like a terrier chasing after ducks, as someone had described it. But Nancy had a strong resolve; for instance, when she was visiting Moscow, she confronted Stalin about his liquidation of the kulaks.

One of the biggest fixtures of the season and Charlie wanted Pamela to manage an invitation in the next four days. Even the most well-connected woman in the country would struggle to get invited to such an important party if she wasn't already on the guest list. Perhaps

Pamela had been too confident in flaunting her social prowess in front of MI5.

It was impossible to manage at such short notice and with such little information. And, if she was being honest with herself, she was feeling a little nervous about such an important assignment after the fiasco at Sibyl Colefax's party. She decided that they were better off with someone more experienced, who would know what kind of information they were looking for. So, she left a note in the dead letter drop for Charlie, sending her apologies. Within a few hours, however, Jenny came into the sitting room with a curious look on her face to tell Pamela that the gardener in the square was asking about the chestnut tree.

Oh blast.

'Really very worried about that chestnut tree, madam,' Fred said to Pamela as he slipped her a note.

Cliveden ball is very important. Must do anything to find a way in. Sources suspect there is someone in this circle who may be the link between London and the German Embassy, passing intel to Berlin. W possibly part of that communication chain. You have been watching her and may know many people at the ball. YOU are perfectly placed to make sense of this link.

Pamela felt frustrated. She didn't know how they expected her to figure out who this 'link' was simply by eavesdropping on conversations. All the information she'd gathered up to this point had been relatively easy, something anyone with social connections could have done. But this was different. Infiltrating Cliveden suddenly seemed impossible and overwhelming. Pamela had no experience in this kind of thing. She couldn't even figure out how to get an invitation – however would she figure out who was passing state secrets to Adolf Hitler? Maybe they would be better off with someone more experienced, who knew what MI5 was looking for and knew how to get it.

But she hated the idea of not living up to expectations. After all, if she couldn't be relied on for this assignment, they might not give her others. She didn't want to have seemingly built herself up to be important to this mission, only to reveal herself as being disappointing and insignificant. A little woman. A wife who only knew about frocks and parties and shopping and Coco Chanel.

What would Aunt Constance say?

What would Sylvia Pankhurst say?

She considered all the people she knew who could find a way of getting her into Cliveden at the last minute. She decided to go to the person who was most likely to help her out of an impossible spot: Percy. He was always creative when it came to underhanded dealings.

She took a deep breath and rang him up, trying to sound as natural as possible. 'I'm finding myself at a bit of a loss for a big piece for next week's edition,' she began.

'This isn't a very promising start, is it?'

'And I didn't want to fiddle-faddle with something bitty like trends in films.'

'Hmm… no.'

'Or who's seen wearing what on the street.'

'*Vogue* is obsessed with that sort of thing at the moment.'

'Or another piece on weddings.'

'No more weddings. Bored to tears by them. Positively nauseating.'

'I think we need something more… high profile. Very…' she said as she twirled her pen between her fingers and leaned back in her chair, 'society. A big party. Something in a grand setting. Lots of recognisable people.'

'Yes, it's about time we covered something like that. Something to whet people's appetites for the summer season. What do you have in the diary, darling?'

'Nothing very exciting, I'm afraid.'

'That's absolutely shocking, Pamela. Why on earth do I keep you around?'

'So many people have gone off to the countryside.'

'I hate the countryside.'

'Or they're at the races – cars and horses.'

'Sport. Even worse. Je deteste.'

'It's just all a bit of a dead end at the moment. Except…'

Pamela paused. (Percy could never resist suspense.)

'Except…?' asked Percy.

'Lady Astor is hosting a ball at Cliveden.'

'That old bag. Like a villainess from a novel. Absolutely stunning place though. And she does invite a rather interesting crowd. I didn't know you were friendly with Nasty Nancy.'

'Well. I'm not, really. Which is the trouble. I don't suppose you know her?'

'No, but I could call on Bobbie.'

Bobbie Shaw was Nancy's son from her first marriage to her American husband, before she married Lord Astor. He was, as Percy said, on the team. Nancy never seemed to mind and perhaps was relieved that no woman would ever take her favourite son away from her. She had been bereft when he had ended up in prison for hanging around barracks waiting for guardsmen.

'Bobbie does owe a favour to moi,' mused Percy. 'Anyway, I'll fix it for you. Give me a moment and I'll ring you right back.'

Within ten minutes, Percy had secured her an invitation to the Cliveden ball.

'Now go out and get me a ravishing story. And don't do anything I wouldn't do,' he said.

As she hung up the phone, Pamela realised she wasn't sure what that ruled out.

IV

As the car drove up the long driveway, Cliveden loomed into view. The Italianate house and the grounds were even more enormous than Pamela had expected and looked like a grand stage set. It was strange to think it was owned by an American, but then again, it increasingly seemed that everything was now owned by Americans. People were coming and going, automobiles were being unpacked and a battalion of servants was rushing in and out of the house. In the entryway, Pamela tried to get a look at the other guests arriving but was somewhat distracted by the splendour of the place – the greatest, most extravagant dreams of the last century playing out in mirrored hallways, portrait galleries and sweeping staircases.

Pamela was not usually one to fall prey to being impressed or intimidated – she prided herself on being unflappable. However, the fact that she had only managed to find a way to get herself invited to the ball at the last possible moment through Percy's finagling made her feel like some sort of imposter. It didn't help that Jenny knew they were there under odd circumstances and that something was amiss. Pamela could feel her nerves as if she was receiving them on radio waves.

It was clear the Cliveden servants had only been told about the addition to the party at the last minute. Pamela and Jenny were led to the wrong room and ended up walking in on Lady Rothermere changing for the evening. Pamela was so flustered that she accidentally trod on the hem of Lady Rothermere's gown and then, trying to back away, knocked a box of face powder off the dressing table, making a terrible mess. She felt more like a character in a slapstick film than a secret agent.

Later that evening, Jenny convinced Pamela to wear her dove-grey, silk organza Poiret with a Grecian neckline. As she did her hair, she looked curiously at Pamela in the mirror of the dressing table.

'Feeling a little better now, Madam?' she said.

'Yes, Jenny, thank you. It's just that early train and all the last-minute packing.'

Pamela could see Jenny didn't quite believe her as she silently finished up with the curling iron.

'Jenny, will you keep an ear out in the servants' hall for... anything interesting?'

'Anything in particular?'

'Yes. I'm thinking of doing a piece about the trend for German fashions. Germans in London. What people are saying about German politics.'

Pamela and Jenny made eye contact in the mirror. Jenny's eyes were such a pale blue they looked almost light grey, piercing. Pamela could tell she wanted to ask her a question but remained silent.

The evening began with cocktails, as waiters walked through the crowd passing out drinks on the terrace. Pamela sought out Bobbie Shaw to give him her thanks. Tall, debonair and exquisitely dressed in white tie, he kissed her hand.

'So, *you're* the "Agent of Influence"!' he said cheerfully in his Mid-Atlantic accent, martini in hand. 'I do so enjoy your column. Very sharp. Are you going to put me in your story about the fabled Cliveden ball? And before you ask, my tailor is Frederick Scholte.'

Bobbie turned around, showing off his tailcoat.

'Thank you very much for arranging for me to come this evening. Very kind of you.'

'Anything for darling Percy. Besides, Mother invites everyone. Politicians, ambassadors, artists, film stars, tennis players, race car drivers... every old rag-tail critter,' he added in a southern accent. 'Come. I'll introduce you to her.'

They walked across the terrace to Nancy, who was speaking to a group of people. Pamela recognised Lords Lothian, Halifax and Rothermere and realised that Geoffrey Dawson was standing next to the Viscountess. She had known that this might happen but still felt her stomach tighten. Dawson looked at Pamela with surprise as Bobbie introduced her to Nancy, explaining that she was covering the ball for *The Times*.

Nancy turned to Dawson. 'You naughty man,' she said in her American drawl. 'You didn't tell me you were sending someone from the paper to ferret out gossip from my guests.'

Dawson frowned and looked at Pamela.

'My friend Percy Blakely – you remember Percy, Mother,' interjected Bobbie.

'Do I?' Nancy drawled as she looked Pamela over.

'Yes, Mother, you do. He felt certain an account of the social season would be incomplete without Cliveden and asked to send someone especially.'

'Mr Blakely is one of our editors,' Dawson explained, looking slightly uncomfortable.

Nancy looked at Pamela pointedly. 'You should know that I don't approve of women drinking alcohol. I don't approve of anyone drinking alcohol but I find it especially unbecoming on a woman.'

Pamela couldn't imagine anyone would want to put up with Nancy Astor sober.

'Lady More, your husband is Sir Francis? He sits in the Lords, does he not?' Nancy asked.

'He does, Viscountess,' Pamela replied.

'Where is your husband tonight? I also don't approve of women going to parties without their husbands,' she said sharply.

Pamela felt as if she was back in finishing school with the most popular girl picking on her.

'Oh Mother! How tiresome and old-fashioned you are! And since when do you care if you're seen without Father? You don't even know where he is right now, do you?'

'He's in Scotland, playing golf,' Pamela replied curtly to Nancy.

Nancy then lost interest and returned to her previous conversation. Bobbie spotted someone he knew and trotted off, leaving Pamela behind to listen as the discussion continued.

'Britain has no primary interests in Eastern Europe,' said Lord Lothian.

'In twenty years, I've never known Philip to be wrong about foreign policy,' replied Nancy.

'And the League is a broken vessel,' added Lord Rothermere.

'It has no authority at all now,' snapped Nancy.

Dawson looked thoughtful as he lit a cigarette. 'I think it's most prudent if we focus our energies on our own sphere of influence – the Dominions. On maintaining unity throughout the Empire. And maintaining peace in Europe, of course.'

'I was recently in Germany,' interjected Lord Halifax. 'I must say, though some might find the lengths to which they've gone to keep out the communists somewhat severe, banning the KPD and so forth, they've done quite a job of it. Quelled the riots, no more fighting in the Reichstag.'

David Stern's words echoed in Pamela's mind.

'I read in the *Manchester Guardian* that the Nazi Party has thrown all the communists in prison. The ones they haven't executed, anyway,' she said.

Everyone turned to look at her in shock.

Then Lord Rothermere laughed. 'The *Manchester Guardian*! I say, that's rather amusing.'

'It wasn't meant to be,' Pamela replied coldly.

'Geoffrey! Are you hiring communist sympathisers to write for *The Times* now?' Nancy exclaimed.

Dawson looked at Pamela in consternation and said, 'Lady Pamela doesn't write political material.'

Pamela smiled and said lightly, 'Just harmless things about parties and fashion, really. Besides, how many communists do you know wear Paris couture?' They all laughed. 'Though,' she added, 'I don't think it makes me a Soviet infiltrator to say that I would hate to live in a country where I could be jailed or executed for belonging to the wrong political party.'

The laughter stopped. Dawson's mouth was set in a tight line as he gripped his champagne glass tightly. Pamela looked up as a flock of starlings flew overhead and into the brilliant sunset.

'No one's being executed, dear,' replied Nancy. 'That's Jewish propaganda. Enormous exaggerations. After all, Adolf Hitler has been in prison himself and suffered a good deal in his life.'

'I daresay if we were in Germany's position, with the Soviets breathing down our necks, we might take much the same position. Rather natural to try to defend one's country. What's standing in the way of peace talks with the Germans is the press,' said Halifax.

'Don't look at me, old boy. The *Mail* and the *Mirror* are very much in favour of peace,' protested Rothermere.

'We try to take a balanced view at *The Times*,' said Dawson as he gave Pamela a warning look out of the corner of his eye.

'As for the Jewish Question,' said Lothian, 'one imagines trying to achieve internal national unity is a logical response to so many external threats.'

'Like I said, propaganda,' Nancy insisted. 'Drummed up by Jewish interests, who did rather well off the war. Munitions, black market, playing both sides with investments. It's that silly little Charlie Chaplin moustache I can't abide.'

Pamela was reminded of what Charlie said, about how the power of the coalition of people sympathetic to Germany could split the Conservative Party and weaken the country. Pamela was surprised. She would have expected people like Dawson and Lord Halifax to have held the line for more British values – healthy debate, democracy, the rule of law. She couldn't imagine how she was going to be able to find the link between London and Berlin when it seemed as if it could be anyone and everyone at Cliveden.

Realising she should probably keep a clear head that evening, Pamela walked over to the railing and subtly emptied her champagne glass into the garden when no one was looking.

As she walked around, surveying the party, she heard two people speaking German. She saw a man in Nazi uniform speaking to a woman in a rose-coloured gown. The woman turned her head to the side and she saw that it was Princess Stephanie von Hohenlohe. Pamela remembered what she had told her about introducing Lord Rothermere to Adolf Hitler, and what Rothermere had just said about his papers giving good press to Germany. The Princess spotted Pamela and waved.

Pamela walked over and got a better look at the gentleman standing next to the Princess. His imposing Nazi uniform seemed like an aggressive intrusion in the sea of elegant evening gowns and tailcoats. His posture was ramrod straight and he kept his hands folded behind his back as he bowed to Pamela.

'Herr Rosenberg, this is Lady Pamela More. She wrote an article about Mrs Simpson for *The Times*. Not only an elegant woman known in society but also a talented journalist!'

'It is a pleasure,' said Rosenberg.

'Likewise, Herr Rosenberg,' Pamela replied.

'Herr Rosenberg is head of foreign policy for the National Socialist Party and has many connections to London. He travels here often. The Viscountess is very welcoming, especially to those visiting the German Embassy,' the Princess said. 'I would imagine, an important woman in society such as yourself has been to many of Lady Astor's parties.'

'It would have been remiss of me not to cover the highlight of the season.'

'We have many fine houses in Germany and Austria but nothing that can compare to this,' the Princess said. 'What I would not give to live in such an excellent residence!'

'Princess, we do not want Frau More to think we do not have many beautiful castles in Germany, much older and more magnificent than this,' said Rosenberg.

Pamela decided to try a new tactic. 'I've never been to Germany. If only I could persuade my husband to go. He's not very fond of travelling. I think it would be marvellous to see the…' she thought quickly, 'Summer Olympics. In Berlin.'

Their faces lit up as if she had mentioned Christmas.

'I was telling Lady Pamela that she must come to Berlin to visit,' said the Princess.

Rosenberg nodded. 'The Olympics will be a very special occasion indeed. The entire city is being transformed as we speak. Impressive. You must see it.'

'Many of your countrymen will be coming, I think,' said the Princess. 'We have so many English visitors. You see, we Germans—'

'The Princess is not German,' interrupted Rosenberg, smiling at Pamela.

The Princess glanced at him with a quick, unreadable look. 'It was what the British call a… object of speech?'

'Figure of speech?'

'Yes, a figure of speech. I am, of course, Viennese, but I meant the Germanic peoples. Who are such natural friends, allies of the English. We hope to build a stronger bond between our two countries. There is so much that can be shared between us.'

'I have always admired this country. Herr Hitler wrote that brutality and tenacity make Britain the best possible ally.'

Pamela wondered how many British people would consider this a compliment.

'And on this subject, we were discussing the new ambassador to Britain Herr Hitler has appointed,' said Rosenberg. 'Herr von Ribbentrop.'

Pamela suddenly remembered the suspicious death of the previous

German Ambassador in London in April, and what Francis had said about the suspicions surrounding the death of his counterpart in Paris months before that.

She took a deep breath and said, 'He must be a very loyal Party member to win such an impressive appointment, no?'

Rosenberg smiled, looking pleased at her observation. 'But of course. And he has very many friends in English society. Perhaps you are acquainted?'

'I'm afraid not.'

How likely was it that this Herr von Ribbentrop had had a hand in the death of his predecessor?

'*Mrs Simpson* is an especial friend of our new ambassador,' added the Princess as she took a sip of champagne.

Now they were getting somewhere.

Rosenberg looked at Pamela's glass. 'May I get you another drink, Frau More?'

She said yes, thanked him and he walked off. The Princess leaned in and whispered in Pamela's ear. 'I do not personally approve of Herr von Ribbentrop. I find him a low, gauche person. As you English say, he has come above his station, yes? He can be quite coarse and rude. He does know many people in society in London but the trouble is, they also know him.'

Pamela was beginning to understand how Princess Stephanie lured people in and determined to find out more about her relationship with Lord Rothermere, as well as how many other powerful men she had under her spell.

'Herr Hitler is never mistaken but I believe he doesn't understand the effect the new ambassador has on people. Rather forceful. Too German for polite British society.'

'And Mrs Simpson?' Pamela asked innocently. 'Why is she such an especial friend of his then?'

The Princess leaned in another inch and said, 'He is rather fond of her and it is sometimes hard to resist when a gentleman shows his fondness. And I suppose he is not an unattractive man.'

It was interesting that there seemed to be dissent within the Nazi ranks and Pamela made a mental note to see if she could cultivate a friendship with the Princess, who seemed to be a font of information. No wonder there was a leak from Buckingham Palace that ran straight to the German Embassy – and possibly more than one.

She spent dinner making polite chatter whilst trying to listen in on people's conversations. Pamela had been seated next to the American interior designer Elsie de Wolfe, who knew Wallis and seemed to think she hadn't been invited because Nancy felt threatened by the ascendance of a rival American hostess. Elsie herself was notable for the fact that her husband Charles most likely received a knighthood for retrieving letters from a gigolo blackmailing the Duke of Kent, who, interestingly enough, was seated across from them at the table. At one point, the two of them engaged in a conversation about the merits of the Nazi government and Pamela wondered if the ball was really some kind of propaganda exercise designed by Joseph Goebbels.

Pamela watched for interesting pairings as the dancing began. The classical quartet that had played over cocktails was replaced by a modern jazz band. She noticed Herr Rosenberg wrinkle his nose in distaste. (Was there anything enjoyable the Nazis weren't morally opposed to?) Pamela found it a challenge to mingle, pretend to be chatting to people about her supposed piece on the ball for the paper, avoid Geoffrey Dawson and Nancy Astor, dance and keep an eye on her suspects. Nevertheless, she managed to observe:

1. The Princess dancing with Rothermere
2. The Princess dancing with the Duke of Kent
3. Duke of Kent flirting with Bobbie Shaw
4. Rosenberg dancing with Nancy Astor
5. Nancy chatting with BUF leader Oswald 'Tom' Mosley
6. Mosley dancing with Baba Metcalfe
7. Baba dancing with Halifax
8. Baba dancing with a dark moustachioed and goateed man

The man with the dark goatee turned out to be the Italian Ambassador, Dino Grandi. Pamela hadn't expected Irene Curzon's younger sister and the wife of Fruity Metcalfe, the King's best friend, to be at the centre of the evening's political intrigue. Baba was Mosley's dead wife's sister, who he had been carrying on with for years, in addition to Diana Mitford, whose marriage to Bryan Guinness he had had a hand in destroying. Diana, however, was nowhere to be seen, which wasn't a surprise, considering Mosley was known to like to keep that relationship as quiet as possible.

Fortunately, Francis had known Fruity in the war and Pamela knew Baba somewhat through Irene so she made her way over to them as they chatted away to Bobbie. As they began to talk, Pamela was reminded of how bossy, and with an irritatingly self-assured head girl manner, Baba was. She had been known as the prettiest deb in her season and was still a beauty. Pamela had to admit that Baba looked stunning in an elegant, dark red, bias-cut silk gown that hugged her figure and revealed her back. Fruity watched her with the look that less attractive husbands give their gorgeous wives – pride mixed with anxiety. Pamela quickly looked around the room to see who was watching and noted Halifax, Mosley and the Italian Ambassador continued to look over at Baba. (Poor Fruity.)

Bobbie explained how Pamela was there to write a piece on Cliveden. Baba's eyes lit up. She slipped her arm through Pamela's and told Bobbie and Fruity that they were going to take a turn around the room.

'I read that piece you wrote about Wallis Simpson,' Baba said. 'I thought it was very good. And made her seem rather more interesting than she actually is. Now that she's the King's favourite, she thinks she's Madame de Pompadour.'

'Yes, well… Americans…' Pamela replied, as noncommittally as possible.

'Pamela, I was wondering if you'd be interested in writing about Tom Mosley. Perhaps you could show how the Blackshirts have become so fashionable these days.'

'*Have* they?' asked Pamela.

Baba stopped in a corner of the ballroom and locked Pamela in her gaze, her eyes glittering. Pamela looked over her shoulder at the mirror on the wall and caught a glimpse of her own reflection. She thought of the Blackshirts giving speeches in Hyde Park, how loud and aggressive they were, the kinds of people they attracted. Francis had always said that the British Union of Fascists wasn't a real political party. At best they were a nuisance detracting from serious politics. And at worst, a bunch of hooligans.

Pamela gritted her teeth at the thought of spending any time with Mosley but said, 'I suppose I could interview him.' He was dreadful but might be an unwittingly useful source of information.

'Oh, yes!' replied Baba delightedly.' You could speak to him about the party and what he's done to reinvigorate politics. He's a man of the future, you know. I really do think he could be the next prime minister. I think it's magnificent the way he managed to recover from his grief when my sister Cimmie died.'

Yes, and with you there to comfort him, thought Pamela acidly.

'Although I can't promise it will be published. You see I don't really write about politics.'

'But they published that marvellous interview of yours with Mrs Simpson.'

'Well, we were mostly discussing her wardrobe…'

'I'm sure you could write something rather entertaining and fun about Tom. Do you know, some women think he looks like Rudolph Valentino!'

Write something fun about the leader of the British Union of Fascists? Pamela smiled politely but said nothing.

Baba saw Mosley and gestured for him to join them. He came over, walking with a slight limp but trying to hide it – a wartime accident, from what Pamela could recall. Although Mosley was wearing a tailcoat like most of the other men in the room, he still managed to look as though he was wearing his rigid and uncomfortable Blackshirt uniform. He looked Pamela up and down, his small moustache bristling as he kissed her hand. He actually looked less like Valentino and more like a ghoulish cinema villain.

Baba sent them off to dance together and Mosley held Pamela more closely than she thought was entirely appropriate. After a purely perfunctory period of asking her polite questions about possible mutual acquaintances, Mosley launched into his pitch for the BUF like a used car salesman.

'We are, in fact, the *only* viable party in the country for the average working man.'

'And for women?'

'We have a Women's Section, started by my own mother. We've become very popular with the ladies. And they are essential to our campaign work,' he continued as he pulled Pamela in more tightly.

She had been studying Mosley's face and noticed that his eyes were slightly too close together, his nostrils flared when he spoke and his moustache seemed almost crooked.

'And we even have several women running for seats across the country under the BUF banner. We like women with spirit,' he said as he inched his hand down Pamela's hip.

Pamela didn't want to cause a 'scene', drawing attention to the two of them, but suddenly felt desperate to escape Mosley's clutches. Could she find an excuse to bolt? A headache? A stitch in her side? Or would she have to suffer through it until the end of the number?

Then all of a sudden, someone tapped Mosley on the shoulder.

Bunny Russell-Jones. What the devil was he doing there?

'Mind if I cut in, old chap?'

A look of irritation crossed Mosley's face. His moustache bristled as he pursed his lips tightly. 'Not at all,' Mosley replied. 'Let's continue this another time,' he said to Pamela, winking, as he slinked away.

'Bunny,' Pamela said, arms crossed.

'Don't look at me like that, old thing. You're even more ravishing than when I saw you last. Twice in only a matter of days! I am a lucky man, aren't I?'

Things clearly weren't going well for him. He looked more dishevelled than when she saw him at Argyll House and she could smell the alcohol on his breath and see its effects in his eyes. For once, she felt somewhat sorry for him. And deeply grateful that she was not the woman who had married him.

'Didn't know you were friendly with this crowd, Pamela. I'd almost say you were following me,' he laughed.

Or you were following me.

Pamela paused for a moment, wondering how likely it was that Bunny *was* following her. Was he keeping tabs on her for old time's sake, because he was newly divorced and dredging up old affairs? Or was there another reason? Was it possible he had been planted? After she had encountered him at Argyll House, knowing Bunny was back in London and she could possibly run into him again, Pamela asked Jenny to look into what had happened in Kenya. After he had ended their engagement, Bunny had become engaged not long after to a coffee heiress. Since the family business was in Kenya, he and his new bride returned to the plantation so he could learn how to manage it and then take it over once her father had retired. However, according to Jenny, it turned out that things had gone terribly wrong. Bunny had made himself out to be more adept at business matters than he really was. A drinking problem soon followed, as well as a number of affairs with the wives and daughters of other local landowners. Which is why his wife Eleanor took comfort in the arms of a dashing, recently widowed British colonel and filed for divorce.

People were talking about his retreat from Africa. Clearly his morale was low, if the drinking was anything to go by. And his current state of financial affairs was unclear. Was it outrageous to think that he could he be in the pay of the Germans?

'I'm here on an assignment for the paper,' she replied as Bunny tried to put his hand on her arm and she moved it away.

'So I've heard. I've also heard you're here without your awfully decent chap of a husband.'

Pamela froze. How did he know? She was tempted to get away as quickly as possible, but didn't want to look suspicious and also didn't want to look as if she was intimidated – for the sake of her cover, as well as her pride and reputation. She was no longer the wide-eyed young woman she had been ten years ago. And as she stood and faced Bunny, she realised he was quite drunk.

'Oh, yes? And where did you hear that?'

'Bobbie Shaw, old thing. We belong to the same club. He was trying to get me to come to this shin-dig to make it a bit less dull. He mentioned you were coming so you could write about it in your column. Without his Lordship. So, I thought you might be in need of an escort. We could twirl about on the dance floor, for old time's sake.'

Bunny was no German spy trying to catch Pamela in her undercover mission. He was simply a desperate man, looking for attention.

'Come on, old thing. Don't say it won't be rather fun,' he said as he attempted to draw her closer.

Bunny was standing very close to Pamela so she put a hand on his arm, looked directly into his eyes and smiled. 'No, I don't think that would be *fun*. Fool me once, shame on you. Fool me twice, shame on me.'

'Eh?'

Pamela moved in closely and lowered her voice. 'To say your behaviour was beyond the pale is the understatement of the year. You treated me appallingly, Bunny.'

Bunny's face fell and he wiped his brow with a handkerchief. 'Yes, you're right. What I did was unforgiveable. I don't blame you for not wanting to speak to me again. I was a complete cad. Worse than a cad. Losing you, treating you as I did, might be my greatest regret. I've missed you, old thing. And I didn't realise how much until I saw you at Argyll House last week. I was young and a fool. What else can I say?'

Pamela put her drink down and looked Bunny in the eye. 'Let us have no illusions about what happened; you ended our engagement for reasons neither of us need go into. You made your choice, and both of our lives moved on. I'm sorry if yours has been a disaster. I can't say I'm at all surprised how things have turned out. You were selfish and foolish and had no interest in what anyone else had to say. You always got whatever you wanted and now you're getting what you deserve. Good for your wife for giving you the heave-ho. But if you think I'm going to jeopardise *my* marriage – and my reputation – for another dalliance with you, then you are even more of a deluded idiot than I thought.' She paused for breath. 'And you reek of gin.'

Bunny stared at Pamela in stunned silence, his face white as a sheet. She realised the jazz band was playing a song she recognised from a Fred Astaire film, though she couldn't remember the name of it. Before he had a chance to reply, Pamela turned on her heel and walked off. She felt dizzy with the energy it took to stand up to Bunny's advances, but she also felt as if she could take on anyone, that she was no longer a young and vulnerable woman but a force to be reckoned with. And she had nothing to fear.

She strode down the side of the ballroom, trying to make her way to the exit while pushing past dancing couples, groups of people talking and footmen with trays of drinks. She suddenly felt suffocated by the overfed opulence of the house, the gilded moulding, the chandeliers, the paintings, the marble floors, the enormous fireplaces. She passed room after room at a rapid pace, hoping to get away from everyone at the party as quickly as possible.

Finally, she reached the library. It was cool, quiet and empty so she went in, hoping to gather her thoughts. One of the windows was open so she went over to it and sat down, looking out the window on to the expanse of elegant, perfectly manicured lawns and gardens. She took a cigarette from her evening bag and lit it, letting the smoke trail out the open window into the evening breeze.

Suddenly, Pamela heard voices and a couple entered the room. They whispered and closed the door behind them. She was about to make her presence known when, on recognising her red dress and his tiny moustache, she realised that it was Baba and Mosley. She quickly threw her cigarette out the window, pulled the drapery on her side of the window across herself and hid, hoping the lighting was dim enough they hadn't noticed her. However, they were so engrossed in each other she hardly thought they had noticed anything at all.

Baba grabbed Mosley's face, started kissing him and then pushed him against a wall.

'Is this what you want?' said Tom, playing with a strap on Baba's dress.

'We haven't much time before they noticed we're gone,' she said breathlessly as she closed her eyes, clearly waiting to be kissed.

'I wouldn't worry. Your husband doesn't seem to notice much of anything,' Mosley said drily.

'You seem displeased with me,' she said, frowning.

'I need you to be my champion.'

'I *am* your champion.'

'I need you to believe in me.'

'I *do* believe in you.'

Baba went in for another kiss but Mosley angled his head out of range and looked crossly over her head, out the window.

'There's only so much I can do, you know,' she whined. 'I think you're a genius. People just don't understand you, that's all.'

Mosley looked at her suddenly, sharply. 'What do you mean?'

'I just mean, you may not be getting the support you deserve, the followers you deserve, because people don't understand you. And you can be a little…'

Aggressive? Boorish? Obnoxious? Pamela thought as she watched from behind the curtain.

Mosley started to pace back and forth across the room. He went over to the fireplace and lit a cigarette, standing underneath a portrait of a long-ago Astor matriarch. 'I can be a little… what?'

Pamela attempted to be as still as humanly possible, doing her best to ignore an itch on her nose and a cramp in her leg.

'Sometimes I think you could use a softer touch,' Baba said as she approached the fireplace. 'For instance, earlier with Lady Pamela.'

Pamela froze.

'I think you could have been a bit more… subtle. I only want to see you rise to power, to be the man I know you can be,' Baba said, stroking Mosley's arm. 'I think certain people have been depleting your energy. And perhaps have had a less than desirable influence on you.'

Mosley smiled and touched Baba's cheek. 'Now, now, don't be jealous, sweet. It isn't becoming on you.'

'I'm not jealous.'

He reached around and put a hand on her backside. 'A man like me must take every opportunity to feed his spirit and body. There *is* something you can do for me, darling. Something very important. Your friend at the Italian Embassy… I need you to tell him that the Party needs more money.'

Friend at the Italian Embassy. It was clear that Mosley meant Dino Grandi, who Baba had been dancing with earlier. Were the Italians funding the BUF?

Slowly, Pamela quietly massaged her calf through her stocking to try to relieve the cramp, which by then had become quite painful. She wondered how much longer this was going to go on for.

'We need the money now more than ever, especially since you know that rich Jews are urging their working-class brethren to attack my Blackshirts.'

'Well—'

'They're trying to provoke us into retaliating violently so non-Jewish opinion will be shocked and turn against us.'

'Tom—'

'It makes perfect sense.'

'That's a rather odd theory, darling.'

'It makes perfect sense, I tell you.'

Mosley leaned against the wall and sulked. Baba took a step away from him and straightened her dress. She then took out a compact and checked her makeup.

'Will you speak to him?' asked Mosley, picking at his fingernails.

'Who?' replied Baba, refreshing her lipstick.

'Grandi, of course.'

'Yes, Tom. I'll speak to him,' she sighed.

'Tonight, I mean. Now.'

Baba gave Mosley a look of exasperation and they left the library.

Quickly, Pamela searched for a piece of writing-paper on the desk next to the window and wrote a note. She then went out into the corridor and ran into a fresh-faced young footman in livery and stopped him.

'You there, hello.'

He seemed surprised and briefly looked around.

'Yes, you. A favour, please. My name is Lady More. My maid is called Murphy. I'd like you to give her this please.'

Pamela handed the footman the note and he disappeared with it down one of the many passageways in the house.

Several hours later, after what had felt like the longest evening of her life, Pamela finally retired to her bedroom and rang for Jenny. As Jenny helped Pamela undress, she reported back on what she had discovered below stairs.

'I managed to cosy up to Palmer, Lady Metcalfe's maid, and my word! Doesn't she talk ever so much! Apparently, Lady Metcalfe has been having it off with...' Jenny paused. 'Sorry, Madam.' Jenny reddened.

'"Having it off" is perfectly accurate. Do carry on,' said Pamela as she removed her earrings.

'She's been... having relations with quite a number of men. Jock Whitney, the Earl of Feversham, Walter Monckton—'

'The legal advisor to the King.'

'Lord Halifax—'

'So, it *is* true.'

'The Italian Ambassador—'

'Just as I thought.'

'And Oswald Mosley.'

Suddenly, there was a knock at the door. Jenny and Pamela looked at each other.

For one awful moment, Pamela worried it might have been Bunny. She opened it, however, to reveal Mosley himself leaning against the doorframe, his top button undone and white tie hanging around his neck in a louche fashion. How many other rooms had he tried that evening before coming to hers?

'I thought you might like some company,' he said with his crooked smile and crooked moustache.

To Pamela's surprise, he pushed past her into the room but stopped when he saw Jenny. Mosley's crooked little smile collapsed, making his moustache droop.

'Thank you, Sir Oswald, but as you can see, I am indisposed.'

He took a step towards Pamela and leaned in. 'Why don't you send her away?' he whispered seductively.

Jenny looked at Pamela and then looked questioningly to the door.

'I'm afraid I'm going to have to send you away instead,' Pamela replied.

Mosley looked at her in surprise.

'We're leaving tomorrow, you see, and we have rather an early start.'

'I could return later?' he muttered quietly.

'Thank you, that won't be necessary,' she replied briskly, as if declining his offer to light the fire or turn down the bed.

Pamela and Jenny stared at the leader of the British Union of Fascists as he stood in the middle of the room, opening and closing his mouth, like a fish flopping around on a kitchen floor. He whipped his tie off his neck and fiddled with it in his hands as he looked back and forth between the two women. Then he gave a small bow and left the room, trying to cover his limp.

'You don't want to be getting involved with *him*,' Jenny said. 'He's having it off with Lady Metcalfe *and* Diana Mitford! And Diana Mitford is having it off with the Italian Ambassador too!'

Baba would not have been pleased to know she was sharing not one but two lovers with Diana.

'Oh goodness gracious no, Jenny,' Pamela said as she sat down on the bed, feeling suddenly quite exhausted. 'Imagine! Me with Tom Mosley! What do you think of me?'

Jenny looked down at her hands and twisted the fabric of her skirt nervously. Pamela suddenly realised how strange everything must have seemed to her.

'Jenny,' Pamela started. 'I can't go into detail and I probably shouldn't be telling you this in the first place… but I've been asked by some people in the government to gather information. About those who may be close to, or sympathetic to, the Nazi regime. It's all rather complicated and I've most probably said too much already.'

'Blimey,' said Jenny, eyes wide.

'And if you'd rather not implicate yourself in such a scheme, just say. I won't be offended.'

'I can get you whatever you need, Madam,' she replied, cool as a cucumber.

'Oh. So, you don't mind? Being involved in something like this?'

'If you don't mind me saying, this is very exciting. I've read an awful lot of detective books and this is just like an Agatha Christie mystery. A country house. Intrigue. Villains. Now all we need is a murder.'

'Don't tempt fate, Jenny.'

Jenny looked as if she could hardly contain her excitement. She got her notepad out, flipped through it quickly and then looked up. 'If this is the game we're playing, then it might be worth telling you that Palmer said Mosley is getting money from the Italian Embassy because of Lady Metcalfe and the Italian Ambassador. But he's also getting money from the Germans through Diana Mitford because her sister is a special friend of Mr Hitler.'

'Excellent work, Jenny. This is rather good.'

'Thank you, Madam.'

'It is rather secret though, you understand? You mustn't tell a soul.'

'You have my word, Madam.'

V

All the scurrying around, the subterfuge and the lying was starting to make Pamela feel as if she was having an affair. She had never had one before. Francis, though somewhat oblivious, was a sensitive man and she would never want to hurt him. And besides, it had always seemed to her to be an awful lot of trouble. The secrecy, getting messages back and forth to one another, finding locations for the assignations where neither person would be recognised. The various and sordid possibilities for exposure were endless.

Pamela recalled the scandal caused by Lettice Wakefield's affair with Giles Langdon. A group of them had gone to Quo Vadis for Lettice's birthday, but her husband Ashley insisted on inviting Giles to the party (as he was an old friend of the family), which Lettice couldn't discourage without raising suspicion since half of Lettice and Giles's friends knew what was going on. It had been an awkward dinner, with Lettice and Giles pointedly avoiding each other. However, at the end of the evening, Lettice disappeared and when Ashley went looking for her, he found her outside on the kerb in an embrace with Giles.

Which just went to show that one had to find a suitable candidate for an affair. Someone not intimately connected to one's spouse or social circle. And then one had to decide whether a bachelor or a married man was preferable. One didn't want to intrude on others' marriages but then again, a bachelor might not understand the importance of discretion (Giles, for instance). And then there was the issue of trying to figure out how to broach the subject.

Pamela and Charlie met at their usual bench facing the Serpentine in Hyde Park to debrief about Cliveden. Since the weather was warm, he had swapped his usual trench coat for a linen suit with a light blue tie and a white carnation in his buttonhole.

'I gather Cliveden was a success?' he asked.

'I've come to some conclusions,' Pamela said as she took a cigarette from a case in her handbag and lit it.

When she was finished reporting on the ball, she handed him a long list of anyone she had encountered who had expressed interest in Hitler or Mussolini within her earshot.

Charlie looked at it carefully, folded it up and put it in his pocket.

'That list reads like Burke's Peerage,' Pamela said. 'But the question is, who is influencing who? It's all rather murky, what with all the people flying back and forth between London and Berlin, the informal diplomacy going on at balls and dinner parties, the various love affairs and the money, the investments people are making. And the thing of it is that these people seem to believe that they're doing the best thing for Britain, forming alliances with Germany and Italy. That it will make the country stronger. They don't see it as a betrayal. But then again, they're all quite easily influenced. I think they like the recognition. Being made to feel important. Since the war, so many of them have come down in the world, either financially or simply in terms of political influence. And the Germans, well, they seem to be rather good at making them feel needed.' Pamela paused. 'That's my theory, anyway.'

For a brief moment, Pamela couldn't help but wonder who Charlie was, out in the world at large. What did he do? Was this his full-time position, working in the shadows for the government? Or did he have some other line of work that acted as a cover? Did he have a family? Was he married? He didn't wear a wedding ring. Or perhaps he took it off when he was working to help inspire other men's wives to gather information for him.

'It's an interesting theory. Perhaps more than just a theory. Though I can't imagine our masters in Parliament and Whitehall would be thrilled to hear it,' he continued.

'Because many of *them* are probably in Hitler's pocket too,' Pamela said, remembering the presence of Lord Halifax.

'Many people are simply blind to the threats this country is facing. And it's going to take quite a lot of evidence to convince them. Which leads me to my request, which is that we'd like you to continue to meet Mrs Simpson, occasionally. Find excuses to see her. Befriend her, gain her confidence. And also, that of this Princess von Hohenlohe.'

'I will do my best. But I have a suspicion there might be another additional route in…'

Pamela arranged her skirt and then leaned in slightly. Charlie put an arm across the back of the bench and leaned in too. He tilted his head.

'A route into what?'

A child's ball rolled over and landed at their feet. A little boy in a sailor suit came running over and looked at them with wide eyes. Charlie kicked it back to him and the boy ran off in hot pursuit, an exhausted-looking elderly governess trailing along behind him.

'From speaking to the Princess, I get the impression there's some discord in the ranks within the German Embassy. Not only does she seem to dislike von Ribbentrop, she gave me the impression she's not the only one, both in German diplomatic circles and in British ones. Perhaps this is something that could be… exploited?'

Charlie looked into the distance, frowning. He ran a hand through his wavy brown hair.

'Of course, if you think I shouldn't be—'

'No, you probably shouldn't. And officially, I haven't given you orders to look into it.'

Charlie stood and Pamela felt a small stab of disappointment as she too stood up. Charlie looked around.

'Of course, *unofficially* perhaps there are things you can discover. Purely by chance, shall we say. And while you're at it, perhaps you could see if you can learn who this source might be.'

'Source?'

'Of the rot. Who's driving the campaign to recruit Burke's Peerage. If there is a source. Unofficially, of course.'

VI

It was eerily quiet at Francis's brother Henry's house in Yorkshire. All Pamela had heard the entire weekend had been the birds and, of course, the persistent sound of wind and rain against the window panes.

Henry was a kind man, but rather taciturn, benign and frustratingly wholesome. He never came down to London if he could help it and considered a day-trip to York rather an adventure. Henry was in the war like Francis, and turned to god when he was discharged and had become involved in the local parish. Francis insisted they attend church with him when they came to stay, even though Pamela generally ended up falling asleep in the pews. (The vicar's voice sounded like the drone of a car engine.)

Pamela felt sorry for Henry's wife Alice. She had never been well and the births of each of her five children had always been followed by periods of deep despondency. Alice only came downstairs once, the night Pamela and Francis had arrived. A petite woman, she looked extremely wan, tired and with dark circles under her eyes. She joined everyone for dinner and then retreated to her bedroom for the remainder of the weekend. Pamela considered going up to her room to visit but was afraid of disturbing her.

Pamela was still mulling over the ball at Cliveden when she and Francis were reading in the sitting room after Henry had gone to bed early, as he normally did. It was unseasonably cold so they had a fire going.

'Francis,' Pamela started.

'Yes, darling?'

'What's the reputation of Mosley and his BUF lot in the Lords? He was there, at Cliveden, being received wholeheartedly. But he seems such a nasty sort.'

'Yes, well,' said Francis, 'he *is* a nasty sort. Couldn't stick to one party or another. No real scruples. Complete megalomaniac. And the less said about his personal life the better. The appalling manner in which he treated his wife when she was dying...' He puffed on his pipe thoughtfully and gazed into the fire.

'But, politically, how are they seen?'

'In political circles, the BUF doesn't have the numbers to be taken seriously. They just have a handful of local councillors, no MPs. Membership has been going down. They hardly lasted a year in Northern Ireland, not surprising given that they were agitating for reunification.'

'Aren't they meant to be rather thuggish?'

'Yes, and many branches are simply criminal gangs. Their Newcastle secretary was convicted of burglary and their Brixton branch was operating as a house of ill-fame.'

'Diana Cooper says that's what Hitler's people are like,' she added, 'thugs and criminal types.'

'And, unlike Germany, I rather think it's been all this talk of Jew-hatred that's been turning people away – civilised people, anyway.'

'I've overheard some things recently, some not very nice things about Jews, in what one might call civilised circles. Lady Astor's party, for instance. And a rather glowing reception for Hitler's ideas too.'

Francis harrumphed and frowned. 'People are often much worse than one expects.' He knocked his pipe against the grate, emptying out the dregs of the bowl into the hearth. He remained kneeling by the fire for a moment. 'We're not as evolved or enlightened as we'd like to think we are – it doesn't take much to push us back down into the muck.'

'We are all in the gutter, but some of us are looking up at the stars,' mused Pamela.

'What's that from?'

'Oscar Wilde.'

He nodded, stood and said, 'I've become quite tired all of a sudden. Probably the heavy roast we had for supper. And all this fresh country air.'

He kissed Pamela goodnight and she watched as he went upstairs. Pamela knew from experience that there was never really anything she could say to lift his mood when Francis had a dark spell. Sometimes they were merely passing moments and sometimes they lasted days, or even weeks. Back when they had just become engaged, Henry had told her that Francis was very changed by the war, a comment she hadn't understood until later.

July 1936

I

Percy and Pamela were in the women's wear department at Selfridges, incognito. She wore a silk headscarf from Liberty's and he wore a pair of spectacles and an ugly porkpie hat.

'Capes. That's the third woman I've seen in a cape in the past hour,' Percy said.

'It's one of those things that keeps coming back round,' Pamela replied.

'Puffed sleeves. I'm seeing lots of puffed sleeves.'

'Bangles. Stacked bangles. Maybe I should do a piece on accessories. I've hardly done anything on accessories since the winter.'

A plump saleswoman arched an eyebrow at them as she walked past.

'Norman Hartnell wants us to do a piece promoting British fashion,' said Percy, leaning against a wall.

Pamela absent-mindedly picked up a scarf with a geometric print from a rack, looking it over. 'What's the point when all anyone wants are French labels?'

'That *is* the point, Pamela. To try to get people talking about *British* labels. Boost the economy and so on.'

A tall, slim blonde walked over to the mirror next to them, wearing a shapeless mauve day dress. Pamela was tempted to tell her it did nothing for her figure.

'Can't you be patriotic for a minute?' Percy sighed.

'King, country and Norman Hartnell.'

Percy rifled through a rack of skirts, peering at the different fabrics. 'What are you doing tonight, darling? I'm having a party. There will be lots of interesting people. It will be fun.'

'We have reservations at Quaglino's with some friends.'

'Come after. Francis will leave early and you'll be bored. Besides, nothing starts before ten.'

When Pamela arrived at Percy's party in Bloomsbury later that evening, it was nearly midnight and she was already a bit tight. As usual (and as Percy predicted), Francis had gone home early and left her to her own devices. The band hadn't been very good and, frankly, she had become tired of watching couples dance, dancing with friends' husbands or fending off unwanted advances from strangers.

Someone had left the door to the flat open so she entered, unannounced. It was packed to the gills and, even though all the windows were open, steaming hot; at least two dozen sweaty bodies were pressed up against each other, drinking and smoking like chimneys.

Pamela spotted Percy, wearing his usual cravat, standing by a window next to a man wearing eyeliner.

'Panda!' he exclaimed drunkenly. 'I didn't think you'd come.'

'Percy, I wish you wouldn't call me that when you get whizzed.'

'Why *does* he call you that?' asked the friend, who was also so intoxicated he had to prop himself up against the wall.

'Because it's easier to say when I'm bevvied than Panela... Pam... Pamela... Vogue us up, ducky,' said Percy to his friend, who then lit his cigarette. 'We *must* get you a drink,' Percy announced as he grabbed Pamela's arm and trotted her over to the drinks trolley.

As he mixed her a martini, Pamela realised there were men everywhere. Far more than she had ever seen at one of Percy's parties. Men wearing eyeliner, mascara, rouge, lipstick. Men with permanent waves and dyed hair. And one gentleman in a dress.

He caught her staring at him and said, 'Can I help?'

She eyed the teal-coloured georgette frock with matching bolero again and said, 'Is that a Charles Creed?'

He looked surprised and said, 'Why yes, it is.'

'Last year's spring/summer collection?'

'Doesn't she have an eye?'

'Well,' Pamela said as she preened in the mirror on the wall next to her, 'I do write a fashion column for *The Times*.'

'Oh, *you're* Lady Pamela! I absolutely *adore* "Agent of Influence",' he gushed as he stood and came over to Pamela. 'I read it to Mother every Tuesday. It's ever so amusing!'

Pamela felt the warm glow of appreciation as Percy handed her a martini. She winced as she realised how much gin Percy had put in it.

'Why thank you, Mr...?'

Pamela felt a bit odd calling a person in a dress Mr anything.

'The name's Donald but everyone here calls me Betty. You can call me Betty,' he replied.

'Why does everyone call you Betty?'

'It's his camp name, darling,' said Percy. 'Mine is Ethel. Yours is Panda.'

Betty eyed Pamela's gown. 'Is that a Vionnet you're wearing?'

'You know, I wasn't altogether sure about the collar when I first bought it.'

Betty inspected the square folds of the neckline of the long, purple satin gown with his manicured hands. 'Absolutely gorgeous.'

Pamela turned to Percy and whispered, 'Percy, why are there so many... gentlemen here?'

Percy waved at someone across the room and said, 'There's no need to whisper, darling. The sisters are here because the police raided Billie's the other week.'

'What's Billie's?'

'Billie's was a club for people like us,' Betty said as he gestured to the party with his hand. 'Until the orderly daughters broke up the party. Very disappointing. So glad I decided to go cottaging in Hyde Park that night instead. When I have a yen for a delicious guardsman in uniform...'

'You and your rough trade,' chided Percy.

'I *do not* like rough trade. My guardsmen are very well behaved. You don't see me trawling for sailors down on Waterloo Road. Or at *the docks*. Not like Mary over here,' Betty retorted, gesturing to Percy's friend in the eyeliner.

'I like the real thing or nothing,' chirped the man called Mary.

'I quite like the well-educated, well-bred types myself,' said Percy.

'That's because you're working class, so you would, wouldn't you?'

'Lower-middle, if you please,' said Percy, indignant.

Pamela looked down and realised she had somehow finished her martini already. She made a mental note not to have another until she had sobered up a bit.

'And what kind of... people do *you* like, Lady Pamela?' Betty asked her with a mischievous look on his face.

Percy turned to Betty and said, 'Darling, Panda is *repressed*.'

'I am *not* repressed.'

Percy raised an eyebrow. 'When was the last time you had sexual intercourse?'

Pamela blushed terribly, like a schoolgirl. A man pushed by her to get to the drinks trolley. He wore rouge and a lavender cravat. He gave Pamela a wink.

'See?' said Percy. 'Sexually repressed.'

'It's not that I don't fancy it!' she blurted out.

Mary and Percy laughed.

Pamela adjusted the strap on her dress that had fallen down and said, 'Stop laughing, you two. It's not funny. It's just that... well, I'm like a camel!'

'Is that because you only have two humps?' asked Mary.

'No, it's because I can go ages without it. You know, like a camel, with water,' she explained as she felt a wave of gin hit her.

'Why would she *want* to?' Mary said to Percy. 'Why would you *want* to?' he then asked Pamela.

'You're not a camel, darling,' said Percy. 'You just don't fancy your husband.'

'That's not—'

'He's a very nice man, a real gent. But he wants to dim her lights, as it were,' Percy explained.

'What do you mean?' Pamela asked.

'It's obvious he feels threatened by you,' said Percy.

She was about to argue with him but the gin slowed her down and she let the thought slide around in her brain.

Then Princess Elena walked over, arm in arm with a thirty-something woman with dark, closely cropped hair wearing a man's suit.

'Pamuchka! How are you?' she said as she gave Pamela her customary three cheek kisses.

The woman in the suit looked Pamela up and down.

'This is my friend, Josephine Nolan,' said the Princess.

She shook Pamela's hand firmly and in an Irish accent, said, 'Jo. Pleasure to be acquainted.'

'Percy says Francis wants to dim my lights,' Pamela said grumpily to the Princess.

Percy said, 'All I'm saying is that Panda's husband feels intimidated by her sparkle. But it's not as if she married him for love, did she?' He hiccupped.

'This is normal, no?' said the Princess. 'All the time people marry those they do not love.'

Jo lit a cigarette in a holder and said, 'Christ, I don't know how anyone can stand it. No wedding bells for me, thanks.' She leaned over and, much to Pamela's surprise, kissed the Princess.

Standing there, in the overcrowded little flat, feeling the gin flow through her bloodstream, Pamela was suddenly hit by an inescapable, sinking feeling.

'What if I've made a terrible mistake?'

'That's why divorce was invented,' replied Mary.

'But I don't like the idea of being a divorcee,' she said as she looked vacantly into her empty glass.

Betty took the glass from her hand and said, 'This woman needs another drink.'

'Better than being a widow,' said Mary. 'Like Queen Victoria. So terribly gloomy. And even worse, you'd look naff.'

'Naff?'

'Not Available for Fu—'

Mary started but Percy shot him a warning look.

The Princess took a drag from Jo's cigarette and said, 'I wish I was a widow. Prince Maxim is in Berlin, driving a taxi, and he still wires me asking for money for his drinking and his whoring. It would be better if he were dead.'

'Drinking and whoring in Berlin,' Betty said wistfully as he returned with another martini for Pamela. 'Those were the days.'

'You'll never stop boring everyone about your Berlin escapades, will you?' Percy said.

'Because they were the best escapades of my life. Berlin after the war. The golden age. Before the Nazis started beating up the queers. They call it "sexual Bolshevism", which is ironic, considering the Soviets call it "fascist perversion".'

They all laughed in a half-hearted way. Pamela took a sip of her drink and felt for her hair clip, which was sliding out of place. She tried to put it back in but gave up, deciding it didn't matter how her hair looked.

'Mind you,' said Mary, 'it's not much better here. Remember when I didn't come out to the Shim Sham Club last week?'

'You said you were ill,' said Percy, still hiccupping.

'I'd been at that pub in Wapping, with Dick, my regular little chicken, and we...' Mary faltered a moment. 'We had an *encounter* with Mosley's queens from BUF. I was a bit worse for wear for a few days. Even slap couldn't cover the bruises.'

'Do you mean to say they hit you?' Pamela asked, incredulous.

'These are not very nice people, darling,' said Percy.

Mary straightened his cravat and smoothed his dyed blond hair. Pamela could see his roots were showing and it made her feel a bit sorry for him.

'And do you know what the worst thing was?' he said. 'The worst thing was what they said. The two of them said, "Just you wait, you Nancy-boys. Just wait until Mosley's in charge. He'll have you all hanged".'

'They said that?' Pamela asked.

'Well, yes,' said Mary, 'but with terrible grammar because they were complete imbeciles.'

'My husband – he sits in the Lords – says they have rather a small following.' She paused. 'And they don't even have a single MP.'

'The problem is, Panda,' said Percy, 'there are quite a lot of people in this country who might not be wearing black shirts, but they share their opinion. I think if Hitler invaded tomorrow, they'd be perfectly happy to watch him string us all up.'

'Lucky for me they didn't know I was Jewish!' Mary said as he finished off his sherry.

'Did you hear Isherwood's story? From a couple of years back,' Jo asked as she leaned against the wall.

She had been so quiet Pamela had forgotten she was there.

'Terrible, wasn't it?' said Percy.

'What happened?' asked Betty.

'You're *always* the last to know,' replied Mary tartly.

Betty pouted and arranged his dress primly. 'I used to be on rather friendly terms with Christopher.'

'He was at Harwich, at the port, trying to get into the country with his German fella Heinz. I think Auden was there too,' said Jo.

'I remember Heinz! Absolutely gorgeous! Very German-looking, rugged, healthy. You could picture him yodelling in the Alps,' said Betty.

'Isn't that Switzerland?' asked Mary.

Percy gave them both a stern look and said, 'Ladies, please.'

Jo continued. 'They were all coming from Berlin and Hitler had already come to power by then, so they were trying to smuggle Heinz out of Germany. Auden and Isherwood got through but at the last moment…'

'Oh no…' Betty said sadly.

'…Heinz got turned away. The immigration official had sniffed them out. The bastard knew what they were. It was just sheer fucking malice.'

II

Pamela awoke the next morning on a sofa. She slowly sat up and felt her head pound, as if there were tiny men inside taking tiny hammers to her brain. She looked around the room, trying to make sense of where she was. The flat was small and crowded with books, pictures and knick-knacks. On the small dining room table lay a series of sketches of women's clothing, as well as coloured pencils, samples of fabric, a pair of shears and spools of thread. Though there were signs of damp on the walls and a crack in the ceiling, the rugs and furniture were exquisite antiques. When she saw the small Russian icon hanging on the wall, Pamela knew she must be in the Princess Elena's flat above her shop in Marylebone.

She stumbled over to the window to open it and let some air into the hot and stuffy room. She looked out and saw people walking in the street below, going about their Saturday. Pamela briefly wondered what it would be like to live on her own in a tiny flat like this. She rummaged around in her handbag for a cigarette and, finding the last precious one in her cigarette case, lit it. She felt slightly ill at the first drag but carried on anyway. She looked down at her beautiful

Vionnet and was relieved to find it was crumpled but none the worse for wear.

Suddenly, she heard arguing from the next room growing louder and louder. Elena flung open the door, a look of frustration on her face. Then she saw Pamela and her expression softened. 'Ah, the sleeping beauty is awake!'

Elena looked effortlessly elegant in a dove-grey silk pyjama set, her red hair piled on top of her head. Jo emerged unsmilingly from the bedroom behind Elena, in her suit from last night and her stocking feet, carrying her shoes.

Elena gestured to Jo, saying, 'Pamuchka, do you remember my friend Josephine? From the party?'

'Judging by how battered she was, probably not,' said Jo with a wry smile.

Elena looked at Jo sharply. 'Do not be rude to my friend, please.'

'I think I rather overdid it, didn't I?' Pamela said.

'You had a whale of a time,' Jo replied. 'And you were quite the hit with the ladies. When you sang—'

'Sang?' Pamela enquired with a sense of creeping dread.

'Ah sure,' continued Jo, 'you sang half of Cole Porter's repertoire while Michael played the piano.'

'I did…?'

Jo sang a few bars of 'Let's Misbehave'. Pamela cringed.

'Oh god… Wait, who's Michael?'

'You'll know him as "Mary".'

Pamela suddenly felt woozy and sat back down on the sofa. 'My head…'

'You were very charming!' exclaimed Elena, sashaying over to the kitchen. She boiled a kettle while Jo put on her shoes.

'Look at it this way, you were no worse off than the rest of those degenerates,' Jo laughed as she ran a hand through her short dark hair. 'Right, I'm off. I'll leave you to take care of the invalid. Take a couple of these.' She opened a kitchen cabinet, took out a bottle of aspirin and tossed it to Pamela. Then she turned back to Elena and said, 'Don't let's be angry, pet.'

Jo attempted to kiss Elena, who turned her cheek to one side. Jo sighed and left the flat.

The sun changed its angle slightly enough that it hit the sofa, bathing Pamela and her hangover in excruciating sunlight. She lay back down for a moment and closed her eyes while the tiny men carried on hammering at her brain.

'Who turns up at a party full of strangers, gets ludicrously drunk and sings Cole Porter? Cole Porter!'

Elena brought a pot of tea in a delicately engraved silver teapot over to the coffee table. 'Not to worry. Percy's friends are very nice people. Eccentric English.'

'Were they... are they all... musical?'

'I think you are the musical one!'

'Oh no... I mean do they all like the company of other men?'

'There are not many places people like us can go.'

Elena pushed a glass of water in Pamela's direction. She sat up gingerly and took two aspirin.

'My father would sing Russian folk songs when he drank too much. Always at dinner parties. It drove my poor mother mad.'

Elena had never mentioned her family before. Pamela was at a loss for what to say, so instead looked at the teapot and said, 'This is beautiful. Is it a family heirloom?'

'I bought it from some other poor Russian in Paris. We waited too long, until it was almost too late to leave. We didn't believe what was happening. And then all I could take were two suitcases. And the Virgin.'

Elena crossed herself and gestured to the icon on the wall.

'How terrible.'

'We escaped with our lives. Many in our family did not.'

Pamela covered her eye with her hand to block out the sunlight and got a better look at Elena. Her face was impassive, betraying nothing. The sun hit the silver streaks in her chestnut hair and Pamela briefly wondered what she must have looked like as a young woman. Pamela's hand found a hole in the upholstery of the sofa and she looked around the small flat. An overwhelming sense of sadness crept over her. To leave one's home, country, family, to flee with a suitcase, what must that be like? To end up in a foreign land, having to begin from nothing.

'We had been banished to France, many years ago, before the Revolution. My grandfather did not approve of my mother,' Elena continued, sipping her tea, looking like a duchess in a second-hand shop. 'When he finally forgave my father for marrying her, we returned to Russia. We should have stayed but what did we know? No one knows how quick things change. But I do not have to live with Nikolai any longer, and that is a blessing. He will not give me a divorce but he stays away.'

She shrugged, rose and went to the kitchen.

'Does it feel strange? You in one country and your husband in another?'

'We were married very young. It was arranged by our families, just before the Bolsheviks turned our lives upside down. He is a fool and a drunk. But he does what he likes with his life and I do the same.'

Elena looked at Pamela wonderingly and smiled. 'But perhaps you know this kind of marriage yourself?'

Pamela was about to protest when she remembered what Percy said to her the night before. Instead, she sipped her tea quietly and shielded her eyes from the sun.

III

'...and Parliament can still suspend the government in India! It's a farce. They've been given hardly anything. Which is the way Westminster and Whitehall want to keep it,' said Aunt Constance as she stalked up and down in Pamela's morning room.

Pamela, who had been midway through reading out a guest list for Aunt Constance's fundraising gala, paused, sighed and put the list down.

'Aunt Constance, if you could just—'

'We treat them like children who can't be trusted with their own country, which we stole from them!'

'I'd like you to have one more look at—'

'Yes, well, if *everyone* wanted their country back, the whole enterprise would collapse, wouldn't it?' said Sylvia as she sipped her tea on the divan.

Aunt Constance went over to the window and looked out on to the square. It was the third or fourth time she had done this in the past hour and Pamela was starting to wonder if she was looking for something – or someone – in particular. She also noticed that her aunt had worn a surprisingly smart-looking frock that day, which looked new. Though, much to Pamela's exasperation, she had paired it with a jade-green turban.

'Aunt Constance, shall we try to finish the guest list?' asked Pamela, waving her list in the air.

Suddenly, the bell rang and Jenny announced that Mrs Brackenberry had arrived. (If there was one thing Flossie knew how to do well, it was throwing a party.)

'I absolutely adore your turban!' enthused Flossie to Aunt Constance.

The four women spent the morning writing up the guest list, brainstorming venues, sketching out a budget and deciding menus. Just before luncheon, the bell rang again and Jenny announced a Mr Dekhale.

'A Mister Who?' asked Pamela.

Aunt Constance leapt up from her seat in excitement. 'I invited my friend – the one from India!'

Wearing a pale grey suit and a blue bow-tie, an Indian man of medium height and middle age entered the room. He gave a small bow to the four women.

'May I present Mr Sardar Chandra Dekhale. We met in India. He is on the committee for the new school and an absolutely wonderful man. He's on a visit to Europe, researching girls' education,' Aunt Constance said excitedly while pressing the hand of Mr Dekhale, who looked somewhat embarrassed.

'I thought he could speak at the event and talk to everyone about the importance of educating future generations of Indian women,' she continued, still holding his hand. 'Wouldn't that be wonderful?'

Even Mr Dekhale looked a bit surprised. 'No, no, Miss Plumbly, I couldn't possibly—'

'Nonsense! You'll be wonderful.'

'What an excellent idea,' said Sylvia. 'You must. That's settled then.'

Flossie, still looking a bit awe-struck, said, 'Are you enjoying your trip to Britain? Is it terribly hot in India? And is it true that practically everything can kill you?'

'Yes, it is very hot in India. And yes, we do have numerous serpents and insects. Many spiders.'

'Spiders! I can't stand spiders. Are they very large?'

'Yes, we do have many large spiders.'

'I would have to shake out my shoes every morning, just to make sure something hadn't made its home inside them!' said Aunt Constance, beaming at Mr Dekhale.

Flossie recoiled in horror. 'But that's simply dreadful!'

'One gets used to such things!' said Aunt Constance. 'Besides, the stunning countryside more than makes up for it.'

'Pamela and Francis and my husband and I are going down to Cowes this weekend for the sailing,' said Flossie. 'You must join us! All of you! Especially you, Mr Dekhale!'

Mr Dekhale blushed at Flossie's sudden insistence. 'No, thank you, Madame. That is very kind of you to make such an offer. However, I am not at liberty to leave London this weekend. I have many people to see.'

'Of course, you do, yes. But if you change your mind!' Flossie turned to Pamela. 'Pamela, you will bring your aunt and her friend, won't you?'

'Thank you, dear,' said Sylvia. 'Very kind of you but I get terribly seasick.'

Pamela didn't quite know what an entire weekend with her aunt in tow would be like; she also didn't know what to reply until Aunt Constance exclaimed, 'What fun! I haven't been sailing in ages!'

IV

Instead of the traditional summer retreat to Balmoral, the King had gone yachting in the Mediterranean with Wallis Simpson, so yachting had become all the rage that summer. Pamela, Francis and Aunt Constance had hardly set foot in Flossie and Albert's cottage in Cowes when Flossie began telling them that they had all been invited to a luncheon on the Duke of Westminster's yacht. She clapped her hands, explaining Albert knew him from the Anglo-German Fellowship.

'Won't it be fun to see such an absolutely enormous boat?' Flossie exclaimed.

'Yacht,' corrected Albert.

A round man of medium height with ginger hair, a pale complexion and freckles, he looked just like Flossie. (Pamela always found it odd when people married spouses who looked as if they could be their siblings.) He was good-natured, but came across as over-eager and eager to please, giving the impression of someone who was often left out of the fun as a child. Social engagement did not come naturally to Albert, who tried desperately hard to join the right clubs, meet the right people and generally fit in.

'What's the Anglo-German Fellowship?' asked Aunt Constance.

Pamela remembered what Flossie had told her about the Fellowship several months ago. She briefly glanced at Francis to gauge his reaction and saw his face had clouded over. He looked as if he was about to say something when Nanny Flynn bustled in with the children. Both Albert and Flossie lit up, Albert taking Margaret by the hand, Flossie doing the same with Elizabeth and Nanny holding baby George.

'Say hello to my friends, darlings!' said Flossie to her children.

'The AGF,' said Albert, 'is a little club that promotes trade and goodwill between our two countries. Marvellous chaps.'

'Between Britain and Germany?' Aunt Constance asked.

'We hope to do our bit to bring some life back into the British markets. Pamela, your editor-in-chief is a member!'

Pamela considered Dawson's presence at Cliveden. As she made a fuss over the Brackenberry children, she wondered how deeply involved Albert was in this cabal. Did he play a significant role? Or was it superficial – merely another club to join in order to meet and impress people? She turned again to Francis but he had become absorbed in baby George.

The Duke of Westminster's yacht, the Cutty Sark, was gigantic and seemed better suited to its original purpose of fighting naval battles than hosting sailing parties. Surprisingly, Albert looked as if he was in his element, chatting away happily to the other guests about banking and the stock exchange. Flossie looked slightly dazzled by the enormity of the yacht and the patina of the crowd and kept grabbing Pamela's arm to point out one social luminary or another.

Aunt Constance kept complaining to Pamela about how extravagant the surroundings were and how many people they could feed with the amount of food that appeared throughout the afternoon, seemingly forgetting her own younger years spent at even more opulent, pre-war society functions. Francis, however, was unusually quiet throughout the afternoon. The luncheon felt to Pamela like an encore to Cliveden, with many of the same crowd waxing lyrical about the German government.

Princess Stephanie von Hohenlohe made an entrance in a large, peach-coloured hat accompanied by two men. One in a cream linen suit, the other in seersucker, both wearing Nazi pins on their lapels. Everyone turned as they entered and the Duke of Westminster greeted them enthusiastically. The man in the linen turned out to be Joachim von Ribbentrop, the new German Ambassador, and the other introduced himself as a secretary in the German Embassy. Pamela remembered what the Princess had told her about von Ribbentrop and his special relationship with Mrs Simpson. Looking at his grim, pursed lips and unsmiling face, Pamela wondered what that relationship could be.

Princess Stephanie spotted Pamela and came over. 'Have you seen Wallis in recent days?'

'Unfortunately, not,' replied Pamela, omitting the incident at Sibyl Colefax's where the King shouted at her. 'But I hear she and His Royal Highness are on holiday in the Med on Lady Yule's yacht, the Nahlin.'

'Ah yes. Very romantic, is it not?'

Pamela took a closer look at Princess Stephanie, noting that her dress – like all her others – was clearly the product of fine material and excellent tailoring, most likely Paris-made. And her jewels – an emerald cocktail ring and a diamond bracelet – were most certainly genuine, and probably worth a small fortune. Was the Princess less likely to be a spy because she had no need for the kind of status and financial incentive that would come with assignments of international espionage? Or was it the Nazi government that was, in fact, paying for her expensive tastes?

She looked over the Princess's shoulder and discovered that the man in the seersucker suit, von Ribbentrop's secretary, was watching her from across the table. Remembering the suspicions surrounding von Ribbentrop and the death of the previous ambassador, she felt a small shiver down her spine and looked away. Did 'secretary' really mean henchman? How far would people like this go to get what they wanted?

Francis, who had been speaking to Albert and one of his AGF colleagues, excused himself and stood up. He leaned in to Pamela and said quietly, 'Pamela, I'm going to absent myself. Please give my apologies.'

Pamela realised the German in the seersucker suit was still looking over at her. Feeling another wave of unease, she decided that perhaps it was time to absent herself too. She made her apologies to the Princess and asked her aunt if she'd like to take a stroll. As they walked the upper deck together, Pamela suddenly noticed Aunt Constance was looking around nervously. She was about to ask if she was all right when she saw that the man in the seersucker suit had reappeared and seemed to be following them. She took her aunt's arm and ushered her towards the prow.

'Shall we take a view of the…' Pamela hesitated, unsure of nautical terms, 'the… front of the ship?'

Aunt Constance was so distracted that she simply nodded and smiled. As they walked on, the seersucker man slowly made his way in their direction. Pamela began to wonder how they could possibly escape, if it came to that. Jump into a lifeboat and row to shore? Hail a passing speedboat? She heard the man coming down the stairs behind them. Her mind raced as she tried to pretend to take in the view of the water. If the man was spying for the Nazis, how long had he been following her? Since she had come aboard? Since she had come to Cowes? Pamela was suddenly struck by the frightening thought that he could have been following them all the way from London. After all, if he was involved in faking the death of von Ribbentrop's predecessor, what might he do to an enemy spy?

And now, there she was, with her innocent, unsuspecting aunt who had the bad luck to find herself caught up in a situation with which she wasn't involved at all. All because Albert Brackenberry had wanted to raise his social profile in the eyes of German businessmen. Because the Princess von Hohenlohe had wanted to insert herself into aristocratic English society. Because Adolf Hitler had wanted the attentions of the King of England.

As the seersucker man approached Pamela and her aunt, she felt her heart pounding in her chest and sweat starting to trickle down her back.

There he was. Right behind them.

Pamela didn't know what else to do, so as he approached, she turned to the railing and said loudly, 'Oh, what a gorgeous view! Aren't you just in love with this view we have?'

Aunt Constance looked at her as if she had gone mad. Pamela saw the seersucker man approaching out of the corner of her eye. She suddenly remembered that she had once been told that if a man ever tried to attack her, she should shout loudly so as to make him worry that she would draw attention to the two of them.

'It's simply an exquisite view!' Pamela shouted. 'Would you look at how the sun is hitting the water? I've never seen anything like it in my life!'

Aunt Constance gripped her arm tightly and hissed, 'Pamela, what are you doing?'

'I bet if we stand here long enough, we could see a seal! Or a whale! I bet you don't have whales in India!'

At this, her aunt clapped a hand over Pamela's mouth and turned to see the man walking up behind them. They both stiffened in fear.

The man stopped, looked at them through his sunglasses, tipped his hat and said, 'A beautiful afternoon, isn't it?'

And then walked away.

Aunt Constance took her hand off her niece's mouth and breathed a sigh of relief. Pamela looked down and saw her hand half-pulling something out of her pocket. To her shock, she realised it was the handle of a revolver.

'Aunt Constance...'

'Yes, dear?'

'Is that a revolver in your pocket?'

Aunt Constance quickly tucked the gun into her pocket and folded her arms. 'What revolver?'

Pamela turned her towards the railing and whispered, 'You know perfectly well that there is a *gun* in the pocket of your dress. Now what on earth are you doing with a gun?'

'I need it for protection.'

'Protection against what?'

'I didn't want to drag you into this.'

'Drag me into what?'

'Mr Dekhale and I... we are involved in some political action in India.'

'What do you mean, "political action"?'

Aunt Constance looked around nervously. 'The Movement for Indian Independence. It's why we had to leave India.'

Pamela saw Aunt Constance fiddling with the gun in her pocket, and, worried she would end up shooting one of them accidentally, took her hand.

Suddenly, it all made sense. Aunt Constance's nervousness the last week. The looks she had given Mr Dekhale.

Aunt Constance thought someone was following her – Scotland Yard, Special Branch, MI6.

And she was in love with Mr Dekhale.

'You're in love with Mr Dekhale!'

Aunt Constance blushed like a schoolgirl. 'He has been my... companion... for several years now.'

'That story about coming to England to raise funds for a girls' school was a lot of rot. You're on the lamb!'

'Well, there *is* a school. The best way to liberate a people is to educate them. But some of the money will go to—'

'Gandhi?'

'Yes. In a way.'

'Whatever next? A gala ball in aid of Irish unification?'

'As a matter of fact—'

'Alright, alright...'

Pamela leaned backwards against the railing, took out her cigarette case and lit a cigarette. She offered one to her aunt, who gratefully accepted it.

'And now you think you're being followed?'

'I wouldn't be surprised if it was Special Branch. I wouldn't be surprised at all if they have a whole file on me by now, dating back to my suffragette days. They're doing everything they can to keep India. The jewel in the crown!'

'But Aunt Constance, that man is a German working in the Embassy. Why would he concern himself with India?'

'If I've learned anything in my time abroad, it's that you never really know who people are, especially when it comes to the British government.'

Pamela took a long drag on her cigarette. 'What do you mean? That he's a British agent in disguise as a Nazi official?'

'Stranger things have been known to happen.' She looked at Pamela. 'Do *you* know that man?'

'I've never seen him before in my life.'

'So why were you shouting? You looked frightened.'

Pamela considered for a moment. She could lie. She could concoct an elaborate but plausible story. But she didn't want to lie to her aunt. It didn't feel right, lying to Aunt Constance when she had just confessed her deepest, darkest secrets.

In for a penny, in for a pound.

Aunt Constance listened carefully while Pamela told her the whole story, starting from when she first suspected that she was being watched, to her recruitment by MI5.

To Pamela's surprise, Aunt Constance embraced her. 'Darling! How terribly exciting for you!'

'You mustn't say a word to anyone. Not a soul.'

'My lips are sealed!'

'You really must promise, Aunt Constance.'

'Yes, I promise. Mum's the word!'

'And I think it's best if you give me your revolver.'

Aunt Constance looked taken aback. 'But it's for my protection.'

'Do be a sensible thing and hand it over.'

Aunt Constance reluctantly handed Pamela the gun and she tucked it into her handbag.

Pamela sent her aunt back to the luncheon and decided to find a deck chair and sit for a while in silence until her nerves had settled. She saw a few in a row, close to the railing, and walked towards them. But once again, she heard footsteps behind her. She turned to look ever so slightly over her shoulder and saw the seersucker man. She considered running but knew there was nowhere to go. She looked over the railing of the ship, down into the water, aware that he could push her overboard and say it was an accident. Pamela started to panic again, but then remembered what she now had in her handbag. She quickly opened the clasp and felt around for it.

'There's no need for that, Lady Pamela,' the man said calmly, removing his sunglasses and revealing his dark blue eyes. He took a step towards her and she took a step back. 'Please do not make a scene.'

'Don't take a step closer, sir. I have a weapon and I'm not afraid to shoot you,' Pamela said as the revolver shook in her hands.

'Lady Pamela, you must calm yourself!'

'*You* calm *yourself*.'

He put a hand on her arm and she felt the cold railing pressing into her back and a sudden wind whipping up her hair.

'We work for the same people, don't you understand?' he said with a worried look in his eye. 'I am not a Nazi. I work for your government, in secret.'

'What?'

The man took a step back and inclined his head towards Pamela. 'Wolfgang Gans zu Putlitz. Since last year, you might say I have been serving two masters. I began diplomatic work under the Weimar government – quite a different time. Many people in my position – of the old world, people who have been educated, who have travelled, who have many friends in other countries – we felt something must be done to put a stop to what has been happening to Germany. And so, we use our positions... *exploit* our positions for good. The good of my country, and of yours. Rather than leave the diplomatic corps, I decided to offer my services to the British.'

Pamela looked at this seemingly ordinary-looking man with a large nose, a cleft chin and a receding hairline. Who was he? What must his life be like? Was he afraid of being caught?

'But how did you know who I was?' she asked.

'I was of course aware of your work through my connections on our side.' He hesitated. 'You see, the Embassy has a dossier on you. They are not aware of what you are doing with regards to Mrs Simpson, but they know that you are an influential, well-connected Englishwoman. They would be very pleased to have you as someone who could help promote their cause.'

'They have a whole *dossier* on me?'

'It is because of the Princess von Hohenlohe. Hitler's lieber Prinzessin. She has recommended you to some very high-ranking people.'

'How dreadful…'

'Sometimes one must pretend to be someone one is not, no?' Putlitz said and smiled wryly.

Pamela looked out past the ship and into the blue waters of the Solent.

'The King is not an intelligent man but Frau Simpson is canny. A frequent guest at the Embassy. She too has a dossier, but she has already been recruited successfully.'

'Is it true? About the Simpson woman and your ambassador? That they have some sort of… relationship?'

'It is highly suspected.'

Putlitz took out an elegant, monogrammed, silver cigarette case and offered Pamela a cigarette, which she accepted.

'So, if Mrs Simpson and von Ribbentrop, who is an agent sent directly from the Führer, are carrying on, in one way or another, that means she might be a conduit for Nazi influence,' Pamela said, thinking aloud.

'A country's leader, whether that is the prime minister or the king, he establishes the tone for the country, the discussions people have, the culture, the way people behave towards one another. Germany's fate is sealed. But there is still hope for Britain, Lady Pamela. Your government should strike while they are able.'

'What are you saying?'

'If you were to declare war on Germany now, Hitler would be completely unprepared and would certainly lose.'

'Declare war? But Herr Putlitz, that's mad!'

Pamela waited for an explanation but Putlitz simply put his sunglasses back on, bowed and tipped his hat.

'If you ever need anything, please do not hesitate to ask.'

He handed Pamela a card with an address and the number for a telephone exchange.

'Herr Putlitz...?' Pamela asked, fingering the card. 'Is it true? About the previous ambassador? That he was... murdered? Like the ambassador to France before him?'

'With crimes of this nature, of course no proof exists. Ambassador von Hoesch was a decent man, of the old guard. There are fewer and fewer these days. He was a good statesman, much liked by your politicians, and greatly missed in the Embassy. And he was suspicious of von Ribbentrop – he thought he was greedy, with a lust for power. The final straw, as you British say, was when he denounced the occupation of the Rhineland. He thought it was foolish and reckless, very bad for peace in Europe.'

'But conveniently, he died a month later.'

'As I say, Lady Pamela, your country's government must strike now, while they can.'

V

Long after evening had set in, Francis and Pamela were finally alone in Flossie and Albert's guest room. Pamela found the sudden and forced intimacy that arose when she and Francis were obliged to share a bedroom felt strange. When they were first married, he had asked if they could do away with the convention of separate bedrooms. They had tried it but it hadn't been a success. Pamela enjoyed reading before bed and Francis preferred to put out the light straightaway and go to sleep. And then of course there were Francis's nightmares. A remnant from the war.

Francis sat down on the bed and looked at Pamela. 'I'm sorry I dismissed you, darling.'

'Dismissed me? When?'

'A few weeks back, when we were at Henry's. You had been to that ball at the Astors'. You were concerned about the BUF.'

Pamela sat next to him. 'Oh?'

'There's far more support for Germany than I could have imagined. Shocking, really.' Francis paused and fiddled with his cufflinks. 'I know the Brackenberries are your friends, but I cannot condone such an appalling regime, even if only in the name of trade and economics. Nazi officials...? My god, what next?' He looked at his hands in bewilderment. 'I asked Albert how he could associate with such people. He told me it was just business.'

A familiar sentiment these days, thought Pamela.

'And he said I was overreacting, that the war is over now.'

A sea breeze drifted in through the open window, ruffling the curtains.

Pamela took Francis's hand. 'He is younger than you. He was only a child during the war. Like me.'

'How do you know that woman? The one connected to the German Embassy, who came in with von Ribbentrop,' Francis asked Pamela.

She felt guilty about the lie by omission she was going to tell, suddenly realising what a double life she was leading.

'I met her when I interviewed Wallis Simpson, for the paper. I saw her again at Cliveden.'

'I sincerely hope she isn't a friend of yours now.'

'What do you take me for? Unity Mitford?'

'Who?' Francis asked.

'Oh, you know, Lord Redesdale's daughter, the one who's obsessed with Hitler.'

'Lord Redesdale has a daughter who's obsessed with Hitler?'

'More than one! How can you be married to a woman who knows everything about London society and know so little?' Pamela laughed.

As Francis laughed with her, Pamela realised how rarely she heard his laugh these days. All at once, she leaned over and kissed him. Though surprised at first, he embraced her.

VI

Pamela tried to make sense of her newfound information. Charlie had wanted Pamela to find the source of the recruitment from the ranks of British aristocracy to the German cause. And even though she officially wasn't meant to be prying into the goings-on within the German Embassy, Charlie was encouraging her to do so. Putlitz had wanted her to know she could rely on him but didn't want her to let on that the two of them knew each other. Clearly Wallis was a threat to the Palace, but how dangerous was she? Now that Pamela knew Princess Stephanie was a go-between for the Nazis and the British (perhaps one of many), drawing people into her web, was she even more of a threat than Wallis?

And now she had Aunt Constance's double life to worry about. Was she being followed by Special Branch? Was she really involved with Ghandi? Pamela knew she shouldn't have told her aunt about her mission, but she felt she didn't have any choice. As with Jenny. (Jenny had proven to be rather useful, though.) And Putlitz, though she supposed that wasn't actually her fault as he already knew who she was. Did all secret agents know each other already?

Pamela found she was starting to become paranoid, worrying about dossiers and plants and people following her, spying on her, trying to recruit her. Or maybe it wasn't paranoia, but rather a growing awareness of a need for caution. At times, her new life felt like a hall of mirrors.

She wrote to Charlie about her knowledge of Princess Stephanie and Putlitz, though not her aunt's activities as a foot soldier of Gandhi.

Charlie was surprisingly unsurprised at Pamela's revelations, and was, in fact, encouraged enough by her recent encounters to instruct her to try to find out who else Princess Stephanie had recruited and what other information she had about Wallis.

Memorandum from a reliable source making the rounds warns that Italy and Germany are not only recruiting British subjects but actively positioned for sabotage within Britain. Will ultimately render diplomatic relations impossible.

Pamela remembered Putlitz had told her how Britain should declare war on Germany now, so as to have the upper hand. She wondered if the reliable source was, in fact, Putlitz.

VII

Later in the week, Pamela received two more interesting letters.

The first was from Diana Cooper, who had been on the infamous cruise on the Nahlin with Wallis and the King. She and Duff were annoyed that the King wouldn't land to view the antiquities in Greece and called Delphi 'Delhi'. Wallis was 'wearing very badly' and Duff was completely fed up with having to listen to the King's ill-informed opinions on the different countries they'd visited and from having to apologise to every foreigner he offended. Diana wondered if she should cut the trip short before she threw them both overboard.

How had the pair of them managed to keep their affair out of the foreign press? After all, it was one thing to sneak around dinner parties in one's own city but quite another to dock in half the countries on the Mediterranean in an enormous yacht.

The second letter was from Pamela's friend Diana Vreeland, who had been making a splash in New York ever since she and her husband moved back from London earlier that year. She had somehow effortlessly managed to get herself a column at *Harper's Bazaar* simply because the editor spotted her out dancing in a white lace Chanel gown. Diana wanted to know how on earth the British public was taking the news of their king being in cahoots with a married American.

Pamela was confused at first, until she realised that it was the American press who had been covering the Nahlin cruise, as well as the French, the Italian and several other countries. Apparently, every American was completely captivated by the fact that their compatriot had caught the eye of the King of England – a fairy tale come to life. Diana was amused by it all, having known Wallis from her days running a lingerie boutique in Mayfair.

Darling, of course I knew about the affair, having sold her corsets and garter belts for years… but what are other people saying? The British are so terribly prudish about these things.

Practically every paper in the world had scooped the British press on the story about their own monarch. Pamela found herself furious about the whole thing. Everyone in the world knew their business, but because of people like Beaverbrook, Rothermere and even Geoffrey Dawson kowtowing to the Palace, the British public had been kept in the dark. Pamela wondered what else they were being kept in the dark about.

VIII

Francis and Pamela went to Wigmore Hall that evening to hear a programme of Schubert string quartets. Though she didn't particularly care for classical music, the couple had an arrangement: Francis took Pamela dancing to jazz bands and she accompanied him to classical concerts. Picking up their tickets in the lobby, they ran into Mr Stern who was accompanied by a serious-looking woman a little older than Pamela with dark-red hair pulled back at the nape of her neck and a light spray of freckles across her nose. Pamela introduced Francis to Stern and Stern introduced them to the young woman; she turned out to be his cousin, who had, until recently, been living in Berlin.

'How long will you be in London?' Pamela asked her.

'Fräulein Eisner is staying with my wife and myself for a period of time. Her English is somewhat limited, I'm afraid. She hopes to improve it and then find employment here.'

Francis said something in German to Stern's cousin. They spoke for a moment, both very animated. She seemed to relax, being able to speak to a stranger in her native tongue.

Switching back to English, Francis said, 'I studied in Germany for a period, before the war. I have very fond memories of Freiburg. I hope your cousin is able to make herself at home here in England.

I can imagine how difficult it's been for her. The situation can only be described as intolerable.'

'Lotte was a cellist in the Berlin Staatsoper,' said Stern. 'She is an exceptional musician. But because of certain laws that continue to be passed, she is no longer able to play professionally anywhere in Germany.'

Francis said something to Lotte Eisner and she shook her head. He frowned and nodded, then said, 'I hope to hear her play here in London before too long.'

As they took their seats, Pamela said to Francis, 'I feel so sorry for her. How horrible. Do you think she'll be able to return to Germany?'

'Only when there's a new government in power, I imagine.'

The next morning, Pamela was having coffee in the paper's canteen, pouring over the day's news, including the worrying headlines about Abyssinia and Spain. The communists had been burning down churches and farms and Franco was bringing in troops from Morocco. The British navy had sent warships to Gibraltar to evacuate British citizens. She spotted Stern drinking a cup of tea, also poring over that day's paper. She walked over to his table.

'Mr Stern. Hello.'

He looked up. 'Mrs More. Good morning.'

'Am I interrupting?'

'Not at all. Please join me,' he said as he made space at the table, moving aside his wire-rimmed spectacles, pen and notebook. 'What a pleasant coincidence to run into you and your husband yesterday evening. His German is very good.'

'He very much enjoys any opportunity to speak it. He and I were very sorry to hear of what has happened to your cousin. She was made to leave the orchestra because she's Jewish?'

'There is a kind of musicians' guild now under the Reich. The Reichsmusikkammer. In order to pursue a career in music, any musician or conductor or composer must belong to it. But of course, you cannot belong to it if you're Jewish. I hear it's common now for orchestras to play the Horst Wessel Song before concerts. At least Lotte no longer has to do such a thing.'

'How terribly insulting for her. To have worked so hard. What does it matter, if one is Jewish?'

'The musicians, the conductor, even the music must be Aryan. It's the same across all fields now in Germany. People are leaving in droves; not only musicians, but other artists, architects, scientists, doctors. If they can leave. In that sense, Lotte has been very fortunate.'

'I suppose, at least we have people reporting on conditions in Germany. I know some other papers don't.'

'Beaverbrook and Rothermere think the race laws are a German problem. And it's more important to maintain peace in Germany than worry the British people about German domestic issues. But it is a worry how the British press – in fact, the European press – are covering emigration from Germany to other countries.'

'Jewish emigration?'

'Indeed. The coverage is quite negative, which only encourages public hostility. Very dismaying.'

'I was thinking about what you said, about Dawson having a conflict of interest because of his relationship with the Prime Minister. But the Astors also support the Hitler regime. And Dawson answers to them. And perhaps that is worse.'

'There will always be conflicts of interest where money and ownership of the press is concerned.'

'But if we are working for these people, doesn't that make us complicit?'

'Do you think it does?'

'Well, for instance, Dawson has told us not to write about the relationship between the King and Mrs Simpson. But their yachting trip was covered by the foreign press. Which means we're keeping the British people in the dark about their own monarch. What else aren't we telling them?'

'I'm sure the secrecy of that relationship is unlikely to last, whatever Geoffrey Dawson says. The truth usually comes out.'

Pamela's strange mood and general sense of unease continued into the evening so she cancelled her plans to go for cocktails with Flossie and Jack Harris and instead stayed at home with Francis.

After dinner, Francis closed the door of the library where they had been listening to the wireless. 'Pam, I'd like to speak to you about something.'

Pamela felt immediately apprehensive.

Francis stood stiffly in the middle of the room with his arms behind his back. 'I know this isn't your favourite topic of conversation, which is why I thought it might be easier if I spoke to a women's doctor, who specialises in... matters of fertility.'

'Francis, you spoke to a doctor I don't know, who's never met me, about my health?'

'I thought you might be relieved to know that this kind of thing is quite common for women of your age.'

'Women of my age?'

'And that Doctor Lindsey generally recommends a good deal of rest, not too much stress or activity.'

'Too much *activity*?'

Francis looked down at his slippers awkwardly. 'Anyway, he said that you *could* give up some of the things you've been doing, perhaps stay at home a bit more – though I'm not saying that you should feel *obliged* to do those things. And of course, there's a special diet he recommends as well. And some other medical things such as taking your temperature at the right time and so on.'

Pamela carefully put down her book and rose from her armchair. She paced back and forth across the library, so angry she hardly knew what to say. She stood in front of the window with her back to Francis while she composed herself. He walked over to her and put a hand on her shoulder. She spun around to face him.

'Francis, are you telling me that you went to see a specialist about having children?'

'I thought it might help, if you didn't have to face the burden alone.'

'But you did it behind my back.'

'Darling, it has been four years…'

'Yes, I know that but didn't it occur to you that perhaps this might have been a conversation you should have had with your wife before you had it with a stranger? And besides, what am I supposed to do? Give up everything I enjoy in life? Being out and about in town? Going dancing? Travelling? The column?'

Francis smoothed his hair with his hand, which shook, as it always did when he was rattled. 'I didn't say that.'

'It seems to be what this *specialist* is saying.'

'Pamela, I'm not asking you to give up everything you enjoy. It's just that, whenever I try to broach the topic with you, you change the subject. I thought perhaps you were embarrassed—'

'Embarrassed?'

'Or ashamed.'

'Of what?'

'Well, I assume that it must be more difficult for you than for other women to have children. And that must be hard on you.'

Patricia, who had been lying on the carpet, sensed Francis's distress and came over to rub her face on his leg and whine softly. He leaned down to pet her with his shaky hand.

'*Do* you want children, Pam?'

Pamela realised it was the first time he had ever actually asked her the question. She went to the door and was about to open it when she felt a stab of guilt. She turned around to face him.

'Everyone wants children. What I don't want is my husband making plans with a doctor for my life, without my knowledge.'

Then Pamela turned and left the room, and then the house, and went out into the night to walk without any idea of where she was going.

August 1936

I

As usual, no one was in London in early August. Francis had gone to play golf in Scotland with his brother while Pamela went to stay with Lettice Wakefield in her chateau in the Loire Valley. Like many marriages in their circle, Pamela and Francis's was rooted in the kind of politesse and mutual accommodation that resulted from a particular kind of upbringing; however, when tested, these tendencies turned to froideur and avoidance. Francis had, of course, apologised to Pamela, and she had, of course, accepted his apology. And while they didn't speak of the argument again, the gulf between them had widened.

Though after a few days with Lettice, Pamela was grateful things weren't worse. The episode with Lettice's lover Giles and her husband Ashley had ended badly. Ashley was asking for a divorce and had spitefully decided to name Giles as the other party, instead of doing what most people considered the decent thing and going to a hotel with a tart. Lettice had been in a terrible state for months and had come to France at the beginning of the summer to recover. Lettice wasn't what one would expect from a glamorous, notorious social casualty; she was petite and a little near-sighted (thus prone to squinting). But Pamela was sorry to see the normally meticulously coiffed, perfectly attired, green-eyed, raven-haired beauty reduced to slumping around the house in dowdy old blouses and trousers.

The chateau had been in her mother's family for over a hundred years and had become a dumping ground for every stick of furniture, objet d'art and keepsake forgotten and/or unwanted by various and sundry Barreau relatives. Lettice had decided to busy herself with organisation, renovation and removal. Pamela's visions of sunning herself in the garden, long afternoons spent reading and shopping trips to Paris had been usurped by the reality of going through dusty, old boxes in the attic, hauling around furniture and painting walls. It was a dirty, sweaty business and Pamela was relieved there was no one to see them, apart from a skeleton crew of three servants.

Lettice had been drinking quite a bit, though Pamela couldn't say she could blame her. Not only was Ashley being distastefully public about the divorce proceedings but Giles had managed to slink away from it all, keeping Lettice at arm's length. He hadn't been returning her letters and always had an excuse to cut their telephone calls short. Pamela kept trying to gently steer Lettice away from phoning him, especially after she'd had a few drinks.

'I just wanted to say hello, that's all. Just to say hello and hear his voice,' Lettice said as she refilled her glass with a bottle of Bordeaux from the wine cellar. 'Why is it that men are so content to hang about when it's fun and games, but the moment things become serious they disappear faster than you can say "Jack Robinson"?'

She sat on the floor of the living room, half-heartedly sorting through boxes of family photos. *'Celine, another bottle of wine, please!'* she called out in French to her maid. 'You're lucky, Pam. Francis would make such a wonderful father. It's too late for me now. I'm ancient – thirty-three! Who will want me now? A dried-up divorcee, the object of derision and scandal. And once the scandal is forgotten, I'll just be an old hag. An old hag who's alone.'

Celine entered with a new bottle of wine but looked to Pamela first for confirmation. Pamela shook her head and Celine turned around and left. Lettice drained her glass and looked around.

'Celine? Celine!'

Celine returned and looked at Pamela again, an anxious look in her eye. Pamela shook her head again. Celine began to depart again but hesitated.

'Lettice, darling, it's only two o'clock. Perhaps we can wait until supper to open another bottle?' said Pamela.

Lettice hoisted herself up from the floor, waved Celine over and took the bottle from her. Celine gave Pamela another worried look and Pamela shrugged her shoulders. Celine sighed resignedly and pulled a corkscrew out of her apron pocket. Lettice took it from her and opened the bottle herself. Celine went to take the bottle back with her to the kitchen, but Lettice took it from her.

'*No, I'll keep it, thank you*,' said Lettice.

She picked up a photo of her French mother in a pre-war ballgown. 'Wasn't she beautiful, Pam? Even at that age I wasn't half as beautiful as she was. They had such a row about my coming out. Mother wanted me to make my debut in Paris but Father insisted on London. He was so hell-bent on my marrying an Englishman. He wanted to remove any trace of la famille Barreau from me. I can't imagine why he married a French woman in the first place, really.'

She took another swig of wine and Pamela took the glass from her hand.

She looked at Lettice with her dishevelled hair and her rumpled blouse, surrounded by countless family heirlooms, cut adrift from her life, in exile. Paying the price for her adventures, as the French called it. What if Pamela had taken lovers, like so many of her friends had done? Why hadn't she? Was it because she cared for Francis too much, or because she was, as Percy said, 'repressed'? Or perhaps simply afraid. She wondered if she might end up in much the same state as Lettice if she did. One's position as a woman in society was always so tenuous, it was advisable to make as few missteps as possible.

'Perhaps you and Ashley could talk it through together?' Pamela suggested gently.

Lettice took the wine glass back.

'There's nothing left to talk about. The thing of it is, I didn't actually think he'd mind – we've practically been strangers to each other for the last few years. But his pride's been irreparably damaged. And you know what men are like about their pride. Though perhaps you wouldn't understand. Francis is such a lovely sort. A constant man is what one needs, really, perhaps above all else. Don't you think?'

II

Back in London two weeks later, Pamela was relieved to return to civilisation. And after long, hot days of dragging around boxes and climbing up ladders, she was grateful to have an appointment at Madame Fontaine's. Pamela and Flossie waited for their hair to set while Flossie discussed her impending sitting with Cecil Beaton and all the outfits she had picked out for him to reject. (Flossie's taste wasn't reliable. For instance, the Schiaparelli hat that she had worn that day made her look like Robin Hood.)

Mid-conversation in walked Diana Guinness, née Mitford, to which she had reverted since her divorce.

Flossie waved and cried out, 'Yoo-hoo! Diana!'

Pamela groaned quietly. They had never been bosom friends but Diana had become boring and self-important since she had taken up with Tom Mosley. Diana trotted over, wearing a blouse that made her look like a schoolgirl – perhaps trying to compensate for the fact that she was only in her mid-twenties but already had a divorce and two young children to her name.

'I'm so pleased to have run into you, Pamela,' she chirped, as her eyebrows arched sharply. (Poor Flossie did so often get overlooked.) 'It has been ages since we saw each other last, but I suppose there are a great number of people I haven't seen in some time. You see, I've been so occupied with helping Tom with his campaign.'

Diana looked so smug that Pamela was tempted to tell her about her encounter with Mosley and Baba at Cliveden. She reminded herself that she had a job to do.

'Oh yes, of course. It's the BUF, isn't it?' Pamela inquired, as innocently as possible.

Diana's eyes glittered. 'It's the future of British politics. I think Tom could be Prime Minister one day.'

Pamela didn't understand what it was about Mosley that inspired such devotion from women like Diana and Baba, let alone his thousands of followers. But then again, she didn't understand the allure of Hitler either (who was even nastier *and* more popular).

As if reading Pamela's mind, Diana leaned in and added, 'He even has the support of Herr Hitler. They're in regular communication. Tom and I have been invited by Ambassador von Ribbentrop to a party at the German Embassy to celebrate the opening of the Berlin Olympics.' She paused for dramatic effect. 'The Duchess of Brunswick will be there.'

'The Duchess of *what*?' asked Pamela.

'You know, the Kaiser's daughter.'

'Didn't they get rid of the Kaiser?' asked Flossie.

'My sister Unity – she's very close with the Führer, you know – has it on good authority that he wishes for a match between the Duchess's daughter and the King. Tom says it will be marvellous for international relations,' said Diana.

Good luck getting past Wallis Simpson, thought Pamela. She cringed at the idea of spending an evening in the German Embassy with people like Diana and Tom but thought about her mission. If Wallis and the King were rumoured to be connected to the German Embassy, what better way of finding out what they – and other members of British society – were up to than to go there herself. Sniff around. Listen in on conversations.

'Sounds smashing,' Pamela said. 'I do love the Olympics.'

Flossie raised an eyebrow at Pamela.

'It would be such an excellent event to cover for my column. For *The Times*,' she added, for emphasis.

Diana looked at her. (Pamela could see the wheels turning.) 'Yes… you could come and write about it for your little column,' Diana said to Pamela.

Pamela bristled at the word 'little'. Who did she think she was? Diana had ruined a perfectly good marriage to take up with the lunatic Tom Mosley. Conveniently, Cimmie died to make way for Diana, but he still refused to marry her. There were whispers that he forced Diana to have abortions, and if the scene with Baba in the Cliveden library was anything to go by, he would never be faithful to her. Besides, her entire family was mad as a box of snakes. Unity followed Adolf Hitler around like a spaniel. Jessica seemed to think she was a communist. Their father, Baron Redesdale, was a raving lunatic prone to fits of rage. And Nancy seemed to spend most of her time irritating her family by satirising them in novels.

'We met the German Ambassador just last month, didn't we, Pamela?' Flossie piped up as she removed her head from the dryer.

Diana turned to look at Flossie for the first time since she arrived. 'You did, did you?'

'Oh yes! On the Duke of Westminster's yacht, in Cowes.'

Diana peered at Flossie like a snake watching a mongoose from a bush. 'Albert is a member of the Anglo-German Fellowship. We see quite a number of people from the Embassy at those gatherings. It's very interesting, getting to know Boche. They're not as bad as people say, you know.'

Diana smoothed the folds of her blouse coolly and said, 'No one says "Boche" anymore, Flossie.'

Flossie looked stung and pulled her robe around her protectively. 'No, of course not. How stupid of me.'

Pamela glared and resisted the urge to whack her with her handbag.

'Albert and I were invited to the party at the Embassy but we have a wedding to go to. I would *so* have liked to attend,' continued Flossie, trying to redeem herself.

Pamela was nearly as surprised as Diana to hear this.

'How unfortunate,' Diana replied. 'But how wonderful that you're available that evening, Pamela. I'll have an invitation sent to you.'

'Marvellous,' Pamela replied.

'I thought you didn't like Diana,' said Flossie as Diana left the salon.

Pamela opened an outdated copy of *Vogue*, flipping through the pages indifferently. 'I suppose one needs to stay abreast of these things,' she replied. 'The Duchess of Blenheim, etcetera. Might make for an interesting column.'

III

'Herr Hitler likes women to dress modestly but womanly. An emphasis of the curves of the body but not too much sex appeal, yes?'

In the name of research, Pamela held her nose and invited Princess Stephanie von Hohenlohe to tea on the pretext of asking for advice as to what to wear to the German Embassy.

'Although unfortunately there aren't many German designers, if you are able to find a dress by a German label that is encouraged.'

The Princess wore a navy silk dress with a peplum skirt and a long strand of pearls, along with a number of other baubles on her wrists and fingers. Pamela doubted anything she was wearing had been made anywhere but Paris.

A waiter brought a pot of tea as Princess Stephanie daintily nibbled on a biscuit.

'You received an invitation directly from the Embassy, I hope?' she asked between nibbles.

'Actually, I was invited by Diana Mitford. Do you know her?'

The Princess stiffened and looked up. 'We have been introduced, yes. I am acquainted with her sister Unity.'

Pamela added a lump of sugar to her tea. 'She's the one who seems to be lunching regularly with the German Chancellor, isn't she?'

'I should never have told her where he would be dining in Munich. The Führer cannot go anywhere without her following him like a pet dog.' She sighed and rolled her eyes. 'You are... *close* friends with her sister?'

'We've known each other socially for some years. She wanted me to cover the party for *The Times*.'

'A marvellous idea. But of course, *I* can introduce you to many people.'

'She wanted me to meet the daughter of the Duchess of… Oh it's so difficult to keep the names of other countries' aristocrats straight, isn't it?'

Pamela paused, gauging the princess's reaction.

Princess Stephanie sat up, suddenly alert. 'The Duchess of Brunswick, perhaps?'

Pamela tried to appear disinterested and looked around the Savoy's tea room casually. 'The daughter of… was it the Kaiser? Anyway, Diana says Herr Hitler wants the daughter of the Duchess – whatever her name is – to marry the King—'

'Diana knows nothing of what the Fuhrer wants,' the Princess fumed, gripping her pearls with one hand. 'She simply wants to appear as if she is more important than she is, like her sister.'

Like you, Pamela thought.

Pamela dabbed at the corner of her mouth daintily with a napkin, crossed her ankles and smoothed her skirt. 'So, it isn't true then? About the Duchess's daughter?'

'Such an idea is pure fantasy.'

'And I would imagine Mrs Simpson would be rather unhappy if such a match were to be arranged.'

Princess Stephanie threw up her hands in a dramatic gesture. 'It would make her most unhappy! Especially now that her husband is…' Princess Stephanie paused dramatically.

Pamela leaned forward.

The Princess also leaned in. 'This must be kept between the two of us. But Ernest has a lover, in New York, where he has been for his business. Wallis believes it may be serious.'

'Poor Wallis!' Pamela replied. 'How difficult for her.'

'Yes, it is unfortunate in many ways. But if Ernest were to give Wallis her freedom...'

'Her freedom?'

'To marry the King.'

'But I had no idea it was as serious as all that!' Pamela exclaimed, wondering if she was laying it on too thick.

'Lady Pamela, they are two people very much in love. The King has assured our friend that he wishes to marry her and put her on the throne, at his side.'

'But how would it be possible? She's a commoner, an American and divorced to boot.'

Pamela took out her cigarette case and offered one to the Princess, who politely declined. She lit one for herself and watched as the Princess smiled in a feline fashion.

'I believe there is one option that your government may allow. It is some kind of arrangement in the marriage. There is a strange name for it. I can never remember some of these strange English words!'

'Do you mean a morganatic marriage?'

Princess Stephanie snapped her fingers. 'Yes, that is what they call it. Wallis would be so very pleased, as would the King. He really does love her terribly, don't you think? And she would do anything for him. And I am sure that the Führer would be very pleased. He and the King are friendly with each other – he knows how much the King cares for the German people.'

'How sweet of the Führer,' Pamela murmured as she took a drag on her cigarette.

'He is a very kind and generous man.'

'Far be it from any of us to stand in the way of true love.'

IV

Pamela sent Charlie a message, telling him about the developments with Wallis, about Ernest's affair, as well as the invitation to the German Embassy party. She was hesitant to tell him, considering how ambivalent he seemed about any potential involvement with the Embassy and how any complications could compromise their mission. But Charlie encouraged her to attend. Pamela was perplexed at his change of attitude, but assumed that the agendas of intelligence men were as strange and unpredictable as ordinary men.

However, Pamela couldn't stop thinking about the fate of von Ribbentrop's unfortunate predecessor, Ambassador von Hoesch. Nor could she stop thinking about what Putlitz had told her, that the Germans had a dossier on her. Was it in order to recruit her, as they clearly had Baba and Diana? Or because they knew she was a threat to them? Because they knew who she was working for.

But surely, if there was serious danger involved, Charlie would have warned her off going?

Wouldn't he?

Or were MI5 as ruthless as the Nazis? Were they content to use Pamela to infiltrate all echelons of German society in Britain, whether there was a danger to her life or not?

She kept changing her mind. She considered cancelling the whole thing, telling Charlie that she had suddenly fallen ill. But was that what a real spy would do? Turn tail at the first sign of danger? Pamela then reminded herself she *wasn't* a real spy, with real spy training, and wasn't actually prepared for anything that could be dangerous.

Then she remembered her aunt's revolver. It was still sitting in the drawer of her dressing table as she hadn't been sure what to do with it. It was small and fit in her handbag. Pamela tried to imagine herself as a femme fatale, standing in the shadows, her gun drawn. But what if the embassy guards searched her and discovered it? What if it went off by accident? What if she actually *killed* someone?

In the end, Pamela decided to come armed only with a compact, lipstick and cigarette case. She wore a champagne-coloured, backless, satin Balmain and a dark red lip. Francis was still in Scotland, so at the very least she wouldn't have to explain to him why she was going to a party to celebrate the Berlin Olympics in the heart of Nazi London. She told herself that it was of the utmost importance, a matter of national security, that she got to the bottom of the relationship between Princess Stephanie, Ambassador von Ribbentrop and the King. What sort of influence was the Embassy having on the Palace, directly or indirectly?

As she entered the Embassy, she looked around at all the cold marble, the brash red flags of the Nazi party and the men in their grey military uniforms. A stern-looking Brunhilde sung Wagner beside a grand piano. Looking around at who was in attendance, Pamela spotted Diana and Mosley across the room.

Diana played the part of the icy-eyed Valkyrie in a silvery halter-necked gown, while Mosley wore his severe black BUF uniform. They looked positively energised by their proximity to the essence of the Führer and Pamela suddenly worried that this heightened fanaticism might have endowed them with the power to sniff out pretenders and saboteurs. What would happen if they suspected her? Did they too know about the dossier the Germans kept?

Or perhaps someone else at the Embassy already had eyes on her. And what would happen if she was rumbled? Would she be expelled from the Embassy, put on a blacklist and never admitted again? Or would they hand her over to the SS? Was it possible to arrest a British national in Britain? Technically, the German Embassy constituted German soil; if they had no compunction about murdering the ambassador himself, Pamela couldn't imagine they would hesitate to eliminate a foreign spy. Her mind spiralled with anxiety as she allowed herself to envision nightmare scenarios.

Mosley gave Pamela a greasy smile as Diana draped herself over him.

'So marvellous that you could come, Pamela, and pay homage to the darling Führer at such an exciting time like this. Unity says Berlin is simply beautiful right now. All those people from other countries will see how different Germany is these days.'

Pamela remembered what Diana Cooper had said about seeing Hitler at a rally in Nuremberg three years ago. ('Repellent. Flabby little man with a belt buckled tightly over a protruding paunch. Dank, fungoid complexion. Dead, colourless eyes.') She and Duff had gone purely out of curiosity and when they tried to leave early, they nearly got arrested by the Gestapo. ('Utterly terrifying. Thank god for diplomatic immunity.')

Suddenly, Pamela felt a hand on her arm and nearly jumped out of her skin in fright. The Princess Stephanie had appeared beside her, wearing what looked to be half of the display window of Van Cleef and Arpels. Diana's face fell and the Princess gave her a hard, steely smile.

'Princess,' said Diana.

Mosley kissed her hand. 'You're looking ravishing, Princess.'

Diana glared at him.

'Lady Guinness,' said Princess Stephanie to Diana.

Diana stiffened. 'I've been going by Mitford since the divorce.'

'Ah, yes. How could I have forgotten?'

'This is Pamela, Lady More,' Diana said pointedly. 'I was so pleased that I was able to bring her to the Embassy. Pamela and I have known each other for years.'

Princess Stephanie's proprietorial hand still rested on Pamela's arm. 'We too have become rather good friends. We were introduced by Mrs Simpson.'

Diana frowned slightly, pointedly ignored this attempt at social one-upmanship. 'Unity sends her regards, Princess. She thought we might see you here. Of course, she is in Berlin for the festivities. The sweet Führer has become rather attached to her.'

Now it was the Princess's turn to frown. 'We corresponded just the other day. I am sorry to say he is unwell,' she said to Diana.

'Merely a summer cold. Unity told us. She brought him soup.'

'I am certain the Führer has a cook who is perfectly capable of making him soup for his cold.'

'My sister is rather devoted to him. She insisted.'

'I'm sure she did.'

'I am sorry but I want to introduce Lady Pamela to Herr Hesse,' she said pointedly to Diana as she took Pamela's arm.

'I can do that,' retorted Diana.

'Please do not trouble yourself,' replied the Princess sweetly. 'I am certain you have many people to greet.'

The Princess led Pamela over to a nondescript man of medium height wearing wire-rimmed spectacles and a grey Nazi uniform. She introduced him as Herr Fritz Hesse, the press attaché for the Embassy. He looked at Pamela coldly and seemed unimpressed when the Princess explained 'Agent of Influence'. Pamela wondered if they kept an interrogation room in the Embassy cellar.

Von Ribbentrop himself marched by and the atmosphere changed abruptly. It was clear that the embassy staff were afraid of him, some of them backing away and retreating into the party to avoid him as he approached. Hesse and the Princess quickly became deferential, introducing Pamela briefly. She was about to remind him they had already met on board the Duke of Westminster's yacht a few weeks ago when he suddenly turned on his heel to scream in German at an unsuspecting member of Embassy staff and marched away again. Jenny had briefed Pamela while she helped her dress earlier that evening. The ambassador was rather unsound, erratic and prone to shouting. He didn't keep appointments and had a propensity for upsetting ambassadors to other countries. Apparently, he had tried to get his son admitted to Eton but was refused. (One could see why.)

The Princess and Hesse became engrossed in conversation so Pamela excused herself to get a drink from one of the passing footmen. As she reached for a glass, she felt a tap on the shoulder. She inadvertently gave a small yelp as she spun around. A smartly-dressed man, about forty, smiled.

'I do apologise. I didn't mean to frighten you,' he said to her.

'Not at all,' she replied calmly.

'It is such a relief to see a friendly face!'

Pamela took another look at him. 'I'm sorry, you'll have to forgive me but...'

The man reached out a hand.

'Donald Jenkins,' he said before leaning in and whispering, 'but you might remember me as Betty.'

'The Charles Creed gown!'

'No drag tonight, sadly. But look at *your* fantastic frock!' Donald exclaimed as he admired her dress. 'What are you doing in a ghastly place like this? "Agent of Influence"?'

Pamela hesitated and then said, 'Yes… I do find myself in some strange places for my column.'

'I hope you won't say anything nice about these frightful people.'

'What are *you* doing here?'

'Government business,' he replied vaguely.

'Do you work for the Foreign Office?'

'No. Actually I'm the MP for Kennington and Lambeth North.'

'You *are?*'

'Surprised?'

'I don't know if I'm more surprised that you're an MP, or that you're an MP for—'

'Labour?'

'Oh! I was going to say South London, but yes. Aren't you *full* of surprises?'

'Well, I may have one more up my sleeve. It turns out I know your husband, Sir Francis. We're on a kind of committee. Though not entirely en plein air, if you know what I mean,' Donald said quietly as he looked around. 'I assume you *do* know what I mean?'

'Ah, no, I'm afraid I don't…' Pamela said, wondering where this was leading. However, when she saw his face alter, she quickly changed tack. 'You see, Francis is involved in all kinds of things – fingers in lots of pies, as it were. And you can imagine what my life is like, gadding about – parties, luncheons, the paper—'

'Late-night soirees singing Cole Porter?' Donald said with a wink.

Pamela blushed. 'Yes, exactly. So, we're like ships passing in the night, Francis and me…' Pamela trailed off, hoping Donald would open up.

'Well,' Donald said conspiratorially, 'I can't be terribly open about it in the present surroundings. But, entre nous, I am here, at this particular party, because of the committee. Of course, I am apt to be all over the place, making little diplomatic in-roads with various people, but they're normally in more glamorous places, like the French Embassy.' He gestured to his glass. 'At least there they'd give you *real* champagne and not some ghastly Riesling or whatever this is.'

'Mr Jenkins—'

'Call me Betty,' he said, winking. 'I'm only kidding. One whiff of camp and they have you shot, which is pretty ironic considering how camp *they* are. Call me Donald.'

'So, Donald, this committee is why you're here?' Pamela leaned in and murmured.

Donald looked around and lowered his voice. 'I wouldn't want to reveal too much, in case anyone is hanging about. But yes, you could say that. We're a group of like-minded men, who have some opinions on the country hosting this sad little party. And the thing of it is, we seem to be very much in the minority in dear old Westminster. And they don't seem to like us very much, for various reasons, personal and political. But we don't care. As Percy would say, we don't care what people think of us, we only care what we think of other people.'

'This is a committee—'

'Yes, but, officially unofficial.'

'This is an *unofficial* committee on… Germany?'

Donald nodded and tapped a finger on the side of his nose.

'And when you say yours is an unpopular opinion…' Pamela continued.

'We're the opposition. There aren't many of us, but there are others. Which is why we mustn't discuss it here.'

Pamela's mind was spinning. Francis was part of some clandestine group within Parliament, opposed to the Nazi regime, secretly working against their colleagues who, presumably, had more favourable, or at least more neutral views, on Hitler and his government. She had had no idea. But then again, she generally had very little idea of his machinations in the Lords, as Francis was hardly forthcoming about it on the occasions when she asked. What else was Francis up to that she wasn't aware of?

'Have you ever been here before?' she asked.

'No, and I hope never to return. Ribbentrop is a ghastly, boorish man. About as subtle as a whore in church. Everyone is afraid of him, apart from that man over there.'

Donald pointed to Herr Hesse across the room still talking to Princess Stephanie.

'The press attaché?'

'He's more than just a press officer, darling. He's Brickendrop's right-hand, tells him everything. Manages to be everywhere, all at once. Nasty little queen.' Donald turned to look at Pamela. 'How do you know that woman? The Princess von Hohenlohe.'

'Oh, just... out and about. In passing.' she replied vaguely.

'I've heard she's *Jewish*. Married some Austro-Hungarian aristocrat before the war, then divorced him and kept the title, which she's been dining out on ever since. A Jewish Nazi. Have you ever heard of such a thing? Probably why Brickendrop hates her. But then again, they all hate each other here. All the little rats, scrambling up the rat-hole to impress Queen Rat. Or rather, Führer-Queen Rat.'

'Did her husband settle a large amount of money on her in the divorce?'

'No. I think the family money was hers, rather than his, though I don't know if there's much of it left. The Austrians lost a great deal when their empire collapsed, followed swiftly by their economy.' He paused. 'Why do you ask?'

'Every time I've run into her, she's wearing the most extraordinary jewels.'

Donald looked across the room at the Princess and peered at her. 'Well, she is known in some circles to be a bit of a courtesan. I'm sure someone's looking after her.'

Pamela made a mental note to find out who that person was.

'How can she be a Nazi *and* Jewish?' she asked.

'I don't know how she lives with herself, with what Hitler is doing to the Jews. And no one who knows anything that goes on over there can plead ignorance. It's all been happening for such a long time. Brownshirts were terrorising Jews long before they muscled their way into the Reichstag.

'Mary – you remember, from the party – she and I were in Berlin together. She's Jewish, but back then, all of Berlin was Jewish or foreign or homosexual. Or all of the above. A veritable Nazi nightmare. But things began to turn and it wasn't safe for us anymore, especially for Mary. Michael, as she's known in *ordinary* life. We were lucky that we could leave. There were many who couldn't. They really are terrible shits, these people.' Donald spotted someone he knew, sighed and said, 'Apologies, duckie, I do have to make the rounds while I can still stomach this place. Doing a little recce, for the boys. Keeping my ear to the ground. See what I can see, or hear. Which reminds me... watch what you say in the khazi.'

'The what?'

'The ladies, love. They say they're all wired... someone listening.' Donald kissed Pamela's hand theatrically. 'Bona nochy, ducks!' He then leaned in and whispered, 'And be careful...'

As he walked away, Pamela saw Putlitz across the room. He glanced at her briefly and then turned away. Pamela felt a chill – for the first time, she knew she was truly alone. Even if something were to happen, Putlitz wouldn't be able to intervene without blowing his cover. Ditto Donald. She would have to fend for herself.

Pamela took a deep breath and decided to take a walk to calm her nerves. And to see if she could overhear an interesting conversation or two. She headed through the main reception area, making her way past people chattering away in English and German, pausing to listen to discussions about the economy, manufacturing, unemployment, the state of European politics and so on. Strains of the Beethoven being played on the piano echoed down the darkened corridors, following her as she explored the other rooms in the building. Upon turning a corner, she spotted von Ribbentrop, who was standing alone in a doorway smoking a cigar. Just as she was wondering if she should approach him and attempt a conversation, she glimpsed a woman approach him from the shadows, as if appearing from nowhere. Pamela pulled back, hiding behind a marble plinth. The woman's arm reached out and something glinted in the light: a diamond and gemstone cross bracelet.

Pamela gasped.

It was Wallis Simpson.

Pamela tried to get as near as she could to them, slinking quietly closer, gripping her handbag nervously. She couldn't hear what they were saying but she watched von Ribbentrop stroke Wallis's cheek as she whispered in his ear. Then they parted, going in opposite directions down the corridor.

Wallis headed to the ladies' and Pamela followed a few paces behind. When she entered, Wallis was standing at the mirror, refreshing her lipstick.

'Oh, hello, Lady Pamela,' she said. 'What an unexpected pleasure. I wasn't aware you frequented the German Embassy.'

'I'm here on an assignment from the paper,' Pamela replied casually, wondering what Wallis was doing there and who she had come with.

'That reminds me, I did so enjoy "A Week with Wallis". Such a cute little piece.'

Pamela tried not to glare at her.

'What brings you here this evening, Mrs Simpson?'

'Wallis, please! Remember? Well, His Majesty is on very close terms with the German Ambassador.'

'And are *you* on as close terms with Herr von Ribbentrop as His Majesty?' asked Pamela, taking a gamble.

'Joachim is such a lot of fun and the King insists we dine with him all the time,' Wallis said as she smiled. 'Between you and me, I think the ambassador has a little schoolboy crush on me.'

Pamela remembered what Donald had said about the ladies' room being wiretapped.

'Oh, really?'

'But he knows my heart belongs to His Majesty,' Wallis replied, her expertly made-up face inscrutable. 'And I would never do anything to hurt him. He is so fragile, really, like a little boy. He just needs to be loved. He's never really got the love he truly needs. What people don't understand is that his family really is very cruel to him and couldn't give a damn if he was happy or not. I know our little arrangement is a bit inconvenient to some people, but I only want what's best for David.'

(David? She called him *David*?)

'Although sometimes I wonder if it would be better if I disappeared,' Wallis said, looking genuinely unhappy for the first time. 'It would certainly be less complicated. But I have come to feel so very at home here in London. It is a bit odd, not being British, but not really feeling very American back in Baltimore. It's very easy to feel quite alone at times, especially when anyone who's ever laid eyes on you can drop you like yesterday's news. Even David. There's nothing stopping him from walking away, from meeting someone else, someone new. Someone his family wouldn't object to.'

For a moment, Pamela felt a bit sorry for Wallis. She awkwardly reached out and patted her on the shoulder in a way she hoped seemed sympathetic. But then she thought of the regular deliveries of flowers, the new dresses, the yachting, and, of course, the jewels. Pamela looked at Wallis and noticed that in addition to the Cartier bracelet (and what could only be an evening gown by Schiaparelli), she was wearing the most extraordinary necklace: strands of diamonds and rubies were entwined with one another, encircling her neck and sitting perfectly on her collarbone. A tassel of rubies hung down, elegantly adorning her breastbone. Pamela was briefly hypnotised by its radiance as it glowed warmly in the low light of the room.

Ernest Simpson was in no financial position to be buying such extravagant gifts for his wife. And – if Princess Stephanie's report that he had a lover in New York was to be believed – even if he was, he would likely be buying them for someone else. I only want what's best for David, my foot, thought Pamela. I only want what's best for moi. Even if that includes the attentions of the King of England and the Ambassador to the Third Reich. (Only a bit of fun? What *kind* of fun?) For all she knew, Wallis could be making secret night flights to Berlin and carrying on with Hitler himself.

All of a sudden there was a knock on the door and a little voice said, 'Wallis my darling, are you in there? You know your little kingy-wingy can't do his kingly duties without his Wallie-Wallie.'

Pamela felt slightly sick to her stomach. She looked over at Wallis and saw that for a brief moment, her face betrayed her irritation at being hounded from outside the ladies' room. It was clear to Pamela that this must be a regular occurrence, that she was used to being watched and followed and clung on to by the King.

Wallis composed herself, forced a smile and called back, 'I'm coming right out my darling...'

'I do hope you and His Majesty enjoyed your tour of the Mediterranean,' said Pamela.

'It was such a nice escape from England but it is very trying to be constantly confronted with foreign press. I just don't understand why they can't mind their own business, like they do in this country. David was very agitated.'

Wallis excused herself and went off with the King. Pamela felt exhausted and decided she had managed to gather enough information for the evening, and without getting herself into trouble.

Just as she was walking back down the corridor to say her goodbyes, she ran into Mosley. When he saw her, he smiled his crooked smile and advanced unsteadily as what were clearly the effects of alcohol brought out his limp. He was sweating in his belted black tunic and gave off an unpleasant odour.

Mosley grabbed Pamela's arm. 'Lady Pamela, you've been caught.'

Pamela froze. Her annoyance turned to fear. Did Tom Mosley know who she was and what she was doing? Was it possible that he was a Nazi spy?

'I've no idea what you mean,' she said brusquely as she tried to pull away.

'I know what you're up to,' he said unsmilingly.

Pamela's mind raced. She considered screaming but realised it was probably unwise.

'I know what this is about. The game you played at Cliveden,' Mosley whispered as he pushed Pamela against a wall.

She was frozen in fear – he must know what she had been up to. It was all over. She waited for him to call for someone, a Nazi guard or official. To reveal that he had put two and two together and he knew her true motives and alliances. He had probably seen her dossier. Von Ribbentrop would have her taken to the interrogation room in the cellar. And tortured. No one would ever see her again.

Mosley leaned in closely, his breath reeking of schnapps.

'Women like playing games,' he slurred as he attempted to kiss her.

Pamela was relieved. Disgusted, but relieved. Sir Oswald Mosley was a pathetic failure of a man; he clearly hoped that by positioning himself close to powerful people, he could finally grasp that promise of influence and authority. This encounter wasn't about espionage or state secrets; it was about someone's desperate attempt to assert himself.

Pamela straightened up and pushed Mosley away from her. 'I thought I'd made it perfectly clear how I felt the last time this happened. Now get your hands off me.'

Mosley looked momentarily surprised but wouldn't release his grip.

So Pamela stomped on his foot with the heel of her stiletto.

He cried out in pain and released her.

Suddenly, a deep voice behind Pamela startled them both.

'Madame, are you all right?'

They both turned around to see a tall, slender man with brown hair, in his middle or late-thirties, dressed in an officer's uniform.

'My bloody foot is in agony!' Mosley spat as he glared at Pamela.

'Why don't you go tend to it, then?' she snarled as she glared back.

The man in the uniform gazed coldly at Mosley, who, to Pamela's surprise, seemed somewhat intimidated by the stranger. He gave Pamela one last poisonous look before hobbling down the corridor.

'He is not a friend of yours?' the stranger said in what she recognised was a Russian accent.

'No one here is a friend of mine.'

The man smiled, bowed and formally extended a hand.

'Captain Boris Nikolaevich Puchkov, from the Soviet Embassy.'

As Pamela got a better look at him, she saw, with a start, that he looked just like her brother. Older, of course, but about the age William would have been had he survived the war. She felt a pang.

'Madame...?' the man said, looking at her curiously.

Pamela realised she was staring.

'Lady Pamela More, from *The Times* of London,' she replied.

She had never (knowingly) met a Soviet before. Russians, yes, but exiles, nobility chased from their homeland by Bolshevik revolutionaries. And a man who worked for the Kremlin, no less. Looking at his army uniform, with its sage-coloured jacket and navy-blue jodhpurs, she couldn't help but think of the soldiers who had persecuted Princess Elena and her family during the Revolution. He would have been a young man at the time, but perhaps old enough to have taken part. He had a scar on his cheek – a remnant from skirmishes with the White Army? If Pamela's family had been Russian, they surely would have been arrested. Their home and land and property would have been confiscated, they would have been made 'non-persons', as Elena called it. Or they would have been executed, like so many others.

'How do you do?' he said with the neutral formality of a diplomat. 'You are British?'

Pamela nodded, wondering if this made him see her in a more favourable light or not.

'It is not common to see women journalists in this country,' Boris Nikolaevich continued in such a way that it was difficult to tell whether he was making a statement or asking a question.

'Is it common to see Soviet diplomats at Nazi parties?' Pamela replied.

The Soviet inclined his head slightly. 'We have athletes competing in Berlin. And of course, the Soviet people wish for nothing but to be on good terms with our neighbours.'

Boris Nikolaevich watched her in a way that made Pamela feel as if he was looking straight through her. Or did she feel this way because he looked so much like William? She suddenly wondered if she should be seen talking to a Soviet diplomat and army officer – if it might compromise her somehow. She excused herself as politely as possible, feeling a slight stab of regret as she looked backwards at him.

Pamela decided to extricate herself from the party before anyone else could accost her. She breathed a sigh of relief as she exited the Embassy and clattered across Belgrave Square, her heels clicking on the pavement. An unexpectedly chilly wind picked up and she pulled her light cloak around her shoulders.

And all of a sudden, she got the feeling she was being followed. Pamela turned her head discreetly and saw someone lurking in the shadows. The lamplight reflected off his round spectacles and when she saw the grey uniform, she realised it was Fritz Hesse. She broke into a cold sweat but walked briskly onwards. Hesse followed behind her apace. She walked faster. But the faster she went, the faster he went.

It wasn't Mosley who was after her, it was the Germans themselves. After all, they were the ones who had the dossier. Hesse must have figured out what she had been doing there.

All at once, Pamela remembered Stern's warning: what if there was nowhere to hide? And then she began to run.

As they reached the main road, Pamela looked around for passers-by but it was dark and deserted. There was no one to be seen. She heard the attaché's footsteps behind her, running in hot pursuit. She turned a corner into an empty mews, hoping to lose him in the darkness. But it was a dead-end. Her heart was thumping in her chest. She wheeled around.

And there he was.

Hesse reached a hand into his jacket pocket. Pamela closed her eyes and lifted her shaking hands into the air.

'Frau More, your handbag.'

When she opened her eyes, to her surprise, Hesse was standing there, her beaded evening bag in his hand. Had she left it in the ladies'?

'Oh. Thank you. Much obliged,' she replied.

Why didn't I bring the cursed revolver, she thought as she walked away, still feeling Hesse's eyes on her back. But if she had, it would have been in her handbag. Which Hesse would have found.

She turned the corner and out of nowhere, a sports car appeared, pulling up to the kerb. It was Charlie, looking surprisingly dashing in a tailcoat. Pamela nearly cried with relief as she climbed in.

'All right?' he asked so casually Pamela could have killed him.

'Certainly,' she replied with a toss of her head. 'Though I've had quite enough excitement for one evening, thank you very much.'

Pamela lit a cigarette, her hands trembling. She felt rather shaken but exhilarated as they sped along the dark London streets.

V

Pamela and Charlie sat in his MG car with the hood folded down on the top of a hill overlooking the glittering lights of the city. Having just told him everything she could remember from the evening, she took a deep breath and relaxed back into the seat.

'Peppermint?' Charlie asked cheerfully as he offered Pamela a tin of mints.

What a surprise this man is, Pamela thought as she accepted one. She smoothed the folds of her gown and took another look at London at night, wondering how many other people were sitting in smart automobiles contemplating brushes with danger.

'Peppermint is supposed to have calming properties,' he continued thoughtfully.

'I think whisky would do a more efficient job of that,' Pamela countered.

'Do you feel in need of a whisky?'

'Who wouldn't? I was just chased through the back-streets of Belgravia by von Ribbentrop's right-hand man. Hess claimed he only wanted to give me back my handbag; that I left it in the ladies'. But how would he know that? I heard the lavatories at the Embassy are all wire-tapped. Is that true? Do you think he was listening to my conversation?' Pamela took a breath and looked over at Charlie, who was looking at the view of the city. 'You seem unconcerned,' she said as she wiped a bit of dust from the dashboard of the car.

'Lovely view, isn't it?' he replied as he undid his white tie. 'It's difficult to say. Who told you the lavatories were bugged?'

Pamela suddenly felt hesitant to tell Charlie about Donald. After all, Donald had been on his own secret mission and she didn't know if he would want the activities of his (and Francis's) committee known to MI5.

'Just a rumour I heard somewhere,' she said vaguely. 'It's very difficult to tell what's real and what isn't. I don't feel as if I have the experience, the training, the background to understand what I'm seeing and hearing. I'm so nervy these days, sometimes I wonder if everyone is lying about who they are. How does one know who to trust?'

'For those in your – that is to say, our – position, these feelings are entirely normal. No matter how experienced you are, you'll always be wondering who you can trust. If you can trust anyone.'

'But that's the problem, Mr Buchanan; I'm not experienced at any of this. I feel like a bit of a fraud.'

'You'd be surprised how many people there are in the service who are far less adept than you are.' Charlie paused and pursed his lips. 'And over-confident about their abilities. They think because they went to the right schools, belong to the right clubs, know the right people, they're equipped to manage anything, whether that's taking a post in the Indian Civil Service or selling stocks in the City.'

A cold wind swept across the hilltop and Pamela pulled her wrap tighter around her shoulders. Charlie looked over at her.

'Cold?'

'These evening gowns aren't exactly built for windy hillsides,' replied Pamela.

Charlie opened his door and got out. He walked around to the back of the car, opened the boot, pulled out an old tartan rug and handed it to Pamela as he climbed back in. 'This should keep you warm.'

Any other man would have offered her his jacket, Pamela thought as she drew the rug over her knees. But for some reason she was glad Charlie hadn't done what any other man would have done.

'Peppermints and tartan rugs! You're like a little old man, Mr Buchanan,' teased Pamela.

'Yes, people sometimes do tell me that,' he replied with a smile. 'I'm afraid it will probably clash with your lovely dress.'

Pamela put a hand to her hair, suddenly self-conscious at the thought that Charlie liked her gown. Sitting in a racy little car, late at night, made her feel like a young debutante again sneaking out late past the chaperones. She looked at Charlie and realised that when he wasn't wearing his tatty Burberry and bowler, he wasn't bad-looking. Frayed trench coat by day, white tie, tails and smart little car by night. It was a mystery, and one she was enjoying trying to work out.

'And what about you? How did you find your way into this line of work? Right schools, right clubs, right people?' Pamela asked Charlie as she traced the criss-crossing lines on the tartan rug with her finger.

He hesitated and then said, 'Something like that. Family connections to the Foreign Office, initially.' He was silent a moment, leading Pamela to believe that was the end of his brief and un-illuminating personal revelation, and that perhaps she was wrong even to have asked. But then he added: 'Though I assure you, I'm not made from the same mould as those kinds of men.'

Pamela turned to look at Charlie and smiled. 'That's what all the boys say.'

He took out his cigarette case, offered Pamela one, lit it and then lit his own.

'My parents met in South Africa, just before the Boer War. My father was an officer in the Royal Scots Greys but from an unremarkable, far less established family than my mother's, so her parents rejected the marriage. They didn't speak to her for many years, until long after I was born. My grandparents arranged for me to be educated in England but I never fitted in with the other boys. The nicknames and the mania for sport, that sort of thing. I was more of a reader. Perhaps I've always been a little old man,' Charlie finished with a raised eyebrow and a slightly upturned corner of his mouth.

Pamela thoughtfully took a drag from her cigarette and smiled inwardly at this sudden and unexpected disclosure. 'And what, might I ask, do you do now? Or is this all you do? I don't really know how it works.'

Charlie laughed. 'They don't pay us enough to keep us out of other professions. That is, for those of us who actually have to earn a living. I'm a librarian.'

A *librarian*? Though it would indeed explain the peppermints and tartan rug, it certainly didn't explain the smart car, the tailcoat or anything else.

'I used to be a headmaster,' replied Charlie, by way of explanation, but with a look on his face that said he wasn't going to offer a clarification.

'Well, curiouser and curiouser…' Pamela paused and then, emboldened by the rare atmosphere, decided to push her luck. 'Are you married?'

Charlie pulled deeply on his cigarette, exhaled and said, 'Once upon a time.'

'So, no one to wonder where you go at all hours of the day? Speaking of which, how long had you been there? Tonight, I mean. Seems strange I didn't see you.'

'I'm very good at not being seen if I don't want to be seen. Comes with the job, you see.'

'Which job? This one? Or the librarian job?' Pamela said playfully, while realising that Charlie hadn't actually answered her question.

'I think you'd find it's rather useful in both contexts,' Charlie said with a smile. 'It's awfully late. Shall I drop you home?'

Pamela felt slightly disappointed that Charlie was drawing the evening to a close, and then silly for feeling disappointed.

'Yes, thank you. Very kind,' said Pamela. As Charlie started the car, she put a hand on his arm. 'Mr Buchanan, I need to ask a question. *Was* I in danger? Tonight, I mean. Was I being followed? Am I right to be worried?'

Charlie left the key in the ignition and surprised Pamela by taking her hand. 'Lady Pamela, some advice, from one professional to another. In this business, it never helps to be worried. Best to keep moving forward.'

He started the car and drove back in the direction of London.

October 1936

I

'Za vashezdorovye!' they shouted as they clinked their glasses and drank. And then another very long toast was proposed, after which they clinked again and drank again.

Flossie paused from trying on hats, turned to the Princess Elena and asked, 'What on earth was that about?'

'Russian toasts are very long and very dull,' Elena replied as she examined a cropped tweed jacket Pamela was trying on. 'Count Aleksey Sergeyevich toasted the beautiful ladies, how he hopes we will always trouble him. It's a hunting lodge toast.'

'I wish *I* spoke Russian,' Flossie sighed.

It had started out as a trip to Princess Elena's atelier with Flossie, Aunt Constance and Mr Dekhale (who had become quite a fixture in Aunt Constance's life). Pamela had taken her aunt to be fitted for a dress for her charity gala; the fitting had turned into cocktails and cocktails had morphed into a party filled with vodka and White Russians émigrés. It was as if they had been transported to St Petersburg, circa 1913.

Count Aleksey Sergeyevich: formerly one of the most powerful landowners in Russia and a fixture in the court of Tsar Nicholas II, as well as his father Alexander III. He wore a threadbare dinner jacket and a bad wig and held a balalaika. He said he was an antiques dealer, but the Princess whispered that his Chelsea store was, in reality, closer to a junk shop.

Grand Duchess Maria Felixova: she was evacuated on the HMS Marlborough, the ship the British Navy sent for what remained of the Russian Imperial Family in 1919 – an attempt to assuage their guilt for having done nothing to save the Tsar, Tsarina and their children the year before. All her jewels were paste, having sold the real ones (that she had hidden in her son's teddy bear) to buy a modest house in Kent.

Galina Petrovna: the Grand Duchess's faithful lady's maid who had even more vitriol for the Bolsheviks than her mistress. She was now the Grand Duchess's companion but they were both so elderly and frail it was hard to say who took care of whom.

Mrs Tanya Blake: younger than Princess Elena, she was only a girl when the Revolution took hold and fled with her mother and sisters to Paris. Once a costume designer for ballet and theatre, she ended up marrying an English accountant and led a dull but comfortable life somewhere on the suburban fringes of North London.

Pamela was reminded of her encounter with the Soviet diplomat. Perhaps he was too young to have been responsible for the expulsion from their great estates and the murder of their families. But certainly, his fellow diplomats and army officers, older men, seasoned Bolshevik warriors, were liable, in one way or another. Perhaps they had sat on committees and redistributed aristocratic property; perhaps they even carried out executions. How bizarre, almost unfathomable, that London was so vast as to be able to contain two sets of Russians so diametrically opposed. And even more bizarre and unfathomable that someone like Pamela could encounter them in such a relatively short space of time. As she looked at the shabby, outmoded clothing, the fake jewels, the scuffed shoes, she couldn't help but think: there but for the grace of god go I.

'Panda!' Percy arrived, drunk already. He waved a bottle of gin around. 'Who wants a gin? One can only drink *vodka* all night if one is *Russian*.'

Behind Percy entered a more sober man, slight and fair-haired, in a too-large, boxy pin-stripe suit and a pair of well-worn brogues. His face was handsome but slightly blank, as if he could have been anyone.

'Panda, this is Baron Jona von Ustinov, a fellow journalist. He is Russian too. And a bit German. And a Baron! I thought he might find this little gathering intriguing.' Percy leaned in and whispered in Pamela's ear. 'Remember I said I had a friend who was a journalist who's rather good at getting dirt on people…?'

'I was interested in meeting you, Lady Pamela More,' Ustinov said to Pamela as he gave her the customary Russian three cheek kisses.

Percy waved to Jo and trotted over to say hello. Ustinov hung back, watching Pamela closely, his dark eyes and smooth face betraying nothing.

'We have a mutual friend,' he said.

Ustinov's words filled Pamela with an inexplicable sense of foreboding. She suddenly felt hot and removed Elena's tweed jacket.

'Who, pray tell, is that, Baron Ustinov?'

He looked around the room. 'You are acquainted with my great friend Wolfgang zu Putlitz?'

Pamela was surprised at the mention of the German spy. For a moment, she wondered if it was a trap. Who was this Baron Ustinov anyway?

'I'm sorry, but you must have me confused with someone else,' she coolly replied.

Ustinov nodded his head, perhaps in acknowledgement of her tactic. 'Ah, you are concerned. Who am I? What is it that I want? Whose side am I on?'

Pamela was silent, refusing to be drawn out.

'We've known each other for many years,' he continued. 'And we report to the same people, Lady Pamela. In fact, the same people you do.'

Pamela wondered if she should ask for proof of this. But what kind of proof should she ask for?

'Until last year, I was working with Herr Wolfgang at the Embassy. But my politics made things difficult. One cannot be an anti-Nazi press officer for a Nazi government. Zu Putlitz is far better at hiding his true self than I. But we work together, for your government.'

Was *everyone* a spy?

'I thought all these things were meant to be *secrets*,' Pamela replied, mildly exasperated.

'There is no such thing as a true secret, Lady Pamela,' he replied with a quiet laugh.

She looked around the room to see if anyone was watching them, but everyone else was occupied. And mostly drunk. She realised that perhaps she was also drunk, certainly too drunk to be having such a conversation.

'Baron Ustinov, I am too drunk to be having such a conversation.'

'Nonsense. You are enjoying your evening. "Jolly"? Is that what you English say?' He smiled as he guided Pamela gently towards the bar, away from the small crowd that had formed in the centre of the room around the Count, who was strumming his balalaika and singing.

'You are Russian, Baron?' asked Pamela.

Ustinov poured himself a small vodka and listened to the song. 'My father was. He used to sing me that song when I was a child.' He paused. 'When Wolfgang – zu Putlitz – and I met, we pledged to do everything in our power to limit Hitler's influence on your country, if not stop the Reich completely. Your mission is not so different, no?'

There was something compelling about the Baron – his slightness, his demeanour and what she could only describe as a faint air of melancholy.

'You met a young gentleman at the German Embassy. A Russian, working in the employ of the Soviet Ambassador.'

Pamela assumed he knew this through Putlitz.

'In passing, yes,' she replied hesitantly.

Ustinov looked around briefly, took another sip of vodka and leaned in. He took Pamela's arm and turned her away from the party.

'He is willing to trade sensitive information for the promise of asylum in Britain,' he whispered.

'Sensitive information about the Soviets?'

'Stalin and Yezhov – the head of the Soviet secret police – have been making lists of people found to be insufficiently loyal to the Party. The young gentleman worries that it may not be long before he himself is on that list. And to end up on such a list in the Soviet Union can be a death sentence.'

'Why can't he do this via your contacts, if we indeed work for the same people, as you say?' she replied, feeling uneasy.

'Because I have used up all my favours to the Service. And you are not a foreigner. The request will carry more weight coming from a British person.'

Pamela felt a hand on her arm. She turned around to find Aunt Constance had wedged herself in between Pamela and Ustinov. She was breathless with excitement and red-faced from drinking.

'Did you hear the singing, darling? How marvellous it all is! I do so enjoy singing.'

Mr Dekhale stood behind her, looking patient but tired. 'Constance, I think I may take my leave.'

'But we've only just begun! And you haven't even spoken to the Count yet!' Aunt Constance gestured to Count Aleksey. 'His Excellency Count Aleksey Sergeyevich was a cavalry officer in the White Army during the Civil War!' She poured herself another vodka. 'When in Rome!' she exclaimed. She then turned to admire herself in the nearby full-length mirror, smoothing the deep green satin gown. 'I don't usually like green but this is very nice.'

'I love green!' chipped in Flossie (who was wearing a green blouse).

Pamela looked around but Baron Ustinov had disappeared.

Pamela's aunt gestured towards Jo and the Princess. 'Did you know they were… ' she lowered her voice comically, '*lesbians*? I knew some women who were of that persuasion when I was in the Suffragettes.'

Flossie's cheeks had turned bright red, flushing through her fair, freckled complexion as they always did when she drank. 'Pam, did you know the Princess had absolutely *everything* taken from her family in the Revolution? Just terrible, isn't it?'

'Yes, ghastly,' Pamela replied distractedly. She felt as if she was watching everything happening around her, at a remove. She was still thinking about Ustinov's proposal and the Soviet secret police.

'Albert says the same thing could happen with the communists *here* if we're not careful,' Flossie continued.

'I don't think Mrs Leigh is ever going to wake up from that coma, do you, Panda?' Percy said as he reached for his bottle of gin.

'Mrs Leigh?'

'Surely, the longer she's in it, the less likely she is to come out of it.'

'I can't say I really know anything about comas,' replied Pamela.

She looked around for Ustinov again, wondering if he had left the party completely.

As if reading her mind, Percy asked, 'What did the Baron want from you? He doesn't fancy you, does he?'

Pamela was at a loss to think of a plausible lie, but Percy seemed too intoxicated to notice.

'You won't find many socialists here,' interjected Aunt Constance.

'What?' Pamela replied, confused.

'I don't mean in this room. I mean, in this country. Not many socialists, are there?' she continued.

'The problem in India,' Mr Dekhale said slightly drunkenly, 'is… it's that… what was I saying, Constance?'

'Anyway,' said Percy, '*The Times* are strict about budget. You practically have to wait for someone to die to bring anyone new in. And of course, she's not dead yet, but I've convinced Dawson to hire Jo. She's quite a good journalist. Serious. Not like us. And probably far better too.'

'The problem with India is that the British have been *looting* it for years!' cried Aunt Constance.

'That wasn't what I was saying… But I have now had too many of these so I cannot remember,' Mr Dekhale said with a sigh, as he gestured to his martini glass.

'Albert says the key is an alliance with the Germans,' Flossie said loudly to Princess Elena. 'Because you can't trust the Bolsheviks – you never know when they might invade. You of all people understand, don't you?'

The Princess raised an eyebrow as she fixed her cigarette into its holder and lit it.

'Panda, are you even listening to me?' said Percy as he poked Pamela in the side.

'Well, it's true! They have! People here don't know the crimes done in the name of Empire,' Aunt Constance continued.

'And the way he explains it – Albert, that is – it doesn't actually sound as if Mr Hitler is such a bad chap, really,' continued Flossie.

The Princess gave Pamela a sideways look. Apart from the ageing cavalry officer strumming his balalaika and humming to himself, Pamela realised everyone had gone quiet and was listening to Flossie, whose voice was amplified by the silence. And the alcohol.

'After all, who else is going to keep the hoards out? I certainly don't want to see *our* Royal Family shot to death in a cellar.'

The Russians turned to look at her in alarm.

Pamela gently took Flossie's arm. 'Flossie, darling.'

'I can't think of anything more horrifying, can you?'

'Flossie, perhaps it would be best to change the subject to something less… taxing?'

Flossie frowned and crossed her arms. 'Taxing for *me*, you mean.'

'I mean for everyone,' replied Pamela.

'You think I don't know what I'm talking about, don't you?'

'Why don't we sit down for a moment?'

'I'm not an imbecile, you know,' Flossie retorted drunkenly. 'I read things. I have conversations with people. Important people. Maybe my wardrobe isn't as glamorous as yours… and maybe my figure isn't as nice… but I've had three children. How can you maintain your figure when you've had three children? You've never had any children.'

'Flossie, you don't want to go around telling people what a nice chap Hitler is.'

'I don't need to listen to everything you say,' Flossie snapped petulantly. 'I can make my own mind up. Albert says the Germans—'

'Albert is acting a *fool*,' hissed Pamela. 'He is being taken for a ride by some terribly nasty people, don't you understand?'

'How dare you speak like that about my husband?' Flossie cried, trying to wrench herself away from Pamela.

Suddenly, Pamela remembered something.

'Think of Margaret, Floss.'

'What? What about her?'

All of a sudden, the front door banged open and two men appeared in the studio. One was handsome, tall and broad-shouldered, with slicked-back dark brown hair, wearing a grey pinstripe suit. The other was shorter, stocky, with fiery red hair and a reddish-blond moustache. His brown suit was dishevelled and his bow-tie lay open around his neck.

'Dobriyvyecher!' cried the redhead, opening his arms to the party.

As he carried on in Russian, it was clear that he and his friend, like everyone else, were drunk as lords. Fortunately for Flossie, the party had turned their attention to the two men.

'The Nazis have no use for children like her, slow children.'

'What?'

'You told me Margaret isn't like other children her age. Slower to develop.'

'How can you bring that up in public, Pam? How can you be so cruel?'

'Hitler has been having those children taken away.'

'That *can't* be true!' Flossie said with vehemence.

'He's having them sterilised. And killed, Flossie. What if we were in Germany? What if they took Margaret away from you?'

Flossie was shaking and tears had started to roll down her cheeks. 'That isn't possible! You're making that up!'

Jo stepped in and took Flossie by the hand. 'Sorry, pet, but she's right. I've heard the same thing from reliable sources inside Germany. Absolutely criminal what they're doing.'

'Who could do something like that?' Flossie began to cry.

'The Nazis want to keep that kind of thing as quiet as possible, of course. Puts people off doing business with them,' said Jo.

Pamela crouched next to Flossie and whispered, 'I'm sorry my darling, but you must understand – you and Albert must distance yourselves from those dealings with the Germans.'

Flossie, mascara now running down her cheeks, turned to look at her with a mixture of anger and drunken confusion. Pamela tried to stroke her arm but she shrugged her off.

'You must convince Albert to leave the Anglo-German Fellowship.'

'But it's just business. That's what Albert says. Nothing political.'

'Francis says he heard in the Lords that there's a list. Of people who have been forming alliances with Germans. Potential traitors,' replied Pamela quietly. 'Organisations like the AGF and their members are on it.'

Flossie looked aghast. 'Albert's name is on a list? Of traitors? But why?'

'Because if we go to war, the government will need to know who's been collaborating with Germany.'

Flossie had gone as white as a sheet.

Pamela retrieved a handkerchief from her handbag and dabbed at Flossie's ruined eye makeup.

'Albert never said... but he wouldn't get involved with people who would...' she said weakly, tears still streaming down her face.

Jo leaned in and whispered to Pamela, 'Is that true? About the list?'

'It's rather complicated,' Pamela said vaguely. (She could hardly tell them that the list was being compiled by her, to pass on to MI5.)

Then there was a commotion. The striking, dark-haired man who had made a dramatic entrance a moment earlier was speaking loudly to the Princess Elena in Russian, gesturing forcefully. His greasy friend stood off to one side, casually smoking a cigar.

Percy came over to Pamela and leaned in. 'Behind the handsomeness was hollowness, vodka and fear...'

'What?'

'It's what Chanel said about her Russian aristocrat lover. The Grand Duke something. You know, Panda, the one who murdered Rasputin.'

Standing nearby, the Grand Duchess Maria Felixova pointed at him and said to Pamela and Percy, 'The husband – his Serene Highness Prince Maxim Ivanovich.' She clutched at her necklace. 'He is return from Berlin!'

Percy raised an eyebrow. 'He doesn't look very serene to me.'

By this point, Aunt Constance had come over to where they were standing, dragging Mr Dekhale with her. 'What's happening?'

Percy looked back at the Grand Duchess and said, 'Well, what is his Serene Highness saying? Don't keep us in suspense!'

'He say she owe him money. He is come to live in London and she must give him money. She is successful woman with business. Maxim Ivanovich is bad. A bad man. It was bad marriage.'

'Yes, we can see that,' replied Percy, transfixed.

'Constance, we must do something to help your poor friend,' piped up Mr Dekhale. 'I am afraid this man will become violent.'

'Yes, yes, you are absolutely right. We must do something,' said Aunt Constance emphatically as she pushed Mr Dekhale in front of her. 'Sardar, lead the way.'

Mr Dekhale looked surprised but marched over to the Russian drama unfolding by the bar.

'Pamela, come!' Aunt Constance grabbed Pamela by the arm.

Clutching his wine glass, Percy hurried to follow them, with Flossie bringing up the rear.

Prince Maxim was gripping the Princess by the shoulder and shaking her. Jo tried to step in but the Prince's friend pulled her back. Then there was a scuffle and suddenly Prince Maxim had Princess Elena by the neck.

Mr Dekhale took a deep breath and said, 'You, sir! Desist your actions!'

The Prince turned and rounded on Mr Dekhale, shouting in Russian.

'Hit him, Sardar, hit him!' cried Aunt Constance excitedly, clapping her hands together.

'You have no right to accost this woman in this fashion!' he said, clearly alarmed at the prospect of a fight with a drunken Russian.

Pamela looked around and noticed a vase on the table next to her. Percy caught her eye and nodded.

'Go on!' he hissed in her ear.

Pamela took the flowers out of the vase and picked it up. As Prince Maxim pulled his arm back, looking as if he was about to strike Mr Dekhale, she smashed it over his head.

'That will teach him!' cried Percy triumphantly.

Pamela looked down and saw Prince Maxim lying on the ground in a pool of water and broken glass.

II

Later that night, Pamela found herself in her sitting room with Aunt Constance, Mr Dekhale, Percy and Flossie. They drank scotch and sodas, trying to recover from the events of the evening.

'Did you see the look on everyone's faces when he keeled over?' said Percy excitedly.

'It was like a film!' cried Flossie.

'What a brute he is!' exclaimed Aunt Constance as she paced around the room. 'Imagine, just showing up out of the blue to demand money from a wife you've not seen in donkey's years!' She turned to Mr Dekhale. 'Sardar, you were wonderful.' Mr Dekhale had fallen asleep. She shook him.

He awoke with a start.

'How can you sleep at a time like this?' said Aunt Constance.

Pamela ventured down into the kitchen to see if she could find something to feed her guests. She could hear voices, which was unusual, as the servants would normally have been in bed by that point. She opened the door to find Jenny sitting at the kitchen table while the young man in the flat cap was standing up, chattering excitedly.

'And he just went for him! Pow! Right in his gob! Wasn't expecting Pat to be a boxer, did he?'

Sam demonstrated the one-two-punch.

'Sam, sit down,' Jenny said, slightly annoyed.

'Jenny…?'

Jenny looked up, startled. She jumped to her feet. Sam stood still, wide-eyed. He suddenly pulled his hat off his head and gripped it in his hands. On closer inspection, Pamela could see they both looked much the worse for wear. Jenny sported one torn stocking and Sam had a wound on his forehead. Looking at the kitchen table, Pamela could tell that Jenny had been trying to clean it.

'I'm sorry, Madame.' She looked very anxious. 'I wouldn't usually but...'

'Sit, sit. Far too late in the evening to stand on ceremony,' Pamela said as she herself sat down. 'You both look ghastly. What happened?'

Jenny and Sam sat at the table with her. Neither of them seemed eager to explain the situation. Pamela lit a cigarette. She offered one to Jenny, who took it. Then she gestured to Sam. He hesitated and then accepted it. For a moment, they all just sat there smoking. Jenny and Sam avoided Pamela's gaze. The blood from the wound on Sam's wound started to trickle down his face.

'You, er... I don't even know your name.'

The young man, a mop of dark curls and a small gap between his teeth, gingerly held out his hand and shook Pamela's. 'Sam Altschuler, your ladyship.'

'Yes, well, Mr Altschuler, you have a bit of blood running down your...' Pamela gestured to his forehead.

Sam touched his hand to his head. Jenny grabbed the bloody tea towel she had been using before and continued to dab at the blood.

'Ouch!' Sam winced and shied away.

'Stop moving your head,' Jenny said.

'Were you attacked?' asked Pamela, concerned.

'There was a demonstration in the East End,' replied Jenny. 'Blackshirts.'

'Mosley and his thugs wanted to show us who was boss and thought he'd bring his little army to stir up trouble in Stepney,' said Sam. 'But there were lots more of us than there were of them. Thousands and thousands more. Everyone's been talking about it for weeks. No pasarán!' he cried excitedly.

At the mention of Mosley, Jenny gave Pamela a look.

'But why Stepney?' Pamela asked. 'Surely, they'd get more attention with a rally in the middle of town.'

'The BUF's been holding meetings every week just off the Commercial Road for months and months,' Sam explained. 'And then they send them out into the streets to beat up Jews. They wait outside the shuls – synagogues – on Friday nights. Because they know that's when they can find us.'

'Lots of Jews live in Stepney, Madame,' said Jenny. 'And when Sam and his friends go to protect the synagogues or break up Mosley's gangs, the police get involved.'

'I would hope the police would get involved,' replied Pamela.

'They're not there to arrest the BUF. They're always there to arrest us! You'd think it was bloody Germany and the bloody Third Reich.'

Jenny gave Sam a stern look for using coarse language and said, 'Sorry, Madam.'

'That's revolting,' said Pamela, as she stubbed out her cigarette in annoyance. 'Both the actions of the BUF *and* those of the police.'

'Mosley doesn't have any bright ideas of his own. Just imitates his friend Adolf Hitler. But we routed the blighters! Pushed them back west, into the City where they came from. They didn't have a clue how many people there'd be.'

'They'd organised,' said Jenny.

'Who organised?' asked Pamela.

'The Communist Party,' Jenny said.

'Personally, I'm more of an anarchist.'

Pamela raised an eyebrow. Jenny elbowed Sam in the ribs.

'Not everyone there was a Party member. It was the Irish working down at the docks, labour unions. Local people. Women and children too.'

'It sounds as if it was quite dangerous,' said Pamela.

'It was! It was a proper battle. The coppers thought it was, anyway. They were galloping through the crowd like it was the Charge of the Bloody Light Brigade! Wielding their bloody batons at us.'

'Because they were protecting the BUF,' said Pamela.

'They were trying to break up the crowd. We'd stopped the Blackshirts from getting through. There were barricades to the south and the east. Even a tram driver – a Party member – stopped his tram dead in the middle of the street to block them,' added Jenny.

'Thought he could come 'round our streets and we'd hide behind our curtains. He had another think coming, I'll tell you that. We're not going to be driven out by some English Nazis. By another pogrom,' said Sam.

'I have to say, it does sound fairly terrifying. I'm glad you're both in one piece! But Jenny, I'd really prefer it if you didn't spend your Sundays getting into street fights.'

'Had to get her story though, didn't she?'

Jenny looked alarmed and hissed, 'Sam!'

'Her story?' Pamela asked.

Jenny caught Pamela's eye and looked down, embarrassed. 'For the local paper… Sometimes they let me do a bit of writing for them – my cousin works there. It won't get in the way of my work. I promise.'

Pamela couldn't help but feel a swell of pride in that moment.

'I suppose it's a bit unorthodox for a lady's maid, but it's good to show initiative. I can't imagine you want to be in service all your life. But just be careful. One can certainly get oneself into tight spots chasing a story…'

'May I look at your wound, young man?' Mr Dekhale had appeared in the doorway of the kitchen. 'I wanted to see if I could be of service, Lady Pamela,' he continued.

'Mr Dekhale, this is Jenny, my maid, and her friend, Mr Altschuler.'

Mr Dekhale examined Sam's face. 'Having been in many such demonstrations in India, I became accustomed to learning how to tend to injuries of protestors,' he said kindly.

'Well, you two, you may be surprised to hear that I also got myself into a scrape this evening,' Pamela said.

'So I've heard from your friends upstairs,' a voice said from behind them.

Pamela turned around to see Francis standing in the doorway in his dinner jacket. Pamela was at a complete loss for what to say, and still, she realised, slightly intoxicated.

'What's all this I hear about you and a vase, Pam?'

III

Francis watched Pamela from across the sitting room, smoking his pipe, his jacket hanging off the back of his chair. Pamela looked tiredly at the trays of sandwiches, glasses of whisky and empty cups of tea lying around the room.

'You were on the Western Front fighting the Russians whilst our maid was on the Eastern Front fighting the fascists,' said Francis.

'Just one Russian. A Russian prince, in fact.'

'I didn't think there were many of those knocking about these days.' Francis puffed on his pipe a moment, thinking. 'That we should be living in one of the last democracies in Europe and still have to endure this sort of thing. That men like Oswald Mosley, who is so third rate that no other party will keep him, can resort to bashing people up in the streets of London.'

Pamela leaned back on the chaise longue, taking the pins out of her hair and nursing her scotch and soda. She looked out the window into the pitch-black street and wondered what time it was. It was that period between midnight and twilight where everything felt surreal, as if night-time would never end and daylight would never come.

'Is this what the last war has led us to?' continued Francis. 'No one ever asks, you know. Why we sent so many men to their deaths. The ones who survived, we just reminisce about French women and our regiment chums, our commanding officers. Never what it was like. Memories are names on village monuments and pictures kept in drawers by silently grieving parents.'

Pamela stood up, walked over to Francis's arm-chair, sat by his feet and put her head on his lap. He stroked her head with one hand. A few feet away, Patricia slept sprawled on the rug in front of the fire.

'My parents never speak of my brother or my uncle. Most people want to leave all that behind,' Pamela said.

'Everyday life didn't change that much for people here. I suppose, in some ways, the war seemed remote to them. Men disappeared. Horses disappeared. People carried on having dinner parties.'

Pamela didn't know what to say. They sat in silence for what seemed like an eternity.

Then Francis said, 'I heard you went to a party at the German Embassy some weeks ago.'

She was startled. How did he know? She tried to behave casually.

'They were hosting a little celebration of the Berlin Olympics. It was for my column. They're eager for coverage from the British press.'

'Why didn't you tell me?' asked Francis.

'You were out of town and I suppose it slipped my mind,' Pamela lied. Then she remembered Donald Jenkins. 'I suppose your MP friend told you he ran into me?' she said as she rose to her feet and paced in front of the fire.

'Yes, he did.'

Francis stood and followed Pamela over to the fireplace. He knocked his pipe into the grate and then looked at her. She felt uncomfortable, knowing Francis knew she had lied to him by omission.

'Of course, I hardly knew a soul there, so it was nice to see a friendly face. Dreadful bunch of people, obviously.' She paused. 'He told me about the committee you two are on. I think he assumed that you had already told me about it. Which you hadn't.'

Francis looked to the mantle and fiddled with the pictures and objects sitting on it.

'You don't often seem terribly interested in what goes on in Parliament.'

Pamela was about to argue, but then realised he was right. She shrugged and said, 'Perhaps I am now.'

Francis looked down and saw he was holding the statue of Ganesh Aunt Constance had given Pamela. 'What's this?'

'Aunt Constance brought it back from India. I can take it down if you like.'

'I quite like it, actually,' he replied as he put Ganesh back.

'Mr Jenkins told me something of the committee, that it's to do with countering friendly sentiments towards Germany in the Commons.'

'Something like that, yes. There aren't many of us, you see. People who are committed to keeping appeasement off the table. Of course, no one wants to see another war, but...'

'We don't want Nazi stormtroopers goose-stepping through the East End.'

Pamela took the last of her hair pins out of her hair and let her soft but unruly waves fall down past her shoulders. One at the back was slightly stuck, tangled in strands of her hair, and Pamela struggled to unpick it.

Francis put a hand on her arm and said, 'Shall I?'

As he gently untangled her hair, Pamela said, 'Mr Jenkins and some of his friends talked about what it's like in Berlin, for men like them.' She paused. 'Terrible, actually.'

Francis handed Pamela the hair pin and said, 'I often wonder where Germany would be today if President Wilson hadn't fallen ill, after the war.'

'The American president?'

'Yes, he contracted influenza during negotiations at Versailles. He had been a great proponent of the idea that we would stand a better chance at a lasting peace in Europe if we allowed Germany's economy to recover, rather than punishing them so severely with reparations. And when he became ill, there was no one to prevent the French – and us – from doing exactly that.'

'Were the other men on this committee in the war?'

'Most of them were too young to have fought. In fact, most other men on the committee are quite unlike me. More like Jenkins, really.'

Pamela ran a hand through her hair, shaking out her curls. 'Are they all…?'

'A good number of the group, yes. It's part of the reason we've joined together. Men like that, Jewish MPs, too. And some who have simply been to Germany and have seen first-hand the consequences of Hitler's ascendance. They've begun calling us "the Glamour Boys", trying to shame us. Guilt, disreputation by association with men forced to live in the shadows. But support for Franco is growing on the Conservative benches and I'll be damned if I see the same thing happen to Hitler.'

Pamela was deeply moved, suddenly seeing this passion and conviction. She reached out and touched his face, their shadows reflected in the dying firelight. Francis took her hand.

'What is it?' Pamela asked.

'Is there someone else?' he asked gently.

'What do you mean?'

'If there is, I'd rather know than not. I'm not one of those men who happily turns a blind eye, content to lead separate lives. You should know that. You've been so distant these days, out late, so much more frequently. And when I heard about the German Embassy, I realised that perhaps I knew less about where you go and what you do than I'd thought…'

Pamela picked up Ganesh and turned it over in her hands, wondering if perhaps the Hindu deity would bring her wisdom.

'I know men are attracted to you – I'm not blind,' Francis continued. 'And it's been some time since we… Since the summer, I believe.'

'I suppose I've been busy. I've had more to do at the paper. And then of course there's Aunt Constance's gala.' The memory of Charlie's car was still strong in her mind and it made her feel oddly guilty.

So, she changed the course of the conversation and said, 'I was quite upset with you after the incident about that doctor.'

'I did apologise, Pam.'

'And, to be frank, Francis, I don't want children right now. I like my life the way it is.'

Francis looked into the embers of the fire. 'Right now? Or ever?'

'I don't know. But I'm afraid of what would happen. How much things would change.'

Francis took her hand. 'One's life always changes when one has children.'

'I'm sorry, but I'm completely spent. It's been rather a long evening. I really should go to bed.'

'I'm going to stay down here a moment longer, just until the fire is out.'

Pamela touched him gently on the shoulder as she left the room.

IV

The basement club was so dark Pamela could hardly see a thing, except the stage, where a tall West Indian woman sporting a slinky sequinned purple dress and neatly marcelled hair introduced each tuxedoed member of the black jazz band behind her. The bar was packed full of men and women, seemingly from every country and background imaginable. The low ceiling and windowless room meant that smoke practically filled the entire space and the smell of food wafted in from the kitchen. The brand was clearly popular and the atmosphere was electric; a small dance floor in front of the cabaret tables was crowded with sweaty couples (men with women, women with women, men with men). But it was so loud she could hardly hear Baron Ustinov.

Pamela fanned herself with her napkin and said, 'Why did you bring us here if we can't hear or see each other?'

Pamela sat in a circular booth lined in shabby red velvet with Ustinov, Putlitz and Putlitz's valet, a short man in his twenties, who was, apparently, also his lover.

'Darkened clubs where one can neither be seen nor heard have many uses,' said Putlitz, with his hand on his lover's knee.

'And it isn't a common meeting place, for these kinds of things,' explained Ustinov.

Pamela wondered what a common meeting place for arranging intelligence handovers from Soviet officers would be. She hadn't yet told Charlie about this assignation. Would MI5 allow her to stage manage a defection from the Soviet Union? She assumed that such a thing was rather unorthodox, but so far, everything had seemed fairly unorthodox to her. It didn't seem as if there were many rules at all. And she couldn't very well say no to a man in such a desperate situation. What was it they said – better to ask forgiveness than permission? Of course, what exactly she should ask, say or do when the Soviet arrived, she had no idea. She wondered if people were taught how to bargain with defectors for information, or if it was the kind of thing one could simply intuit with experience. Not that she'd received much instruction or training for anything at all anyway.

'A toast, to you, Lady Pamela,' said Putlitz as he raised his glass. 'In congratulations.'

'Congratulations for what?' said Pamela, perplexed.

'Foreign Secretary Anthony Eden himself has stopped sending the King anything of a confidential nature. Certain people have been feeding him information about his politics and the politics of his concubine,' explained Ustinov. 'It has been your intelligence on them that has made the difference.'

'But why didn't anyone tell me?'

'The British never motivate their people with flattery or kind words. They must drive us on with reprimands, like angry nannies,'

Pamela felt the warm glow of admiration but then a sense of unease, wondering if Charlie would have ever said anything to her if Ustinov hadn't. She wondered if there was anything else he wasn't telling her. But before she could speak, Pamela realised that Boris Nikolaevich was standing next to their booth, wearing a slightly too-large dark suit. Out of uniform, he looked surprisingly ordinary and slighter than she'd remembered. And even more like her brother. It was unsettling to be looking at a stranger and feel such a sense of familiarity. He proffered his hand as formally as he did at the German Embassy.

Pamela and Boris exited the gloom of the club and emerged into the gloom of the foggy Soho night. Only the sodium lighting of the street lamps and the neon of the nightclubs weakly lit their way. To an unsuspecting passer-by, they could have been any other couple walking down the street together. Pamela looked around, taking in the tarts, the night-time revellers and the loud drunks spilling out of the pubs. Two burly men in brightly-checked overcoats who looked like gangsters stood on a street corner talking quietly. A woman in a worn-out coat with a mangy fur collar played the violin as people threw coins in the upturned hat on the ground in front of her. A group of young boys ran past them, shouting at each other in Italian.

As she got closer to him under the street lamp, Pamela could see that the Soviet was nervous. She offered him a cigarette. His hand trembled ever so slightly as he lifted the cigarette to his mouth. A little up the street, someone smashed a glass against a wall. Boris flinched. He looked around. Suddenly, he looked as if he was about to run.

'That suit is too big for you, you know. You should really get it tailored,' said Pamela, hoping to distract him.

Boris looked surprised as Pamela reached up and took him by the shoulders and pinched the tops, as if she was eyeing up the fit of his jacket.

'I would take in the shoulders a tad and have someone bring up the bottom of the jacket, ever so slightly. It's a good material, quite salvageable.'

He looked self-conscious and said, 'It belonged to a friend.'

Pamela realised that he was probably a military man and unused to wearing civilian clothing. She felt sorry for embarrassing him.

'My brother was in the army. You look just like him.'

Boris smiled. 'He must be a handsome man.'

Pamela simply smiled back and nodded.

He looked anxious again. He took another long drag on his cigarette and then adjusted his tie. 'I can't go back to Moscow. Will you help me please?'

Boris's face was pale. He laid a hand on the wall next to them to steady himself, looking as if he might be ill.

'Are you quite all right?'

'If there is a protocol that I must follow…' he continued, breathing rapidly.

'Well, as I understand it… you give me… whatever it is you have. And I will arrange a meeting with… our people. And they will speak to you.'

Pamela felt like a fraud. She was worried that this frightened man, who was clearly putting his trust in her, would be better off in the care of someone who actually knew what they were doing.

But she straightened herself up, put her hand on his arm and said, 'Take a deep breath please, Captain Puchkov.'

Boris looked around. 'I'm an officer in the Red Army,' he whispered. 'I am a patriot.'

'Yes, I'm sure you are. But I understand you're in rather a tight spot.'

'The denouncements have no logic. They've been unpredictable. No one is safe. Even our ambassador is afraid to be recalled to Moscow. They are putting many, many people on trial. There are no... assurances, no protections.

'But why would they do such a thing?'

'Stalin wants to ensure absolute loyalty. The kind which only comes from fear.' He stubbed his cigarette out on the wall and looked down at his feet. 'I have a wife and two children here. I'm being sent back. They'll have to join me. I don't know what will happen to them.'

For a moment, Pamela was somewhat frightened herself. What if she was really putting this poor man and his family in danger? Could she really assure their safety? She had no experience with this kind of thing and no guarantee he would be granted protection from the government. One the other hand, she had procured intel that the Foreign Secretary himself had deemed valuable. Surely, that must count for something. Maybe she could repeat the trick. Maybe Boris had information Security Services would find valuable. Besides, it didn't seem as if anyone else was in a position to help him. Or perhaps it was that they weren't willing to take the risk.

'Then, Captain Puchkov, now is not the time for second thoughts. We must be resolute,' she said firmly. 'Are you able to tell me what you have?'

Boris nodded. He turned Pamela's body towards his, pulled something out of his pocket and put it in her hand.

It was an envelope. And it was empty.

He leaned in and whispered, 'There are three dots on the inside of the envelope. They are called "microdots". Tiny images of files that can only be seen through a microscope.'

Pamela looked down at what, at first, appeared to be a plain white envelope, and sure enough, there were three very small dots, almost imperceptible to the naked eye. She quickly slipped the envelope into her handbag.

'These are names of Soviet agents in Britain. If your government grants me protection, I have more information.'

Pamela felt sick to her stomach at the enormity of what she was holding in her handbag.

She took a deep breath and said, 'I will do everything in my power to help you, Captain Puchkov.'

'Boris Nikolaevich.'

'Boris Nikolaevich.'

He looked at her, leaned in and kissed her on the cheek. And all of a sudden, he was gone. Disappeared into the murky, Soho night-scape.

V

When Pamela first began working for Charlie, she didn't think she was cut out for spying. But now, she was starting to worry that it was, in fact, ordinary, married life for which she wasn't cut out. For the first time in their marriage, she had started to wonder how long they would be able to carry on in a strange twilight of a relationship. The other evening they had spent talking felt like it was the first time they had had such a serious, honest conversation in a long time – perhaps ever. And while it seemed to have cleared the air between them somewhat, it also seemed to have brought up even more questions. Would they continue to be so transparent in future? Would Francis continue to push for children? Was the problem that they ultimately wanted two different lives, completely unsuited to one another?

Meanwhile, Pamela hadn't heard from Flossie since the Russian party. She felt guilty for implicating Albert on the list of fascist sympathisers she had given to Charlie, but had also felt obliged to give his name. (Not that Flossie knew what she had done.) She wondered how long it would be before she heard from her, if she was still upset about what Pamela had said about her daughter.

She did have, however, a phone call from Princess Stephanie.

'Lord Rothermere has made a gift of a priceless tapestry to the Führer… perhaps your Mr Dawson would like to make a similar gift of goodwill? Naturally, I would be happy to assist in such an offer.'

Pamela was sure she would.

'I will certainly ask.'

Pamela wondered what the Princess made of the recent clandestine marriage of Diana Mitford and Tom Mosley in Germany – where the sweet Führer was the guest of honour – but restrained herself from asking.

'Have you heard, Lady Pamela? About Wallis and the divorce? Ernest will be the – how do you say? – the lamb, the sacrifice. He will offer his love affair with his lady-friend in America to the courts. Wallis is upset, very strained.'

Pamela felt sorry for this poor woman in New York, whose name was about to be dragged through the mud for the sake of the modesty of a woman who was, in reality, quite an immodest woman, and the dignity of a monarch with little dignity at all.

'Yes, I can imagine. Poor Wallis. How terribly worrying for her.' Pamela paused. 'Of course, she *must* feel she can rely on me for support, count on me as a friend in her time of need.'

For good measure, Pamela wrote a letter to Wallis, extending her sympathies and expressing her support, wondering if she might continue to confide in her. To her surprise, Wallis wrote back right away, telling Pamela how trying it all was, how she was the victim of British approbation. (Apparently, someone had graffitied 'Down with the American whore' on a wall in Scotland.) Wallis's doctor had put her on a week's bed-rest for her nerves and she was contemplating going away somewhere for a while, to get away from it all. Wallis said all she wanted was for everyone to be happy. (Pamela very much doubted that this was *all* she wanted.)

She couldn't help but wonder what the urgency was regarding the divorce. Was it at Ernest's behest? Had he grown fonder of his mistress or simply tired of his wife? Did it have something to do with Wallis's murky dalliances with von Ribbentrop? Was it at Wallis's own urging, trying to make the wheels turn faster in settling her future with the King – though it wasn't as if he had proposed to her.

Had he?

VI

Pamela made contact with Charlie, sending him a note about Wallis's confidences in her, and about Boris Nikolaevich and his offer to defect.

She enclosed the envelope with the microdots. Charlie responded with two directives:

Do your utmost at The Times *to agitate for coverage of the story. If the public knows, there is hope that they will voice their support for their King and his romance. And with public support, the King may be emboldened to push the government to* accept *his proposal of marriage to Wallis Simpson, which will, in turn, push them to understand that this is a very serious situation indeed, thus considering abdication an absolute necessity.*

After some inspection, it seems the intel is genuine. Meet me next Thursday evening, in our usual location. Bring your friend.

VII

Pamela thought about Charlie's directive and wondered how to go about it, especially since it was going to be a difficult task. There was a restriction on coverage of the Simpson/HRH affair that Dawson had been quite adamant about earlier in the year. But perhaps he had softened. Or could be encouraged to change his mind. What case could she make for it, she wondered as she sat in a meeting.

She was starting to realise that some of the staff were becoming discontented with the editorial direction they were being given. For instance, Henry Rake and the coverage of the war in Spain.

'But the public must know what's happening. We *must* report on the atrocities being committed by Franco's men!'

'Mr Rake,' replied Dawson, exasperated, 'there are likely even more atrocities being committed on the side of the Republicans.'

To everyone's surprise, the normally taciturn Henry burst into tears. 'You have no idea what's happening over there. It isn't *your* son fighting with the International Brigades. It isn't *your* son who sends you letters about how brutal the opposition is, how cold and hungry those boys are, how frightened he is…'

Dawson's secretary Doris stopped taking notes in order to come around to the other side of the table and put her arm around him, saying, 'There, there, Henry. It will all be all right.'

But Henry would not be pacified.

As tears streamed down his cheeks, he said, 'Don't you understand how many British men are going to Spain to fight for a cause they believe in?'

'Oh dear…' Percy muttered to Pamela quietly.

Sitting on the other side of Pamela, Jo raised an eyebrow and looked at the two of them in amazement. It was her first meeting at *The Times* and she was somewhat surprised at such goings-on.

'I am sorry, Mr Rake, but we really must continue,' said Dawson perfunctorily.

'Mr Dawson, Nationalist forces are on their way to Madrid, as we speak, as we sit here in this office. And god help the people of that city when they reach it. Why are you so unwilling to allow us to tell our readership what is happening?'

Dawson was beginning to look quite cross, his mouth pursed into a tight little frown.

'We have a good deal of news to cover in the world and our editorial policy on the Spanish War is in line with government policy,' he announced tersely.

Jo leaned over and whispered, 'Which is exactly the problem.'

Pamela remembered what Francis had said about his alarm at the growing support for Franco within the ranks of the Conservative Party.

'We cannot simply fall into line with the government at every turn,' Henry replied angrily. 'Otherwise, how will we as the press hold politicians accountable for their actions? And their inaction. The British government is doing precious little to prevent Franco from jack-booting his way through the Iberian Peninsula, but many people have gone over to fight in the International Brigades from this country. Many children of our readers, who may very well want to know what is happening to their loved ones.'

'Spain is a death-trap. In my opinion, it will do us no good to entangle ourselves in what are, essentially, Spanish affairs. And if young British men are foolish enough to volunteer to enter the conflict, that is their prerogative, sadly.'

'We always gravitate towards the victor, don't we? Because it doesn't much matter who comes begging the Bank of England for loans when everything is over, does it? When everyone is dead. When *my son* is dead.'

The room was so silent you could hear a pin drop. Everyone was looking back and forth between Dawson, who looked very angry, and Henry, who now looked thoroughly drained. He leaned back in his chair and closed his eyes. Doris, still standing awkwardly next to him, gingerly patted him on the shoulder. Dawson finally looked to Doris and asked her for the next item on the agenda, as if nothing at all had happened. Henry got up from his chair and walked out of the room.

Pamela considered bringing up covering the story of Wallis and the King but the atmosphere in the room was heavy. She could tell some people had genuine sympathy for Henry while others thought he was being sensationalist. She didn't feel it was the right time to bring up something so controversial and decided to pursue it with Percy instead.

After the meeting, as everyone exited into the corridor, Percy said to Pamela, 'I can't believe Dawson didn't say anything about Mrs Leigh.'

'What happened?'

'She died,' said Jo, as she fished for cigarettes in her handbag. 'Yesterday.'

'Oh god,' said Pamela. 'How awful.'

Pamela was about to protest when Jo said, 'It's fishy, don't you think? How she ended up in that coma.'

Percy rolled his eyes. 'You're always looking for a story.'

'A perfectly healthy, middle-aged woman, standing *alone* on a train platform, just happens to fall?' said Jo with a raised eyebrow as she lit her cigarette.

'Apparently, it was wet. The platform was probably icy. That man says he thought she slipped.'

'Yes, but he didn't *see* her slip. And just as a train was coming?'

Percy crossed his arms. 'All right, Agatha Christie, you suggesting she was *murdered*?'

'Percy, you don't have to be Agatha Christie to suspect foul play.'

Who would want to kill Mrs Leigh? Pamela thought to herself. Or did she take her own life? But that seemed even more unlikely. It was very odd. She made a mental note to find out when the funeral was and if there was someone to whom she could send flowers.

'Either way, it's terrible.'

'It is… We're going to lose all those readers who only read our section for "A Word in Your Ear",' sighed Percy.

Pamela gave him a smack on the arm. 'Have some decency.'

'Come on, pet. It isn't as if you liked her.'

Pamela thought for a moment and then said, 'I have an idea for increasing numbers.'

'Yes?'

'I know we're not to print anything about the King and Wallis Simpson.'

'No, we certainly are not,' Percy replied as he gave her a warning look.

'But it would increase readership, wouldn't it?'

'No interviews, no gossip, no rumours, nothing. Nada. Nein.'

'Percy, every other paper in the world has been scooping us on Mrs Simpson and the King for months.'

'Yes, I'm aware, but there's nothing we can do about it. Dawson returned from his holiday last month to find a stack of press cuttings from America. Some malicious, exaggerated gossip. Some pure invention. But some of it was true – quelle horreur. And now he's getting letters asking why he hasn't published anything yet. Of course, *I* would like nothing more than to splash their names around and have a good old time of it. *I know* it would do wonders for sales. But we are still under strict orders not to stoke the fire.'

'But Percy, we cannot be complicit in covering up something like this, something so important,' Pamela retorted.

Jo blew smoke in Percy's face. 'Since when are you on the side of the authorities, Percy?'

They exchanged a sharp look but Percy waved her away indignantly.

'She's right, you know,' continued Jo. 'It's a damned cover-up. People have a right to know what their king is up to. Jesus, it's bad enough we still have a king.'

'You've only just started here. I wouldn't go getting yourself into trouble already.'

Looking irate, Percy strode off down the hallway.

'He can be a real shit sometimes,' Jo said to Pamela. 'Dawson's been talking to the Palace. He's in the PM's pocket too, but he also knows it's only a matter of time before everything goes to hell. And won't we end up looking like absolute eejits when all the other papers come out with it first? The whole thing must be making you completely mad,' Jo continued.

'Me?' replied Pamela.

'*You're* the one who could blow the whole story to high heaven. And have your name all over a big scoop like that.'

'I hadn't thought about it like that.'

'Well, if you ever need my help...' Jo said with a smile. 'In Russian fairy tales, the hero usually completes some tasks or helps out some other character – a witch or a fairy or a goblin. And then they help the hero somewhere down the line.' She paused. 'Elena told me that. Thank you, for the other night. Mad bastards, Russians. Not what I expected from the woman who I first saw blind drunk on martinis singing Cole Porter.'

'I've never done anything like that before, you know,' Pamela replied, somewhat embarrassed.

'What? You've never smashed a man over the head with a pot?' laughed Jo.

'Is Elena all right?' asked Pamela.

'She's just about recovered from all the excitement. Though she's not speaking to me again. Politics is the only thing we row about. You can imagine we have different perspectives, me not having grown up on a grand estate of a thousand acres.'

Pamela remembered the argument she heard through Elena's bedroom wall the morning she woke up on her sofa.

'Pamela, you're a clever woman,' continued Jo. 'You must know that things need to change if this country is going to have any kind of future at all.'

VIII

Pamela returned home that afternoon from a day of errands and shopping to find a letter from Mr Dekhale. He wanted to talk to her about himself and her aunt. That she might want to distance herself from the pair of them because they were likely wanted by the government due to all the things Aunt Constance had told Pamela on the Duke of Westminster's yacht. (It struck Pamela as very sweet of him.)

At first, Pamela wondered if they were both simply being paranoid and overreacting. The colonial government probably dealt harshly with rabble-rousers in India, but this was England. Surely, it wasn't as bad as they feared. And Aunt Constance and Mr Dekhale were just middle-aged, armchair revolutionaries who talked a great deal.

As Pamela was halfway through reading the letter, the telephone rang. Jenny announced that Mrs Brackenberry was on the line.

'Pam!'

'Hello, Flossie.'

'I am sorry I was such an embarrassment at the party the other evening.'

'You weren't the one smashing men over the head with vases, darling.'

'That was quite exciting, wasn't it?' Flossie trilled. 'Anyway, I've been thinking about what you've said, Pam. About Albert and the AGF. And I told Albert… I told him about Hitler and the children. About what might happen to us, you know, if people were to know. We had a terrible row.'

'I am sorry, Floss.'

'Gets the blood up, doesn't it?'

'Yes… I suppose it does.'

'I was inspired, you see.'

'Inspired?'

'By you! With the vase!'

'You didn't smash one over Albert's head, did you?'

'No, but I did throw my fork on the ground in a fit. I've never shouted at him before and it was such a great rush. All of a sudden, I found myself standing up at the table, over my eggs in the breakfast room, practically screaming that if Albert didn't leave off with those Nazi murderers that I would leave him and take the children. Isn't it marvellous? Nanny Flynn said she was quite proud of me.'

'This happened in front of the nanny?'

'I've never done anything like that before, Pam. Shouted at Albert like that, or anybody really. I just do what people say most of the time. Of course, I've never needed to shout at Albert before. He is a good man, really. But when it comes to the children... well, you know what I'm like.' Flossie paused. 'Pam, are you still there?'

'What? Yes, I'm here.'

'Albert thinks I've gone crackers but I don't care. He says he'll leave the Fellowship if it makes me feel better. I don't think he understands really, but at least it will all be over and done with.'

Pamela sighed, relieved to know that Albert would no longer risk being called before some tribunal, in some distant future, because of her.

Flossie carried on, talking about Albert and what Nanny Flynn said and something that had happened in the garden. Pamela's eyes drifted back to Mr Dekhale's letter. And then she froze.

'Flossie darling, can I ring you back later?'

Pamela hung up the phone and re-read what he had written. That Aunt Constance had a substantial police record. Which was how she ended up in India in the first place – to evade arrest. Police record? Evading arrest? She knew her aunt had been in some trouble during her suffragette days, but a record? Fleeing the country? What exactly had she done?

Mr Dekhale went on to say that it was possible that they may have to leave England. His sources in London told him that both he and Aunt Constance were being watched. And that it might only be a matter of time before they were both arrested for conspiracy against the colonial government in India and the Empire.

Pamela couldn't think what to do. Part of her wondered if Mr Dekhale was as tightly wound and imaginative as Aunt Constance, that perhaps the two of them had convinced each other that they were more important than they actually were. It could very well have been that Special Branch was keeping an eye on them, but it wasn't likely to be as bad as all that.

Was it?

But what if he wasn't overreacting? What if what he said was true, that her aunt was not only an agitator for Indian Independence but also a fugitive from the law?

Pamela took a deep breath and wrote back to Mr Dekhale, saying to please let her know if there was anything she could do to help. Though, of course, she hoped it wouldn't come to that.

IX

Pamela knew that she should have felt proud of herself, of what she had achieved. She had won the trust of the King's beloved mistress, managed to influence the Foreign Secretary, collected a growing list of possible traitors to the Crown, and arranged for the defection of an innocent Soviet bureaucrat, thereby securing state secrets straight from the bosom of the Kremlin. But instead, she felt unsettled.

She couldn't get the thought of Mrs Leigh's untimely demise out of her head. It was strange that such an ordinary woman would meet with such a terrible fate. And Gertrude Leigh was originally meant to write 'A Week with Wallis', not Pamela. Was it a coincidence? Had someone been trying to stop her? But surely, that was a bit far-fetched, that a tweedy woman known for being an agony aunt who wrote the occasional feature for the Lifestyle section of *The Times* would be murdered for attempting to write a story about Wallis Simpson. Unless...

No.

Pamela knew she was just being paranoid. Just because it seemed as if there were spies around every corner, it didn't mean that was actually the case. She had to keep a clear head and couldn't get distracted by red herrings. Besides, she had more important things to worry about.

It was late afternoon and the autumn sun was beginning to set as she walked to the park to meet Boris Nikolaevich and to make the introduction to Charlie. She brought Patricia with her, who had become something of a regular cover for any suspicious-looking walks she was obliged to take. When Pamela reached the appointed bench, the Soviet was already in place. Patricia sniffed his hand companionably and he petted her head.

Boris smiled, perhaps the first genuine smile Pamela had seen from him. 'What is its name, please?'

'Patricia.' Pamela sat next to him and Patricia sat at her feet obediently.

He repeated her name a couple times while continuing to pat her head before muttering sweet nothings to her in Russian.

'When I was a child, my father, he had a dog, for hunting. We called him Sasha,' Boris said softly.

Pamela felt quite sorry for him, thinking of the family and friends he would be leaving behind in Russia.

Boris looked at her. 'Do you know this man, your contact?'

'Yes, of course,' she replied, wondering if she really did.

'You trust him?'

It was a good question. Pamela hesitated.

Before either of them could say anything else, Charlie appeared from the interior of the park. He looked at the two of them momentarily from a distance, took off his hat and smoothed his hair – the signal. Pamela nodded at Boris. He looked at Charlie and then back at Pamela again, somewhat uncertain.

She leaned down to pet Patricia and whispered in his ear. 'Please do not worry, Boris Nikolaevich. Rest assured, my government is very interested in what you have to offer. You will be a great asset to them.'

Their hands touched momentarily as the Soviet gave Patricia one last stroke. Boris bowed to Pamela before walking in Charlie's direction.

November 1936

I

Pamela received a letter from Charlotte.

Can you believe Peter has gone to Abyssinia without me? He went to meet some Italian business associates and has left me behind with the ghost! Followed your advice and had the priest round while Peter was gone, to assess the situation. Was a very trying experience as he had no English at all. He prayed and did something with incense but whatever it was, it wasn't very effective because the poor girl is still hanging about banging on the walls. And the hotel Peter is staying in sounds utterly ghastly. He says there's a tannery on one side and a brothel on the other! And fleas! Don't they have respectable places for European people? Perhaps there are better quality hotels elsewhere. What was the name of the place where your Mr Waugh stayed?

Pamela had read in the paper the other day that Germany and Italy had formed a pact, and wondered what that would mean for Charlotte, Peter and Peter's Italian business interests. She smiled as she thought of the two of them having to return to England and leave behind their vineyard and their Roman palazzo.

She also received another letter from Wallis, who was most unhappy having recently begun to receive death threats as word of her divorce and romance with the King trickled out. Special Branch had resorted to assigning bodyguards to her.

I wish they would understand that I don't want anything! Merely to make David happy. I'm simply a woman, trying to do her best.

Wallis was outraged that she had been advised to leave the country.

Where would I go? What would I do?

Rather predictably like Scarlett O'Hara. Were all American self-styled femme fatales alike?

She was in fighting mode.

Besides, they don't understand that the King would only come after me regardless of everything. And then they would get a far worse scandal than they're getting now.

And she was enormously indignant having heard that Churchill referred to her as 'cutie'.

What a horribly rude man!

(In truth, Churchill could be an awkward dinner companion; if he wasn't able to address the entire table, he refused to speak at all.)

Then, at the end of the letter, much to Pamela's surprise, Wallis invited her and Francis to Fort Belvedere for the weekend. As if she had already taken her rightful place by the King's side.

And perhaps she had.

II

The next day, Pamela read Mrs Leigh's obituary in *The Times*. Due to the fact that she had been a member of staff and a popular figure amongst the readership, it was quite substantial, taking up half a page. Pamela's first reaction upon reading it was guilt. The woman had been far more interesting and accomplished than she had known. A graduate of University College London and student of German literature. Having had a German mother and a love of German culture, she had been a fluent German speaker and had travelled to Germany on many occasions. Her husband had been a professor of literature himself. She had been a nurse in the Great War. She was survived only by her sister and her sister's family.

Most surprisingly, she had written a number of murder mysteries under a pen name. The Virginia Dalkeith series. Pamela was shocked. She had loved those books as a teenager. Virginia was a strong-willed, convincing female protagonist. Pamela suddenly felt sorry that she had never known. She would have loved to have been able to talk to her about the books, the characters, how she came up with the idea for a twenty-something, Scottish lady-detective.

Pamela now wished she had got to know Mrs Leigh better, that she hadn't been so quick to judge her. When she thought about their interactions, what she realised was that perhaps the woman hadn't been looking down on her, but rather simply trying to push her to do greater things. She had often tried to get Pamela to write about more serious topics, dismissing the notion that fashion *was* a serious business. 'Pamela, you are an intelligent woman – why do you behave like such a flibbertigibbet?' she had said to her once.

Her second reaction was one of a dawning realisation. It was too much of a coincidence. She spoke German *and* was about to take on the piece on Wallis Simpson. And just before she did, she fell into an oncoming train. Alone. In the dark. On a Sunday night. Like a plotline in a Virginia Dalkeith novel

Had Gertrude Leigh been an informant for the Germans? She spoke German, she loved German culture and German literature – she even had a German mother. As a well-known writer for *The Times*, she would have been well placed not only to get information, but also to subtly influence people. Had 'A Word in Your Ear' been some kind of mechanism to subliminally influence the British population and act as a conduit for Nazi propaganda?

Or what if it was the other way around? What if she had been a spy for MI5? Which meant that Pamela would have been her successor. But why would she have been brought on after someone like that? If someone as knowledgeable and accomplished as Mrs Leigh had managed to get herself bumped off, why would MI5 think that Pamela would have done a better job? It didn't make any sense. And it was too incredible.

III

Charlie arranged to meet Pamela at the little café where they had their first meeting many months before. Since it was nearly closing time, the place was as deserted as it was then. Only this time, after Charlie and Pamela sat down, the waitress went over to the front door, flipped over the closed sign and locked the door. The bell on top of the door rang, as if emphasising the finality of the gesture. Pamela knew better than to be surprised to find that a seemingly unassuming café in Marylebone was actually an MI5 safe house.

Pamela also thought about the last time she'd seen him. Although they had exchanged letters, and Pamela had sent Boris in Charlie's direction in the park the month before, they hadn't met in person since they had sat in his car, looking at the view of the city, getting the tiniest glimpse into his life, eating peppermints. There he was, back in his tatty Burberry and bowler, but somehow, he now looked to her as if he was in disguise, and that the MG-driving, white-tie wearing spy was merely hiding underneath. How much had she really learned? It seemed nothing and, at the same time, everything. A librarian (this still flummoxed her) who had had a difficult childhood and an ex-wife somewhere. Or perhaps he was a widower. When Charlie said he had been married 'once upon a time', he could have meant that his wife was dead.

Charlie offered Pamela a cigarette. The smoke from her cigarette travelled up and she looked again at the stain from the leak that was still there on the ceiling. Had it become bigger? Perhaps they were sitting underneath someone's bathtub. She looked back at Charlie, trying to discern whether anything of their relationship had altered in his eyes, or if their late-night rendezvous was a distant memory. Or perhaps it was par for the course for him, that he was used to meeting his agents at odd hours in strange locations. Did he have other agents to handle? And if so, were any of them women? Or was she the only one? But Charlie looked as he usually did, almost preternaturally composed. He wore a navy-blue, three-piece suit, with a striped tie, but clearly none of it was new, and while not as scruffy as his trench coat, it looked as if it belonged to a librarian. Everything he wore had a slightly lived-in appearance; Pamela could just about envision him, walking around the stacks, books in his arms.

She was impatient to ask about Boris. She wanted to be assured that it had all gone off smoothly, that he would be safe in the arms of the British government, away from the dangers of Moscow. But she didn't want to appear anxious.

'Wallis has asked me to Fort Belvedere for the weekend,' she started.

Pamela paused, waiting for something. Any kind word of appreciation or congratulation. She felt both annoyed with herself for wanting praise, like a child, and with Charlie for failing to oblige her.

'The correspondence is going well then, I take it?'

'It seems to be, yes,' Pamela replied as she contemplated her weak tea and stale biscuit.

For the first time, Pamela wondered how long this was going to carry on for. Would she be obliged to trail after Wallis and the King forever? Or just until she had helped push HRH off the throne and into the hinterlands of anonymity. Or ignominy. Or both.

'The Prime Minister has come to us with concerns about the King and Mrs Simpson,' explained Charlie. 'It seems he is worried about a consolidation of power of the opposition, backed by the King, and a subsequent takeover of the government.'

'Like a... coup?'

Charlie thought for a moment.

'Not exactly. Simply a political manoeuvre to shore up his own position. However, the governing board of MI5 have come to deem the King and Mrs Simpson as a security threat and have asked the Home Office to intercept their phone calls.' He paused. 'I thought you might like to know that.'

It was curious, what Charlie wanted Pamela to know and what he didn't. And how he wanted her to feel – *if* he wanted her to feel anything at all. Pamela remembered what Ustinov and Putlitz had told her about Anthony Eden and how he had stopped sending the King confidential documents. She also remembered what Wallis had written to her about the bodyguards, perhaps intended to protect the world from Wallis, as much as she from it.

Charlie cleared his throat. 'Be careful this weekend. See what you can do to exploit their vulnerability. They are likely to be feeling vulnerable, with this new threat of the complete exposure of their affair to the public. But tread softly. Do nothing to make them suspicious.'

He had said this with such stiff finality that Pamela expected him to stand and put on his coat. But then his face softened. Charlie cleared his throat, looked down, fiddled with his cufflinks and straightened his cuffs. Then he looked at her.

'How are you… getting on? Generally speaking, I mean.'

For a moment she parsed through the numerous recent incidences rambling through her head: her twilight reckoning with Francis, her strange but developing friendship with Wallis, her wayward aunt with a criminal record. And the Soviet.

'It's difficult,' she said, 'trying to keep one's personal life, one's… feelings apart from… this. It seems nearly impossible to maintain some kind of distance, from the things one is asked to do, to lie about…'

Charlie nodded. 'I suppose you learn to compartmentalise, to a certain degree. And you learn that the truth is… variable, that it's sometimes a matter of perspective.'

But whose perspective?

Pamela considered asking Charlie about Mrs Leigh. But then suddenly the idea of asking if an Englishwoman working for *The Times* as an advice columnist was seeding Nazi propaganda into her column seemed ludicrous. Asking if she had been fighting Nazi infiltration as an agony aunt for MI5 seemed equally ludicrous. She worried about coming across as paranoid, seeing espionage everywhere. And besides, she had something more important to worry about.

'Mr Buchanan, did it all go off smoothly with... my Russian friend?'

'After we made that initial contact in the park, I arranged for him to meet me for a full debrief, so we could understand more about what he knows. And I'm afraid he didn't turn up.'

Pamela's stomach dropped. The worried feeling she had been repressing came rushing to the fore. She could sense a cold sweat breaking out around her neck.

'What happened?'

'It's difficult to say. He could have had cold feet, changed his mind at the last minute. It's quite an overwhelming thing to decide to do, to decide to betray one's country, to know you can never return to your friends and family. To throw oneself on the mercy of a foreign government.'

'But he seemed so desperate! It seemed like he had no choice.'

'Perhaps that's how he felt in the moment, but had time to think better of it. Everyone has a choice.'

Charlie looked down at his hands, holding his bowler. It was clear that this wasn't what was really on his mind, and that he was as worried as Pamela was.

'*Or...?*' Pamela asked.

'Or... he may have been intercepted.'

'Intercepted?'

'It's possible,' Charlie said, more calmly than seemed rational to Pamela. 'These things happen.'

'Intercepted by whom?' she said, a note of panic creeping into her voice, despite her best efforts.

'Our Soviet counterparts,' Charlie said softly. 'They are said to be quite... attuned to episodes such as this. It's been known to happen before.'

Pamela wrapped her arms around herself and closed her eyes momentarily.

'I knew I didn't have the experience to handle something like this. He should never have trusted me.'

'Lady Pamela...'

'That poor man put his life in my hands and I—'

Charlie reached across the table and laid a hand on Pamela's forearm.

'First of all, we don't know what happened. We have no proof. Second of all, he knew what he was doing – it was his decision, his risk to take,' he said gently. 'His defection was never your intended mission. So, you mustn't blame yourself.'

Pamela nodded.

'I'm very sorry, but I must go. Will you be all right?' Charlie asked gently as he withdrew his hand across the red and white checked tablecloth.

'Yes, quite all right. Thank you,' replied Pamela quietly, feeling anything but.

Charlie slowly rose from the table, picked up his hat and put on his coat. He tipped his hat to Pamela before leaving the café.

IV

Pamela continued to agonise about what might have gone wrong with Boris's defection long after the meeting with Charlie. *Had* he changed his mind at the last minute? And if so, had he gone through with returning to Moscow? Or was it possible he had gone into hiding, somewhere in England, perhaps somewhere in London? If he truly was in as much danger as he suspected, he must have been frightened. At first, she hoped that Boris might get in touch with her again, asking for help, but those hopes diminished with every passing day. And despite what Charlie had said, she felt terrifically guilty. She should never have said yes to helping in the first place. She cursed her overconfidence she had felt that night in Soho, buoyed up by Putlitz and Ustinov's assurances that the intelligence she had gathered about Wallis and the King had influenced the Foreign Secretary.

At first, Pamela felt totally in the dark and totally helpless. Then she thought, what would Virginia Dalkeith do? Gertrude Leigh's fictional creation had inspired her all throughout her teenage years. A savvy woman of derring-do. Virginia wouldn't have fallen at the first hurdle; she would have persevered until she'd uncovered the truth.

Pamela considered who to contact, to try to find out what had happened. Her first instinct was to go back to the men who had connected Boris to her in the first place. But which one?

Putlitz?

Or Ustinov?

Putlitz seemed more solid, reliable, with the authority of the German Embassy behind him. Ustinov seemed craftier, perhaps even more disreputable. But like a man who knew how to find things out. A journalist, in fact. After all, Percy had said Ustinov was a great source for information. So, in the name of discretion, rather than contact him via Putlitz, Pamela approached Percy. She could sense that he was still somewhat annoyed with her for pushing the issue of Wallis

Simpson, so she brought him a box of assorted macarons from a tiny French patisserie in Fitzrovia she knew he loved.

'What do you want with the Red Baron?' Percy asked suggestively, while raising an eyebrow and nibbling on a strawberry macaron. 'Ooo, these *are* sinful. You naughty girl.'

'Marlene Dietrich, of course,' Pamela replied.

'Marlene Dietrich?'

'Yes, it seems all these Germans-in-exile know each another,' Pamela said casually as she played with a pen that was sitting on Percy's desk. 'That's what we were talking about at the party, you know. He seems to be acquainted with quite a lot of émigrés and wanted to know if I would be interested in writing a piece about… oh, I don't know… the luminaries of that social circle.'

Percy looked sceptical. 'And who would those social luminaries be, exactly?'

'That's what I asked. And Baron von Ustinov said there was a possibility he could get me an interview with Marlene – he says she's very keen on raising the profile of Germans living abroad who are anti-Hitler.'

Percy thought for a moment, finished the strawberry macaron and picked up a chocolate one. He contemplated it for a moment and then said, 'Of course, we can't be seen to be getting into politics. Dawson wouldn't want "Agent of Influence" to become a *political* platform.'

'No…'

'I've heard Marlene can be quite outspoken – apparently, she was plotting to assassinate Hitler, armed only with a poisoned hair pin or some such thing. And of course, Ustinov can be a bit of a radical himself.'

'Oh, really?'

'Apparently, he was made to leave his position at the German Embassy when he refused to prove he had no Jewish ancestry. Not that I disapprove,' Percy added hurriedly. 'It's just… well, we don't want to be seen to be getting caught up in all of *that*, you know.'

Percy was so different from his friends like Donald Jenkins and Michael (aka 'Mary'), who seemed so passionate about their opposition to the Hitler government. Though it was often difficult to say where Percy's professional ambitions began and where his personal convictions ended. (Or if he had any personal convictions.)

'Isn't the divine Lola Lola living in Hollywood these days? And besides, it isn't as if she needs the publicity,' he continued.

'Percy, are you saying that if we were offered an exclusive interview with Marlene Dietrich, we would pass it up?' Pamela replied as she crossed her arms.

'Well, no, of course not, but—'

'It seems she comes to London from time to time for shooting films and premieres and what have you. No promises, of course, but he said he would see what he could do. And I was thinking it was about time we sprinkled "Agent of Influence" with a bit of starlet glitter.' She paused and then added, 'Besides, I'm doing my best to find alternatives to the Simpson Affair, as requested.'

Percy leaned back in his chair and peered at Pamela over the top of the reading glasses he made sure never to be seen wearing in public.

'Yes, all right then,' he replied as he removed his full-to-bursting address book from his desk drawer and began to flip through it.

Pamela felt even more justified approaching Ustinov, knowing he had been principled enough to give up his embassy position for the sake of resisting the pressure to conform to Aryan race laws. She phoned him, saying she wanted to ask about a mutual friend who was in town, knowing he would understand what she was referring to. And so, they ended up in Russell Square, sitting on a bench and watching the university students walk and cycle by.

Ustinov looked as blank and smooth-faced as ever, betraying nothing. 'It is not surprising that your handler knows so little. Although Moscow has many spies in London, London has no one in Moscow.'

'What do you mean? That the Soviets are spying on us, but we aren't doing the same to them? Why?'

He shrugged. 'In part, because Russia is not a priority for SIS. Funds are limited and they do not want to waste them on a country they do not find to be an imminent threat. And ignorance, of course. They seem blind to the size of the network of Russian agents in Britain.'

'Are there that many?'

Ustinov nodded again. 'A great many. Far more Russian than German agents. Many in London.'

How was one meant to live one's life if one's city was a nest of spies? She looked around, suddenly wondering how many exactly. Were they simply walking the streets, posing as ordinary Russians? Or perhaps posing as English men and women? Or were they, in fact, English-born?

'They are known to gather in Hampstead,' he continued.

'Soviet spies in Hampstead?'

'In a new building known as the Lawn Road Flats.'

'I've never heard of it.'

'I supposed you wouldn't have. It's very modern. Unusual.'

Pamela felt slighted somehow, that Ustinov thought her to be a woman unaware of avant-garde architecture. That, and the sight of young men and women passing by talking and laughing, satchels thrown over their shoulders and books in their arms, made her feel indescribably old. She felt a longing for the kind of youth she never experienced, but often wished she had. She watched a brunette in a Fair Isle jumper and duffle coat argue passionately with a dark-haired, dark-skinned man wearing tortoiseshell spectacles. Could Pamela have been the kind of bluestocking who went to parties in avant-garde buildings, who discussed the latest volumes of poetry and smoked hand-rolled cigarettes? The brunette looked like the kind of girl who had never been to a debutante ball in her life, yet probably *had* heard of the Lawn Road Flats.

'The network isn't as dangerous as it could be because the Kremlin doesn't trust its own people,' Ustinov continued, bringing Pamela back down to earth, 'so they waste the intelligence they receive because they discount it. They are paranoid enough to think that every agent of theirs has either been turned or is an enemy plant.'

Pamela suddenly felt guilty, floating off into her own mundane fantasies, forgetting entirely why she had met Ustinov in the first place.

'If they are really that paranoid, then…'

As if reading Pamela's mind, Ustinov said, 'I spoke to some contacts of mine. It seems Captain Putchkov has disappeared. He has not been to the Soviet Embassy in some weeks. No one has heard from him.' Previously so calm and unreadable, Ustinov now looked dejected. 'It is unfortunate.'

The clouds above grew darker and a few raindrops began to fall.

'Does anyone know what might have happened?'

Ustinov pulled his coat tighter around him and looked steely-eyed into the distance. 'The NKVD is all-reaching and all-seeing. It was a great risk for him.'

'Does that mean they've taken him back to Moscow. Or…?'

'It is difficult to say. And, sadly, we may never know.'

She suddenly felt naïve, having hoped to get a simple, concrete answer for something so wrapped up in complex political machinations.

She worried briefly that Boris's disappearance was her fault. But she was simply doing what she had been asked. She hoped that wherever he was, he was simply in hiding.

Hampstead. Why was it that Hampstead rang a bell in Pamela's mind? Then she remembered; Gertrude Leigh had been in West Hampstead when she was waiting for the train. Was that simply a coincidence? All of a sudden, it seemed as if there were too many coincidences for Pamela's liking.

'There's something else I need to ask you. There was a woman, working at the paper. She had a very popular column – we had the same editor. I only had the opportunity to interview Wallis Simpson because I inherited her feature when she… fell off a train platform. She's dead now.' Pamela took a deep breath. 'Was Gertrude Leigh a spy?'

Ustinov looked surprised. 'They didn't tell you?'

'Tell me what?'

'She was your predecessor.'

Pamela felt as if her heart skipped a beat.

'My god. I thought I was just letting my imagination run away with me.'

'Maybe they didn't think it was necessary information for you to have.'

'Not necessary for me to know that the woman who came before me was probably shoved in front of a train??'

'And of course, we do not know definitively what happened to Mrs Leigh. She might have slipped that night.'

'Just because it was a bit slippery? Because it was dark? And she was in Hampstead. Another coincidence? What was she doing up there? Doing some shopping? Visiting a friend? Investigating a nest of Russian spies?'

'It is, unfortunately, our fate. Never to be able to see the whole picture.'

It seemed outrageous that Pamela had been asked to risk her life without even knowing what those risks were. But maybe he was right. That she might never know the truth. And she realised people like Ustinov and Putlitz were taking far greater risks than she was, and for a country not even theirs.

She walked home in the hope of clearing her head, until the rain became too ferocious and she was forced to hail a taxi. As they pulled up into the square and outside her front door, she saw the light was on in Francis's study. She suddenly remembered (with an internal groan) that she had to find a way of telling him about the weekend at Fort Belvedere. She went straight to the study, where she knew Francis would be poring over the evening news at his desk, before she had a chance to lose her nerve. Pamela knocked on the door frame and, without looking up, Francis gestured for her to enter.

'Fancy going to Fort Belvedere this weekend, darling?' she said, as lightly as she could manage.

Thinking about the possible fate of Mrs Leigh had made Pamela think twice about going to visit the King and Mrs Simpson alone. It made her think twice about doing *anything* alone.

Francis looked at her strangely. 'Where?'

'You know… the King's residence.'

Francis put his paper down and rubbed his eyes tiredly. Pamela sat on the chair across from his desk.

'What?'

'We've been invited, you see…'

'Invited by *whom*?'

'Oh… just… people.'

'What do you mean by "people"?' Francis peered at Pamela 'And why are you wet? Were you walking in the rain?'

Pamela looked down at herself and saw she was, indeed, soaking wet.

'Er, yes. I decided to walk home through the park and got caught out.'

Francis was looking at Pamela in the way she imagined she looked at Aunt Constance. She realised she hadn't taken off her sodden coat yet and killed a few moments of strained silence by fiddling with the coat, scarf, hat and umbrella. But Francis persisted.

'Pamela, has *the King* invited us to Fort Belvedere?' he asked, suspicious.

'No… Mrs Simpson has.'

Francis stared at Pamela incredulously so she barrelled on.

'Not that I'm friends with her, of course. But she seems to like me for some reason. I thought it might be… interesting.'

'Mrs Simpson?' Francis repeated.

'It isn't as if we're *bosom friends.*'

Francis said sternly, his arms crossed like a headmaster. 'I thought you found her an obnoxious Johnny-come-lately.'

'I do! But I am rather curious. About the situation, you know, with the King. And of course, none of the papers are able – or willing – to cover the story. *The Times* included. Especially since her divorce has become public.'

'Her *divorce?*' Francis said in surprise.

'Yes. And I think it's a jolly good idea to have first-hand knowledge of who the next queen might be.'

'Mrs Simpson isn't going to become queen. It's hardly possible. And it isn't as if he's going to marry her.'

Now it was Pamela's turn to cross her arms and raise an eyebrow. Francis cocked his head to the side.

'He isn't.' He paused. 'Is he?'

'That's what I'd like to find out.'

V

In the end, Pamela had gone alone to Fort Belvedere. Francis declined to join saying he had no interest in getting involved in the intrigue. At first, Pamela was nervous to go by herself, knowing what she knew about Mrs Leigh and the Russians. But once she arrived, she realised it was just a very strange weekend party. Drinks, dinner, music and card playing seemed to occur at random intervals, rather than according to any sort of plan. Almost as if they were all staying in a hotel.

Wallis kept a little notebook by her side at all times that (according to Jenny) the servants called her 'grumble book', noting the successes and defects of every gathering: who was present, who said what, what food pleased her, what didn't, who was on her blacklist. (Though from what Jenny heard, it sounded like the whole notebook was itself a blacklist.) Wallis carried it with her everywhere, perhaps a sign that she took herself quite seriously as the soon-to-be-mistress of the house.

Surprisingly enough, Wallis seemed relieved to see Pamela.

'Pamela, I am so glad you're here. I simply can't trust anyone anymore. Vipers, all of them. Just waiting in the bushes to attack me. I've had to move here to get away from London. My nerves are just shattered.'

'And how is His Majesty?' Pamela inquired politely.

'Oh him?' Wallis replied dismissively. 'He's fine. Happy as a clam to have me here.'

Pamela looked across the drawing room where a small group of people were scattered about, drinking a mixture of afternoon tea and early evening cocktails – which struck her as symbolic of the strange, disordered nature of the weekend itself. A pretence of informality within the context of the most formal kind of environment of all – a royal one. Which was not to say that the King lent any kind of air of occasion or ceremony by his presence. If anything, he seemed to have less authority than when Pamela had last encountered him at the German Embassy cooing outside the ladies'. Certainly, less than when he barked at her at Sibyl Colefax's garden party. He was wearing a shirt and V-necked jumper, looking somewhat like a little boy playing in his toy castle. He waved happily at Wallis but she pretended not to see him.

A maid carried a tray of sandwiches into the drawing room and Wallis snapped, 'You there! What's your name?'

The young woman turned around, startled. 'Harris, ma'am.'

'Harris, those sandwiches are for *later*. Why are they being brought in now?'

'For… afternoon tea, ma'am?' she said, as unsure as Pamela was about the protocol.

Wallis looked at the platter and sniffed. 'People don't need sandwiches *now*. We'll be having supper soon enough. Take them back to the kitchen, please.'

The poor girl slunk away, confused. Pamela had also heard from Jenny that the King had taken to sacking his staff to make up for the enormous amounts of money he was spending on Wallis's jewellery and wardrobe. No wonder the atmosphere in the house was tense – none of those frequenting it knew who would be next to get the chop.

Wallis took out her grumble book and made a note in it. 'Honestly. Just try to find anyone who can follow simple instructions. Do I have to do *everything* around here?'

The King approached them. Pamela bowed. Wallis did not.

'Your Royal Highness,' said Pamela.

He waved a hand at her, as if inconvenienced. 'Wally darling, why did you send the sandwiches away? I wanted one…'

Wallis simply gave him a stern look and the King bowed his head, like an admonished child. Or a pet.

'Why won't they listen to anything I say, David?'

'My darling, there has been rather a lot of upheaval. You do things very differently from what they're used to.'

Wallis crossed her arms and glowered. 'I thought that's what you wanted – to do things *differently*.'

Pamela spotted Tommy Lascelles, the King's Private Secretary, from across the room, looking as irritated as he had when she'd seen him last spring, but even more exhausted. He came over, carrying a stack of papers. He noticed Pamela and looked surprised.

'Lady Pamela. What a pleasure,' he said. And then to the King, 'Your Majesty, if I may, there are some papers that require your attention.'

Wallis glared at both of them.

'At this very moment?' asked the King. 'Really, Tommy, if isn't one thing, it is another. We are quite occupied with our guests at the moment.'

'Surely nothing is so urgent it can't wait,' Wallis told him with a challenging stare.

Tommy caught Pamela's eye and they exchanged a look.

'As you wish…' Tommy gave a small bow and retreated stiffly to another room.

To see such disarray and dereliction of duty was even more worrying than Pamela had expected; it was if the throne was in the charge of a resentful child. Wallis may have been the chief distraction from the King's royal obligations but it was clear as day that he felt there was little to tether him to them in the first place in the house of the soulless fairy king.

Later on, over cocktails, Princess Stephanie appeared and sat herself down next to Pamela. 'Isn't it romantic, to see the two lovebirds together?' she cooed.

'Mmmm,' Pamela murmured noncommittally. 'I hear she is in permanent residence here now.'

'Wallis and Ernest have started divorce proceedings so there is nothing to stand in their way. I am certain they will be married soon,' the Princess replied.

'Of course, it may be difficult to persuade the government, the church and the British public that Wallis and the King should be *allowed* to marry.'

Princess Stephanie waved Pamela away impatiently with a bejewelled hand that dazzled in the light. 'I have told Wallis that the... pardon me, I can never remember the strange English word. The marriage where she would not receive a title but could remain by his side.'

'The morganatic marriage.'

The Princess snapped her fingers. 'Precisely! Of course, our dear friend would prefer a title for herself, but she is willing to make sacrifices for her love. All that she wants is to be happy and be left in peace.'

Pamela looked across the room to the King, who had been looking at no one but Wallis all evening, who, in turn, had been doing little else besides snapping at servants and writing in her grumble book.

'In my personal opinion, I believe this would make good international relations, no?' continued the Princess.

Pamela looked back at her; her attentions now fully engaged. 'Oh?' She lifted her glass and assessed the Princess over its rim while taking a sip. 'In what way?'

The Princess lowered her voice. 'I am certain it will come as no surprise to you that Herr Hitler would be most pleased by the union.

He thinks it would be beneficial for your country to have a commoner as queen. That it will be welcomed by the people.'

Hitler clearly didn't know the British public half as well as he thought he did. Pamela suspected those opinions had been the by-product of Ambassador von Ribbentrop's relationship with Wallis. She looked at the King again and wondered if he knew anything at all about their acquaintance.

'You of course must understand how difficult it is to make a good marriage in the English aristocratic classes, no?' continued the Princess. 'As a woman of the world, like Wallis.'

Pamela turned to look at Princess Stephanie, feeling suddenly deeply uncomfortable.

'I'm sorry but I don't catch your drift.'

The Princess smiled. 'You are not so different, you two. Nor from myself either. We are… complex women. With, how do I say? *Histories.* Life is not always so easy for us, and society is not always kind.'

Pamela's stomach felt distinctly queasy. She sat very still and looked at the Princess, at her diamond earrings, her manicured hands, her exquisitely tailored gown. Was she hinting at what Pamela thought she was hinting at? She shuddered at the thought.

'But surely, life isn't always easy for any woman,' Pamela said as breezily as she could. 'And any woman older than, say, eighteen has *some* kind of history, doesn't she? Despite what our mothers would like to think,' she added with a forced laugh.

She turned back to her martini, took a sip and hoped the Princess would miraculously drop the subject. The Princess laughed quietly and put a hand on her arm. Pamela's heart began to race.

'Yes, but not all women are like us three.' (Pamela shivered at being implicated with the Princess and Wallis.) 'We have *lived* lives. Wallis has been married once before – to a man who dragged her across the world, who treated her cruelly. But she made something of those travels, she became wise. And as for me, I too have been married and divorced. And I have lived in the capital cities of Europe and known many men. I too became wiser for the experience.' Princess Stephanie smiled.

Pamela replied, 'But my little life is hardly as thrilling as all that. I've only been married once. And as damnably dull as it may sound, we're still married to each other.'

Princess Stephanie looked thoughtful. 'Your husband's family must have been very much relieved to have found a beautiful young woman for their son, especially one who had seen so much in the war. And perhaps were willing to look over the fact that she was a – can we say – wise woman too? You had been engaged previously, yes Lady Pamela? To another? Also a cruel man who deceived you?'

It was one thing to look into someone else's personal history; it was quite another to find they have been doing the same to you. The idea that the Princess had been digging into her background chilled Pamela to the bone. How long had this been going on? What else did she know? Was this the dossier on her that Putlitz had referred to on the Duke of Westminster's yacht?

'So, I think a woman like yourself would be in support of Mrs Simpson's cause. Would you not?' She paused, leaned in and looked at Pamela closely. 'Of course, that kind of support would be greatly appreciated by the Führer. And *valued*.'

Another English society lady drawn into the arms of the German Embassy. Or perhaps the Abwehr. Another feather in the Princess's cap. Did she really think Pamela would be made to feel some kind of affinity for her and Wallis by having her youthful indiscretions exposed at a weekend party? Or was she well aware that she was applying pressure on Pamela to collaborate by blackmailing her? After all, this was a woman working for those who had no compunction about murdering not only the ambassador in London but also the one in Paris.

For a moment, Pamela wondered if she should accept. If Charlie would expect her to accept. To become some kind of double agent, like Putlitz. Pamela shivered at the thought of having to live an even more complex, deceitful life than she already was, and having to report to someone like Princess Stephanie, or worse, von Ribbentrop. And then she wondered what could happen if she refused to accept. Would Princess Stephanie go so far as to expose her past and attempt to ruin her reputation if she refused? Of course, she wasn't half as well connected in London society as Pamela was, and there would surely be a good number of people who would find her dubious, if not entirely unpalatable. But even a whiff of gossip like that was like a smell that could threaten to become a stench, following Pamela around, perhaps for the rest of her life. And Francis's as well. Pamela felt ill just thinking about the damage it could cause to the two of them.

She looked around at the room, at the sycophants hanging on to every word of Wallis and the Fairy King, at the tired and frustrated Palace staff, like Tommy Lascelles. And there she saw the bleak future of the country: self-involved hangers-on with no regard for the good of the nation. She wouldn't be able to live with herself if she became complicit in that, simply to save her own skin.

And besides, it would only increase the element of danger for her. The image of Mrs Leigh lying in a coma in a hospital bed loomed large. Though Ustinov said there was no evidence that she had been attacked, that it hadn't been an accident, no one knew for certain.

Who's to say Mrs Leigh hadn't been found out? By the Germans she was attempting to infiltrate? Perhaps by someone exactly like Princess Stephanie.

The Princess was watching her, waiting for an answer. Pamela spun any number of half-baked excuses through her mind, wondering which to feed the Princess without risking losing her confidences or making her feel threatened.

And then she had a thought.

'I suppose you have had the same experience,' she said quietly. 'An outsider trying to make your way into society. Marrying into a title. As a *complex* woman with a history, as you say. And especially as a Jewish woman, I imagine that must have been even more difficult.'

Princess Stephanie's face fell. There was a stony-cold silence. 'That is of no consequence,' she replied finally.

'And it must be somewhat trying to maintain your position with regards to Herr Hitler's society with such a background. I suppose it poses somewhat of a moral dilemma for you. To climb the Nazi social ladder when you find yourself stepping on others – those whose lives are, in fact, in jeopardy.'

The seconds ticked by as they sat without speaking, the party carrying on around them. Then the Princess looked up and rose from her chair.

'You will have to excuse me.'

And then she left the room.

Pamela wondered for a moment if she had made a miscalculation. But then she thought about David Stern's cousin Lotte who fled Berlin and his other relatives still in Germany. If she had ruined her chances as a Nazi spy, so be it.

After dinner, Pamela was already feeling a sense of exhaustion and decided to take a walk while everyone else was playing cards and listening to the gramophone. She looked around at the recently renovated Fort Belvedere and thought of poor Thelma Furness, who put all the work into it only to be jettisoned for Wallis. It was distinct from other royal residences with its gleaming new bathrooms and modern touches of mirror and chrome. It had been practically a ruin when the King took possession of it during his father's reign. And even after King George died, the toy castle given to the Fairy King remained his favoured residence, over all others. A hideaway, far from the demands of the Palace and Westminster.

As she passed a small sitting room, Pamela heard low voices. She paused momentarily to see who it was. And lo and behold, it was Wallis and the King.

'I don't understand why you need *anyone's* permission to marry. You're the King of England, why can't you do what you like?'

Pamela lingered in the shadows, just out of sight.

Wallis was sitting in a chair and the King was kneeling on the floor, at her feet.

'My darling Wallie, you know how it is. Please don't make me sad.'

'We'll be nobodies. Do you understand that? And your family will look down on us. That is, if they ever acknowledge us again, which I doubt. Is that what you want? Is it?'

'But I want *you,* my darling. I couldn't give a damn about the throne.'

Wallis slapped the King's hand and he recoiled.

'I've given up everything for you. *Everything*. Do you understand?' Wallis retorted.

The King laid his head in Wallis's lap. 'But now you have *me.*'

He suddenly cried out softly, as if in pain. Pamela squinted and saw Wallis was pinching his ear.

'Maybe I *should* go away. It seems that's all there's left to do.'

The King looked up in horror, apparently distracted from the pain. 'Wallie, you wouldn't.'

'And after some time, my name will be forgotten and it will all blow over.'

He clasped her hands in terror and she looked away.

Pamela then felt someone behind her and saw a footman approaching. She spun around. 'You couldn't tell me where the telephone is, could you?'

Feeling disoriented and unsettled, Pamela retrieved her coat and went outside to take a turn around the gardens. Despite the winter cold that had settled on the countryside, she felt a sense of relief in the dark, empty grounds. She spied a tower and decided it might be a good place to get some air, clear her head and think. However, when she reached the top, she was surprised to find someone already there. It was Tommy Lascelles smoking a cigarette and staring blankly into the distance.

'My apologies, I didn't realise anyone was up here,' she said. 'Am I interrupting?'

'No, no. Not at all. Have you come with Sir Francis? I haven't seen him this evening.'

Pamela felt a twinge of discomfort. 'Sadly, he is indisposed this weekend.'

'I can't imagine he'd much care for this crowd.' Tommy looked at her closely for the first time, suddenly concerned. 'You aren't here for *The Times*, are you? Because we do have an agreement with Geoffrey Dawson. I know it can't hold much longer but—'

'Oh no, Sir Alan. We are all well aware of the... delicate circumstances.'

Tommy leaned against the parapet and took a drink. 'The whole thing will be called into question if that woman doesn't go abroad immediately – the Crown, the government…'

'Is it as bad as all that?'

'Worse, probably,' Tommy said, looking out in the direction of Windsor Castle. 'As if he wasn't bad enough on his own… calling us day and night with ideas, no routine, keeping all his staff on hand every waking hour yet no loyalty to any of us and paying little attention to his briefings. And now, he thinks of nothing but *her*. He does hardly any work at all and assumes everyone else will do everything for him.'

They were both silent a moment. Pamela lit a cigarette and pulled her fur closer to her neck to brace against the wind.

'What a view,' she said. 'I've heard you can see seven counties from here. What was this place, do you know?'

'It was a folly, just a summer house. But the ruins, which you can see just over there,' Tommy said, pointing, 'are from an ancient temple in Leptis, as it was called, near Tripoli. A prominent city of the Roman Empire before the Berbers invaded and sacked it. And then the Vandals. And then the Arabs. Before it was abandoned altogether and lost in the sands of the desert.'

'That's rather depressing.'

Tommy grunted in agreement as he finished his cigarette and threw it over the parapet.

'Anyone who's read anything about history will tell you that all empires fall eventually. And the greatest ones leave the most destruction in their wake.'

December 1936

I

The Fleet Street blackout regarding Wallis and the King had been broken. A week before, the Bishop of Bradford (a man no one had ever heard of) made a speech stressing the King's need for 'god's grace', admonishing him to go to church before his coronation. Strangely, the Bishop claimed to have had no idea of the royal affair and was simply dismayed that the church was gaining a dissolute, irreligious figurehead. (Though many suspected he was covertly chastising the King for the affair with Wallis.) And suddenly every paper in the country decided that the gloves were off. The Hoover Dam had broken. The press was ablaze.

Chairing another weekly meeting at the paper, Dawson looked grave, the dark circles under his eyes betraying his exhaustion. He peered around the table.

'I know there has been talk of censorship and collusion with the Palace and the Government. And I admit, the Prime Minister has probably seen a great deal more of me these last few months than any other journalist, but that was due rather to an old friendship than to the slightest desire to influence me.'

Everyone looked at each other, eyebrows raised, muttering and mumbling. Pamela was sitting between Percy and Jo, who turned to Pamela with her usual sceptical look.

'The nearest approach to interference from high quarters was probably the customary request from Buckingham Palace that the Sovereign's privacy should be respected by the press during his annual holiday abroad. Something by which we would and always have abided, no matter the monarch. And in the wake of such a monumental event, we will be critical insofar as to estimate the defects of character which have led to this crisis, but we must also give full weight to King Edward's good qualities.'

On this note, the silence was starting to break and snickering was heard throughout the room. Dawson looked around angrily.

'May I remind you, we are, indeed, in a crisis, and this is *not* a laughing matter.'

Percy turned and whispered to Pamela, 'What's got into her bonnet?'

Dawson carried on, a little louder this time. 'As never before, the British Monarchy has a duty to stand as a rock to the world outside amid the seething tides of Communism and Dictatorship. And the public need some definite reassurance if the rock is not to be shaken.'

'What does he want us to do? Lie to our readers?' Pamela whispered to Jo.

'I think you mean *continue* to lie,' Jo replied.

'However, despite all of this,' Dawson sighed, 'the rumours that the King will leave the throne if he isn't allowed to marry Mrs Simpson are growing stronger by the day. People may protest if he steps down, and they may protest if he does not step down. We can only hope that we do not have a revolution on our hands. None of us may play judge to this extraordinarily complex situation, of the incalculable human emotions which are jeopardising the very fabric of these historic institutions. It is well to remember that the King has comported himself with great dignity throughout this sorry business.'

A number of images ran through Pamela's head. The King leaving official papers lying around. Telling off his private secretary in public, and refusing to do any work at all. On his hands and knees, painting Wallis's toenails. With his head in her lap. Loitering outside the ladies' room at the German Embassy.

Great dignity indeed.

'Our King has shown himself brave, completely free from pompousness, chivalrous, conscientious in his everyday public duties and genuinely interested in the condition of the poor. In fairness, none of us can realise how hard is the path of a king in choosing close friends.'

As Pamela looked around the room, she saw that nearly everyone looked annoyed. There was whispering, the rolling of eyes, crossing of arms, some tittering. She wondered what Gertrude Leigh would say. And what Virginia Dalkeith would do.

'King Edward has most of the qualities that would have made a great constitutional monarch. This is not a romance, but a drama of the deepest tragedy.'

Pamela found she could no longer restrain herself.

'I think it's absurd that we have had to lie, to compromise our journalistic integrity, to protect that silly little man and that dreadful woman,' she stated.

Percy looked at her, aghast. Dawson stared at her from across the table, open-mouthed.

'I'm sorry that we've all gone to such trouble to shield them from public judgement because, in fact, it's been a waste of time. Just look at where we've ended up. Speak to anyone working in the Palace and you'll learn about the real character of our king. That he couldn't give a toss about his duties, his people or the… what did you call it? Fabric of these historic institutions? And it isn't as if he's tried very hard to keep his private life private, as if he's carried on with Wallis Simpson in complete secret. It is as if he's been daring us all to say something, to judge him for his selfishness, knowing that marrying her would be impossible and would force a constitutional crisis.'

Pamela found herself standing up. Percy desperately tugged at her sleeve.

Jo whispered, 'Go on, girl.'

'On top of everything, the man is continually sticking his nose into politics, where the monarchy is meant to be neutral. And what kind of politics? It is no secret that our king is a great supporter of the Nazi Party. He seems to think that Oswald Mosley would make a first-rate PM and that, in fact, we might want a dictator of our own one day. And that is the tip of the iceberg where Germany is concerned, which is the true crisis we have been facing. Not the King and Mrs Simpson. Hitler. If the King does decide to abdicate, I say so be it.'

Everyone in the room was staring at Pamela.

'Just because you wrote one piece on Mrs Simpson's wardrobe doesn't mean you have any kind of political understanding. We've no need of your amateur opinions here. Why don't you go back to hats and gowns, Pamela?' retorted Dawson angrily.

Everyone looked at him and then turned back to look at Pamela. She drew herself up to her full height and stared down the table at the editor-in-chief. Percy covered his face with his hands in horror.

'You may think I'm an *amateur*, but my opinions are formed from evidence that I have seen before my very eyes, and I'm not afraid to voice them,' she proclaimed. 'I've met our king on a number of occasions and I think he is a careless, selfish, silly little man who's going to get us all into trouble with that other silly little man in Germany. And I know you think Hitler is quite an A-OK chap, but he is killing people. And he is inspiring quite a bit of violence in our own country. Can we really turn a blind eye to what the BUF did in East London? I know no one wants another war but we might have another war – whether we like it or not – when we find Hitler on our doorstep. After leading our nice, quiet, blinkered lives.'

Dawson was purple in the face. There was a good deal of commotion and whispering as Pamela put on her hat and coat and tried to make an exit as gracefully as possible. She felt both indescribably relieved, but also rather worried. It was almost certain she would be sacked after such an outburst. She would miss the paper a good deal – and she wondered if she had somehow jeopardised her mission, no longer having a cover.

Francis was up north playing golf with his brother and Pamela couldn't bear to return to an empty house in a mood like that. So, she decided to do something she had never done before in her life.

She went to a pub.

Pamela chose an average, nondescript place around the corner from Printing House Square. As she entered, she looked around at the clientele, a decidedly ordinary bunch of Londoners. Some Fleet Street newspapermen, a couple of girls out early from the typing pool, some old men playing darts, a rather scruffy-looking gentleman with a terrier. Pamela hung up her coat, went to the bar and ordered a whisky from the barmaid, a stout woman of older middle-age with vibrant dyed red hair.

'You all right, love?' asked the barmaid. 'You look a bit peaky.'

Pamela, who had been gazing into the distance, caught her reflection in the mirror above the bar and saw that in fact, she did look peaky. She was also a mess, with her thick, wavy brown hair threatening to escape its confines. She tucked an unruly strand behind her ear and looked up at the barmaid, who was looking at her, concerned.

'To be perfectly frank, I think I've got myself into trouble.'

Although she had just poured Pamela's whisky, the barmaid unscrewed the cap on the bottle and poured her another serving. She then looked Pamela up and down.

'Does the father know?'

Pamela's eyes blinked open in surprise. 'Does the father...? Oh!' she exclaimed, embarrassed. 'No, no, not that sort of trouble.'

'Well, thank Christ for that!' exclaimed the barmaid. 'Something to drink to, I should say.'

'I should say so too,' Pamela replied.

The barmaid poured herself a whisky too (albeit a much smaller one) and toasted Pamela. Then she reached across the bar to shake her hand and said, 'Mabel. Pleased to make your acquaintance.'

Pamela placed her handbag on the bar, took a seat, shook Mabel's hand and said, 'Pamela. A pleasure.'

'So, what's the trouble, then?' asked Mabel.

Pamela thought for a moment, wondering if she should keep shtum and respect the blackout that was still, technically, in effect. And then she realised that since she was unlikely to still be an employee of the paper anymore, and the news was about to break anyway, there was no need to respect anything. So, she told Mabel the whole story of Wallis and the King (minus Charlie and MI5).

'Good on you! Speaking your mind, not letting some old windbag who's up himself tell you what to do. Not often you get a chance to stick it to gents like that.'

Pamela felt herself agreeing with Mabel but also privately worrying what the fallout from the confrontation would be, and if she should have held her tongue instead of giving in to her hot-headedness. It wasn't often a woman – any woman – spoke like that at the paper. Or ever, really. She knew Dawson would be feeling angry. Could he expose her somehow?

'That Mrs Simpson sounds like a right piece of work. And, let me tell you, I wouldn't give tuppence for *him*! Very handsome of course – like a film star – but any woman with eyes can see he's a bounder. When his father King George died and he came to the throne I said to myself, "Mabel, this one's trouble". A King should be married, not gadding about with Americans. And why isn't he married already? Why isn't he settled, with children? Because he's a bounder! I don't know anything about that Mrs Simpson but she'll learn sooner or later what she's landed herself in. Every woman knows you can't change a man.'

While Mabel regaled Pamela with stories of a dizzying number of beaux and husbands, Pamela thought about the men she herself had known. Her father, a quiet but sensible gentleman of few opinions who always deferred to his wife. Her brother William, an intelligent, handsome and strong-willed young man who was becoming a hazier and hazier memory with each passing year. Bunny, a charming but deeply manipulative and selfish man, bent on self-destruction. Francis, principled but withdrawn, scarred by the war, he had always seemed so mild but had, as Pamela was only now realising, hidden depths. And Charlie. A quiet librarian with a mysterious past who kept mints in his glovebox and rugs in his boot. Who had been married at one point in his life but showed no evidence of a current, existing romance. A strange man with a strange allure.

A couple hours (and a few stiff drinks) later, Pamela began to walk west down Fleet Street, heading towards home, hoping to clear her head, or at least allow the cold December air to cut through the fog of whisky. It was late enough that she had missed the crush of bankers, clerks, secretaries, salespeople, market hawkers and others who worked in the densely packed square mile. She passed the Royal Courts of Justice, exiting the darkening City and entering the bright lights of the West End; the shops and office buildings had closed but revellers ate and drank inside the pubs and restaurants that lined the Strand. The streets seemed strangely quiet to Pamela until she remembered that the theatres whose marquees illuminated that central London artery hadn't yet released their audiences into the evening.

And then she got the creeping sensation that she was being followed. If it had been an hour earlier or later, when the crowds of drinkers, diners and theatre-goers filled the streets, she might never have detected the shadow and the footsteps that had begun to dog her. A year ago, she wouldn't have noticed anything at all, but her experiences over the past few months had taught her enough to know when she was being tailed. Pamela began to think about Fritz Hesse, Princess Stephanie, Soviet spies, even people working for Buckingham Palace. It could have been anyone who had begun to find Pamela a thorn in their side, someone to be watched closely. Was this what had happened to Mrs Leigh? She had proved inconvenient so someone pushed her in front of a train under the cover of darkness? Pamela's heart began to pound. Every face she passed in the darkness had the potential of menace and danger. The footsteps behind her grew louder. How could she have been so stupid? Walking home alone, in the dark. She had made herself incredibly vulnerable and now there was someone following her. In order to harm her. Kidnap her.

Eliminate her.

Pamela looked around desperately for a taxi. Fortunately, she saw one immediately and hailed it. She felt a moment of relief when she climbed in, knowing she was leaving whoever had been following her behind. But then she got the sensation that the taxi driver was looking at her. She kept catching his eye in the rear-view mirror. Was she finally safe? Or was it possible he was working for whomever had been following her? She tried to get a glance at him to see… what exactly? If he had a shifty or menacing look? If he was signalling to someone outside?

Pamela sighed and sank back into the seat. She pulled her coat tightly around her and wondered if her mind had been playing tricks on her. If she was simply being paranoid. If all the things weighing on her, combined with the drinks she'd had, had conspired to make her see and hear things that weren't there.

As they drove west, they passed Trafalgar Square, St James Park and Buckingham Palace. Pamela gazed out the window at the pillared fortress, encircled by its high fences and soldiers. She wondered if the British people would ever know the truth about Wallis and the King, or if their secrets would forever be as tightly guarded as the Palace itself.

As the taxi let her out in front of her Belgrave house, Pamela found herself hurrying towards her front door feeling somewhat exposed in the dark, deserted square. As she reached out for the door handle, she felt a hand on her arm. She let out a shriek.

To her great surprise, it was Charlie.

'What… what are you doing here?'

She felt confused. Had Charlie been the one following her? Surely, by now she had the trust of MI5. Or did she? Did they still feel the need to tail her at every turn? After all, Charlie had been shadowing her at the German Embassy. Pamela felt confused and found herself wishing she hadn't had quite so much to drink.

From under the brim of his bowler, Charlie looked around, surveying the area. 'I think we've lost him.'

'Lost who?'

'You were being tailed. I tried to follow him as closely as I could without being seen, but he's disappeared.'

So, she *had* been followed. Pamela's heart began to pound again. The exhausted calm that had descended on her in the taxi evaporated.

'Oh my god…'

'Try to calm yourself.'

'Did you see who it was?'

'No, it was difficult to—'

'Was it Hesse? Or do you think it was a Soviet?'

'Lady Pamela—'

'Am I in danger?' she cried. 'I don't want to end up like Gertrude Leigh!'

Charlie clapped a hand over her mouth.

'Pamela, take a deep breath. Over-exerting yourself won't help anything.' Charlie took his hand off her mouth. 'Now, I need you to act as if everything is perfectly normal before anyone at home sees you.'

'There's no one… Francis is away, it's Cook's night off and Jenny has likely gone to bed,' she replied, feeling the pounding in her chest start to slow.

Pamela struggled slightly to unlock the front door, feeling both intoxicated and terribly unnerved. She tried to remind herself that she was safe now that Charlie was here. And, of course, that she didn't want him to see her lose her wits completely. After all, she had come this far without seeming like a hysterical woman.

She led him into the library, poured both of them a brandy and closed the door. As they sat next to each other on the sofa, Pamela found her hand was shaking.

'I don't know that I'm cut out for all of this anymore,' she said. 'Being followed, alone at night. Risking my life. Never knowing when or if I'm really safe. Do you think it was the Germans? Have I made an enemy of them? Or the Russians? Maybe some kind of revenge for trying to help one of their people?'

'I don't know who was following you – it was dark and I couldn't get a good look without getting too close to be seen. Try not to worry.'

'Try not to worry? Try not to worry! Don't worry about men following you, perhaps intent on abducting or murdering you?'

'Lady Pamela—'

'Don't "Lady Pamela" me!' Pamela was suddenly angry at Charlie. 'I know what happened to Mrs Leigh. I know I was brought in to replace her. And no one told me what had happened. *You* didn't tell me. That *I* could be the next victim. That *my* life would be in danger. What if *I* was pushed into an oncoming train or bus or car?'

For once, Charlie looked caught off-guard. 'We don't know what happened to her. It could have been an accident.'

'And I'm the Sultan of Constantinople! If I had known, if I had known the risks, about her... I would have been more careful. I was stupid, really, letting my guard down, getting drunk, alone in a pub. And after what I'd done!'

'What did you do?'

'I was an absolute fool in the meeting at the paper! I told Geoffrey Dawson exactly what I thought of him and his editorials and how he's been protecting Wallis and the King. I can't believe the things I said.'

'Not entirely the plan, was it?' replied Charlie, as he took a sip of his brandy.

'I couldn't help myself! How should I call myself a journalist if I can't report anything that's actually going on in the world? Are royals above the rest of us? Can they simply do what they like, without consequences?'

'There are a great number of people in the world who are able to act with impunity, who will never face consequences. Royals, politicians, those with a great deal of money,' Charlie replied, looking around the well-appointed library.

For a moment, Pamela felt chagrined. 'Perhaps I'm one of those people? Just another wealthy aristocrat with nothing to risk and no consequences to face.'

'Well, I can't imagine there won't be consequences where Dawson is concerned,' Charlie replied with a smile.

'No, I suppose I'll get the sack. I can't imagine he'll allow Percy to keep me after my little demonstration.'

Charlie hesitated, looking up at the ceiling for a moment, as if he was holding something back.

'What is it?' asked Pamela, fearing some kind of reprimand was forthcoming.

Loosening his tie slightly, he looked back at her and said, 'I don't necessarily blame you, for what you did. I can imagine it was deserved. You stood up for the truth. You tilted at the windmills of powerful men with complex and vested interests, like Geoffrey Dawson, and like his overlord Astor, and many others like him – Beaverbrook, and so forth. But if no one did, where would we be? What kind of country would we be living in? I probably shouldn't be encouraging you… but it was rather a brave thing to do.'

Pamela blushed and looked down. To her surprise, she realised she was still wearing her fur coat. She put her drink down, awkwardly wrestled her way out of it and threw it on a chair.

'I'm sorry, I... well, I've had a bit to drink already, as I'm sure you can see,' she said.

Charlie shrugged. 'It sounds like you've had a time of it today.'

Pamela walked over to the gramophone and looked through the records. 'Do you like jazz?' she asked Charlie.

'I'm more of a classical aficionado, myself. I used to play the piano,' he replied.

Another piece to the puzzle, and yet it told her nothing of him or who he was. Pamela looked over at Charlie in his sombre, dark grey three-piece suit. A lock of hair had fallen over his forehead and he pushed it back.

'What now? Now that I'll no longer have a useful cover story, no more "Agent of Influence", no more *Times* columnist,' Pamela said sadly, holding a record in her hand.

Charlie crossed one leg over the other and thought for a moment. 'It's difficult to say. You see, the reason why I wanted to find you in the first place, the reason why I wanted to intercept you – before you began to be followed – was that I wanted to convey a message of thanks, from those above me. In addition to the flurry of press attention, your information about Wallis being in league with von Ribbentrop and Princess Stephanie has ultimately helped tip the scales in favour of the government rejecting any proposal from the King to marry her and remain on the throne.'

'And now... what? What happens next?'

'It means that the King will likely abdicate, leaving his brother the Duke of York to reign.'

'A stable family man with no apparent penchant for yachting, American divorcées or fascists,' Pamela quipped.

'One hopes.'

'So… the plan worked? He abdicated for her?'

'Yes, as far as we know, it's been a success. *You* have been a success, Lady Pamela,' said Charlie as he toasted her with his brandy glass.

'So, I haven't been a complete disaster, as it were?'

'You may have made some enemies, at least at *The Times*, but you've certainly proven your mettle where your mission is concerned.'

For some reason, Pamela felt herself begin to cry. She quickly turned around and busied herself with the gramophone. She put on a record and then wiped her eyes.

'Bizet's *Carmen*?' asked Charlie. 'Another femme fatale? Is this in honour of Mrs Simpson?'

Pamela tried to laugh but found she was crying. Charlie stood up from the sofa and walked over to her.

'That was a terrible joke, but there's no need to cry,' he said softly.

'It's just that… I feel as if I've been spending my life living as someone else. What I mean is, I feel like I've discovered that I'm a stranger to myself. Well, that's not exactly what I mean. I just feel… maybe I don't really know myself, or perhaps I do better now than I ever did and all the things that seemed important, what made me happy, or what I thought made me happy, none of them seem to matter now. And I don't know if it's because I agreed to this blasted mission, or if it was all going to fall apart regardless, if it was just a matter of time.' Pamela paused for breath. 'I'm sorry. I don't know what's come over me.'

'You are a remarkable woman,' said Charlie, standing very near to her.

'Though I suppose that doesn't matter. Because now it's all finished. Everything is finished. You've no more need for me. And I've lost my column. And I'll simply have to return to my old life. So, it doesn't matter if I'm remarkable or not.' Pamela turned to him and found herself holding onto the lapel of his jacket, crushing it under the grip of her sweaty fist. Then she released it and smoothed the fabric. 'Sorry, I'm sorry.'

As Carmen began her aria to the toreadors, Pamela began to turn away. But Charlie looked into her eyes and put a hand on her cheek. And then they kissed, tentatively at first, then with intensity. And it suddenly seemed like they were the only people in the world, protecting the country against the forces of evil. Or at least the only people kissing in a library while listening to Carmen.

As she continued to kiss Charlie and he continued to kiss her, as they undressed each other, Pamela's mind swam in a sea of whisky and brandy. She kept thinking: Was Charlie the matador and she the bull? Or he the bull and she the matador? Or perhaps Pamela was the bull and the matador and Carmen all at once.

As she climbed on top of him on the sofa, she thought: Olé.

II

Waking up next to Charlie the following morning, Pamela didn't feel half as sorry as she should have.

Pamela and Francis had always been quite fond of each other. And he was as solid as a rock – as much as any man she knew; as much as any man could be. But they were rather different people, which seemed to matter a great deal more now than it did when she was younger. In her youth, Pamela had just assumed that men and women were so vastly different that any man she would marry would naturally be completely unlike her. But at least Francis was kind, understanding of her whims and her need for independence, who seemed contented to allow her to live her life as she liked, more or less. Even as a younger woman, Pamela had been no fool. She had seen other marriages fail due to the ways in which the lives of her friends had become constricted and constrained by the dictates of their husbands and their husbands' families. But over time, Pamela and Francis's lives had become more and more separate; there seemed to be less and less that they shared as a couple. And then, of course, there was the issue of the children Francis so dearly wanted, which seemed to be cutting between them like a knife.

Pamela had had a good number of admirers in her first two seasons as a deb; there had always someone to dance with or to take her motoring. There were, of course, people who thought she was a bit fast, but she had a jolly good time, nonetheless – and being ladylike was never very much fun. And then she met Bunny Russell-Jones who said a number of things to make her forget herself entirely. Pamela knew it had been silly of her not to have been more careful. Tongues wagged, as they always did. Alma had feared her daughter's reputation would be damaged beyond repair when Bunny inexplicably called off the engagement. (Alma didn't know the reason for certain and didn't want to ask.) Pamela's mother had feared she would never be married and would, instead, end up like her sister Constance, rejected from society and living the life of a spinster in a far-off country.

Pamela and Francis had been seated next to one another at a dinner party five years before. There were whispers that he'd had a 'bad war'. An injury, a long time spent convalescing in a hospital somewhere, shattered nerves that never fully repaired. A broken engagement with a woman he had loved greatly followed. And then a broken heart.

Francis had been rather quiet most of the evening, and Pamela had had a devil of a time getting him to participate in conversation with her. At first, she had thought Francis had been invited to make up the numbers but then she realised that he had been invited for her. Or perhaps she for him. As she looked at his face in the candlelight of the dinner party, she remembered thinking Francis had been lucky – he could have been one of those poor fellows who returned from France or Belgium blind from mustard gas or with half his face missing.

They had both been long in the tooth when they became engaged – Francis especially. There hadn't been fireworks, like in the novels. But, as Pamela often reminded herself, novels aren't real life, are they? And while he was older than most of Pamela's friends and her friends' husbands – more serious, far less enthusiastic about staying out all hours drinking and dancing – he carried a kind of quiet conviction that was often so lacking in others of her generation.

Francis didn't know about Pamela's condition. No one knew, except Doctor Merriweather. He had been kind enough to keep the little operation a secret from her mother. But then again, he had made rather a hash of things. He had said it hadn't gone the way he'd planned. There had been unfortunate complications.

As a result, Pamela could never have children. But she tried not to think about it. It was easier that way.

III

The King had abdicated. (Long live the King.) He finally accepted that neither the government nor the church would allow him to marry Wallis – since divorced people could not marry if the previous spouse was still living.

Pamela found herself having to feign surprise as she and Francis listened to the abdication on the wireless in the sitting room, with Jenny and Cook hovering in the doorway. She had nearly forgotten that the general public had little idea of what was transpiring underneath their noses until it was all over. People were bewildered. Why was the King stepping down? Who was Wallis Simpson? What the devil was going on? Pamela couldn't help but think how unfair it was that something so monumental could have happened with the British people in the dark about it the whole time.

Wallis had fled to France, and the paparazzi had given chase. It was rumoured that her bodyguards worried she might flit off to Germany in the dead of night. The Duke of York was reported to have sobbed when he heard of his brother's decision.

The only supporters left of the love affair was a strange combination of Oswald Mosley, various Communist MPs and Winston Churchill. David Lloyd George had also been in favour, but was indisposed (on holiday in Jamaica with his mistress). And, of course, the German Embassy; von Ribbentrop was furious. He believed that the government opposition to the marriage was symbolic of their opposition to Hitler, but also that the abdication itself was the product of nefarious Bolshevist machinations.

Noël Coward (who had been snubbed by the King since he played for him at Sibyl Colefax's party) said that statues of Wallis should be erected around the country as gestures of thanks from a grateful nation.

'Well, I'll be damned,' said Francis, puffing away on his pipe.

'I don't understand. Who is she, anyway?' said Cook. 'Who's ever heard of Mrs Wallis Simpson?'

Jenny and Pamela tried not to look at one another.

'I take it this was the upshot of the weekend at Fort Belvedere… ?' Francis asked Pamela with a raised eyebrow.

For a moment, Pamela wondered if he suspected her involvement in the whole thing.

'Yes, well, I suppose so,' Pamela replied vaguely.

'What's she like, ma'am? If you don't mind my asking,' said Cook.

'Oh… well, unremarkable, really. American. Good taste in clothing. Very petite,' she said.

'I don't understand it. With all those princesses and society ladies he could have married, and he gives up the throne for an American!'

'Obstinate man… ' Francis muttered to himself as he knocked his pipe into the grate. 'I suppose we can count ourselves lucky that the government is still standing. The whole thing could have been a good deal worse.' He paused. 'Back when he was serving in the Guards during the war, he said, "What does it matter if I am killed? I have four brothers".'

Cook looked alarmed. 'Heavens…'

'He never wanted the crown in the first place.'

IV

A Christmas carol had been making the rounds:

'Hark! The herald angels sing,
Mrs Simpson's pinched our King!'

January 1937

I

Pamela was, indeed, sacked from *The Times* and Percy was treating her as persona non grata. She had to admit to Francis what had happened, who was surprisingly sanguine about the whole episode. Even a little bit pleased.

'Sometimes we have to make sacrifices for our principles,' he had said cryptically. 'I imagine I would have done the same thing in your position.'

Pamela had been expecting him to be grateful that she had been relieved of her duties at the paper, that she'd now be able to spend more time with him, perhaps even be goaded into more discussions about starting a family. But Francis encouraged her to seek out other opportunities at other papers and magazines. It surprised her. Then she remembered the secret committee he was on and wondered if they were continuing to meet behind the backs of their whips and party leaders. If so, their agenda was likely at odds with Dawson's editorial policy and likely took up a good deal of his time.

'Don't you have a friend working for some glossy fashion outfit in New York? Perhaps she has some pull somewhere,' he said.

Diana Vreeland. Why hadn't she thought of it herself? Although Pamela wrote to her to tell her what had happened (a simplified, expurgated version), she felt somewhat wary at making an attempt to enter back into the journalistic fray, to be at the mercy of the political and personal leanings of yet another editor-in-chief. But then again, she wasn't going to have to labour under the added burden of using her writing as a front for an intelligence operation.

Pamela had thought it would be a relief to be free of the pressures of working for MI5. Writing secret notes and having secret meetings. Constantly having to lie and hide things. Finding ways of cajoling her targets into giving her information. Pretending to fawn all over people she found loathsome. Acting as if she knew what she was doing when she was mostly improvising. Worrying about being watched or followed. Wondering if someone was going to shove her off a train platform.

And while life now was certainly less exhausting, it was also less exciting. It was quite thrilling, feeling as if the fate of the monarchy was resting on one's shoulders. Infiltrating grand parties and spying on prominent guests. Running from Nazis through the streets of London.

As she had heard nothing further from Charlie after their assignation, she was forced to conclude that sadly, her involvement with MI5 was over. Her mission had been successfully accomplished: the King had abdicated and was currently making plans for his future life in France with Wallis. Pamela couldn't help but wonder if what she had done – a tryst with her handler – was a black mark on her record. Everything had ended so abruptly. In the morning, Charlie had left, kissed her goodbye and said that someone would be in touch for a debriefing at some point. But there had been no debriefing.

Was that it? Without so much as a by your leave? Or even a thank you. After all that. She had been good. Better than good. Pamela knew she had been excellent, whether they told her or not. They had asked her to gather information that would help unseat the King of England, and she had done it. Surely, anyone would consider that a success. Especially by a woman such as herself, with no background or training. Who hadn't even wanted to be involved in the first place. She couldn't help but wonder how they would have treated her if she had been a man.

In the end, Pamela was no longer a journalist, and no longer a secret agent. It felt strange and uncomfortable, knowing so many things when most others were in the dark. Knowing she would never be able to reveal the secrets she kept. Except, of course, to the only two people who already knew: Jenny and Aunt Constance.

Pamela couldn't tell if Jenny was more dejected at the prospect of the end of their involvement with *The Times* or with the end of the intelligence mission.

'Oh, I am sorry,' Jenny had said. 'What will you do now?'

Pamela had simply shrugged. 'Well, something will come along. And if I find another opportunity – journalistic I mean – would you be interested in continuing to help me?'

Jenny smiled. 'I've had another piece published in that paper I've been writing for. It's not much, but it's a start.'

Aunt Constance was outraged.

'This is an outrage!' she cried. 'How dare Geoffrey Dawson try to silence you in such a fashion? Well, don't give up, my dear girl. You have a sharp mind and it mustn't be wasted on dinner parties and nightclubs.'

Diana Vreeland had written back, patently unsurprised at the turn of events.

That's the British press for you! Corrupt to the core. I'll have a nose around and see what I can do. Of course, there's always a place for you here at the Bazaar, *if you ever fancy upping sticks and coming to the Big Apple. You simply haven't lived until you've lived in New York.*

For a brief moment, Pamela wondered what would happen if she did just that – move to America and install herself in its fashion capital. Get to know the metropolitan set. Live in a skyscraper. After all, a part of her felt as if her life in London was finished. And she felt so changed she didn't quite know what to do with herself anymore. Of course, besides Diana and a handful of other acquaintances, she didn't know anyone in America. And she would be leaving behind all her friends and family in Britain. And what of Francis? He certainly would never cross an ocean with her to begin a new life. It was as if everything was possible and yet nothing was.

One thing had stuck with Pamela, lodged in the back of her mind like a dull but persistent throbbing: Boris Nikolaevich Puchkov. She was still hoping against hope that he would turn up somewhere having gone into hiding for his own safety. And Pamela knew she couldn't rest until she had discovered what had happened, so, not knowing what else to do, she made contact with Ustinov for the final time.

'I am sorry to be the bearer of tragic news – I hadn't wanted to tell you. But Comrade Puchkov's body was recently found in the Thames. A gunshot wound in the back of the head, his hands tied behind his back. The kind of assassination the NKVD is known for. You must not blame yourself.'

But, of course, Pamela did blame herself. After feeling so smug about the abdication, she felt terrible about Boris. If she had refused to facilitate his defection, would he still be alive? Or would he have been forced to go back to Moscow and been executed anyway? And what had happened to his wife and children in London? She felt almost duty-bound to try to figure out who was responsible. Was it really some shadowy Soviet assassin? Or had someone closer to home been to blame? Could Boris have been murdered right under her nose? Was it Putlitz? That didn't make sense. A German posing as a Nazi diplomat, working undercover for the British. Why would he murder a Russian defector?

Or was it Ustinov? He was, after all, a mysterious figure, with origins and motivations even more obscure than Putlitz's. A supposed freelance journalist working for British intelligence, with a mixed German and Russian background who, for no discernible reason, goes to great lengths to help a young Soviet diplomat pass sensitive information to the British government. How had he even known Boris to begin with? And who was to say he wasn't doing exactly what Putlitz was? Working for two masters at once – both the British and the Soviets? It seemed fantastical but what other answer was there?

II

'I know it's not much, but it's very good for developing pictures,' said Johnny, by way of apology.

Pamela looked around at the small, spare basement flat in Chelsea. The walls were covered in photos by famous photographers. There was little else besides a table, two chairs, a bed and a shabby sofa. Pamela shuddered as she felt a chill creep in under the windows – the flat was damp and freezing.

'One has to start somewhere,' Pamela said, trying to be encouraging.

'I'm sorry to hear about…' Johnny trailed off, embarrassed.

Pamela waved a hand and said, 'Don't worry, Johnny. It wasn't meant to be. Besides, I rather think "Agent of Influence" had run its course. I'm just sorry I may have blackened your name by association at *The Times*.'

'Quite all right, Lady Pamela. I was just grateful for the opportunity.' A gentleman to the last.

'If I find myself in another position, I'll put in a good word for you,' she said.

'Thank you, Lady Pamela. Would you like to see the photos now?'

Johnny led Pamela through to the bathroom, which doubled as a dark room. She had asked him if he could develop some photos for her from some recent events they had attended together. She had promised a sulky Percy to bring the best ones to him as a final parting apology. Although Pamela was irritated with him for not fighting her corner, she was also well aware that he was such a terrible gossip, one never knew whose ear he had or what he would say. It seemed the better part of wisdom to keep things on an even keel.

They squeezed into the tiny darkroom (which doubled as his bathroom) together, where Johnny had set photos in the bathtub to develop. He swirled the photos around in the water and watched the images emerge. It had been a Christmas-time charity gala, in aid of orphans displaced by the war in Spain. As photos of women in evening gowns and men in tailcoats came into focus, Johnny hung them up one by one. Pamela looked around the room, distracted momentarily by the other pictures already hanging up to dry.

There was a series of what was surely Johnny and his friends at Cambridge on graduation day. A group of happy, smiling young men in caps and gowns, arms over each other's shoulders, horsing around, making silly faces and hand gestures. A few more sombre ones, of the boys with what must have been university lecturers, older men with moustaches, beards and spectacles. And then, Pamela thought she saw a familiar face. She blinked and squinted into the reddish darkness. Was this a picture of Johnny and two of his friends with... Charlie?

'Johnny, tell me about these darling photos from... is this your university graduation?'

Johnny looked up and walked over to where Pamela was standing. 'Oh, yes, they're nothing special.'

'Well, I think they're quite charming. I rather wish I had gone to university sometimes.'

Johnny looked at Pamela in surprise. 'It was quite dull. Lots of reading and old men droning on. I wanted to go to art college but Father wouldn't hear of it,' he sighed.

Pamela looked at Johnny out of the corner of her eye and asked casually, 'And these are your boring old men then?' She pointed at the image of Johnny with his lecturers.

He nodded. 'That one wasn't so bad. He liked to point out the racy bits in Greek plays.'

Pamela then pointed at the photo of Charlie. 'And who's this? He doesn't look like a boring old man.'

'Oh, him. That's Mr Buchanan. He wasn't one of my professors. Quite a nice chap. One of the librarians. Always very friendly with us.'

Pamela breathed a sigh of relief. She knew so little about Charlie. She somehow felt safer, less exposed for what she had done, knowing Buchanan *was* his real name, that he *was* a librarian at Cambridge. There was something to hold on to that was concrete, real. Because sometimes Pamela wondered if it had all been a dream. If she made the whole thing up. Not that it made a difference now, of course. She looked at his face in the photograph, at the familiar crinkles around his eyes, at the lock of hair that had been blown by the wind across his forehead.

III

Pamela looked at herself in the fitting room mirror. 'You've truly outdone yourself this time, Elena.'

She was wearing a reproduction of an eighteenth-century French court gown the Princess had made for one of her clients who was going to a fancy-dress ball. (Parties imitating the court of Louis XVI had become all the rage lately, which Pamela found odd considering the fate that had been met by the French court one hundred fifty years ago.) She stroked the rose-pink silk and admired the impeccable detail in the lace trim around the elbows and bodice.

'But you must try it on with the wig!' exclaimed Elena as she handed Pamela an elaborate powdered headdress.

Pamela duly fitted it over her own hair and looked back in the mirror again, seeing perhaps some long-ago Georgian ancestor of hers looking back at her. 'It is absolutely gorgeous, Elena. But I think I need to sit down...' Pamela put her hands on the sides of her corseted waist, feeling faint.

Elena took her hand and guided Pamela to a chair. Pamela tried to sit but found her wide panniers wouldn't allow her.

Jo, who had been sitting across the room, cocktail in hand, said, 'Thank god we don't have to wear constricting shite like that anymore. You can't move, you can't breathe, you can't even sit down!'

(Jo and Elena, it seemed, had managed to make up and were once again an item, much to Pamela's surprise.)

Elena waved a hand at Jo impatiently and led Pamela to the sofa. 'Beauty comes at a price in every age,' she retorted, straightening her own outfit, an elegant but simple bias-cut dress with long sleeves in a deep, blood-red.

Jo, who was wearing her usual uniform of blouse, jacket and wide-legged trousers, replied, 'If women want to torture themselves with girdles and stockings and that sort of nonsense, that's their business.'

Elena and Jo knew Pamela had been feeling dejected since her sacking from *The Times*, and had been trying to cheer her up. The Princess had locked up her shop for the evening and the three women had been trying on clothes, drinking cocktails and eating a spread of zakuski – Russian hors d'oeuvres that Elena had bought from a nearby Russian deli: caviar on black bread, pickles, salads and slices of cured fish.

Elena handed Pamela her vodka martini and sat down next to Jo. She looked at Jo and then back at Pamela, saying matter-of-factly, 'I do not know what is the matter with Josephine today. Pamela, she has an excuse, she has lost her column, but Josephine, I don't know why you are frowning. All day, she is somewhere else!'

Jo took a sip of her drink and looked around the room, seeming uneasy. She shifted uncomfortably in her chair and then got up. She walked to the window, pulling back the blue velvet curtain to peer out into the Marylebone street.

'See? Do you see how she is behaving?' the Princess said to Pamela.

Pamela leaned back on the sofa and watched Jo, who did indeed look a far cry from her usual confident self.

'What is it, ducky?' Pamela asked Jo.

Jo turned back to them and crossed the room slowly, the ancient wooden floorboards creaking under the Turkish carpet. She absent-mindedly ran a hand over the dressmaker's model as she passed it, and then took a piece of rye bread with cream cheese and cucumber from the table. Jo nibbled on it and looked off into the distance.

'I had a pretty queer experience last night. You know when something happens to you but you're not even entirely sure what just happened because it's so surreal?'

Pamela knew exactly what she meant but said nothing.

'I went to see a friend in Hampstead yesterday,' Jo continued. 'He's just moved into a great big new building – one of those modern jobs. Looks like an ocean liner, if you ask me.'

Something rang a bell for Pamela.

'Utopian, socialist project, communal living, that sort of thing.'

Elena scoffed. 'People are fools. Who would *choose* to live in a kommunalka?'

'All very state-of-the-art, apparently,' replied Jo. 'Though as much of a socialist as I am myself'– Elena rolled her eyes – 'it did feel pretty close, people living cheek by jowl. And, curiously, everything was made out of plywood.'

Pamela sat up and took off her cumbersome wig. 'You said this building was in Hampstead? What was it called?'

Jo thought for a moment. 'Er... the Lawn something-or-other.'

'The Lawn Road Flats?'

Jo pointed at Pamela. 'You heard of it?'

Pamela thought back to her conversation with Ustinov about the building being a nest of Soviet spies.

'Simply that there seem to be quite a lot of liberal Hampstead artist-types living there.'

'That's one way of putting it! Jesus, I mean…' she paused, seeming uncertain. 'So, there I was, having a drink with my mate who's just moved in – he's a writer himself and a bit of a socialist too. I guess you could say he fits in with that lot. And he gets a knock at the door, and it's this neighbour of his. This woman, think she was from Vienna. And we're all gabbing away about politics. Unemployment, the corruption of businessmen, the shame of poverty in this country – that sort of thing. And I've had a bit to drink so I'm being gobby as usual. Down with the Royals, down with capitalism. You know what I'm like. And my friend leaves the room for a moment and this woman makes me an offer. The woman basically asked me, brazen as you like, if I was interested in lending my services to the flippin' Soviet Union!'

The Princess dropped her glass, which smashed on the floor.

'What?' she cried in horror, and then said something angrily in Russian. 'She asked you to *spy* for the Bolsheviks?'

'She said there were others like me, people sympathetic to the socialist cause, who were aiding Russia. That it was the only way to push back against the capitalist machine, to fight the fascist menace. And wasn't Russia the only country lending its support to the poor brave souls fighting in Spain?'

Elena continued to mutter angrily to herself in Russian as she crouched on the floor with a brush and pan, cleaning up the broken cocktail glass. 'Yes, they are so righteous! Protecting the poor! Fighting for the Spanish! Turning people out of their homes and murdering their families!'

She suddenly cried out, having cut her finger on a piece of glass. Jo took her by the arm, pulled her up from the floor and inspected her finger.

As Jo helped Elena wrap her bleeding finger in a tea towel, Pamela tried to process what she was hearing. So, it *was* true, that the Lawn

Road Flats was a magnet – or perhaps even a breeding ground – for Soviet spies. And, it seemed, not just Russians but people from other countries as well. If they tried to approach an Irishwoman, surely they were doing the same to British citizens. With a sudden jolt, Pamela realised that the person who had eliminated Boris Nikolaevich had not necessarily been Russian. And perhaps it wasn't a German spy that had caused Mrs Leigh to meet with her untimely demise in West Hampstead.

'What did you say in reply?' asked Pamela.

'I didn't want to make a fuss – because god knows what those people are likely to do – but I told her that wasn't really my cup of tea. I was happy to write articles and campaign for causes but anything beyond that was a bit... much.

'And she even tried to press me on the Irish Question, about what loyalties did I have to Britain as an *Irishwoman*? I'm surprised she didn't go as far as to bring up the fucking famine and all. Still, I was firm but polite. What I *wanted* to say was, "are you out of your mind, you lunatic?" Can you imagine? I thought it was just Cambridge where that kind of thing went on.'

'Cambridge?'

'Socialist student unions, professors of Russian or history or some such thing. Being in love with Stalin, singing the Internationale. But they're fantasists, people like that. In their own little world.'

Pamela felt her breath grow shallower and shallower and began to feel faint again. She felt at the dress for the buttons so she could loosen the stays, but couldn't reach them.

'You all right, pet?' Jo looked at Pamela as she began to fumble around for the buttons.

Pamela tried to breathe in, fighting a sensation of dizziness, perhaps even panic. She couldn't tell if it was the dress that was the cause or the mention of Cambridge. She started to hyperventilate.

'Steady, steady, I'll get you out of this contraption in no time,' Jo said as she peeled back the bodice of the gown and started to unlace the stays of the corset. 'Take a deep breath.'

Pamela breathed in as she felt her lungs expand. She leaned back on the sofa, with the gown half undone.

Elena came over and sat on the other side of Pamela and stroked her hair. She looked at Jo. 'Sneaky. Sneaky bastards! Never trust Russians! They always have something going on, some plot, some scheme. Russia has always had spies, secret police. Even in the tsar's time there was Okhrana. They spy on their own people, they spy on everyone else's! It isn't enough they chase me, my family from our estates, making us fight for our lives, now they come here! To England! To London! How do they dare? I will crush them myself! With my bare hands!' The Princess was wild, gripping the end of the sofa with the hand that hadn't been injured. 'Josephine! You must write an article exposing these common criminals! You must alert Scotland Yard!'

Jo looked deeply uncomfortable, sitting on Pamela's other side. 'I don't know if that's such a good idea. You don't know what these people can do…'

Elena stood up. '*I* don't know? I don't know what "these people" can do? Me?'

'Sorry, love, sorry… I didn't mean that. I just meant…' Jo trailed off, running a hand through her Eton crop. 'It could be dangerous, to expose them. I think I'd be playing with fire. I don't want to make an enemy of people like that. If I wrote a story about it, and put my name to it, I'd be sticking my neck on the line. And I'd have made myself an enemy.'

Pamela thought about what happened to Boris and knew Jo was right.

February 1937

I

Pamela found herself living in a paranoid twilight state. She couldn't help but continue to obsess over her suspicions about Charlie. Could it be possible that Charlie, her MI5 handler, was secretly working for the Soviets? Or was she just grasping at straws?

She kept running through the events of the past year. There were things he had said at the time that had stuck in her mind. For instance, when she had handed him a list of people she knew – or at least suspected – to be sympathetic to the Nazi agenda. When she had hesitated, telling him she was worried about betraying her friends, Charlie had encouraged her, emphasising that 'the threat from within is the most dangerous one'. And who would have understood such a notion as well as a man who was himself a traitor to his country?

Pamela was reminded of his anger at the British establishment, at those who abused their wealth and power, at those who could evade the consequences of their actions. And, of course, there was the Cambridge connection – maybe someone there had recruited him? Or perhaps he himself had been to the Lawn Road Flats? Maybe he knew this mysterious Viennese woman who lived there?

There were the ways in which he had persuaded her to think about the truth, as a malleable notion, a concept flexible enough to accommodate multiple versions. But wasn't this what everyone who worked in intelligence did? Manipulate the truth?

She thought about his willingness to bend the rules, to go around the dictates of her mission and of MI5 protocol: for example, encouraging her to stoke tensions between people associated with the German Embassy in order to uncover the divisions within the Nazi Party – a highly risky manoeuvre she now realised to be well beyond her original assignment. Wouldn't such a tactic be in keeping with the Russian strategy? After all, information on the inner workings of the German government was just as useful to Moscow as it was to London.

And that evening at the German Embassy. Had Charlie been shadowing Pamela to make sure she didn't get into trouble? Or was he there on a mission from his Soviet handlers? Perhaps specifically to tail Boris and discover if he would try to make an approach to someone at the party? And when Charlie had swooped in to pick Pamela up in his car, was he truly rescuing her from the clutches of Hesse? Or had he seen her speaking to Boris and had been hoping to find a way of learning what they had said to each other?

Pamela was reminded, with a shock, of the evening not so long ago when she thought she was being followed home from the Fleet Street pub, which Charlie confirmed. When all along, perhaps it was, in fact, Charlie alone who had been following her. A shiver ran down her spine. He had been tailing her for who knows how long, to catch her on her own doorstep, perhaps knowing no one would be at home. Perhaps knowing she would be feeling low, certainly knowing she had been drinking, was lonely. Vulnerable. And she was the fool who had invited him into her house. Who had drunkenly confessed her weaknesses. Who had tumbled into bed with him, willingly, enthusiastically, unapologetically. Why had he done it? To throw her off the scent? Purely to manipulate her? As some random gratuitous act? Or had he felt a genuine attraction that evening?

And, of course, there was the defection itself. Which Charlie had encouraged, even though he knew Pamela was practically an amateur, untrained, inexperienced in handling such delicate situations. Putlitz and Ustinov had approached her because they knew she had her own connection to MI5, hoping she would be well placed to aid Boris. If Pamela was right, if all her suspicions were correct, Boris would have fallen straight into Charlie's hands. When she passed the intelligence on to him, he would have seen the names of Soviet agents, perhaps one of them being his own, and would have known that Boris would be a prize to hand back to the Kremlin.

And what had happened to Gertrude Leigh? Why was she in Hampstead? Had she known about the whole thing? Was that why she too had to be eliminated?

Worse, if all this was true, Pamela had been playing into Charlie's hands for months. She felt a cold stab of fear at the very thought. Was the game over now? Or was he still following her?

II

Hoping to somehow find a subtle way of getting more information out of Jo about the Lawn Road Flats and the Cambridge set, Pamela invited her for drinks at the Café de Paris. But because of Pamela's own gloomy mood and Jo's equally melancholy countenance (Elena was, once again, not speaking to her), the two women had found themselves at odds with the bar's lively, upbeat atmosphere. Instead, Pamela invited Jo over for a late supper.

Out of the blue, Jo said, 'I've been meaning to thank you.'

'For what?'

'For speaking your mind, to Dawson. You only told him what the rest of us wanted to. Only you could do it because you don't have to worry about losing a job and having to go back to Ireland, penniless, with your tail between your legs.'

'No,' replied Pamela. 'I suppose not. Though I seem to be doing a number of things that are rather out of character for me these days.'

'Oh?' said Jo, looking curious.

Pamela desperately wanted to tell her about her mission, but of course she could not. Instead, she settled for confessing to having an affair, which even in itself, felt like a kind of relief.

'Happens to the best of us,' replied Jo, looking unphased. 'Who was the lucky feller?'

'No one in particular,' Pamela replied vaguely. 'I suppose I rather lost my head one evening.'

'Ah well, marriage is a bourgeois construct designed to oppress women. And speaking of marriages,' said Jo, 'how *did* you know so much about Wallis and Edward?'

Pamela hesitated. 'I have some friends who have been sending me reports from America. That's all really. Just an inside track from some like-minded gossips.'

Jo raised an eyebrow and Pamela could tell she didn't believe her.

And then the doorbell rang. Jenny entered the dining room, looking alarmed, with Aunt Constance trailing after her carrying a suitcase, as well as Mr Dekhale (also carrying a suitcase) and Sylvia Pankhurst.

When Aunt Constance saw Jo, she looked alarmed. 'Oh! I didn't know you would have company!'

'Well, you didn't exactly give me any notice you were coming. What's all this about?'

'The time has come, Lady Pamela,' announced Mr Dekhale.

'The time has come for what?' Pamela replied.

'We are going to need your help, my dear,' Sylvia said to her.

Mr Dekhale's letter had proven not to be hyperbole, but, in fact, an accurate prediction. His source (a mole inside the Home Office) tipped them off that they would be arrested that night, giving them a head start to make a getaway. To Ireland, according to Sylvia. (Thank heavens it was an evening when Francis was going to be at his club until late.)

'I have some friends – in a particular political organisation – who I think will be accommodating to those who are escaping the clutches of the British authorities,' said Sylvia.

Jo, who had been quiet until that moment, said slowly, 'I don't suppose those friends of yours are in the IRA now, are they?'

Sylvia turned around, surprised. 'I'm sorry, but I cannot say,' she replied primly.

'I don't think you're going to get the warm embrace you're expecting,' Jo said.

'I beg your pardon?'

Jo stood, clearly not intimidated by this titan of suffrage. 'They're having problems of their own these days. Since the assassination of that admiral Somerville, De Valera's made it clear he doesn't want any more trouble. I can't imagine they're going to be pleased to harbour anti-Empire revolutionaries.'

'Excuse me, but I don't know who you are but I have it on good authority that—'

'They might very well turn them away at the border, you daft cow!' growled Jo.

'Oh dear!' cried Aunt Constance.

And then everyone started shouting at each other.

Cutting through the din was Pamela's realisation that her aunt's flight from the country could be complicated by her own secret, imperilled life. What if Charlie was still watching her? Could he know about Aunt Constance and Mr Dekhale? Was it possible that he could jeopardise their escape? And all of a sudden, this burst of fear crystallised into an idea.

Several hours later, Jo had driven the five of them down to the coast to Dover. Aunt Constance and Mr Dekhale were to take the ferry to France, where they would stay for a time with Lettice Wakefield until they could decide what to do next and where to go. Knowing she was still rambling around her house in the Normandy countryside, redecorating, stewing about her failed marriage and drinking the contents of her family's cellar, Pamela had wired Lettice with a desperate request. Fortunately, her friend had seemed to think it sounded like rather an adventure and told Pamela to send the fugitives to her straightaway. Pamela had felt that the farther they could get away, the better, and the safer they would be.

They all stood on the dock in the dwindling darkness and the freezing cold, waiting for sunrise and the first ferry of the morning to appear. Pamela walked over to where Aunt Constance and Sylvia were having a tête-à-tête and took her aunt's arm.

'What's all this about you having a criminal record anyway, Aunt Constance?'

'Your aunt was arrested for protesting the war, rather publicly,' interjected Sylvia. 'Someone threw a rock at her and she fought back. There was a scuffle with a policeman and that was that. The problem was that she already had a record – from our suffrage days – so the potential consequences, if she was convicted, were more severe than we had anticipated. I posted bail, but her parents refused to hire a solicitor.'

'Your grandparents and your mother were so very angry,' said Aunt Constance, who was beginning to tear up. 'They had cut off all communication with me by then. Because both your uncle and your brother had been killed at the front, they felt I was dishonouring their memories. I saw it completely the other way round. That I was memorialising them, and the absolute shocking waste of their lives, through protest. So, I could try to end a war that was killing so many other sons and brothers. "You cannot overcome evil with evil", they used to say. But they didn't understand. I felt I had no future in this country, you see. I had a friend who was going to India to be a teacher, so I joined her.'

Pamela looked at her aunt, whose face was barely visible in the darkness and what little light had been provided at the ferry terminal.

'You got yourself arrested, more than once, jumped bail, fled to India, where you then got involved in illegal revolutionary activity, then came back to England to further that illegal activity, and now you're having to flee again?' Pamela said slowly, almost disbelieving.

'It isn't *my* fault that the wheels of oppression continue to turn! After all, India was assured independence if they fought in the war alongside the British, and what did they get? Broken promises. Lies. We are not exceptional people, simply the ones most often holding the guns. We are a greedy, corrupt, war-mongering nation, Pamela.'

Pamela felt somewhat indignant on Britain's behalf but did not think this was the time to argue.

Aunt Constance took her aside. 'You must come out with what you've learned in your… travels. This must be public knowledge. The

King, the affair, the cover-ups, the dance of death with Germany.'

'Aunt Constance, I've signed the Official Secrets Act.'

'That doesn't matter. The British public are being lied to. About some very serious things. And only you can make this right.'

'No one can know about this. *You're* not even supposed to know about this.'

'If people knew the truth about their own country—'

'If they knew the truth, that there are Nazis living in our midst, running our newspapers, sitting in Parliament, sitting right in Buckingham Palace... what? They would rise up?'

'You never know!'

Pamela looked at her hopeful face and wondered what would happen to her if she did tell the truth. If she wrote a great exposé about her mission. She would probably end up like her aunt, on the run from MI5 and standing on a dock at five in the morning.

She sighed and said, 'I will do what I can.'

Aunt Constance hugged her and said, 'I know you will, darling girl.'

'Aunt Constance, will we ever see each other again?'

'Darling, of course we will! Don't be silly!' said her aunt, though the tears in her eyes betrayed her true anxieties.

Pamela stood silently with Sylvia and Jo as they watched Aunt Constance and Mr Dekhale sail across the Channel into an unknown future.

Sylvia sniffed. Jo pulled a flask from her pocket and offered it to her. Sylvia hesitated momentarily and then accepted it.

'She's a one, your Aunt Constance,' said Jo.

'You have no idea,' replied Sylvia.

Pamela felt tears start to form in the corners of her eyes as she looked out towards France, realising how much she was going to miss her aunt.

March 1937

I

Pamela had made up an excuse to see Johnny and asked him if he knew anything about communist lecturers recruiting students. She claimed that she had a friend whose son wanted to go to Cambridge but her friend didn't want him ending up in a hotbed of political radicalism. Johnny said he knew one or two students in the history department who had fantasies of being barricade-building freedom fighters and that this kind of thing wasn't uncommon across the different colleges. But he didn't know if university staff were involved. He said he hadn't experienced anything of the kind. But then again, Pamela couldn't imagine Soviet agents setting their sights on dreamy, easily distracted art history students.

She then asked Jenny to find out if she or Sam or anyone in the Communist Party circles had heard anything about Russians or Russian spies operating in Britain and recruiting British people to the Soviet cause. Neither of them had heard anything, but people had certainly given them some funny looks when they asked.

Pamela even went up to Hampstead a few times and staked out the Lawn Road Flats. She didn't entirely know what she was looking for and she had no idea what the mysterious Viennese woman looked like. But at least she could try to see if Charlie was paying visits to anyone there.

Pamela had thought about going back to Ustinov or Putlitz, to ask them about Charlie and voice her fears, but she hesitated. She worried it might bring trouble to them, perhaps even make them targets. She didn't want any more people ending up in the Thames.

Then one day, she received an anonymous letter that she was to meet someone at the National Gallery, in front of 'Judith in the Tent of Holofernes' by Johann Liss. Clearly, her digging for answers hadn't gone unnoticed. She felt a mix of excitement and apprehension. Was it Charlie who had written to her or was it someone else? Were her suspicions totally unfounded about Charlie or did they have a basis in some plausible reality? Did she have reason to be afraid or had she become irrationally paranoid in these last two months of trying to work out what had happened?

And then, for a brief moment, Pamela had a horrifying thought: that her aunt's escape and her part in it had been discovered. She wasn't meeting anyone to discuss her own mission, but rather facing charges for aiding an insurrectionist in fleeing the country. If they had been discovered, surely, Special Branch would have turned up at her door. Wouldn't they? Pamela realised she didn't know anything anymore.

Regardless, by the time she arrived in Trafalgar Square at the National Gallery, Pamela was nervous – about who she might meet, about finding the correct room, about being able to identify her contact. As she entered one of the rooms containing Renaissance paintings, she spotted it. A woman wearing a headscarf and a loose white blouse showing her muscular back looked over her shoulder, confronting the viewer. Holofernes' severed head, spurting blood in a startlingly realistic fashion, demonstrated the fruits of her labours.

Judith was holding the head aloft, grasping a tuft of dark, curly hair while a deadened eye rolled back in its socket.

And then she heard a cough. She turned around and there was David Stern.

'Mr Stern!' she exclaimed, surprised. 'You'll have to forgive me, but I'm supposed to be meeting someone.'

He smiled and replied, 'I believe, Lady Pamela, that someone is me.'

Pamela hardly recognised the now sharply dressed David Stern, wearing a three-piece suit and a silk tie.

He nodded at the painting and said, 'I've always found it interesting that Judith was helped in her mission to execute the Assyrian general by her maid. You can just about see her eyes in the background, there. In the Gentileschi version, the two women behead Holofernes together.'

Then he smiled at Pamela, who was speechless. *David Stern* had been the man behind the curtain the entire time?

'Congratulations on your achievements thus far,' he continued, as he sat on the bench behind them. 'I was right about your potential.'

Stern invited Pamela to sit next to him.

'*You* were right about my potential?'

'Yes,' he replied. 'After all, I am the one who recruited you.' He paused, looked around at the nearly empty gallery and leaned in. 'We had been watching you for a long time.'

Pamela felt suddenly uncomfortable and exposed. She arranged her scarf nervously. 'How long, exactly?'

'Of course, I cannot say *exactly*, but I will say that we approached someone you've known for some time before we made the invitation.'

Someone she'd known for a long time? Who on earth did she know would have connections like that? Percy? Of course, he and Stern had been at the paper together for a while, and Percy had his strange connections, but it didn't seem likely. Jo? She was a dark horse too but had only known Pamela since last year. Was Princess Elena involved in MI5? Was Flossie secretly a government agent? Don't be ridiculous – your mind is racing, she thought.

Pamela crossed her legs primly at the ankles, sat up straight and said, 'I would ask who this person is but I imagine you can't tell me that either.'

Stern shrugged, clasped his hands in his lap and smiled.

'In the same way that no one could tell me that I had replaced Gertrude Leigh,' Pamela added acidly. 'I understand that secrecy is of the utmost importance, but I replaced a woman who met a rather grisly end.'

'We don't know that. It may have been an accident.'

'I don't think it was an accident. And I don't think you do either.'

'We have no proof, Lady Pamela. Unfortunately, these things happen, from time to time. And it is often difficult to ascertain whether an accident is simply an accident or...' He shrugged again. 'It is very unfortunate. Mrs Leigh was a friend of mine. She was at university with my younger brother. I'd known her for a great many years. She was a very clever, courageous woman. And being a German speaker, she had been quite useful to us. She too was tasked with infiltrating circles of British people sympathetic to the German cause.'

'I'm a rather different person than Gertrude Leigh, Mr Stern.'

'Yes, you certainly are. But you have been incredibly helpful in allowing us to take a slightly different approach because of who you are, your social standing, your connections.'

'I was in the right place at the right time...'

Pamela felt a bit dejected. Mrs Leigh had been chosen for her intellect and abilities. Pamela simply had the right social connections.

'Yes, there is that. But you have proven yourself to be an asset to us. A valuable asset. We had time to prepare Mrs Leigh for her mission. But her unfortunate accident left us with precious little time to prepare you. We have been rather pleased with the work you've done. I sometimes feel people's efforts go unnoticed, especially with the women we engage. But you have risen to the occasion and provided a great service, despite the lack of training.'

Pamela felt both pleased and, at the same time, terribly guilty. How much did Stern know? Did he know about Boris? What about her affair with Charlie? It seemed unlikely he would be unaware of what had happened.

Gripping the handle on her handbag, she said, 'Mr Stern, I have something I must discuss with you. I don't know what the protocol is for this kind of thing but...'

Stern watched Pamela, his brow furrowed behind his spectacles. She looked up at Judith, and Judith looked back at her. She wondered briefly if she could be capable of such a thing herself.

'Go on please, Lady Pamela,' Stern said gently.

She took a deep breath. 'Are you aware of my contact with a gentleman who worked in the Soviet Embassy?'

Stern nodded and suddenly looked grave. 'I wasn't consulted before you were approached to facilitate that... arrangement. Which was quite a risk for all involved to take.'

'I'm sorry, Mr Stern. I didn't know what to do. My contacts seemed to think it was quite a dire situation and, at the time, I wanted to help.' Pamela paused a moment, wondering how far she was able to take this conversation, if she had the nerve to verbalise her suspicions. She closed her eyes a moment and then said, 'I've been having misgivings lately, about... someone we both know. It began as a kind of gut feeling, and then I started to piece together some experiences I'd had.' She paused. 'I realise how serious an accusation it is that I'm about to make. I don't have any concrete proof. Though I have noticed a number of coincidences – more than coincidences – that have led me to believe what I'm about to say.'

The gentle chatter from a tour guide floated in from the next gallery. Pamela found she had been gripping the metal handle of her handbag so tightly that her palms were sweating. Stern had turned his body towards her and was listening intently. The light from above reflected on his spectacles.

'Go on.'

'Mr Buchanan may be a double agent for the Soviets.'

Stern frowned, took off his spectacles and rubbed his eyes. 'Yes, I've suspected this myself for a little while now.'

This was not the reaction she had been expecting. Incredulity. An attempt to reason with her wild allegations. Reassurance that she was imagining things. An explanation, perhaps rooted in the fact that she was too inexperienced to understand what was really happening, some kind of double-cross or double-bluff or double-blind. A secret plan cooked up by Security Services.

'Your Soviet acquaintance...' started Stern. 'It is more than likely that Charles Buchanan was responsible for his unfortunate end. I do not know exactly how, but it's probable that he gave the poor man's name to his NKVD handler. This man, this Russian, had intelligence he was planning on bartering in exchange for asylum?'

'Yes. He told me that he had a list of names of Soviet agents, here in Britain.'

'Of course. And Buchanan was possibly on that list. By informing on this man, he killed two birds with one stone. He appeased his

Soviet handlers and their tremendous paranoia about their own people, while also protecting himself from exposure.' He paused and looked at Pamela. 'But he didn't count on you – his go-between – to cleverly work out what he had done.'

'Mr Stern, Mrs Leigh, she was in West Hampstead when the accident happened. And from what I've learned, these Soviet agents often meet in Hampstead. Is it possible Mr Buchanan is responsible for her death as well? Could she have, perhaps, stumbled on to what he has been doing, as I have?'

'It is possible. But we don't know. We cannot know. As I said, it is impossible to prove what happened to her.'

Pamela looked back at Judith, who watched her with hooded eyes. Judith pretended to seduce Holofernes in order to behead him. Charlie seduced Pamela and got away with murder.

'And I must admit too, that I have done something that may have clouded my judgement. We became… intimate. I suppose we formed a relationship which wasn't appropriate.' Pamela couldn't bear to look Stern in the eye.

Stern looked at Pamela kindly, patted her hand and replied, 'These things happen far more often than you might expect. And perhaps this intimacy *didn't* cloud your judgement. Perhaps, in fact, it *allowed* you to see Buchanan more clearly. And, of course, it was never your mission to uncover enemy agents in our midst. So, in fact, you have gone above and beyond your calling. We only began to suspect something was wrong partway into your mission.'

'What happens now?'

Stern shrugged and opened his palms to Pamela. 'Nothing.'

Surprised, Pamela stood. 'Nothing? What do you mean? Has he fled the country?'

Stern stood up from the bench and thrust his hands into his pockets.

'Rather the opposite. He's still here in England. And continues to work for us.'

Pamela approached Stern and said softly, her voice trembling, 'How is that possible? How can you let him get away with this? He'll only continue to betray us!'

Stern looked around the gallery and seeing a handful of people passing through, put a finger to his lips.

'First of all, like you, we have no concrete proof, only suspicions and circumstantial evidence. Secondly, even if we did, our hands would be tied. It is far more useful to track him, watch his movements, listen to his conversations, find out who he reports to and what kind of information he's passing on, than to unmask him. Besides, for it to become public that MI5 has had a traitor in their midst for many months... Well, I'm sure you can imagine.'

Pamela nodded and absent-mindedly stroked her scarf with one hand. She was suddenly overcome with a great sense of loss.

'I still cannot help but feel I've made such a terrible mess of things.'

Stern briefly rested a hand on her shoulder. 'You weren't to know.'

'But I'm responsible for a man's life being taken,' she whispered.

'An occupational hazard, Lady Pamela. We cannot control rogue elements. And we certainly couldn't have expected you to anticipate the machinations of the Kremlin,' he said with a smile. 'You had no training and you used your instincts. After all, one must often handle unexpected situations in the field. We wouldn't have chosen just anyone for that mission – we knew you were a clever and capable woman. And your relationship with Buchanan may come in handy at some point in the future.'

Pamela looked at him in surprise. 'In the future...?'

'If we are to catch him, we'll need to lay a trap. And for all we know, there may be others like him. Double agents. Both native and foreign-born. More importantly, for the time being, keep in contact with Mrs Simpson. Preserve her trust. She is nearly friendless now, and will likely be keen to maintain the relationship. We may call on you again someday.'

II

One evening several nights later, Pamela and Francis had gone to a dinner party, but Francis had spent the whole time acting as if he was elsewhere. Whenever someone asked him a question, he seemed completely distracted. Pamela wanted to find out what was wrong but Francis so often had these dark spells that she knew never to pry, to make him feel self-conscious. As she was getting undressed in her bedroom, there was a knock on the door and Francis entered, looking serious.

'Francis, what is it?'

He came in and sat down in the armchair by her fire. 'I feel it's time I was honest with you, Pam.'

Pamela felt a shock run through her. Honest about what? She turned away from her dressing table to look at him.

'Darling, no one likes phrases such as "I feel it's time I was honest with you", which is about on par with: "We need to have a chat".'

Francis seemed curiously both apprehensive and also nonchalant. He unlaced his shoes as he sat in the chair. 'I'm sorry, I didn't mean to alarm you.'

'Is there something wrong? Are you going to tell me you've somehow lost all our money whilst you unlace your shoes? Or that you're having an affair?'

Francis looked at Pamela curiously and she immediately regretted that last question.

'What must you think of me? No, nothing like that. I just felt it was time to make a clean breast of things...'

'Make a clean breast of what, exactly?'

'I know things have been... different lately, between us.'

Pamela took her cigarette case out of her handbag and was about to light a cigarette when Francis said, 'I do hate it when you smoke.'

She put the cigarette back in the case and snapped it shut. 'Well, why didn't you just tell me?'

Francis shrugged. 'I don't like to get in the way of the things you enjoy – you know that.'

Pamela thought again of Charlie and started to feel guilty, something she hadn't felt previously. She realised she knew what Francis was going to say and decided to relieve him of the burden of having to say it, yet again. Maybe it was the fact that so much else had changed in the past year, but she felt as if she was standing on the edge of a precipice and finally needed to take a leap.

'Francis, I know you'd like me to see this... doctor, this specialist.'

He looked confused. 'What?'

'You don't have to say anything, because I know we haven't spoken of it in some time. And I know you're impatient to start a family. But it's no use.'

'What do you mean, "no use"?' asked Francis.

Pamela took a deep breath. 'I can't have children.'

Francis rose from his chair, walked over to the bed and stood over Pamela. 'I don't understand. What do you mean?'

Pamela suddenly felt very sad, took his hand and stood up. 'I'm not able to have children. It's physically impossible.'

'Who told you this?' he asked, searching her face for answers. 'Some doctor? You're a woman in the bloom of health, perfectly fit. We'll get a second opinion. We'll get a—'

Pamela took his hands off her shoulders, clasped them in her own and sat Francis down on the bed next to her.

'I'm sorry, I shouldn't have lied to you. I didn't see anyone. I've known for a long time that I can't have children.'

'What do you mean?' Francis looked around the room, as if searching for answers. He paused and scratched the back of his neck. 'Do you mean to say that you were born... infertile?'

'When I was young, I had been foolish and careless. I didn't know any better. No one tells you anything when you're that age. At least, no one tells *girls* anything. They're afraid even the mention of sex will corrupt you. You see, I did a very silly thing, something I shouldn't have done. Something I very much regretted. But I was only twenty years old.'

A look of comprehension dawned on Francis's face. He took his hand away from Pamela and sat back, taking her story in.

'I had been engaged before. We've never spoken of it, but I know you'd probably heard, as people do talk.'

Francis nodded. 'Yes, I've always known there was someone before me. Not that it made any difference, of course.'

'And because he and I were engaged, at the time, I thought... well... I don't know what I thought. Maybe I thought it was... safer? That it was expected, even. But things happened, as they sometimes do, well before the wedding was meant to take place. And so, I had to have a...' She paused, feeling as if time had stopped as her breath hung in the air, as Francis sat there, watching her, waiting. 'An abortion.' The word reverberated around the room. 'And it all went a bit

wrong. Doctors never know what they're doing, do they? So now…
it just won't be possible to… It just won't be possible.'

Francis looked at Pamela with what she could only interpret as a
mix of pity and alarm. She closed her eyes. She couldn't bear to look
at him. The guilt washed over her like a cold bath. There was a deathly
silence. The fire cracked and popped in the grate. A motorcar drove
by in the street outside.

'Why didn't you tell me?' he asked her quietly.

'I didn't know how. What could I have said? Besides, if I had, you
wouldn't have married me.'

'That's not true.'

'Yes, it is. You want children. You've always wanted children,
Francis. You want a wife that can give you children and I'm no
good to you.'

He stroked her cheek and smiled. 'You're not an old cart horse I'm
going to send off to the knackers, you know.'

Pamela laughed, despite herself, and protested, 'Francis… don't!'
She paused. 'Does it bother you?'

'No,' he replied softly, 'I just wish you had said. Does it bother *you*?'

'I don't know. I suppose it's something I've become used to, over
time. One of those things you can't change. Of course, if I could go
back and…'

Francis absent-mindedly ran a hand over his head and said, 'There
are always things we all wish we had done differently. We are human,
after all. And you're not the only person with a wretched story of a
failed engagement. A youthful romance that crashed on the rocks.' He
smiled slightly. 'She didn't like who I was when I returned from the
war, not that I could help it. Not that I could help who I'd become.
Not that I'd even wanted to go off to fight in the first place. But then

329

again, I don't think I much liked who I'd become either. I was a very different person before I went to France. Most people were.'

Pamela looked at Francis and took his hand. They sat watching each other for a moment, and then kissed.

Francis pulled back. 'You know, this conversation hasn't gone the way I'd planned at all.'

'What do you mean...?'

'None of that was what I had intended to speak to you about this evening, Pam. I knew you had a secret, but I didn't realise *that* was what it was. I thought it was your mission, with the King and his Mrs Simpson.'

Pamela froze.

'This may come as some surprise, but I do know what you've been up to. Stern said it was all right to discuss it, now that he's debriefed you.'

'What?!'

'I know about your mission. Stern asked me before he recommended you.'

Pamela stood, pulled her robe around her and folded her arms in front of her chest. 'Francis, what are you saying? That MI5 asks the husbands of women they recruit if they have their permission to recruit them?'

Francis looked apologetic. He cleared his throat. 'Well, only if those husbands are themselves working for MI5.'

Pamela's mind swam. She grasped the bed post to steady herself. Francis had been working for MI5 all along? First Stern, now Francis? What kind of secret agent was she, if her own husband had been working for the same agency as she had, right under her nose, and she hadn't suspected a thing?

'I know it's a bit arcane,' Francis said, 'but considering female civil servants are forced to resign their posts when they marry, I suppose—'

'*Arcane*? It's absurd! This is absurd, Francis!'

Pamela paced around the room.

'Darling, are you angry?'

'Angry? Am I angry? I'm... well, I don't know! This is completely ridiculous! *I* was supposed to be the secret agent! *I* was supposed to be the woman of mystery! *I* was supposed to be the one with the exciting life! Not you – me! Why on earth are *you* working for MI5?'

Francis sat on the bed, patiently watching Pamela stalk back and forth. He sighed. 'You *are* angry...'

'They asked you for *your* permission to allow *me* to carry out a top-secret mission, which concerned the very fate of our nation! As if I'm a child!'

Francis was about to interject when Pamela realised something.

'And why did you give your permission for me to work for them?'

'I beg your pardon?' Francis looked confused.

'Why did you agree to let me be used for this mission, when you knew – you must have known – that I was replacing a woman who had been taken out violently in the midst of the exact same one?'

Francis tried to interject again, but Pamela kept on.

'And before you tell me that the death of Gertrude Leigh was an accident or there's no way of proving what happened or how it happened or who did it, save your breath. It wasn't an accident. I think we all know it's rather likely the poor woman was pushed. But you decided that your wife could very well do the job. That she was expendable.'

Francis put his hand up, forcing Pamela to pause.

'Darling, I don't think you're expendable. But I knew you were up to the task. And besides, wouldn't you have been angrier at me had you known I had thought you *weren't* up to it? That you weren't clever and daring and resourceful enough for a job like that?'

'Wouldn't I have been angrier at you for not considering me up to spying on...' Pamela huffed. 'This is absurd, Francis.'

'The thing is, practically speaking, that they couldn't very well make an approach to you without me knowing, because that would have made everything rather more complicated. It wouldn't have been sensible.'

'So, they can tell the *husband* about the *wife* before they recruit her, but they don't feel any need to tell the *wife* about the fact that her *husband* has already been engaged in espionage for... how long exactly?'

Francis looked down at his hands.

'Francis?'

'Oh... I suppose... on and off for... a couple of years?'

'A *couple of years*?!'

Pamela walked to the bed and towered over him.

'Darling,' he began, 'you're not allowed to let anyone know what you're up to if you're working for the Security Service. As I'm sure you yourself can appreciate...'

Pamela thought about the past year, the great pains she'd gone to in order to make sure Francis hadn't found out about her mission, the lies she'd told, the places she'd gone in secret, the things she'd done.

'So, all those times when you left a party or a club or a dinner and mysteriously flitted off somewhere, where you having a meeting with someone?'

Francis smiled. 'Yes, sometimes. And sometimes I rather just wanted to go home.'

'Perhaps this is a silly question, but did your people... did they listen in on our telephone calls?'

'Yes, they did. How did you know?'

'Clicking, on the line. Jenny said it was wire-tapping, but I thought that sounded a bit far-fetched.'

'Jenny said…?'

'Apparently, she has a friend who's a telephone operator.'

Pamela flopped back down next to Francis on the bed, suddenly exhausted. 'This *is* absurd. Darling, we're like Nick and Nora Charles!'

'Who?'

'Oh, you know… from that film, *The Thin Man.*'

'But weren't they detectives?'

'I suppose *we* could be detectives.'

'I think we'd make quite good detectives.'

'Maybe you would. Clearly, I'm rubbish at this. *You're* like the Scarlet Pimpernel.'

Francis smiled. 'That's a very flattering comparison. I think I prefer the dashing, eighteenth- century English aristocrat to the moustachioed American… gumshoe? Is that what they call them?'

'I don't know,' replied Pamela. 'Is it?'

She sighed loudly and collapsed backwards on the bed. As she looked up at the ceiling and the shadows created by the flames from the fireplace, she thought about all the things she had done. And wondered how much Francis actually knew. Did he know about every mission she had gone on? About her encounters with the Princess von Hohenlohe and Mosley and von Ribbentrop and Wallis and the King? Did he know about Charlie and what had happened between them? Did he know about Boris? Did he know that she was instrumental in a failed defection? To top it all off, her confession about her youthful indiscretion and the subsequent fallout had been entirely unnecessary. If she hadn't jumped the gun and insisted on bringing up pregnancy, she might not have had to say anything.

She considered prodding Francis, trying to get a better sense of what he knew, but she was far too tired. It could wait another day, if she had the heart to face it. Especially her affair with Charlie. They had covered more than enough ground for one evening.

Francis stroked her hair. 'Stern asked what I thought, that he had been keeping an eye on you for a while and felt you had a good deal of potential, but wanted to know if I felt you were up to the job.'

'And what did you say?'

'Of course, I said you were extraordinarily clever and resourceful. And had a flare for the dramatic, so would probably be enticed by the prospect.'

Pamela gave Francis a playful slap. '"A flare for the dramatic"!'

Francis lay down next to Pamela and put his arms around her.

'How did you…? I mean, who recruited you?' she asked.

Francis was silent a moment as he buried his face in her hair. 'Of course, I can't say exactly who, or how, but suffice to say it was in connection to this secret committee I'm on.'

Pamela stroked his hand and replied, 'I see. So, in connection to monitoring German sympathisers? Something like that?'

'A chap in the Lords has a friend – they know each other from school, and they're both members at White's.'

Pamela couldn't help but remember what Charlie said about a certain type of man who worked in intelligence, who was recruited by the exact same type of man, who had gone to the same schools and belonged to the same clubs.

'And,' he continued, 'it seemed I fit the bill. They wanted someone who was in the Lords, so had involvement with Parliament and a connection to the Commons, yet without being in the Commons and having to worry about elections, that sort of thing. A military background helped. A knowledge of German and Germany. Both my year in Heidelberg, as a student. And...'

Francis paused. Pamela stiffened, anticipating what he was going to say.

'... my time spent in the prisoner camp, during the war. They saw it as an advantage, that kind of insight. They wanted someone who could monitor the growing feelings, either in favour of, or in opposition to, the German government.'

Pamela turned to face him. 'So... doing the same job I was asked to do. More or less.'

Francis smiled.

May 1937

I

One day, much to her surprise, Pamela received a phone call from Madge Garland at *Vogue* inviting her for tea.

As they sat in her office, Pamela looked around at the sketches, photographs and fabric samples pinned to the walls, at the stacks of recent issues of the venerable magazine and proofs of upcoming articles and fashion spreads. The editor-in-chief wore her hair neatly waved, and sported a double strand of pearls and a smart suit. Business-like but effortlessly chic.

'I always did enjoy "Agent of Influence". It was just about the only reason I ever read *The Times*. What a sense of humour you have! And believe you me, we all need a sense of humour these days.' Madge sighed. 'Diana Vreeland told me what happened with Geoffrey Dawson. Sticking two fingers up at someone like him and leaving in a cloud of whale dust is one way of getting everyone's attention, pet. She says you're thinking of leaving us for New York and working with her, for all those Americans.'

Pamela opened her mouth to correct her, and then thought better of it. Clever, clever Diana. Instead, she paused, busying herself with arranging her skirts while she thought quickly.

'Yes, well, the idea has crossed my mind once or twice. Might be the new fashion capital, New York.'

Madge laughed out loud. 'New York? They'll never be any competition for Paris, and you can put money on that. I'd even say they'd be hard-pressed to pass up dreary old London. All they do is copy the Paris models and modify them for the American market. Try to make the housewives who shop at Bendel's happy. No, no... you'd be wasted on the Americans. I think you should come and work for us. Start with a column, something like "Agent of Influence", and then maybe we can give you something to really sink your teeth into.'

Pamela's eye caught a gown hanging alone on a rail. Long, ivory satin, bias-cut, a plunging V-neck with a built-in cape. Looked like House of Patou.

Then she had a thought.

'You're right... New York will never be Paris. Only Paris is Paris. I lived there for a year. Mother insisted I was finished in Paris, but then, of course, regretted it when she realised I'd spent the year running around Montparnasse after midnight.'

Madge looked at Pamela with a raised eyebrow and leaned back in her chair. She put a finger to her blood-red lips and was silent a moment. 'Speak French?'

'Tolerably well. Though I admit my pronunciation could use some polishing.'

'And how would you feel about doing that polishing in situ, Lady Pamela?' asked Madge with a smile.

Pamela felt her stomach flutter. She took a sip of tea to steady herself. 'Yes, well, I always feel languages are best practised on native soil.'

'We need an extra hand to cover the Paris seasons. One of our girls has gone off to get married and settle into the countryside some-where – don't ask me why.'

'And give up *Vogue*? Unthinkable,' Pamela replied. She then took a deep breath. 'Of course, I could always write a few editions of "Out and About with Lady Pamela" from the bosom of the City of Light.'

'"Out and About with Lady Pamela"? That has a nice ring to it.'

Madge stood and reached a hand across her desk. Pamela put her tea cup down, got up from her chair and firmly shook her new editor's hand.

As evening drew in and the last of the late spring light kissed the city, Pamela was both so surprised and so delighted by this sudden turn of events she practically floated home. Paris. Why hadn't she thought of it before? The year she was 'finished' had been a delightful one of Left Bank cafés, jazz bands in caverns and glamorous new French girlfriends. Pamela thought back on it with great fondness.

Maybe that was what she needed now, she thought as she reached her entryway. More frequent trips to Paris, a few fittings here and there, an excuse to attend the shows for all the big couture houses. Francis's voice echoed down the corridor. And perhaps he would be happy to join her, from time to time. Maybe it would be a chance for the two of them to start again. A stay at the Ritz. A walk down the Seine. Late dinners at Maxim's.

As she took off her jacket and walked in the direction of Francis's study, she was surprised to hear other voices. Whoever could it be? Francis never had people over – Pamela couldn't even say for certain if he had any friends per se. She knocked on the study door and he opened it, looking far more bright-eyed and invigorated than she had seen him for a long time. Pamela peeked around the corner and spotted Donald Jenkins, who winked at her.

'Lady Pamela!' he cried. 'What a welcome surprise!'

As Francis augustly opened the door for her, Donald got up and kissed her on the cheek.

'I see you two have already met,' said Francis.

'I told you, I know *everyone*,' quipped Donald.

Francis gestured to a slim-built man about Pamela's age, with dark hair and a kind smile.

'Ronald Cartland, MP for King's Norton.'

'Oh! Are you Barbara's brother?' asked Pamela as the man kissed her hand.

He looked surprised and said, 'Yes, do you know my sister?'

Donald interjected, saying, 'Darling, she knows everyone too.'

Pamela noticed a fourth man, standing in the corner of the room. Round spectacles and a serious face, he looked somewhat more ill at ease than the other two.

Donald turned around, looked at him and said, 'It's all right, Robert. She's one of us. Lady Pamela, this is Robert Bernays. Lucky duck has just been made secretary to the Minister of Health in the new Chamberlain government. Or unlucky duck. Who's to say yet?' He gave Pamela a knowing but mysterious look.

The bespectacled man bowed solemnly to Pamela.

These must be the Glamour Boys Francis mentioned. The secret committee, dedicated to fighting Hitler, forced to operate in the shadows. This was how Francis himself became involved in MI5. And how Pamela became involved as well. She looked around the room at these mismatched, unusual men and wondered if any of them were involved in any secret missions of their own.

She turned to Francis and said, 'Darling, I don't want to interrupt you, I just wanted to say hello and…' She was about to tell him her news of Madge Garland and *Vogue* and Paris, but thought better of it. Perhaps later, over supper. 'Well, just say hello, really.'

Francis hesitated and then replied, 'You're not interrupting.' He looked back at the three MPs standing behind him. 'Would you care to join us for a drink?'

Donald clapped his hands together and said, 'What a wonderful idea!'

'Are you quite sure?' asked Pamela.

'Quite sure,' said Donald firmly as he took her by the arm.

'In that case, I'd be delighted,' she replied as Francis smiled and closed the door behind her.

Acknowledgements

The Socialite Spy was inspired by a story told to my mother by my grandmother that Wallis Simpson was not the love of Edward VIII's life, but, in fact, a plant devised by the CIA and MI6 to remove him and his fascist politics from the throne. At a time when only Fleet Street was observing a government-mandated blackout, the rest of the world was following the story; then as now, American readers couldn't get enough of a Royal soap opera. I owe a debt of gratitude to my grandmother for coming up with this theory all those years ago, and my mother for telling me.

This book started its life as the one-woman show *Agent of Influence*. Commissioned by Fluff Productions, the play made its way to the Edinburgh Festival, back down to London and then went on to a national tour of the UK. This book wouldn't exist without the support and invaluable creative input of those who were involved in *Agent of Influence*: Jessica Back, Katharina Reinthaller, Phil Hewitt and most importantly, Rebecca Dunn – the original Pamela.

Having spent my entire life in the theatre world, the realm of fiction was enticing but daunting. My agent Gaia Banks at Sheil Land has been a tireless champion of this book from the beginning, but also of me and my journey from playwright to novelist.

A big thank you to the team at Lume Books, not only for the enthusiasm they have showed for Pamela, but also the care they took with the publication: the fantastic editors, the marvellous marketing team and the excellent designer who went back and forth with me endlessly on the cover, patiently taking on board all my references to 1930s collage art.

I am endlessly grateful for the love and support of my excellent friends, those in the UK, the US and beyond. They have been generous with their affection, enthusiasm and time, from listening to ideas to looking at titles and book covers. Many have also been the most wonderful artistic collaborators, supporting and building on my creative practice as a writer, theatre-maker and storyteller, without which I would never have been able to write this novel. A special shout-out to Stephen Laughton for being the cheerleader who helped me find an agent in the dog days of the pandemic, when no one was particularly optimistic about anything at all.

Lastly, words cannot express my appreciation to my parents for the love, care and endless encouragement they have given me over the years. Miss you, Dad.

About the Author

Sarah Sigal is a London-based American writer, dramaturg and director working across fiction, theatre and film. She has written and collaborated on numerous plays and performance events across the UK. In her academic life, she adapted her PhD into the monograph *Writing in Collaborative Theatre-Making* (Bloomsbury, 2016). *The Socialite Spy* is her first novel.

9 781839 015311